For the Love of Grace

Ginna Gray

QuestMark
CONTEMPORARY
ROMANCE

Questmark Inc.

Published by the QuestMark Book Group
Questmark Inc., 15 Paradise Plaza #351, Sarasota, FL 34239
www.questmarkinc.com

FOR THE LOVE OF GRACE

A QuestMark Romance / Published by arrangement with the author.

www.ginnagray.com

Cover design and interior text design by Jeanie James | Shorebird Media.

Cover image: © Dwight Smith | Dreamstime.com
Back cover: © CJ McKendry | iStockPhoto.com

ISBN: 978-0-9798856-2-4

PRINTED IN THE UNITED STATES OF AMERICA.

10 9 8 7 6 5 4 3 2 1

Dear Reader:

Don't we all love stories of courage, redemption and triumph? Of struggling against insurmountable odds and winning? Combine all of those elements in one book and I'm in heaven. And where better to set such a story than in a small town?

The dynamics of small town living have always fascinated me, particularly small towns in Texas, since I am a native of that state.

As so often is the case, beneath the placid surface of these sleepy little hamlets, where everyone knows everyone else, and secrets seldom remain secret long, there is intrigue, scandal, fierce rivalries, and rivers of seething passions. Inevitably, there are also distinct social lines, and a right and a wrong side of town.

Being the bad boy from the wrong side of the tracks is never easy. When you are accused of a heinous crime such as murder, life can seem hopeless. Add to that mix the hero's love for the most respected and admired woman in town, and his seemingly impossible struggle to overcome the stigma of his birth and prove his innocence, and you have, I hope, the makings of one heck of a story.

I hope you enjoy reading it as much as I enjoyed writing it.

Sincerely,

Ginna Gray

One

ȣ

HE'D FORGOTTEN THE SAWDUST SMELL.

Forgotten, hell. More likely he'd blocked it out of his mind, right along with everything else about this place that he possibly could.

Entering Cedar Grove from the south, Jake Paxton eased his sputtering pickup down Main Street in low gear. The truck backfired and coughed twice. "Dammit to hell." Jaw clenched, he pumped the gas pedal harder.

It was nearing twilight and the town was almost deserted. After five everyone went home and the town practically rolled up the sidewalks. He'd passed only two or three cars, poking along the street at a speed that would drive big-city dwellers mad. None had been driven by anyone he recognized.

Just as well, Jake mused. He was about as welcome in this town as the plague.

They'd find out soon enough that he was back.

He managed to coax the pickup as far as Clyde Ledbetter's Texaco station and brought the wheezing vehicle to a halt in the side drive. The engine died with a shudder before he could switch off the ignition. "Great. Just great."

He climbed out and slammed the door, but halted when he got another whiff of the pungent smell coming from the sawmill. His nostrils flared and his eyes narrowed. Some people liked the scent of sawdust, but for Jake it brought a rush of bitter memories.

He had awakened to that odor every day of the first nineteen years of his life. The sharp, resinous aroma permeated everything within a ten-mile radius and served as a constant reminder that in this part of Texas, Ames Lumber Company was all powerful. One way or another, every living soul in Cedar Grove depended on the sawmill for their existence. Without it, the town would dry up and die . . . a fact the Ames family never let anyone forget.

Jake's gaze swept the main street. Cedar Grove's business district covered a mere six blocks, and the entire town boasted one traffic light. That had been installed over fifty years ago, mainly to slow the traffic on the old highway that had cut through the heart of town in those days, and perhaps to snag a few customers for the local businesses.

Years ago the new interstate, and any hope of growth, had bypassed Cedar Grove. Now the traffic light was merely a nuisance, but no one was willing to do anything about it, simply because it had been there so long. Change didn't come easy here.

The same hodgepodge of two-storey brick and sandstone structures lined the street. Purdee's Pharmacy still occupied the northeast corner of Main and Elm. The bank, Elbertson's Feed and Grain, and the City Cafe took up the other three corners.

From where Jake stood he could see the barber shop and the bench out front beneath the red awning where the Ackerman brothers spent their days playing dominoes and keeping an eye on the town.

Across the street, Ida Mae's Beauty Emporium, with its garish pink neon scissors sign in the window, still sat squeezed between the pharmacy and Humphries Hardware.

Beside the bank the area's only medical facility, known simply as the Clinic, looked as time worn as ever. Jake couldn't remember when the trim on the red brick building hadn't needed a coat of paint. The simple shingle old Doc Watley had hung out more than forty years ago was so faded you could hardly make out the words.

Orville Snead's Saddlery and Shoe Repair, the Five and Dime, the drygoods store, Martha Peabody's Dress Shop, even Clyde Ledbetter's Texaco station, with its old-fashioned grease pit and pumps, all appeared frozen in time. There was not a new building, or even so much as a new street sign in town.

One corner of Jake's mouth twisted. He wouldn't be surprised to learn that the sale ads taped in the windows at the Piggly Wiggly were the same ones that had been there ten years ago, when he'd shaken the dust of this place off his boots and lit out.

He'd also be willing to bet the last seventy bucks he had to his name that the locals' opinion of him hadn't changed by so much as a hair.

A showroom-perfect 1980 maroon Cadillac crept into the station as Jake headed toward the telephone booth. The driver, a tiny gray-haired woman, looked absurd in the huge car. She could barely see over the steering wheel.

Well, I'll be damned, Jake thought. Harriet Tucker. He was surprised she was still alive. The starchy harridan had been elderly twelve years ago. Hell, she'd seemed ancient to him when he'd been in her fifth-grade class.

Sitting ramrod straight, gripping the wheel with white-gloved hands, not a silver hair out of place, Harriet gave her car horn an imperious blast. An instant later Billy Bob Wheatly came sauntering out of grease pit area, wiping his hands on a filthy orange rag.

That Ledbetter's service station still offered full service somehow came as no surprise to Jake. Not here. He could not imagine Harriet Tucker pumping her own gas. If any fool ever dared to suggest to her that she do such an outrageous thing she'd probably whack him over the head with her purse for impertinence. Proper ladies like Miss Harriet did not engage in such common activities.

And Cedar Grove, Texas was full of Miss Harriets.

"Be right with you Miss Har . . . ri . . . et" Billy Bob did a double take and nearly stumbled over his own feet when he spotted Jake.

Ignoring the man's slack-jawed stare, Jake walked past him without a word, stepped into the old-fashioned telephone booth, and pulled the door closed behind him.

From the corner of his eye he saw Billy Bob come to life and scurry around the Cadillac. He stooped to Miss Harriet's level, talking a mile a minute. An instant later the old woman's head snapped around in Jake's direction.

He turned his back, dropped coins into the telephone and punched out the number written on the slip of paper he'd fished out of the pocket of his denim jacket.

News spread like wildfire around these parts. Within minutes tongues would be wagging. Not because of Miss Harriet. Spreading tales was as reprehensible to her as defacing a book or throwing spitballs in class—although, in this instance, she would no doubt feel it her duty to inform her family and close friends of his return.

Billy Bob, however, was sure to telephone his mother, and Ida Bell Wheatly was the biggest gossip in ten counties. By nightfall the whole town would be buzzing with the news: that no-good, murdering Jake Paxton, was back.

Two

"Hello."

"Josie? It's Jake Paxton."

"Jake! Where are you?"

"At Ledbetter's station."

"Oh, Jake, I'm so glad you decided to come back. You're doing the right thing. I know you are."

"Yeah, well, right or wrong, I'm here. And I'm staying. I'm through butting my head against a stone wall." He paused a beat, gritting his teeth. Jake had been on his own all of his life. It galled him to ask, but he had no choice. "Is that offer of yours still good?"

"Of course. Just tell me how I can help you."

"For starters, I'm going to need a job and a place to stay. Someplace cheap. Finances are pretty thin."

"I've already talked to my dad about hiring you at the mill—just in case you did decide to come back. He agreed to give it a try."

Jake could just imagine how reluctant Hank Beaman had been to agree to that. Josie's father was basically a good man, but it wasn't easy to go against popular opinion, not in a place like Cedar Grove. Not unless you were a born rebel-rouser and a social activist like Josie.

Even back when they'd attended Cedar Grove High School, plump, serious-minded Josie Beaman had had a penchant for lost causes and underdogs. It hadn't surprised Jake to learn that she'd become a social worker.

Hank Beaman had always shaken his head and patiently tolerated his only child's causes and crusades, but luckily for Jake, the man had always been putty in his daughter's hands.

"A place to stay may be a bit more difficult to come by," Josie went on. He could almost see her tapping her forefinger against her pursed lips, they way she used to when plotting some strategy to win people over to her latest cause.

"Although . . . I have been working on Grace for months to rent out the garage apartment behind her house. The place has been sitting empty for years, and Lord knows she could use the money."

"Grace Somerset?" It was crazy, but even now, after all this time, Jake got a knot in his gut just saying her name. "Shit, Josie, you've got to be kidding. No way in hell is she going to allow an accused murderer to live on her property."

"Don't sell Grace short," Josie advised, and Jake didn't miss the defensive edge in her voice. "She may be the soul of propriety on the outside, but my cousin has a good heart. Besides, can you think of anyone more apt to give you the benefit of the doubt than the minister's daughter? Don't you worry about a thing. You just leave Grace to me."

ꟸ

GRACE'S EYES WIDENED WITH SHOCK, and her hand tightened around the telephone receiver. "Josephine Beaman, have you lost your mind? I can't possibly rent the apartment to Jake Paxton."

"Why not?"

"You know perfectly well why not. The people of this town would have a conniption if I let a criminal move in here."

"Jake isn't a criminal."

"He spent almost two years in the county jail."

"Only because that narrow-minded, biased old bigot Judge Abrams denied him bail. As if Jake represented a danger to the community. Huh! They tried him twice, and both times the prosecution's case against him was so weak the trial ended in a hung jury. That doesn't mean he's guilty."

"It doesn't prove he's innocent, either."

"Come on, Grace. You know Jake was blamed because everyone around here had branded him trash from the day he was born."

"That may be, but the point is, everyone here believes that he raped and murdered Carla Mae Sheffield."

"You and I never believed it."

"For heaven's sake, Josie, twelve years ago we were seventeen-year-old girls, full of righteous zeal and sympathy for the underdog. What did we know?"

She could almost see Josie stiffening. "Are you saying you now believe he is guilty?"

"I . . ." Grace felt the sharp gnawing of her conscience. She sighed and rubbed her forehead with her fingertips. "No. No, I don't. But almost everyone else around here does. If I rent him the apartment I'll bring the wrath of the whole town down on my head."

"I know, I know. But you can handle it. Grace, you have to rent him the apartment."

Her head snapped up. "Why? Why should I stick my neck out for Jake Paxton?"

"Because it's the right thing to do!" Josie fired back.

The answer scored a direct hit, and Grace caught her breath. Closing her eyes, she groaned. Darn Josie. Her cousin had always known exactly which buttons to push with her.

"And because if you don't he'll be out on the street. No one else will rent to him."

"Why doesn't he move in with his mother?"

"Lizzie?" Josie made a rude sound. "He hasn't spoken to her in twelve years."

"That's terrible!"

"Not really. Remember how the woman treated him when he was growing up. She didn't even bother to show up when he was being tried for murder. What kind of a woman would let her nineteen-year-old son go through that alone?"

"Even so . . . she is his mother."

"Oh, Grace, you are such an innocent. In my line of work you learn quickly that just because a woman gives birth doesn't mean she gives a damn about her kid."

"All right, so he can't stay with Lizzie. Why doesn't he just move on? He wouldn't have this trouble in some other town where they don't know him. Why come back here? He's just asking for trouble."

"He has as much right to live here as anyone else. Besides, he came back to clear his name, once and for all."

"You're kidding! How?"

"I don't know. But I'm going to help him in any way I can, and so should you."

"Oh, Josie, I don't know—"

"C'mon, Grace. If you have any doubt, just ask yourself one question. What would your father have done in this situation?"

Grace winced. Oh, she was good. Really good. Grace's father had been the kindest, most tolerant man who ever lived. The Reverend William Somerset had believed in the basic goodness of mankind, in giving second chances. And in doing what was right, no matter how difficult. Most of Grace's life had been spent striving to be like her father. She had always wanted to make him proud of her.

"Darn you, Josie. That's playing dirty, and you know it."

"Tough. A man's future is at stake here. Besides, if the people of this town will listen to anyone, it's you. You never take a step wrong. Everyone in Cedar Grove respects and admires you. Shoot, you're the closest thing to a saint this town has. If you set an example, some of the others might follow. Just stand your ground and make them listen to reason."

"Huh. Easy for you to say," Grace grumbled.

"I know it won't be easy, but you can do it." An expectant pause followed. "So how about it? Will you rent him the apartment?"

Grace gnawed at her lower lip, but she was no match for that beseeching note in Josie's voice. She sighed and her shoulders sagged. "Oh, all right."

"Thanks. I knew I could count on you. We'll be there in twenty minutes."

Grace was shaking when she hung up the receiver. She paced the length of the parlor, wringing her hands. How in heaven's name did one greet an accused murderer? What did you say?

Hello, Jake. It's been a long time?

She grimaced. It certainly had been that. Twelve years, two months, and nine days, to be exact, since Jake had been arrested for the murder and rape of Carla Mae Sheffield. Somehow, though, she doubted that he would appreciate being reminded of that.

Pausing before the parlor mirror, Grace stared at her reflection and assumed a pleasant but distant expression. "Hello, Jake. It's nice to see you again."

She bit her lower lip: She never had been able to tell even the tiniest lie without it showing all over her face.

The truth was, she wasn't looking forward to coming face to face with Jake Paxton again. Neither was she thrilled with the prospect of becoming his landlady.

Almost from the day he was born, everyone in Cedar Grove had been predicting that he would come to no good, and as far as they were concerned, his arrest had proven that consensus to be accurate.

Everyone was going to be enraged over his return.

When they found out that Grace had provided him with a place to stay, a lot of that outrage was going to be directed at her. There was no way around it; there was going to be hell to pay.

Especially when Verna got wind of the arrangement. Her mother-in-law would flutter and have hysterics. And Lyle Ames, Charles's cousin, would rant and carry on and try to order her around, as though it were his right.

Grace sighed and rubbed the dull throbbing in her temple.

She had just returned from turning on the heat in the apartment when the doorbell chimed. She jumped, and her gaze flew to the glass oval in the front door. Through the etched and wavy glass she saw two blurry shapes, one short and a trifle plump, the other tall and imposing, with shoulders so broad they almost blocked the light.

Her stomach fluttered.

She pressed her balled fist against her midriff and raised her chin. She could handle this. After all, she was a mature woman of twenty-nine now, a widow of two years, and a respected member of the community, not the shy girl she had been when she and Jake had attended Cedar Grove High School together all those years ago.

After casting one last glance at her reflection, she drew a deep breath, ran her sweaty palms over the green wool slacks covering her hips and headed for the entrance.

The instant Grace opened the door she knew she was in trouble.

Nothing could have prepared her for the shock that slammed through her when her gaze locked with those familiar, insolent green eyes.

"Hi. I know we're a little late," Josie declared in her usual breathless rush. "I had to give Jake's truck a push to get it started. That idiot Billy Bob wouldn't let him leave it at Ledbetter's. I swear, the mentality of some people in this town makes me want to scream. And of course, it never fails, when you're in a hurry everything goes to hell in a handbasket. I hope you weren't worried that we were late."

It took a moment for Josie's chatter to register. Grace dragged her gaze from Jake and gave her a weak smile. The March air held a biting chill, but Josie's round face was flushed and perspiration beaded her upper lip. She was one of those people who charged through life, always with a million things to do and short for time. Her energy and enthusiasm were admirable, but Grace sometimes found them exhausting.

"Uh . . . no. I, uh . . . I hadn't noticed the time." She had been too busy fretting.

Like a moth is drawn to a flame, Grace's gaze returned to Jake's. Something flickered in those green depths—something very male and dangerous. Her heart gave a little bump.

Though she had known that Jake Paxton was now thirty-one years old, somehow she'd still thought of him as the sullen, handsome boy who had swaggered through Cedar Grove, Texas with a chip on his shoulder.

He was still handsome, in a tough-as-nails kind of way, and if the set of his chiseled lips was any indication, still sullen, but he was no longer a boy. He had become a man—a man with whom only a fool would tangle.

Evidently he had spent some time during the past twelve years working out. The skinny boy was gone. He was still lean, but now his long, lanky frame was corded with muscle. He wore scuffed cowboy boots, jeans and a cheap cotton shirt beneath a denim jacket. The white cotton strained across his impressive shoulders and chest, nearly popping the buttons from their gaping holes and revealing glimpses of the mat of hair that covered his chest. Oddly, the sight of those shadowy curls interfered with Grace's breathing, and she dragged her gaze upward to his face.

It came as something of a shock when she saw that Jake's black hair was now peppered with strands of silver at the temples. It was also longer than it used to be, curling at his nape, almost down to his shoulders. His features were the same—strong jaw, chiseled lips, finely molded straight nose, lean cheeks—but his face was older now, harsher, more unyielding. Those green eyes had always been intense. Now they were downright unnerving, filled with smoldering emotions and an awful world-weary cynicism.

This was the face of a man who had endured the worst that life could throw at him.

Grace's heart began to beat faster. Was she making a grave error? She had barely known the boy Jake had been. She didn't know this man at all.

"Well, well, well. If it isn't little Mary Grace Somerset." Unsmiling, he gave her a slow, thorough once-over.

A frisson raced through her at the bold assessment. As the daughter of a minister, Mary Grace Somerset-Ames had never been subjected to such a look from a man, and she had never expected to be. No gentleman of her acquaintance would have dared.

Then, no one had ever said that Jake Paxton was a gentleman.

"Hello, Grace." His voice was low and raspy, as though from disuse. Which, Grace thought, was probably the case. Yet somehow he had managed to infuse those gravelly tones with an intimacy that sent goose flesh rippling over her skin.

She swallowed and nodded. "Ja-Jake."

His name came out breathless and quavery, but considering the way her insides were trembling she was lucky to have a voice at all. "And it's Grace Ames now," she tacked on, raising her chin, disgusted with herself for letting him get to her.

It didn't seem possible, but his face hardened even more. "Yeah, right. So I heard. My condolences."

Grace wasn't sure if he was expressing sympathy over Charles's death or her misfortune in having married him. From the look in his eyes, she suspected it was the latter. She opted to ignore the slur—if that was what he'd intended.

"Thank you. And uh . . . forgive me for being so tardy, but welcome home, Jake."

"Home." He glanced around and snorted. "Yeah, right."

He stood with one hip cocked, a muscled arm braced against the door frame. His denim jacket gaped open with no regard whatever for the cold or the sharpness of the March wind. The thumb of his other hand was hooked in the pocket of his jeans, drawing her gaze to his flat belly and narrow hips. A small duffle bag sat on the porch at his feet. He looked confident and defiant . . . and sexy, in a disreputable way. And dangerous.

". . . dear, would you look at the time. I'm really sorry, Grace, but I've got to go. I'm running late, as it is. Anyway, I'll drop by in the morning and see how things are going. I promise."

Grace was so distracted she barely caught the tail end of her cousin's breathless rush of words. By the time their meaning clicked, Josie was halfway down the steps.

"Wait a minute! You're not leaving?"

With one booted foot on the bottom step, Josie stopped and looked back at Grace. Her wholesome face seemed a study in exasperation. "Weren't you even listening? I said I've got to be in Bedalia by four. I have to look into a suspected case of parental abuse."

"But . . . but you can't just leave." Grace's voice bordered on hysteria, but she didn't care. She had been depending on Josie to help her through the first awkward few hours. She certainly didn't want to be left alone with Jake.

"I'm sorry, Grace, but this is important. Besides, you don't need me to show Jake the apartment." She glanced at the man's watch dangling from her wrist and made a harried sound. "Look, I gotta go. I'll see you in the morning."

"No! Josie, wait!" Grace could have saved her breath. Her cousin hot-footed it down the brick sidewalk, her loose knit sweater fluttering, the full denim skirt that made her hips look enormous swishing around the ankles of her Western boots. Grace stared after her like a shell-shocked victim.

From behind her Jake drawled, "Well, well. Looks like it's just you and me."

Three

The statement, issued in that rough-edged voice, drew her attention back to Jake. She glanced at those intense eyes and received a shock. He was staring at her breasts!

Grace quickly looked away, seeking aid. With a sinking feeling, she watched Josie's battered compact car bounce down the drive at her cousin's usual breakneck speed. At the end she barely slowed before careening out onto the gravel road heading back toward the highway.

Gripping her hands together, Grace pressed them against her midriff. "Yes. I . . . that is . . . it looks that way." She bit her lower lip and gazed again in the direction Josie had taken, willing her to return. The fluttery sensation in her chest was almost suffocating her.

"Well? Are you going to ask me in? It's damned cold out here."

"Oh. Yes. Yes, of course. Sorry, I . . . I was wool gathering." She stepped back and waved him inside. "Please. Won't you come in."

She didn't want him in her home. She didn't want him within a mile of her, and it had nothing to do with the murder charge. Even when they'd been children, Jake had made her uneasy. Now he unnerved her so she couldn't think.

He slung the duffle over his shoulder and sauntered inside, bringing with him the crisp, cold scent of outdoors and a disturbing aura of maleness. As she closed the door he looked around. His face remained hard and impassive but those sharp eyes took in every detail.

"If you'll follow me, I'll show you the apartment."

She was so nervous she was slightly nauseous. She glanced at him out of the corner of her eye. The smirk that curved Jake's lips told her he knew it, too.

Grace had barely known Jake when they were growing up, though she had noticed him, of course, especially during her teenage years, but she would never have dared to associate with a ruffian and trouble-maker like Jake. Unlike her sister Caroline, Grace had never had that kind of nerve.

She glanced at Jake's profile again. He was older now, harder, tougher, but he still exuded that "go to hell" attitude which, twelve years ago, had infuriated adults and made the hearts of teenage girls flutter.

Oh, yes. Grace had no doubt at all that, had Caroline not been six years older than him, she would have been interested in Jake, all right, if for no other reason than to shock the locals.

Jake said nothing, but she was acutely aware of him walking beside her. She could feel his gaze on her as they passed by the dining room and her father's study. Unable to resist, she glanced his way again, and nearly gasped when she encountered that disconcerting gaze.

A slow smile curved his mouth. It also did startling things to that harsh face and made Grace's chest tighten painfully.

She looked away quickly, stepped up her pace and pushed through the swinging door into the old-fashioned, high-ceilinged kitchen.

Grabbing a sweater from the coatrack beside the back door, Grace slung it around her shoulders on the way out. The instant they stepped onto the back porch the north wind sliced into them like an icy knife.

"Oh, my. It's getting colder." A late March norther had blown in that afternoon. Pine needles and debris skipped across the back yard before the blustery wind. The air was heavy with moisture, dank and bone chilling. An ancient oak beside the kitchen window swayed and moaned, its bare limbs rubbing against the house with an unearthly screech.

Striding along beside her, Jake glanced back over his shoulder. "This is a nice place, but it needs some work. Like a paint job, for one. And that tree ought to be trimmed."

"Yes, I know. I keep meaning to get around to those things." Lack of time and skill to do the job and the money to hire it done had been the main reason.

Grace hugged the sweater closer and looked up at the gunmetal gray clouds scudding across the sky. "It looks like we're in for another blue norther. It will probably be freezing by morning."

Jake's only response was a noncommittal grunt.

His silence rattled her. So did his closeness. The path was narrow, and with every step, the sleeve of his jacket brushed against her arm. Despite the chilly weather, the contact sent heat zinging through her body.

She studied him out of the corner of her eye. He appeared impervious to the weather, but she knew he had to be cold. She wondered if that thin denim jacket was the only coat he had.

Before she could look away he turned his head and his gaze locked with hers. This time there was no mistaking that look; it was blatantly sexual.

Grace jerked her gaze forward. "Here we are," she said in a rush, and hurried up the outside stairs leading to the apartment.

"As you can see, this used to be a carriage house, but it's been used as a garage for the past seventy years or so. It's much larger than the normal garage, so the living space over it is more generous than the usual garage apartment. It's nothing fancy, mind you, but it's clean and everything is in working order. I think you'll be comfortable here."

She was babbling and she knew it, but she couldn't stop. Her nerves were humming like a plucked string on a cheap guitar.

Her hand trembled so it took three times for her to fit her key in the lock. Warmth hit them in a gentle wave when she finally got the door open and they stepped inside. Jake walked to the middle of the living room and turned slowly, his face as impassive as stone. Grace stayed by the door, holding one hand behind her, on the doorknob.

He remained silent for a long time. She shifted from one foot to the other. Finally she blurted out, "If it's too warm in here for you, the thermostat is right over th—"

"It's fine." he said without looking at her. He continued to inspect the apartment with an intensity she found strange.

The furnishings were of no particular period, a mix of castoffs of several generations of Tuckers and Somersets. Most pieces were old and a trifle shabby but still comfortable and sturdy—a navy blue sofa and a couple of wingback chairs in navy and rust plaid, an old platform rocking chair that had once belonged to Grace's grandmother, a leather ottoman, a few bird's-eye maple end tables and rustic lamps.

An enormous braided rug covered most of the polished pine floors. Rust, blue and cream pillows were piled against the arms of the sofa and an afghan she had made lay draped across the back. In one corner of the living room, next to the counter that separated it from the kitchen, sat a round oak table.

Jake stared at the room so long the silence began to tear at Grace's already frayed nerves. She gestured toward the television. "Uh, that set is old and sometimes cantankerous, but you can still get a decent picture on it."

He didn't respond, and her nerves stretched tighter. "As I said, this place is nothing fancy."

He turned his head and looked at her. "Compared to the shack where I was raised and most of the places I've lived in since, this looks like a frigging palace."

A blush crept up her neck and stained her cheeks. She was certain he'd used the vulgarity deliberately to shock her. He was as uncouth and rude as he'd been twelve years ago.

Jake nodded toward the door on the opposite side of the room. "You want to show me the rest?"

That wasn't what she wanted at all. She wanted to return to the dubious protection of her own home and lock the doors. She wanted to escape those piercing eyes, to put an end to the fluttery sensation in her stomach and ease the uncomfortable tightness in her chest.

Steeling herself, she reluctantly released the doorknob, marched across the living room and led the way down the hall.

"This place was originally built to house the handyman and his family. There are three bedrooms, though one is so tiny it hardly merits the name. The bathroom is right through there," she said, pointing toward the door at the end of the hall.

"How about showing me where I sleep."

There was no mistaking the taunt in his voice. The last thing Grace wanted to do was walk into a bedroom with Jake, and he knew it, darn his sorry hide. He obviously expected her to dither and flee, as she had always done back in school whenever she had caught him staring at her. Which had seemed to happen all too often.

Well, he could think again. She was by nature a nonaggressive person. In all probability she would never be the take-charge, stand toe-to-toe kind of female the women's liberation groups touted, but she was not spineless. Six years of marriage to Charles Ames had honed her survival skills. If she had learned one thing from that hurtful and humiliating experience it was to hold her head high and endure, no matter the provocation.

She lifted her chin. "Certainly. Right this way." She marched past Jake down the hall and into the largest bedroom. "This is it. I think you'll find the bed comfortable, and there are extra blankets on the shelf in the closet if you need them. Now, if there's nothing else you require, I'll leave and let you get settled."

Jake made a sudden move beside her and she jumped and let out a shriek.

"For God's sake. I was just going to pull down the window shade."

"I . . . I'm sorry, I—"

"What's the matter, Grace? Afraid you're going to end up like Carla Mae?"

"*No!* No, of course not! If I thought you had murdered that poor girl I never would have agreed to rent you this apartment."

He looked surprised. "Really? You believe I'm innocent?"

"Yes. Of course. Josie and I have always thought so. Now, if you'll excuse me."

She made it as far as the door when Jake's arm shot out in front of her and his hand slapped the frame, barring her way. "Then why the hell are you afraid of me?"

"I'm not!"

"Really? You could've fooled me. You act like you think I'm going to jump your bones any second."

Grace gasped. Scalding heat rushed to her cheeks. "That's not . . . How could you even think . . . I never thought any such—"

"Sure you did. But you can stop worrying. I'm not going to."

Whatever faint relief she felt was dispelled an instant later when he added in a soft voice, "Not yet."

"Wha-what?" She gaped at him, alarm streaking through her. Then she realized that was exactly what he intended.

Grace snapped her mouth shut and raised her chin another notch. "You have a lot of gall, talking to me that way, Jake Paxton. Especially under the circumstances. But then, I suppose I shouldn't be surprised. You always did go out of your way to annoy people and stir up trouble."

"Is that what I do? Funny. I always thought trouble found me without any help." That intense gaze roamed over her face, taking in every detail.

It was then that Grace became aware of how close they were standing. Across her chest she could feel the heat radiating from that muscled arm stretched out in front of her, and along her side his body heat warmed her like a furnace blast. With every breath she drew in his scent, musky and male.

Her nose twitched and her scalp prickled as a wave of goose flesh rippled over it.

He must have sensed her reaction. His pupils expanded, then a hint of a smile tugged at his mouth. "What's the matter, Mary Grace? Do I make you nervous?"

There was no point in evasion. Besides, she wasn't good at lying. Even the tiniest fib made her feel guilty, and it showed all over her face. "Yes," she admitted. A fresh wave of heat wash flooded her cheeks but she brazened it out, looking him right in the eyes. "You always have."

"Really. Interesting. Now why do you suppose that is?" Smiling, he reached out and trailed his forefinger along her jaw. Grace jerked away from his touch as though she'd received an electric shock.

"Stop it, Jake. I don't know why you're being deliberately provocative, other than the fact that you've always taken some sort of perverse pleasure in rattling me. But we're not kids anymore and I won't stand for it. If you persist in this behavior you will leave me no choice but to withdraw my offer to rent you this apartment. Then you'll be on the street."

He did not look in the least worried. "You could do that," he conceded. "But you won't. You're much too tenderhearted. You always were." His smile taunted. So did the look in his eyes. Taking his time, he dropped his arm and moved aside, giving her room to get by.

Grace knew when she was beaten. She was no match for Jake Paxton. She never had been. Forget enduring; she just wanted to put some space between herself and this disturbing man.

Without a word she stepped around him and hurried down the hall. In the living room she headed for the door with the desperation of a doe escaping a forest fire. She almost reached it when from behind her he said, "Tell me one thing, Grace."

With her hand on the doorknob she stopped and turned reluctantly. "What?"

"Why did you agree to let me have this place?"

"I told you. I never believed you killed Carla Mae."

"Why not? Everyone else in this town does. After all, the evidence showed she'd had intercourse several times that night. My skin was found under her fingernails, and my back still bore her claw marks when they arrested me."

Confusion swirled through Grace. Why was he doing this? "You never denied having sex with her. You said it was consensual. I saw no reason not to believe you."

"The question is, why? Why would you take my word, knowing what the people around here think of me? To them, I'm nothing but sorry, river-bottom trash and a troublemaker to boot."

"I can't give you a logical reason. I just don't think you are capable of killing that girl, especially not in that brutal way."

Jake shook his head slowly. "You're too damned trusting for your own good. Your faith in me is based on nothing more than some foolish belief in man's intrinsic goodness. Hell, for all you know, I could be a rapist and murderer."

Grace shivered, but she stood her ground, her eyes locked with those intense green ones. "Are you?" she managed at last.

"Do you think I'd admit it if I was?"

The trembling in her belly grew worse, but with it came anger. "Why are you doing this, Jake? Why are you deliberately trying to put doubts in my mind?"

"Maybe I'm just trying to make you wake up to reality. The world is full of vicious bastards. It's not smart to be too trusting." He shrugged, and his mouth twisted in what might have passed for a smile. "Or maybe I was testing to see just how deep that trust of yours runs."

Grace's mouth fell open. "You . . . you were just . . . what a rotten thing to do!"

"Yeah, well, I've done worse. Go home, Grace. Now, before I'm tempted to show you what I mean."

Four

SHE STARED AT HIM, her blue eyes glittering like sapphires.

Jake watched her pull herself together, squaring her shoulders and standing as tall as her small frame would allow. She still looked fragile as hell, but it was obvious she wanted to rage at him. Instead, without so much as a word, she gave him one last withering look, turned and walked out.

When he no longer heard her steps on the stairs he turned out the living room light and walked to the window. Night had fallen. There was no moon, and he could barely make out her shadowy form scurrying back to the house. He watched her hurry inside and slam the back door behind her.

The big country kitchen in the Somerset farmhouse had numerous windows but the curtains were tied back, ruffled things that afforded him a bird's-eye view of the interior. He supposed, since the farm was so isolated, privacy had never been a concern. He could see Grace pacing back and forth, alternately raking her hands through her long, golden brown hair and holding her arms tightly folded over her midriff. From that distance he could not hear anything, but he'd bet she was talking to herself.

He stared at her for a long time. Mary Grace. How many times over the past twelve years had that name echoed in his mind? How many times had he dreamed of her, thought about her? A million at least. Maybe more.

When he'd heard that she had married that son-of-a-bitch Charles Ames, it had made him sick. The thought of sweet, gentle Grace living with that puffed up little maggot, sharing his bed, had seemed the worst kind of blasphemy. He didn't care if it was wrong—when he'd heard that Charles had been killed in an auto accident he'd been glad.

He had feared that marriage to the son-of-a-bitch would have changed her, but it hadn't, thank God. She was still the same gentle soul he remembered, as giving and compassionate as ever. He turned his head and glanced around the darkened room. The fact that she would rent him this place was proof of that.

She was going to catch hell for it from the rest of the town. He regretted that, but it couldn't be helped. He'd had twelve years of trying to forget, trying to succeed, and getting nowhere. He'd started over in so many new places he'd forgotten half of them. No more. It was time—past time—to take a stand.

GRACE REACHED THE END OF THE KITCHEN, swung around and paced the other way. What a fool she'd been. She had expected gratitude, perhaps even a deferential manner from Jake. Nothing could be further from reality. He was as insolent and insufferable as he'd been twelve years ago. Maybe more so.

She jumped when the telephone rang, then groaned. She was still shaking from the encounter with Jake and in no mood to talk to anyone, but she had never been able to ignore a ringing phone.

"Hello."

"Lock your doors and windows at once."

"Aunt Harriet? Why? What's wrong?"

"Don't question me, child, just do as I say."

"But I don't understa--"

"Jake Paxton is back. I saw him with my own eyes at Ledbetter's station."

Grace sighed and glanced out the back kitchen window at the lights coming from the garage apartment. "Yes, I know."

"Oh, horse feathers! Someone else has already told you. I tried to call you earlier, but your line was busy. So who told you?"

"Uh, I learned about it from Josie." Grace rubbed her forehead with her fingertips. She should have known that Jake couldn't set foot in this town without someone seeing him. Not that there was any hope of keeping his presence a secret for long.

But she had hoped to have a little more time, especially before word spread that he was living over her garage.

Grace dreaded the furor that was going to erupt. She hated strife and confrontation. She was by nature a peaceful person who went out of her way to avoid conflict. Now, thanks to her cousin, she was going to be caught in the eye of the storm.

"Josie!" her aunt exclaimed. "How did she come by the news? When I tried to call her a few minutes ago, she was gone."

"Yes, she was on her way to Bedalia when I talked to her earlier," Grace said, wincing at the half truth.

"Humph. I keep telling that foolish girl that a young woman shouldn't be running around at night alone. Especially not now, with a killer on the loose."

"Aunt Harriet, I'm surprised at you. Jake Paxton was never convicted of murder," Grace admonished gently.

"Maybe not in court, but everyone in this town knows he's guilty."

"That's a terrible thing to say. And so unlike you." It was the kind of thinking she would have expected of Lollie, her father's sister, but not Aunt Harriet.

She heard a sniff on the other end of the line. "Well . . . maybe. But better safe than sorry. Now, I want you to do as I say and lock yourself in tight just as soon as you hang up. Do you still have your father's old hunting rifle?"

"Yes, I think it's on the shelf in his closet. Why?"

"Get it and keep it next to your bed. And be sure it's loaded."

"Aunt Harriet, really. You don't seriously think Jake is going to attack me, do you? Or that I could actually shoot him, if he did?"

"If it's you or him, you darned well better, young woman. Now I've got another call to make. You take care, like I told you, and I'll talk to you tomorrow."

When Grace hung up the telephone her gaze strayed out the window again to the lights above the garage. What a mess.

The apartment had been empty for years. From the start Grace had not been keen on the idea of renting it. She loved the solitude and peace of the old family farm and wasn't thrilled with the idea of having an outsider living on the premises. However, as her cousin had pointed out, she did need the income.

Grace had given in to Josie's badgering and gotten the apartment ready for occupancy only the day before. Now she fervently wished she had followed her first instinct.

Of course, this was typical of Josie. Her cousin had been born a social activist. All her life she had championed one cause after another, usually dragging Grace into the fray with her. Now she'd done it again. Grace was now in the unenviable position of being landlady to the most hated and feared man this town had ever known, a hard, bitter man—a man who, to boot, had always had the power to unnerve her with no more than a look.

Grace glanced at the apartment again, and this time Jake's silhouette against the bathroom window shade captured her attention. All the windows in the apartment were long, extending to within a foot of both the ceiling and the floor, and the one in the bathroom was no exception. It provided a stunning full-length view. She told herself to look away, but she could not. She stared, mesmerized, as he shucked his shirt, then his jeans and underwear. His back bowed as he leaned down, balancing on first one foot, then the other. She assumed he was removing his socks. When he straightened again he flexed his shoulders, stretched and arched his back. Grace's mouth went dry.

She laid her hand over her breast. "Oh, my."

Though all she saw was a black silhouette, his physique took her breath away. Broad shoulders and chest, tapering down to a slender waist, a corded abdomen, powerful arms and thighs. She never seen a more perfectly formed male body, not even on a Michelangelo statue.

Finally she gave herself a shake and managed to drag her gaze away from the fascinating silhouette. Mercy. She fanned her hot face. One thing was certain, she was going to have to get a thicker shade for that window.

An odd flutter wafted through her. Jake Paxton. She had never expected to see him again.

All of his life he'd been labeled "no good" by the citizens of Cedar Grove. To be fair, other than proving himself a hard worker, he'd done nothing to make anyone think otherwise.

As a child Jake had run wild with no supervision, a ragged, unkempt urchin who had learned at an early age to fend for himself. With a mother like Lizzie Paxton, he'd had little choice.

As a teenager, Jake had been a defiant young man with a wild reputation. He had seemed to go out of his way to ruffle feathers and stir up trouble.

Grace remembered how he had roared through town on his motorcycle with belligerent disregard for the disapproving scowls and mutters that followed him.

He'd bought the motorcycle with money he'd earned working part time at the sawmill for Josie's father. Hank Beaman had managed the mill for the Ames's family for as long as she could remember. Uncle Hank had been the only one in town willing to take a chance on the surly young man from the wrong side of the tracks.

Jake had attended school only sporadically, and when he had, his attitude had been one of boredom. Even so, she and Josie had privately thought that, beneath his "go to hell" manner, he was really quite bright. He had managed to make passable grades with little or no effort, something no one else in town had seemed to notice.

When Jake hadn't been in school or working at the mill, he'd hung out at the Rip Saw, a seedy poolhall/beer joint out on the edge of town where the loggers gathered, especially on Friday nights after getting paid.

Grace remembered her father preaching a sermon on the evils of that establishment one Sunday years ago. He had so thoroughly impressed her that she had never set foot in the place. To this day, she still speeded up whenever she drove by there.

Grace poured herself a mug of coffee and sat down at the table. Like a moth to a flame, her gaze went back to the window. This time there was merely a yellow glow in the window. Had any two people ever led more opposite lives than she and Jake?

His youth had been spent drinking beer, getting into brawls and striking fear in the hearts of the Cedar Grove mothers of teenage daughters.

A wry chuckle escaped Grace as she recalled that many of those daughters, even the ones from so-called good families, had been irresistibly drawn to Jake's bad-boy image. That was partly the reason she had never believed that he had killed Carla Mae Sheffield. The whole town knew the girl had been chasing him for months. Jake would not have needed to resort to rape to have sex with Carla Mae.

Cradling the steaming mug of coffee between her hands, Grace let her mind wander back to those teenage years. She had to admit, she'd been as aware of Jake as all the other girls at Cedar Grove High School, but he had always made her uneasy. Even when he'd been a lanky teenager, she h felt that aura of danger and raw masculinity about him.

Back then, whenever she had been around Jake she'd experienced a panicky sensation in the pit of her stomach. Especially when she'd caught him staring at her, which had seemed to occur all too frequently. She had always pretended not to notice those piercing stares, just as she had pretended not to notice Jake.

Nevertheless, regardless of how much he unnerved her, she had always sensed that there was a core of goodness in Jake, one he went to great lengths to hide.

She had no concrete reason for her faith in him. Maybe it was because, once, in the school yard, she'd seen him protecting a weakling from a bully. Or maybe because she knew from Josie's father what a hard worker Jake was.

Or maybe, it sprang from all those times she had seen him at the library with his nose stuck in a book. He had always been huddled in a remote alcove, as though hoping no one would see him. Of course, she'd never had the nerve to intrude or even speak to him. Back then, she'd gone out of her way to avoid Jake. But she'd wondered about his obvious love of reading. It was not an activity one expected of someone with Jake's reputation.

Whatever the reason, Grace had never been able to accept that he could have committed so heinous a crime.

Carla Mae's body had been found at Neeson's Cove on Lake Kashada, one of the favorite "make-out" spots for the local teenagers. She had been stabbed seventeen times, the word "Bitch" scrawled in blood on her forehead. She had also been brutally raped. Within hours, Jake Paxton had been arrested.

When picked up by the police and questioned about his whereabouts that night, Jake himself had hurt his case by at first denying that he had any sort of personal relationship with Carla Mae.

Unfortunately, at least two witnesses, her late husband Charles and his cousin Lyle, had seen them together the night of the murder.

Carla Mae had been killed after midnight. Her parents had forbidden her to have anything to do with Jake. As the only child of one of Cedar Grove's more well-to-do families, Carla Mae had never been denied anything her heart desired, and she had desired Jake. According to him, they had been meeting on the sly for several weeks before her death.

Jake claimed that on the evening of the murder he had dropped Carla Mae off a block from her house at ten-thirty, her curfew on week nights, and he had been at home asleep by eleven. Unfortunately for him, the only person who could have verified his story was his mother, and, as usual, Lizzie Paxton had been dead drunk at the time.

The blood and tissue found under Carla Mae's fingernails had been Jake's and he'd had fresh scratches on his back. However, the semen in her body had not been his, but that of two other men.

Jake had not denied having sex with the girl, but he had claimed it was consensual and that he had used a condom.

The prosecutor had argued that Jake could have had—must have had—accomplices who had not used any protection.

It was pure conjecture without a shred of evidence to back it up. The judge should never have allowed it. Jake had always been a loner, and as far as anyone knew, the sheriff never even made an effort to identify the so-called accomplices, but that didn't matter: everyone in Cedar Grove knew that Jake was guilty.

The public defender assigned to Jake's case did manage to get a change of venue, which was probably the only thing that saved him from going to prison for life, possibly being executed for murder. Evidently, the discrepancy about the semen was enough to raise some doubt in the minds of some of the jurors. The good people of Cedar Grove were outraged when the first jury deadlocked and the judge declared a hung jury.

The prosecution had immediately filed the charges again and petitioned the courts to continue to hold Jake without bond.

The vengeful attitude of the locals had reinforced Josie and Grace's belief that Jake had been found guilty because he was who he was—that sullen, no-account Paxton kid from the wrong side of town.

When the second trial ended the same way, the state elected not to waste any more of the taxpayers' money. After spending almost two years in jail awaiting his trials, Jake was finally released.

She and Josie would have been happier if he had been found innocent, but they'd been delighted that he had gained his freedom, no matter the circumstance. Grace still believed in his innocence, despite Jake's obnoxious behavior, but that didn't mean she wanted him living practically on her back doorstep.

Grace sighed and rubbed the dull throbbing in her temple. She hated controversy and strife. She especially hated to be in the position of having to defend her actions. She didn't want to be involved in this, but she had given her word. Besides, her conscience would not allow her to put Jake out on the street.

With a sigh, Grace rose and put on an apron to prepare dinner. She had spent her life striving to do the right thing. Most of the time it was easy, the lines between right and wrong clear, but not this time, she thought as she pulled a large pot from the cabinet. She only prayed she was not making a mistake, taking this chance on Jake.

An hour later the savory aromas of beef stew and baking biscuits filled the kitchen. Grace had just given the stew a stir when a knock sounded on the back door. She nearly jumped right out of her skin.

A quick glance over her shoulder confirmed her fear. The light spilling through the window in the door revealed Jake standing on the back porch, his shoulders hunched and the collar of his denim jacket turned up against the frigid night wind.

Five

GRACE'S HAND SHOOK as she replaced the lid, and it clattered against the cast-iron pot. Wiping her hands on her apron, she forced herself to walk to the door and opened it partway. "Yes?" A blast of cold air whooshed in but she made no move to step aside and invite Jake inside.

"I was wondering if I could borrow a few things."

"What things?"

"Oh, maybe a can of soup and some crackers. Some butter, if you can spare it." He jerked his head toward the apartment. "The cupboard up there is bare and the Piggly Wiggly is already closed."

"Oh." Grace wanted to tell him that the Dairy Queen was open, but she couldn't bring herself to be so ungracious. "Yes, of course. Wait just a minute and I'll get it."

She hadn't invited him in, but before she could close the door, Jake stepped inside. Grace hurried toward the pantry, but halfway there the timer on the oven buzzed.

"Excuse me a moment," she said, flashing him a look over her shoulder. He stood just inside the door, watching her every move. Grace turned off the oven and removed the pan of biscuits, but when she turned with it in her hand he was sniffing the air appreciatively.

"Mmm, something sure smells good in here."

She glanced at the pan of steaming biscuits, then at the stew pot simmering on the stove, and her conscience pricked her. It seemed rude, even downright mean, to send him home with a can of tomato soup when it was obvious that she had enough food for several people.

"Uh, why, uh . . . why don't you join me," she said with a decided lack of enthusiasm. "It's nothing fancy—just beef stew and biscuits, but it beats canned soup."

"Are you sure you have plenty?"

She was tempted to lie, but she couldn't. "Yes, of course. Please join me. If you want to wash up, there's a bathroom through there, first door on the right, down the hall."

"Thanks." Jake shrugged out of his coat and hung it next to her sweater on the rack beside the back door and left the kitchen.

As she set a place for him at the table she heard the water running in the bathroom. She closed her eyes and pressed her palm against her stomach. Her heart thumped madly. Now she'd really done it. The last thing she wanted was to have Jake in her home, sitting across the table from her. She must be losing her mind.

When he returned she dished up two bowls of stew and put them on the table, along with the basket of steaming biscuits and a pot of butter and two glasses of water. To her surprise, Jake held her chair out for her before seating himself.

As was her habit, Grace bowed her head and offered a short blessing. The action seemed to take him by surprise, but after a brief hesitation he followed her lead and lowered his chin until she was done.

"Mmm, this is delicious," he said after a few bites. "You're not only beautiful, you're a good cook, too."

The comment on her looks merely served to make her more nervous. She sent him a wan smile. "Thank you."

After that an excruciating silence stretched out. For a long time the only sounds were the clink of the silverware against the bowls. Grace searched for some neutral topic of conversation, anything to fill the void and ease the awful tension. Jake beat her to it.

He paused to butter another biscuit and looked around. "This is a nice place. Real homey. It's funny, I've known you all of my life, but today is the first time I've ever been in your house."

"Really? I hadn't realized."

But she had.

It wasn't so surprising, really. In a small town like Cedar Grove the social lines were clearly drawn. Growing up, Jack Paxton and Mary Grace Somerset had been poles apart. She was the minister's daughter, and the great-great-granddaughter of the town's founders. Jake was the son of Lizzie Paxton, a drunken slattern who lived down on Tobin Road in the poor area along Jasper Creek, known around Cedar Grove as the Bottoms.

Some even said that Lizzie was a whore who sold herself for money, though Grace preferred to give the woman the benefit of the doubt. However, it was true that no one, not even Jake, knew who had fathered him.

A blush warmed her cheeks. She lowered her eyes and pretended to concentrate on scooping up a bite of stew, but she knew the lie was written all over her face.

It was rude of her, she supposed, not to offer him a tour of the house. In Texas, that was considered the polite thing to do when someone showed an interest in your home. The old Victorian house had been in the family for five generations, and normally she delighted in showing it off, even in its current shabby condition. But in this instance, Grace simply could not.

Keeping her gaze fixed on the bowl, she methodically dipped up one bite of stew after another, but she didn't taste a thing. She was so tense she felt as though she would fly apart at any second.

"Josie told me about your father. I'm sorry."

She started, but the statement brought her head up. The look in his eyes was sincere, and she experienced confusion.

Somehow, she hadn't expected thoughtfulness from Jake. "Thank you."

Jake shrugged. "He was a good man. He and Hank Beaman were the only ones in this town who ever gave me the time of day."

Pride swelled Grace's heart. She smiled. "Yes. Dad was a fair man."

"He was the only visitor I had during those two years I was in Bedalia."

Her spoon clattered against the bowl. "My father came to see you in jail?"

"Every week."

"He never told me that." Deeply moved, Grace impulsively reached across the table and put her hand on Jake's arm. The hard muscles tensed beneath her touch. "I'm glad he believed in you, Jake. Truly. I am."

His green eyes darkened. He looked from her face to her hand, small and feminine against the dark skin of his forearm and the sprinkling of dark hairs that covered it. When his gaze captured hers again the remoteness was back.

"Yeah, well, I'm not sure that he did, but he thought I ought to have some moral support. Like I said, he was a good man. Although he was probably too tender-hearted. And too damned trusting for his own good. You're just like him."

Whether he knew it or not, Jake could not have given her a better compliment.

Grace had adored her father. She'd spent most of her life trying to emulate him. The Reverend William Somerset had been the kindest, most compassionate man she had ever known. He had believed in the basic goodness of mankind, in giving whatever help he could, and most especially in giving second chances. Once Grace thought about it, she knew she shouldn't be surprised that he had gone out of his way to befriend Jake.

"You know, Jake, there's nothing wrong with having a good heart," she chided gently.

"Except that it makes you a sitting duck for every asshole that wanders by. And take it from me, the world is full of assholes." He watched the color flood into her face, a tiny smile curling his lips as he reached for another biscuit.

Grace ducked her head and applied herself to spooning up more stew. She knew he'd deliberately used the crude expression, and probably for the same reason he'd stared at her so intently all those years ago: to rattle her. What she didn't understand was why.

The silence returned, taut and nerve jangling. She was so tense, when Jake spoke again she jumped.

"I was surprised when Josie told me you had moved back to the farm. I would have thought, as the wealthy widow, you'd still be living up at the Ames place."

Grace frowned. There was a barb in there somewhere, she just couldn't quite put her finger on it. She shrugged. "Not wealthy, actually. Charles had no money of his own, only the allowance his mother gave him. Everything belongs to Verna."

"Ah, I see. So, what do you do for a living? I noticed your land is lying fallow. You're obviously not farming."

"Hardly," she replied with a chuckle. "I wouldn't know where to start. My mother's family were the farmers. My father tried his hand at it in his spare time, but he wasn't brought up on a farm like Mom and was never very successful at it.

"After Charles was killed, I used his insurance money to open an antique store in town. It's called Things Remembered. I'm not setting the world on fire, but I'm managing. Most of my trade comes from tourists and the wealthy people who own second homes on Lake Kashada."

"What about all this land. I'm surprised you haven't sold it, or at least part of it."

"I'll admit, I've thought about it, but I just can't. This farm has been in my mother's family since the first settlers came to Texas. It would be like selling my heritage."

"Hmm. I don't have a heritage, so I wouldn't know about that. Although I guess I can see your point. Must be a helluva tax burden, though."

"Yes. It is sometimes difficult, but I manage." Barely. If her business didn't pick up soon she might be forced to lease some of the land just to pay the taxes.

Grace ducked her head, aware suddenly that she had talked with Jake more during this meal than she had the entire rest of the time she had known him. The thought made her uneasy and self-conscious, but as the silence grew once more so did the tension.

After a while she couldn't stand it any longer. "Uh, how did you happen to get together with Josie? I know she wrote to you while you were in jail awaiting trial. Have you two kept in touch all these years?" If so, Josie certainly hadn't mentioned it to her.

"No. As it turns out, we have a mutual friend. Professor Haily, at U.T."

"You know Professor Haily?"

"You look surprised. What's the matter, Mary Grace? Don't you think someone like me would be friends with an educated man like Thomas Haily? Or are you just surprised that I have a friend at all?"

"No! That is—" That was exactly what she'd thought, on both counts, and Jake knew it. The look he sent her left no doubt of that. Embarrassed, Grace ducked her head and murmured a miserable, "I-I'm sorry."

"Yeah, well, I'm used to it. Anyway, one night a month or so ago I was visiting the professor at his home when Josie dropped by for a visit. At the time I mentioned that I was thinking of coming back here, and she offered to help me find a job and a place to stay."

"I see." But she didn't see at all. Why would he come back to a place that could hold only bad memories for him, a place where everyone hated and feared him?

Of course, his reasons for returning were none of her business. If he wanted to subject himself to the kind of animosity he was sure to encounter in Cedar Grove, that was his choice and no concern of hers.

She stared at her bowl, following the circular motions of her spoon as she stirred the stew around and around in endless circles. It was no use. She had to know. The spoon hit the bowl with a clatter. She gripped the edge of the table with both hands and said in a desperate voice. "For heaven's sake, Jake, why did you come back?"

"Didn't Josie tell you?"

"All she said was that you had come back to clear your name."

"Mmm. That about covers it. That's one of the reasons, anyway."

"But how can you? Surely you don't think you're going to turn up any new evidence after all this time."

"Probably not. But I'm going to give it a shot." He smiled slowly, but it was a hard smile that reminded her of the angry young man he'd been all those years ago. "At the very least, I'll set the small-minded bigots in this town on their ears."

"Oh, Jake." She shook her head and looked at him sadly. "You haven't changed at all, have you? You're still bent on thumbing your nose at people and stirring up trouble. Why subject yourself to all that unpleasantness? Wouldn't it be better, and easier, if you just put what happened behind you and start fresh somewhere else."

"I tried that. But for the past twelve years, no matter where I've gone or what I've done, my life has been crap. I finally realize that I'm not going to have any kind of decent future until I've dealt with the unfinished business from my past."

"You're just going to bring more trouble down on yourself. And for what? Without hard evidence, you're not going to change the minds of the people around here."

"Maybe not, but at least I'll make some of them uneasy. I may even plant some doubt in the minds of a few people. Besides, I'm tired of running away."

"Jake, you—"

A sharp rap on the back door made her jump. Her gaze flew to the glass pane, and the face she saw made her heart sink. Before she could rise, the door opened and Lyle Ames stepped inside. "Hi, Grace. I guess you've heard about that animal, Ja—"

He stopped short, his face going slack with shock as Jake, whose back had been to the door, turned in his chair and looked at him. Disbelief, then fury chased across Lyle's features. "What the hell are *you* doing here?" he exploded.

"Lyle, you don't understand," Grace began, but he wasn't paying any attention to her,

"Get out! You son-of-a-bitch! You've got ten seconds to haul your sorry ass out of here!"

"Oh, yeah?" The legs of Jake's chair scraped against the pine floor as he stood up. "And who's going to make me leave? You?" His tone and the disdainful curl of his lip were both challenge and insult.

"Why you—" Lyle bristled and took a step forward, and Jake braced for battle, a look of unholy anticipation in his eyes.

"Stop it! Stop it, both of you!" Grace quickly stepped between them and placed a palm against each man's chest. "I won't have this kind of behavior in my home."

"Fine. We'll take it outside."

"You'll do no such thing. There will be no fighting!"

"Don't worry, Grace. I'm not going to sink to this animal's level. I'm going to call the sheriff and have him thrown out."

Jake's lip curled. "I didn't think you had the balls to back up that mouth of yours."

"Why you scum. I'll—"

"Lyle, stop it! *Stop it!"* Grace shoved against their chests with all her might. Short of squashing her, Lyle had no choice but to obey. She immediately turned a warning glare on Jake. "And as for you, just shut up."

His eyebrows rose, but a second later his mouth twitched, and she felt his taut muscles relax.

"There's no reason for you to get involved. I'll handle this, Grace."

"You'll do no such thing. Lyle, listen to me. You're being unfair. Jake is here because I invited him to dinner. He's my tenant now. I've just rented him the apartment above the carriage house."

"You did *what?* Have you lost your mind? Well, I won't allow it."

"You won't allow it? What do you mean, you won't allow it? You have no say in the matter."

At that, Jake, who had been listening to the exchange with interest, stepped back, crossed his arms over his chest and waited to see what would happen next.

"Grace, I'm not going to argue the matter with you. I will not stand for that man living here, and that's all there is to it."

"Well that's where you're wrong. You can't come into my home and start issuing orders."

"Grace, I am head of the family now, and as such it's my right and duty to look after you. I simply cannot allow you to make foolhardy decisions. Now why don't you just run along upstairs and let me handle this."

Grace had been trying to hold onto her patience, but the condescending statement made her see red. Stepping closer, she narrowed her eyes and poked his chest with her forefinger.

"You listen to me, Lyle Ames," she practically hissed at him. "You may be the only living Ames male but you have no authority over me. None whatsoever. Do you understand?" she demanded, giving his chest another poke. "I am a grown woman and I make my own decisions. This is my property and I will decide who lives here, not you. If I want your advice or help I'll ask for it. Until then, you keep your nose out of my business."

"Grace, don't be ridiculous."

"Ridiculous? All right, that's it. Out. Get out of my house right now."

"Now, Grace—"

"Out! I mean it, Lyle. If you don't leave this instant I'll call the sheriff and have him run *you* off."

"You don't have to do that, Grace," Jake drawled. "I'll be happy to oblige."

She tilted her chin at Lyle and gave him a cold look. "You hear that? Go—now—before I'm tempted to let him."

Furious, Lyle looked from Grace to Jake. The hard eagerness in those green eyes stopped whatever retort he wanted to make. His jaw clenched tighter. "All right. I'm going. But this isn't the end of it. We'll discuss this again when you're in a more reasonable mood. In the meantime, whatever happens, don't say I didn't warn you." He whirled around and stomped out, slamming the door behind him with enough force to rattle the glass.

Grace's shoulders slumped. Suddenly she felt very weary. "Well, well. That was a surprise. I didn't know you had it in you."

Turning, she was chagrined to find Jake watching her with a speculative gleam in his eyes. A rush of hot color flooded her face. She was so embarrassed by the display of temper she couldn't quite meet his eyes. "I . . . I'm sorry about that."

"Hey. Don't be. Lyle Ames is a prick. He always was. Anyway, I'm intrigued. You were always such a retiring little thing, I didn't think you ever even raised your voice. This is a whole new side of you."

"Not a very nice one, I'm afraid."

"Oh, I don't know. A little temper can be a healthy thing, if you ask me."

"Well, I don't. So could we just drop the subject, please."

"Sure." He picked up his empty bowl and carried it to the sink.

"Wait. You don't have to do that," she exclaimed, hurrying after him. "I'll take care of the dishes."

"That's okay, I'll give you a hand. You want them in the sink or the dishwasher?"

"The sink, I guess. There aren't that many things to wash."

While she drew the dishwater, Jake wiped off the table, then picked up a dishtowel. Grace's protests had no effect, and after a while she resigned herself to having his company for a while longer.

She had never been so nervous in her life. She was horribly aware of him, standing mere inches away. Occasionally his hand brushed hers when he reached for a dish. She could feel his steady gaze boring into the side of her face.

"Why did you marry that slimy asshole, Charles?" he asked quietly out of the blue.

She looked up, surprised. "Wh-what?"

"When Josie told me, I wanted to puke. How could you do it, Mary Grace?"

"Now see here—"

"Was it for the Ames money?"

She stiffened. Drying her hands on her apron, she turned and stalked to the back door. A icy blast of air whooshed in when she jerked it open and held it wide. "I think you should leave. Good night, Jake."

He studied her set face for a moment, then shrugged and tossed the dishtowel on the counter. Taking his time, he retrieved his denim jacket and shrugged into it. "Just answer one question," he said, pausing in front of her at the door.

"What?"

"Did you love him?"

She started to reply with an emphatic yes, but she could not. Firming her mouth, she looked away from those penetrating eyes and stared over his shoulder into the darkness.

"In the beginning I did." Her tone was resentful and as close to belligerent as Grace could achieve.

"How long did it take you to see what a bastard he was?"

Her mouth firmed and she cut her eyes back at him. "I won't discuss my marriage with you. Now will you please leave."

"Sure." Hunching his shoulders, he stuffed his hands into his pockets and stepped out onto the porch. Before Grace could close the door all the way he turned around and caught the edge, stopping her.

Panic fluttered up in her throat. He was immensely strong. If he chose to, he could overpower her with little effort. "Let go," she demanded, tipping her chin up at a commanding angle, but the quaver in her voice spoiled the effect.

"In a second. First there's one other thing. The murder charge isn't the only reason I came back. You're my other unfinished business, Mary Grace." He smiled and touched her sagging chin with his forefinger. "Just so you know—I've wanted to make slow, sweet love to you ever since you were about fourteen."

He turned and loped down the porch steps and melded into the dancing shadows cast by the swaying limbs of the oak tree. She stared after him, so shocked she didn't feel the freezing wind whipping in through the open door.

Six

AFTER AN ALMOST SLEEPLESS NIGHT, Grace awoke the next morning to the sound of a cantankerous engine grinding. The noise seemed to be coming from right beneath her window.

Lifting her head from the pillow, she squinted at the bedside clock and groaned. It was barely seven.

The balky engine fired, coughed and sputtered briefly, then backfired like a pistol shot and died. The starter ground again, but the sound quickly tapered off to a pathetic *"unh, unh, unh"* then stopped.

A car door slammed and Grace thought she heard cursing. With a sigh, she tossed back the covers. Her second-floor bedroom was on the northeast corner of the house. She padded barefoot to the window on the driveway side of the room just in time to see the cause of her sleepless night pushing a dilapidated truck up the drive.

A funny feeling whispered through her as she watched him push the truck, that lean, well-honed body straining. *"I've wanted to make slow, sweet love to you since you were about fourteen."* The words echoed through her mind, just as they had all night long, keeping her awake and restless. And, though she hated to admit it, excited.

She couldn't believe he'd actually said that. Jake Paxton, attracted to her? That possibility had never occurred to her. If anything, in the past his attitude toward her had always seemed slightly disdainful. Grace had always assumed that if Jake had any feeling for her at all, it was dislike.

Her own reaction to him she chalked up to nothing more

than that fatal attraction women feel toward dangerous men.

Somewhere around three in the morning she had decided that he was merely trying to rattle her, the way he used to do when they were in school, though to what end she had no idea. It was the only possible explanation that made sense.

Jake disappeared out of her line of vision. She hurried over to the back window and watched him push the pickup through the open doors of the carriage house.

Grace frowned. She could have sworn that those doors had been locked the night before. Folding her arms beneath her breasts, she watched him pull them closed from the inside. He certainly had a lot of nerve, using the carriage house without permission. She had a good mind to go down there and tell him so.

Although . . . it was freezing out. It would certainly be more comfortable working inside, even as big and drafty as the carriage house was. The only thing she used it for these days was to garage her car, and that took up only a fraction of the space. It seemed petty—even mean—to deny him use of the building.

With a sigh, Grace turned away and headed for the shower. Maybe Jake was right. Maybe she was too tender-hearted.

When she came downstairs an hour later the garage doors were still closed and there was no sign of Jake. Grace's gaze strayed out the window every few seconds as she put on the coffee and made herself a slice of toast, but nothing had changed. She could not even be sure he was still inside.

She had just taken her first sip of coffee when someone banged on the front door.

Grace sighed and headed down the hallway. She had a feeling the trouble was about to begin.

She was right.

Through the frosted glass oval in the front door, she could make out the diminutive shape of her great-Aunt Harriet.

The elderly woman rapped the front door two more times with her cane, then let herself in before Grace got there.

"Sakes alive, child. I thought I told you to lock your doors. You could have been killed in your bed."

"I must've left it unlocked when I stepped out to get the

morning paper. And good morning to you, too, Aunt Harriet." Grace kissed the papery cheek the old woman offered and took her coat.

"What brings you here so early?"

"Humph. I'm here because I finally got that communist hippie cousin of yours on the telephone this morning. I couldn't believe what she told me." Harriet scowled and jabbed Grace in the midriff with a bony finger. "Well, my girl. Is it true? Is that no-account Jake Paxton really living in the apartment above the carriage house."

"Yes, Aunt Harriet, he is. And how many times must I tell you, Josie is neither a hippie nor a communist. She's a social worker. She's merely a concerned person doing her best to make a difference."

"Humph. All her life she's been carrying signs and going to rallies and protesting God knows what. Always beating the drum for some cause or jumping on the government about something or trying to help some n'ere-do-well. You ask me, that's communist."

"Well, it isn't," Grace said matter-of-factly and hung the coat in the entry closet. Harriet Tucker was a strong-willed, strong-opinioned woman. Grace had learned long ago that her great-aunt would walk all over you unless you stood up to her—gently but firmly, of course. Anything less and you might as well save your breath. Come on too bossy or authoritative, and she would bash you with her purse.

"Oh pish tosh, who cares. I want to know what you think you're doing, renting the apartment to that man? And don't try to distract me."

"Why don't we talk in the parlor? You go on in. I'll get us some coffee."

"Don't be silly. We'll go to the kitchen as we always do. Now, come along, come along. I want to get to the bottom of this. You've got a lot of explaining to do, my girl."

Silver head high, she stomped away down the central hallway, her cane thumping rhythmically. With a sigh, Grace accepted her fate and trailed after her. She had hoped to keep her aunt away from the back windows, just in case Jake was in the carriage house and decided to come outside. Though her aunt knew about him, Grace thought it would be best if she didn't actually see him.

The elderly woman eased herself down into a chair, propped her cane in front of her knees and stacked her hands over the top. She fixed Grace with a gimlet stare and thumped the cane against the floor. "Would you please explain to me why you let that person move into my family home?"

"He did not move into the house, just the apartment."

"Humph. Same difference."

"Not quite. The apartment wasn't even there when you were growing up in this house."

"Don't split hairs with me, young woman. Just answer my question. Why did you rent to him?"

Grace pulled an exquisite bone china cup and saucer from the cabinet and filled it with coffee. Harriet Tucker did not drink from a crockery mug. She placed the cup on the table before her aunt. "If I hadn't rented him a place to stay, no one else would have."

"That's right. And good riddance, too, I say."

Taking a deep breath, Grace struggled for patience. Before she had a chance to reply, the front doorbell rang.

"Excuse me," she said, and headed down the central hallway with leadened feet. It was starting.

The instant she opened the door her father's sister bustled inside in a dither, her hands fluttering like a pair of caged doves. "Please tell me it's a vicious lie."

Lollie Somerset Madison was the exact opposite of Harriet.

At eighty-three, Grace's great-aunt on her mother's side was a tiny dynamo, feisty and stern, but level-headed and as independent as they came. Harriet still lived alone, she still drove her own car, and she took care of her own affairs, thank you very much. She also didn't put up with any sass nor did she hesitate to tear a strip off of anyone if she thought they deserved it, from the mayor right on down.

Lollie on the other hand was, as Grace's father had affectionately described his only sibling, a flibbertigibbet. She fluttered and fussed and went into hysterics over the least thing. She was a vain and silly creature and totally helpless. Though she stood a good five inches above Grace's five feet four and absolutely towered over Harriet, she had always appeared wary of the tiny woman.

"May I take your coat, dear?"

Without a break in her chatter or the least acknowledgement that she'd heard Grace, Lollie surrendered the coat. "It can't be true. It simply can't be true."

"What can't be true, Aunt Lollie?" But Grace knew. She was there for the same reason as Aunt Harriet, for the same reason her mother-in-law was there, Grace thought with a sigh, watching through the window as Verna drove up.

"That that killer is living here, that's wh— Oh, good. Here comes Verna. I'll bet she'll get to the bottom of this."

Grace had the door open for Verna by the time she reached the top step. "Come in. You might as well join the party."

"Brrr. I do believe it's gotten colder over night," Verna exclaimed, sailing in the door in a dramatic fur-trimmed cashmere cape, tons of jewelry and trailing a cloud of perfume. "Hello, Lollie. Good morning, Grace." She bestowed a quick kiss on Grace's cheek as she handed over her wrap. "I'm sorry to drop by so early, but I heard the most disturbing news from Lyle this morning. Dearest, we have to talk."

"I know. Why don't we join Aunt Harriet in the kitchen. She's here for the same reason. That way you can all gang up on me," she said with a rueful smile.

The instant they trooped into the kitchen, Grace glanced out the window at the closed doors of the carriage house and sent up a cowardly prayer for Jake to remain inside, if, indeed, he was still there.

"Then it's *true?* You really have rented your apartment to that . . . that . . . murdering fiend."

"Of course it's true, Lollie," Harriet snapped. "Why else do you think I'm here at this hour of the morning?"

As though to underscore the statement, at that moment the carriage doors opened and Jake strode out, wearing a tool belt strapped around his middle and carrying several pieces of lumber.

"There he is now! Oh! Oh! What shall we do? Oh, this is terrible." Lollie sank down onto one of the kitchen chairs and pressed one hand to her heart. "I can't bear this. It's just too awful. I think . . . I think I'm going to faint."

Harriet's cane thumped the floor. "You'll do no such thing, Lollie Madison. Stop that foolishness this instant. We're here to talk some sense into Grace, not witness your silly theatrics."

"Well!" Lollie huffed, shooting Harriet a look of deep affront, but she said no more.

"What is he doing?"

Grace followed Harriet's gaze, and received a surprise. As she watched, Jake tore out the rotten step on the stairs and began to hammer a new one into place. "Why . . . it looks like he's repairing the apartment stairs."

"Humph."

"Grace, how could you do such a thing?" her mother-in-law asked in a pathetic voice. "Taking in that vicious criminal."

A murmur of agreement came from the other women, and Grace sighed. "Ladies, please. May I remind you that Jake Paxton was never convicted of a crime?"

"Well, he should have been. Lord knows, my poor Charles did his best to see that he got what he deserved. And you taking him in this way is an insult to my son's memory," Verna said in a quavery voice. She dabbed her eyes with a lace-edged hanky and gave Grace a reproachful look. "I'm hurt, Grace. Truly I am. And very disappointed in you."

The comment was typical, and no more than Grace had expected. In her genteel, Southern-belle way, Verna was a lovely woman, and certainly she had always been a loving mother-in-law. Grace was fond of her, but she wasn't blind to her faults. Manipulation and emotional blackmail were her mother-in-law's stock and trade. Verna never raised her voice or used harsh words. She didn't have to, when tears and a bit of deftly applied guilt worked so well.

"Oh, for heaven's sake, Verna. The only thing either Charles or Lyle could tell the juries in both trials was that they had seen

Jake with Carla Mae that night. It's not as though he witnessed the murder."

Verna sniffed and shot Harriet an offended look. "I'll have you know, it was my son's testimony that led to Jake's arrest. And if Grace had any respect for his memory or any concern for my feelings, she wouldn't allow that man on her property, much less rent him an apartment."

"Verna, dear, I didn't mean any disrespect or insult. Please try to understand. I'm simply trying to do what's right."

"Humph. I should have known," Harriet muttered.

"By taking in a murderer?"

"Aunt Lollie, please—" Grace began, but Lollie was on a roll.

"And you living all alone out here on this isolated farm. Why, it'll be a miracle if he doesn't cut your throat in your sleep some night."

"Now, Grace, you know I think Lollie is a silly, pious fool."

"What? Why, I never—"

"We've never seen eye to eye on anything, and you know it," Harriet went on, ignoring Lollie's indignation. "But, bad as it pains me to do so, I'm afraid I have to agree with her on this." She reached across the table and laid her spotted, gnarled hand over Grace's, and her voice gentled with concern. "Child, I know you always strive to do what's right, and I couldn't be prouder of you for it if you were my very own daughter, but you're taking a terrible risk, putting your trust in Jake Paxton."

Grace bit her lower lip. Were Verna and her aunts right? Was she making a mistake? Her gaze went once more to the man in the yard. Jake had finished the repair to the stairs and was working on the sagging carriage house door. She smiled softly. No. She didn't think so.

"A risk! That's putting it mildly," Lollie scoffed. "The girl's being downright foolish."

Grace tilted her chin. "I don't think so. My father would have done exactly what I am doing had he lived, and you know it."

"Oh, I don't doubt it for moment. But that's just the problem. You're just like that foolish brother of mine, too softhearted and compassionate for your own good. It's just too bad that your dear mother died of a broken heart at so young an age. Perhaps she could have made him take off his rose-colored glasses and see people for what they are."

"Mother died of an aneurysm in the brain, not a broken heart."

Lollie sniffed. "I don't care what that old fool, Dr. Watley, and all those fancy doctors down in Houston said, I know what I know. When that wild sister of yours ran off with a married man at age seventeen it broke poor Madelene's heart and killed her."

"You're a fool, Lollie Madison," Harriet declared with a thump of her cane. "Pay no attention to her, Grace."

Grace didn't, but it infuriated her they way Lollie never missed an opportunity to crucify Caroline.

"A fool, am I? Well just let me tell you—"

"Oh do hush up, Lollie! I swear to goodness you'd blame the Crucifixion on Caroline if you could."

"Harriet Tucker!" Lollie gasped. "That's . . . why that's blasphemous!"

ಬಿ

The weekend went downhill from there.

Grace had barely managed to convince the three ladies that she wasn't going to change her mind and send them on their way when the telephone started ringing—and kept ringing throughout the day. It seemed that half the people she knew called. They all wanted the same thing: to know if it was true that she had rented her apartment to Jake Paxton. Grace was a patient woman, but after hours of repeating the same thing and answering the same questions over and over, her nerves were frayed.

Which was why, when Edith Hollister, the woman who worked part time at Things Remembered, called that afternoon Grace's hello was a bit abrupt.

"Grace? Is that you?"

"Oh, Edith, I'm sorry. I didn't mean to bite your head off. Is there a problem?"

"Well. . yes. I hated to call you. I heard about your new tenant and I know you're probably being inundated with calls, but. . ."

"But what?"

"It's Charley Sneed."

"What about him? Don't tell me he didn't show up for work?"

"Oh, he showed up, all right. Six hours late and stinking drunk. He's passed out in the storeroom right now."

"Oh, no, not again." Grace leaned her forehead against the wall beside the kitchen telephone. This was all she needed.

Charlie was her handyman. He ran errands, made deliveries, stripped furniture and supplied the muscle it took to move the heavier antiques. The last time he had gone on a binge she had warned him that if it happened again she would have to fire him. Now she had to follow through on that threat, although how she was going to manage without a handyman she didn't know.

"All right," Grace sighed. "I'll be right there."

Jake was working on the picket fence that surrounded the yard when she stepped out of the back door. She didn't want to talk to him, but she couldn't just walk right by him and not say something. Reluctantly, she paused by the fence.

"I appreciate all you've done today, Jake, but you don't have to work around here, you know."

He glanced at her over his shoulder, and went right on pounding a nail into place. He was wearing his denim jacket over a plain white T-shirt, and his face was ruddy from the cold. "I know. It's no problem. Since I don't have the parts I need to fix my truck, I might as well do something useful."

"I see. Well . . . if that's what you want . . ."

He didn't seemed inclined to talk, and after an uneasy moment she said good-bye and left.

At the store Grace called her friend Harley Newcomb, the county sheriff, to come and get Charlie. Between them, she and Harley managed to rouse the drunken idiot long enough for Grace to give him his walking papers, then Harley hauled him off to detox.

By then it was getting late. Grace helped Edith close up the store, then, not anxious to return to the ringing telephone and Jake, she decided to have dinner at the City Diner. That turned out not to be one of her better decisions.

Since she knew almost everyone in town she had to answer more questions, not just about Jake but about Daniel Street, the man whom she had been dating for the past few months.

Normally on Saturday nights she and Daniel went out, and her presence alone at the diner aroused curiosity. Daniel was the young minister who had taken over her father's congregation after his death, and most of the parishioners were pleased that they were seeing one another.

The exception was Verna. Lately her mother-in-law had been doing her best to promote a romance between Grace and Lyle. The very idea made Grace shudder.

Among the many calls Grace had received that day had been one from Daniel to tell her that he had to go to Bedalia to be with a family whose young child was critically ill.

Grace had hopes that she and Daniel could build a future together. Daniel was precisely the sort of man she had always hoped to marry, the type of man she *should* marry.

He was good and kind and decent. He was dedicated to his calling and his congregation, and they got along beautifully. He was also good-looking, and they had a lot in common. If he didn't exactly make her heart go pitty-pat or leave her breathless and all hot and bothered, well, what did that matter? Six years of marriage to a spoiled, self-centered, verbally abusive, philandering husband had pretty much cured her of any silly schoolgirl notions of love and romance.

Daniel was a wonderful man and he would make a good husband and father, and Grace wanted children. Lots of children. Enough to fill up her family home and make it ring with laughter once again.

It was dark by the time Grace returned to the farm. Much to her relief, the only sign of Jake was the glow of lights from the apartment windows.

That relief was an illusion, she discovered the next morning when Jake knocked on her back door as she was about to leave for church.

Surprise flashed through when she opened the door. She had never seen Jake in anything but jeans, but this morning he was dressed in a charcoal suit, a crisp white shirt and a maroon, black, and white tie. He looked gorgeous. She blinked several times, then shook her head and said with a touch of impatience,

"Yes?"

"Good morning. I'd like to ask a favor."

"I'm sorry, Jake, but I don't have much time. I'm on my way to church." She already had her coat on and her purse in her hand. Surely he could see that.

"That's why I'm here. I'm going to church, too. I wondered if you'd mind giving me a ride."

Seven

"WHAT'S THE MATTER, MARY GRACE? Cat got your tongue?" A slow grin curved Jake's mouth as he reached out and lifted her sagging jaw with his forefinger.

She jerked her head back, breaking contact with that warm finger, but shock still reverberated through her. Good Lord. Take Jake Paxton to church with her? She could just imagine what kind of reaction that would provoke.

The unholy gleam in his eyes told her he knew exactly just what a spot he'd put her in, too. Like just about everyone else in town, many in the congregation were convinced that he was guilty of murdering Carla Mae, and they would not take kindly to having him in their midst.

While Jake had lived in Cedar Grove, to her knowledge, he had never set foot in a church, and she was dubious about his reasons for wanting to now. She strongly suspected that he simply wanted to stir up trouble. The way he always had.

He had, however, effectively backed her into a corner. How could she refuse to take someone—*anyone*—to church?

The answer, of course, was, she couldn't.

THE EXPERIENCE was every bit as horrendous as Grace had expected it would be.

They were late, and when they entered the sanctuary she could feel the shock waves ripple through the congregation. For the first time in her life, Grace regretted that the first pew had traditionally been reserved for the Tuckers and Somersets. Instead of taking a seat in the back of the church, as she had hoped he would, Jake stuck by her side. The walk down that long aisle with him solicitously holding her elbow seemed interminable. Gasps and mutters and snippets of outraged remarks followed in their wake as they made their way down the aisle.

Her two aunts were already seated, and Grace slipped into the pew next to Harriet with a wan smile of apology. When Jake took the aisle seat on Grace's right Harriet started, but Lollie gave a squeak of alarm that was heard on the back row.

"What is that man doing here," Harriet hissed in Grace's ear.

"He asked for a ride to church," she whispered back. "What was I to do?"

"Humph." Leaning forward, Harriet glared at Jake. When satisfied that he'd gotten her warning, she sat back, straight as a marine drill instructor, stacked her hands atop her cane and folded her mouth in a firm line.

On Harriet's other side, making desperate little noises, Lollie fluttered and fanned herself and cast repeated terrified glances Jake's way, as though she expected him to leap up and attack her at any second. Only when Harriet gave her a sharp whack with a rolled up church bulletin did she hush.

From the pulpit, Daniel cocked an eyebrow and gave Grace a quizzical look, but he did not seem upset.

For Grace the entire service passed in a blur. She could not have told you what hymns they sang or what Daniel's sermon was about. She went through the motions by rote, following Harriet's lead, rising and sitting and bowing her head in prayer when her aunt did. Sharing a hymnal with Jake so unnerved her she had to leave it to him to turn to the right page, and she merely mouthed the words when the congregation sang. Even if she could have gathered her wits enough to read the lyrics she was in such a state of high anxiety she feared the only sound that would come out was a croak.

All she could think about was the man beside her. Even in scruffy jeans and T-shirt Jake drew the female eye, but he was stunningly handsome in a suit and tie. He sat on the padded bench seat, his thigh pressed against hers. Standing, sharing the hymnal was no better. With each tiny movement the sleeve of his suit coat brushed her arm, and the slight abrasion sent tingles rippling over her skin. She was acutely aware of that dark suited arm and the masculine hand extending from the snowy white cuff, the warmth of his skin, the clean smell that emanated from him, a heady combination of soap, shaving cream, starch and male.

At the close of the service Grace tried to delay their departure long enough for everyone else to get out, but Jake took her arm and led her right into the crush of people heading down the center aisle.

Some people, though obviously uneasy, nodded or murmured a polite, "Hello." Others of slightly less charitable nature at least had the good manners to simply ignore him, but Grace knew that they weren't going to get off that easy. They were in the minority, thank goodness, but among the congregation was a small group of pious, holier-than-thou types who were sure to react to his presence with hostility.

Daniel, standing in the doorway, greeting his parishioners individually as they filed out, was, bless him, his usual gracious self. "Hello, Grace," he said in a warm voice, taking her hand in both of his. "I'm sorry about last night, but I really needed to be with the Conners."

Grace could feel Jake's eyes on her and she sensed his sudden alertness. "Don't worry about it, Daniel. How is their little girl?"

"Not good, I'm afraid. It's just a matter of time before they lose her." He shook his head sadly. Then with a determined effort he shook off the mood and turned his gaze on Jake and offered his hand. "You must be Jake Paxton. Grace told me she'd rented you her apartment. Welcome to our church."

Suspicion narrowed Jake's eyes, but after a brief hesitation he clasped the reverend's outstretched hand and gave it a shake. "Thanks."

More people were waiting behind them to speak to the minister, so the two moved on, stepping outside into the sunshine and the cold wind.

"Grace, we want to speak with you." Ida Bell Wheatly and a cluster of her cronies, which included Verna and Lollie and several of the church deacons, were waiting at the bottom of the steps as Grace and Jake descended. The hostility of the group was almost palpable. "In private," Ida Bell added, casting Jake a hate-filled look.

"Certainly. Jake, would you mind waiting for me in the van? I won't be long."

"You sure?" He looked from one to the other of the hostile group. "I'll stay if you want."

"No, that's okay. You go on."

He shrugged. "Suit yourself."

Head high, he walked away through the milling people in the church yard. Giving him a wide berth, they stepped aside at his approach, and he passed through them like Moses parting the Red Sea.

"How *could* you, Grace?" Ida Bell snarled. "How could you bring *that* man to God's house?"

"The church is open to everyone, Ida Bell," Grace replied patiently.

"Not to people like that. Not to killers."

The others murmured agreement, adding dark comments of their own.

"Jake isn't a killer. I never thought so from the start. Neither did our courts."

"Then you're a fool. Those people in Houston who served on his juries didn't know anything about Jake Paxton. But the people in this town know exactly what he is. No good trash."

"Even if that were true, that doesn't prove he killed that girl. Nor is it a reason to bar him from attending services." Though gentle, Grace's smile held unmistakable reproach. "The church isn't for saints, Ida Bell. It's for sinners. Isn't that why we're all here?"

A few in the little group, especially the deacons, shifted uneasily and looked shamed-faced, but Ida Bell's mouth drew up as though she'd just sucked the juice out of a lemon. "Are you comparing me to Jake Paxton?"

"No. I'm merely saying that none of us is perfect. So who is to say who can attend and who can't? Now if you'll excuse me, I really must go."

Grace walked away with an unruffled expression on her

face. As she wound her way through the after-church crowd she was hailed by various groups, and each time she stopped briefly to exchange pleasantries. She smiled and chatted and answered questions about Jake in a gracious manner, but inside she was annoyed—with her friends and relations for their judgmental attitude, and with Jake for putting her into such a ticklish position.

"Grace, dear, wait."

Grace stopped and turned in time to see Verna detach herself from Ida Bell's group and hurry after her. When she reached Grace she put her hand on her arm. Her expression was woeful and her eyes swam with tears. "Grace, dear, you're not . . . you're not thinking of bringing that . . . that vile creature to my home, are you?"

Grace sighed. Until that moment she had forgotten that she and Daniel were supposed to go to the Willows, the Ames family home, for Sunday dinner. With all that had happened in the past few days it had slipped her mind. The dinners had become almost a weekly ritual ever since Grace had moved out of the Ames mansion. She did not enjoy the visits, mainly because her mother-in-law spent the entire time pressuring her to move back into the Willows.

"No, Verna. Of course not," she replied with as much patience as she could muster.

"Oh. Well good. That's good. I just wanted to be certain. You're so tender-hearted and forgiving, one never knows. Not that those aren't admirable qualities, my dear," she added quickly. "They are, of course. But, well . . ."

"Never mind, Verna. I understand."

By the time Grace reached the van she was thoroughly put out, and the sight of Jake slouched in the passenger seat as though he hadn't a care, somehow irritated her more.

He had removed his coat and tie and rolled his shirtsleeves up. The sight of those muscular forearms, liberally sprinkled with dark hair sent a little shiver through her, and she slammed the door harder than she'd intended.

"Something wrong?"

"Of course not. What could possibly be wrong?"

He raised his eyebrows at the honeyed sarcasm in her voice,

but before he could speak, Daniel tapped on the window on the driver's side.

"Hi. Sorry, I forgot to mention, I'll be by to pick you up in about half an hour. Is that okay?"

Grace could feel Jake's eyes on her, and she shifted on the seat, anxious to be gone. For some reason she didn't understand, she didn't feel comfortable making plans with Daniel in front of him.

"That's fine. I'll see you then."

Eight

From the church yard, cold eyes followed the departing van. Fury built inside the watcher.

So . . . Jake was back, was he? How, after all that had happened, did he dare show his face here again?

He would pay for this. Oh, yes, he would pay. He could not be allowed to get away with such an affront.

Nine

"IS THE GOOD REVEREND YOUR BOYFRIEND?"

Grace darted a cautious glance at Jake out of the corner of her eye and turned onto main street and headed north. "We've been dating, if that's what you mean."

"Are you sleeping with him?"

"What?" Her jaw dropped and she shot him an appalled look then had to slam on the brakes to keep from rear-ending the car in front of her when it stopped at the traffic light. "May I remind you that Daniel Street is a man of the cloth?" she replied huffily.

"So? He's still a man."

Grace gritted her teeth. "Just because men of your caliber have no control that doesn't mean all men are the same."

"He's a saint, huh. Must be damned dull."

She stared straight ahead and refused to dignify the comment with a reply. The light changed, and Grace stepped on the gas. In less than a minute they were out of town and speeding down the highway at a much faster clip than she usually drove.

The silent treatment did not deter Jake. Turning sideways in the bucket seat, he hooked his arm over the back and studied her profile. "So, Saint Grace has found her match. I'm curious. Just how do two saints make out?"

"Do you think you could refrain from being so disgusting? And don't call me that."

She turned onto the country lane that led to the farm and drove the last half mile without so much as glancing his way. At the farm, she stopped the car in the driveway and waited in offended silence for him to get out.

Jake didn't budge.

Finally she turned her head and found he was watching her. "Would you please get out?"

"Sure." He opened the door and climbed from the van, then turned and grinned at her across the seat. "Have fun. Oh, and be sure and give my love to your mother-in-law."

He closed the door and sauntered away and climbed the stairs to the apartment, his suit coat hanging from one finger and slung over his shoulder.

Grace watched him with a myriad of emotions squeezing her chest, mostly exasperation. Fun was the last thing she expected to have. And if she dared to relate his message, Verna would keel over and die.

Resting her head back against the car seat, Grace gazed out at the gathering twilight and let her mind float. She could do that with Daniel; he was such a peaceful person.

"Tired?"

She rolled her head on the back of the seat and looked at him, smiling softly. "Mmm."

He was such a handsome man. With his blond hair, neatly parted on one side and perfectly cut, his pale blue eyes and even features, his slender physique, he had a clean-cut, ultra-civilized look that inspired trust.

Unlike that dangerous, slightly disreputable aura of Jake's that sent little prickles of fear and excitement through her nervous system whenever she was within six feet of him.

"Well, you have a right to be. Verna was a bit of a trial today."

Grace chuckled.

Daniel released the steering wheel with one hand long enough to reach over and pat her arm. "But, as usual, you handled her very skillfully."

"Mmm. What you were watching was the result of years of practice."

A bit of a trial was putting it mildly. Verna had been in fine form. Her mother-in-law was put out with her, and as usual, Verna's disapproval had taken the form of self-pity and repeated attempts at emotional blackmail.

She had even tried to solicit Daniel's help over dinner.

"Reverend Street, perhaps you can talk some sense into Grace. Lord knows, I've tried, but this foolish child just won't listen to me, even though she knows I'm worried sick about her. Why, last night I had one of my migraines I was so upset just thinking about her being out there on that isolated farm with that man.

"I've tried my best to be a loving mother to her, but she obviously doesn't care about my feelings or my health. Perhaps you can persuade her to have the sheriff evict that horrible man. She should never have allowed him on her property in the first place."

"Well . . . actually, Mrs. Ames, I'm afraid I can't do that. You see, I trust Grace's instincts."

"What? Do you mean to say you're taking the side of that criminal?"

"Not exactly. I don't know Mr. Paxton. The murder and the trials happened long before I came to Cedar Grove. However, from what I've been able to piece together, the only thing of which the man is guilty is being born poor."

Verna shot Daniel an annoyed look and sniffed. "He's also a bastard."

"That is hardly his fault, now is it?" Daniel said with gentle reproach.

"Well . . . no. Of course not. But no one even knows who his father is. And breeding will tell, you know."

"I wouldn't know about that. But I have to say, I applaud Grace for her compassion. Not many people would give a man a chance in the face of so much opposition." He smiled at Grace across the dining table, and a warm feeling spread through her. Daniel was such a dear man.

Verna's face had taken on that pinched, martyred look she assumed whenever she was losing an argument. "Yes. Our Grace always did have a soft heart," she had agreed, but somehow she'd managed to make the trait sound like a shortcoming instead of a virtue.

"Perhaps it's my imagination, but I get the feeling that Verna doesn't really like me."

Surprise flickered through Grace. She hadn't realized that

Daniel was so perceptive. "Oh, I wouldn't worry about it. It's nothing personal."

An amused smile tilted the corners of Grace's mouth. Poor Verna. Where Daniel was concerned, she was caught between the proverbial rock and a hard place. She was not at all happy about the developing relationship between Grace and the reverend, but she had no choice but to hide her feelings and be polite to him. He was, after all, a highly respectable, decent man, an excellent minister and an ideal catch, especially for someone with Grace's background.

"Oh? Well, that's good to know. But if it's not me, personally, then what is the problem? I haven't done anything to offend or hurt her as far as I know."

"No, of course you haven't." Grace sat up straighter in the seat. She hesitated, not sure if she should tell him, but she didn't have much choice, other than a lie, and she wouldn't do that. "Verna wouldn't approve of anyone I dated, unless it was Lyle. She wants me to marry him."

"Ah, I see. And are you considering it?"

"Heavens no! I'd rather kiss a toad."

Daniel threw his head back and laughed. "And have you told her that?"

"Repeatedly. But no matter how many times I tell her that I'm not interested in Lyle, that I will never be interested in Lyle, Verna just keeps right on trying to promote a romance between us. My mother-in-law, in her fluttery, genteel way, is a control freak. She refuses to accept that she can't always make things go her way, so she tunes out what she doesn't want to hear."

Looking back, Grace now realized that Verna had hand-picked her to be Charles's wife and the mother of future generations of Ameses.

Grace was the great-great-granddaughter of the town's founders and the daughter of a much loved and respected minister. In her mother-in-law's estimation, that had made her a suitable mate for her beloved son.

Verna had encouraged Charles to date her and had welcomed Grace into the Ames family with open arms. Now she was trying to keep her in the family by marrying her off to Lyle.

Grace was flattered that Verna thought so highly of her, especially when one considered the problems many women had with their mother-in-laws. She was, in fact, quite fond of Verna, despite her faults, but there was no power on earth that could make Grace marry Lyle.

She had never liked him. Before Charles's death, he had been the poor relation and Charles's adoring sidekick, and so in awe of his rich cousin it was sickening. Now, as the only relative, Lyle was the heir apparent to the Ames fortune. At Verna's invitation, he had even moved into the Willows. Although, like Charles, his only source of income was the allowance he received from Verna, his elevated position had gone to his head. He was cocky and overbearing, which made him more insufferable than ever.

"Well, at least that explains Lyle's hostility," Daniel said as he turned onto the farm road. "He, I take it, is quite willing to go along with his aunt's wishes."

"Oh yes. For some strange reason, Lyle seems to think that anything that belonged to Charles is now his, me included. I'm having difficulty convincing him otherwise."

Daniel chuckled. "I have faith in you."

Grace turned her head and gazed out at the gathering darkness. Lyle wasn't her only problem. Verna had pressed her again today about giving up the farm. As she and Daniel had been about to leave she had asked to speak to Grace in private. In her study Verna had turned to her with a pleading look and gripped her hands tightly.

"Grace, dearest, won't you please reconsider and move back here. After all, there's no longer anything keeping you at the farm. And I would feel so much better, knowing you were away from that terrible man."

Sighing, Grace had shaken her head. It was an argument she was hearing more and more as time went on. "I'm sorry, Verna, but I can't. The farm is my home."

"The Willows is your home," Verna insisted with a trace of affront. "You are an Ames now."

"Verna, dear, please try to understand. I love the farm. Five generations of Tuckers have lived there. I'm quite happy and comfortable where I am."

Much more comfortable than she'd ever been in the Willows. The Ames mansion was as cold and suffocatingly stiff and formal as her own home was cozy.

"If the problem is that little business of yours, you can keep that. Although, there's really no reason for you to bother. I'm perfectly willing to give you the same allowance I gave Charles."

That was one of the problems. As fond as Grace was of Verna, the thought of being financially dependent on her or remaining under her subtle domination for the rest of her life was unbearable. Shortly after Charles had been killed she moved out of the Willows and back to the farm, telling Verna that her father's health was failing and he needed her.

It had been the truth, Grace remembered sadly. Although at the time she had not realized just how ill her father really was. Ten months after she had returned home he had passed away.

Ever since then, Verna had been campaigning to get her to return to the Willows.

In what seemed like no time at all Daniel turned into her driveway.

The last glow of twilight had slipped away, and the sedan's headlights cut through the darkness, arcing across the wraparound front porch of the ornate old farmhouse. Vines of wisteria, honeysuckle and roses, all sprouting new shoots and heavy with buds, clung to the posts and hung in graceful swags from the fancy fretwork.

The house was in darkness as Daniel escorted her up the brick walkway. She stopped at the base of the steps and turned to him. "Thanks for coming with me to Verna's. I really appreciate your support."

"Anytime."

"And I enjoyed the drive afterward. I've been sort of tense lately, and it was very relaxing."

Daniel smiled and clasped her upper arms, massaging gently. "I'm glad I could be of help. Now, why don't you treat yourself to an early night? You look like you could use it."

"I think I will."

Hesitating, he searched her face, then bent and kissed her. It was an undemanding kiss, soft as spring rain. It held affection and respect... and stirred not one iota of desire in Grace, even though she stepped closer and clutched his suit coat and responded with more ardor than she felt.

When Daniel raised his head, she noted that his breathing, too, was even and slow and she could feel his heart beating against her palm with a steady rhythm. He smiled and touched her cheek with his fingertip. "I'll call you tomorrow."

She climbed the porch steps, then turned to watch him stride to his car. Even in the faint moonlight he looked so tall and lean and so utterly upright. He started the car and backed down the drive. Wrapping her arms around the post she laid her cheek against the twining honeysuckle vine and watched with melancholy eyes as his taillights disappeared. Daniel was so absolutely perfect for her in so many ways. Why didn't he excite her?

"You call that a kiss?"

Grace jumped and let out a little scream. She whirled around and stared into the shadows on the porch and made out the silhouette of a man, lounging in the porch swing. "Jake Paxton! What are you doing there? You scared me half to death!"

She sagged weakly against the post and closed her eyes. Her heart felt as though it was about to club its way right out of her chest.

The swing creaked and the chains jingled as Jake rose. The heels of his boots struck the board floor with slow thuds. He walked out of the shadows and stopped before her. The look in his eyes made Grace's heart rate, which was just beginning to return to normal, take off again.

"Jake? Wh-What are you doing?"

Ignoring her question and the sudden panicky look in her eyes, in one deliberate move he slid his hand beneath the long fall of her hair, cupped her neck in a firm grip and jerked her up against his chest. His other arm wrapped around her and she found herself staring up into those intense green eyes.

Then his mouth claimed hers.

The kiss was like nothing she had ever experienced. It made her head spin and her pulses pound and took her breath away. There was nothing tentative or restrained about the embrace. This was a man taking what he wanted. His mouth rocked over hers, taking her in, devouring her like a starving man devours a feast.

His lips were firm and yet somehow soft at the same time. And hot. Oh, so hot. Grace felt as though she were melting, her body blending into his. She clung to him, on fire and trembling.

He traced her lips with his tongue, and when they quivered and parted he plunged inside. He was a conqueror staking a claim, charting unknown territory. His tongue swirled in her mouth, twined with hers in a sinuous dance, skated over her teeth.

He made a low growl and shifted his stance, bracing his feet wider and pulling her into a more intimate embrace, pressing her tight against his arousal. Then his tongue began to plunge in and out, in and out, in quick rhythmic thrusts that mimicked the rocking motion of his hips against hers.

Grace moaned. She was on fire. Every cell in her body came alive with tingling awareness, every nerve ending danced and hummed. Her sensory perception became so acute she was awash with tactile sensations. She felt each button on his shirt, the buckle on his belt, pressing into her flesh, that hard arm across her back like an iron clamp, the large hand clasping her nape, each long finger buried in her hair and pressed against her scalp. She was acutely aware of the breadth and muscled strength of his chest and the way her soft breasts were molded against that firm wall, in their centers, the nipples puckered into firm little pebbles, so achingly tight and tender.

Like a hot zephyr, his breath eddied across her cheek. Her breathing was erratic and shallow, and with each desperate intake of air she drew in his scent. Its heady maleness made her head spin. She felt the hotness of his skin, the soft cotton shirt, the rough denim of his pants.

Her body quivered and hummed like a struck tuning fork. All she could do was cling to his solid bulk and give herself up to the soul-shattering kiss.

When at last he raised his head she hung in his arms like a

ragdoll, limp and boneless, her lips still parted and kiss swollen, her eyes closed. Her eyelids fluttered open and she looked up into the hard glitter of his gaze.

"That," he said in a gravelly murmur, "was a kiss."

The next instant she found herself leaning weakly against the post at her back, watching him walk away into the shadows and disappear around the corner of the porch. She heard his boots thud down the steps of the side porch.

Then there was only silence and the thundering of her heart.

Ten

OVER THE NEXT TWO DAYS Grace saw little of Jake, merely glimpses as he came and went—and lights in the windows of the apartment. That suited her just fine. After that shattering kiss, she was not anxious to encounter him again any time soon.

The kiss disturbed her tremendously. It had effectively revealed to her something she would never have dreamed possible; she was attracted to Jake.

She didn't like it, not one bit, but she couldn't deny the way he made her body hum. Grace was much too honest for that.

Jake Paxton, of all people. It was ludicrous.

Of course he was handsome as sin, in that dangerous sort of way, and everything about him, from those stormy green eyes to that insolent saunter, oozed sex.

She had no intention of acting on the attraction. The very idea was absurd. She simply didn't know yet what to do to make it go away, except stay as far away from him as she possibly could.

On Wednesday morning Grace had to leave early for an estate sale in Houston in order to get there in time to preview the antiques before the auction began. After the third straight restless night of tossing and turning, she could barely drag herself out of bed when the alarm sounded.

The pearly, half-light of predawn was beginning to seep into the sky when she drove down the long driveway in her cargo van. There were no lights on in the apartment, and Jake's dilapidated truck sat in the circular drive before the house. She would have to speak to him about that. She didn't want that eyesore parked in front of her house all the time.

She glanced at the clock, then in the rear-view mirror at the dark apartment. He would never make it to the mill by seven, she thought. And her Uncle Hank was a stickler for promptness.

Stifling the urge to go back and wake him, she turned out onto the gravel road and headed for the highway. Jake Paxton wasn't her responsibility. She'd done her part as Good Samaritan in renting him the apartment. If he wanted to louse up and get himself fired the first week on the job, that was his problem.

At that hour there was little traffic on the road. All Grace encountered when she turned on the highway were a few eighteen-wheelers and a farmer taking a stock trailer full of cattle to the auction barn.

About a half a mile north of town she spotted a man dressed in jeans and a denim jacket walking alongside the road with his hands in his pockets and his shoulders hunched against the north wind. She wondered who he was and where he'd come from. Her place was three miles north of Cedar Grove and there was nothing between there and town but the fields and woods that were all part of the Somerset farm.

There was something vaguely familiar about that loose-limbed stride and the gritty determination in the man's posture. Grace knew he must have heard her van approaching, but he kept his head down and made no attempt to hitchhike. A split second before she went whizzing past him his identity registered.

Her gaze flew to the rear-view mirror. Good Lord. It was Jake.

Her foot went automatically to the brake. As the van slowed she craned her neck to watch him in the mirror. What on earth was he doing out here on foot? The temperature was near freezing.

She hesitated and chewed her lower lip. Jake Paxton wasn't her problem. Just because she'd rented him an apartment didn't make her obligated to look after him. He was a grown man.

Still . . . the sawmill was two miles on the other side of town. And she was going to go right by it.

Sighing, she pulled over onto the shoulder of the road and brought the van to a halt.

In the mirror she saw Jake's head jerk up. He hesitated only an instant, then trotted up to the van and jumped in.

"I didn't think you were going to stop," he said, as he settled into the bucket seat.

The crisp cold scent of the outdoors clung to him. Mixed with it were the smells of shaving cream and soap . . . and male. Grace glanced at him and caught her breath. He exuded an aura of raw masculinity that hit her like the shock wave from a bomb blast.

Jake's large frame seemed to take up all the space. By his very presence, silent and brooding, he dominated. His steady green eyes made her feel exposed and vulnerable as a trapped doe. What was it about Jake that had such a devastating effect on her equilibrium? And why him, of all men?

He shot her what passed for a smile. "Thanks. I appreciate the lift," he murmured, and slouched down on his spine in the bucket seat to assume his usual, "don't give a damn" attitude.

His long legs sprawled apart, and one jean-clad knee propped against the console gear box just inches from her hand. The wind had tousled his hair but he leaned his head back against the seat and made no effort to tidy it.

"Put on your seat belt, please. I don't want to get a ticket." The request came out sharper than she intended, but Jake made her nervous.

"We wouldn't want that," he sneered. "Sheriff Greely would probably pee all over himself for the chance to lock me up again."

"They don't lock you up for not wearing a seat belt, they just give you a heavy fine. And Oscar Greely isn't sheriff anymore."

Jake's head whipped around. "You're shittin' me. Who is?"

"Harley Newcomb. Maybe you remember him. Tall, kind of barrel-chested, brown hair. He was a new deputy twelve years ago. He would have been in his late twenties at the time. He's fair and honest and a good officer."

"Yeah. I remember him." Jake's sneer eloquently expressed his opinion of all law officers.

His surprise was understandable. So was his bitterness. Oscar Greely had been sheriff of Carver County for longer than most folks could remember. A bigoted, cigar-smoking, beer-bellied, redneck bully, Oscar had used intimidation and brutality to carry out the duties of his office. In Grace's opinion, the man was unfit to wear a uniform, but, because he'd managed to keep most major crime out of the Cedar Grove and the rest of the county, he'd gotten reelected, election after election.

The one black mark on his otherwise perfect record had been the murder and rape of Carla Mae Sheffield. For Jake, that had earned Oscar's undying hatred. Grace was fairly certain that before he'd been transferred to the jail down in Houston he had suffered at the sheriff's hands.

"What were you doing walking to work?"

"My truck won't run. The carburetor needs work. I've tried it every day. This morning it finally started, but I only got as far as the road before it conked out again. I pushed it back into the drive in front of your house and started hiking again."

She looked at him, surprised. "You mean, you've been walking to and from the sawmill for the past two days?

"I didn't have much choice."

"You could have asked me for a ride."

"My shift starts two hours before you open your store. By the way, when I walked through town the first day I looked in the windows. You've got a nice place."

"Thank you." The compliment surprised her into silence momentarily, but she couldn't dismiss from her mind the image of him walking six miles to work every morning in the cold, then walking back again after working hard all day. It was certain no one would offer him a lift.

"Will you be able to repair the truck yourself?" She doubted any mechanic in this town would touch it, not even if he paid him double, and she had no intention of chauffeuring him to work every day.

"Sure. If I had the money for parts. Until I get a payday or two under my belt, I guess I'll just have to hoof it." He shot her a sardonic look. "I'll push the truck back into the carriage house if you want me to. We wouldn't want your neighbors to think I was pulling an over-nighter."

Grace blushed, as she was sure he intended, but she kept her head up. "You know perfectly well I don't have any neighbors. But even if I did, I can assure you that no one would think any such thing."

He turned his head, and she could feel him staring at her. "Hmm. Still Little Miss Perfect, are you."

She shot him a sharp glance. "Of course not. I never claimed to be perfect."

"C'mon, Mary Grace. You've never made a wrong step in your life. Well . . . with the exception of marrying that asshole, Charles Ames. Hell, even when we were in school you were the model teenager. You made good grades, never did anything you weren't supposed to, went to church three times a week."

"How do you know how often I attended church?" He didn't answer for a few seconds, and when she glanced his way his green eyes were trained on her with disturbing intensity.

"You'd be surprised what I know about you, Mary Grace," he said finally in a silky murmur that sent gooseflesh rippling up her arms.

Afraid to ask what, exactly, Grace stared straight ahead at the road and nudged the van's speed a little higher. "Okay, so what if I did those things? I was the minister's daughter, after all," she reminded him pointedly. "I was expected to behave and set a good example."

"Expectations don't guarantee shit. That sure as hell didn't stop your sister from running wild. She's a few years older than me, but from what I heard, she was a regular hell-raiser as a teenager."

Unfortunately, she still was.

The thought brought a troubled frown to Grace's brow. She didn't understand her older sister at all. Ever since she could remember, Caroline had behaved like the stereotypical, bratty minister's daughter. She had been their parents' cross to bear, was the way their Aunt Lollie had always put it.

High-spirited and rebellious, all of her life Caroline had been straining against the strict code of conduct expected of her, both as a teenager and now, as an adult. If something was forbidden, she was hell-bent to try it. The more people, particularly the locals around Cedar Grove, disapproved, the more determined Caroline became.

Typically, Grace had heard from her wayward sister only once since their father's funeral over a year ago, and that had been a brief telephone call in the middle of the night, which Grace suspected had been prompted by a little too much to drink.

She had thought her sister might stick around after their father died, since he'd left the farm to them jointly, but in her usual breezy fashion, Caroline had taken off for parts unknown within hours of the funeral.

She had yet to contribute so much as a dime toward paying the taxes on the old place and Grace had not pushed the matter. Even had she wanted to, most of the time she had no idea how to contact Caroline. One of Grace's biggest fears was that her sister would want to sell off the old place, but so far she'd made no mention of doing so, even though she would be within her rights to demand her share of their inheritance in cash. The last thing Grace wanted to do was put the idea in her head by asking for money for taxes.

Grace glanced at Jake and tried to appear unconcerned. "You're right. But I'm not Caroline."

"Yeah. I know," Jake replied quietly, and she got the uneasy feeling the words were infused with a much deeper meaning.

She gripped the steering wheel tight and tried to concentrate on the road, but out of the corner of her eye she could see his long legs. His jeans were worn and his boots were scuffed and run down at the heels. His hand, resting on his thigh caught her eye. It was rough and chapped from the cold.

She glanced at him again. The denim jacket he wore wasn't even lined. On closer inspection she saw that he was shivering, though he tried to hide it.

"That coat can't be very warm. Is it the only one you have?"

He sent her a sidelong glance. His green eyes darkened to emerald and glittered beneath his black brows. "Are you worried about me, Mary Grace? I like that."

"I would be concerned about anyone who was inadequately clothed for the winter."

For several seconds he said nothing, but she could feel his gaze on her profile. "Yeah, you probably would." He returned his gaze to the highway.

"My father's sheepskin lined coat is just hanging unused in the closet. I'm sure it would fit you. You can have it if you wa—"

"Forget it," he snapped.

"But it's a perfectly good coat. Someone should get some use out of it."

"Then give it to the Goodwill. I don't want your fucking charity."

Grace gasped. She looked at him and saw that he was furious. A tiny muscle wriggled along his clenched jaw, and his face was tight. She realized that she had unintentionally stepped on his pride, and she felt terrible. "Jake, it's not charity."

"The hell it's not."

"No, really. I simply thought someone should get some use out of a perfectly good coat, and since the one you're wearing doesn't appear to be very warm, I thought it might as well be you. I was worried about you."

"Well, stop worrying. This coat's warm enough."

She doubted that, but instinct and the terse note in his voice warned her to back away.

There weren't many people in town at that hour, but as she drove down Main Street she saw Ina Shoemaker in front of the City Cafe. Her pink and white waitress uniform peeked out all around the bottom of her coat, as she bent to unlock the front door. She spotted Grace's van and waved, but a second later her jaw dropped when she noticed Jake slouched in the front seat.

Grace waved back, gritting her teeth.

They got the same reaction when they passed J. T. Brenner, who was cranking up the awning over the front window of the hardware store, and from Titus Monroe as he drove by going the other way. Their slack jawed double takes would have been funny under other circumstances, but Grace knew they were just the harbingers of another storm of criticism that was about to descend on her.

Jake remained silent until Grace stopped the van in front of the sawmill.

"Thanks," he muttered, and got out. As he sauntered around the hood to the driver's side, Sam Norton, one of the regular millhands, was dropped off in front of the gate by his wife. Lunch pail in hand, he started to stride into the millyard, but on the third step he spotted Jake and stopped dead, staring, his face filling with anger.

Without breaking stride or so much as glancing his way, Jake flipped him the bird.

"Must you do things like that?" Grace demanded in a tight whisper when he reached her door.

"Oh yeah," he said without the least contrition or concern.

He gripped the open window and leaned down, his face granite hard. "A piece of advice. Don't ever try to give me anything else. I don't take charity from anyone, and especially not from you."

Before she could reply, he turned away and stalked into the millyard, stubbornly ignoring the angry stares he drew from the other workers streaming in through the gate.

Grace watched his broad back, feeling awful. When he disappeared inside she put the van in gear and pulled out onto the highway again.

What a thoughtless thing to do. She should have remembered that fierce pride of Jake's. He hadn't had much of anything growing up, but he'd held on to his self-respect with stubborn tenacity. She had always suspected that his arrogance and "go to hell" attitude were nothing more than pride, a shield against the world.

She and Josie had certainly been treated to a demonstration of just how strong that pride ran in Jake on the day, twelve years ago, that he left Cedar Grove. She and Josie had happened to be in town that afternoon.

His second trial had ended in a hung jury just that morning in Houston. Sheriff Greely was fit to be tied, but by order of the judge, he was told to return Jake to Cedar Grove and release him.

Less than an hour after he was set free, Jake had ridden his motorcycle up onto the front lawn of the courthouse and shouted for the mayor, the district attorney and Sheriff Greely to come out.

Cautiously the mayor and the prosecutor had stepped out onto the courthouse steps, and across the street Oscar Greely, backed up by three deputies, had swaggered out and stood on the sidewalk in front of the jail. "Whaddaya want, Paxton? And get that damned machine off the lawn before I throw your sorry ass back in jail."

"I came to say good-bye to you assholes," Jake shouted.

He looked from one group of men to the other, revved up his Harley and spun it in a tight circle, right there on the courthouse lawn, tearing up turf and sending dirt flying and making a tremendous noise. All the while he held his right hand high, the middle finger pointing obscenely toward the sky.

Sheriff Greely had nearly had a seizure. His fleshy face had turned the color of a beet as he'd run out into the street, shaking his fist. "Paxton! You sorry son-of-a-bitch! I'll fry you for this!" he'd shouted.

Grace and Josie had stood on the street corner, gaping at the spectacle. Grace had been shocked, but Josie had cheered him on.

He let the sheriff get almost within reach, then poured on the gas and roared away.

It was the last anyone in Cedar Grove had seen of him until five days ago.

In spite of herself, Grace laughed at the memory. Jake hadn't changed.

so

THE ESTATE SALE turned out to be a gold mine. Grace successfully bid on several prime pieces. The smaller ones she had loaded into the back of the van, and she made arrangements for the larger ones to be shipped to her shop by motor freight.

It was a little after three that afternoon as she approached Cedar Grove, and she was feeling pleased with herself and in a good mood. She was even feeling slightly more charitable toward Jake.

His shift had ended ten minutes ago, and she had already

decided that she would keep an eye out for him and give him a lift home.

She heard the wail of several sirens in the distance, but she paid no attention to them at first. The closer she got to the sawmill, however, the louder they got. As she neared the entrance three sheriff's cars came racing toward her from town, red lights flashing and sirens screaming.

"What in the world?" Grace murmured aloud. An instant later her heart began to hammer as, one after another, the patrol cars turned into the sawmill entrance.

Acting on instinct, Grace turned in after them.

Eleven

HARLEY AND HIS DEPUTIES had already disappeared inside the mill when she brought the van to a halt beside the three patrol cars. Grace grabbed her purse and ran in after them.

A crowd of men were gathered on the mill floor by the time clock, shouting and cursing. Mindless of their offensive language, Grace fought her way through the dirty, sweaty men. When she finally squeezed past the men at the front of the crowd, the scene that greeted her was so appalling she came to an abrupt halt, and stared, her hand over her mouth.

Harley and her uncle stood to one side in serious discussion and three deputies had Jake face down, spread-eagle on the floor.

Several of the sullen men standing around showed signs of having been in a fight. Bruises, cut lips and abrasions were in abundance. Two more men were on the floor, one out cold and another rocking back and forth and moaning, nursing what appeared to be a broken arm.

One of the deputies holding Jake had him by the ankles. Another had his knee in the small of Jake's back and held one of his arms twisted up at a hard angle. The third deputy, Frank Sheffield, had a fistful of Jake's hair and had his head pulled back, the barrel of the .357 Magnum in his other hand pressed against the underside of his prisoner's chin.

Carla Mae Sheffield, the girl Jake had been accused of murdering twelve years ago, had been Frank's cousin and he hated Jake.

The language spewing from Jake's mouth was so shocking Grace cringed. Under the circumstances, however, she supposed one couldn't blame him.

Grace's eyes widened when she saw Jake's blood-stained shirt. She skirted around Frank to speak to him but when she saw his battered and bloodied face she gasped again and stepped back.

"What in the world is going on here?" she demanded, but she couldn't make herself heard over the noise of the crowd. At any rate, no one paid any attention to her. They didn't even seem to realize she was there.

The shouts and grumbles from the crowd were ugly and growing meaner by the minute, and they were all aimed at Jake.

"Merciful heavens! Grace, what in the hel— What in thunderation are you doing here, girl?"

She looked around in time to see Ansel Burke, a shift foreman and an elder in the church, push his way through the crowd. Ansel had known her all her life and had dandled her on his knee when she was a baby and he still tended to treat her as though she were a child.

"This is no place for a lady. Come on. Let's get you out of here." He grasped her elbow and tried to lead her away, but Grace snatched her arm free.

"I'm not going anywhere."

"Now, Grace—"

"Don't 'Now Grace' me. I want to know what happened, and I want to know right now."

"Now, now, this is nothing for you to trouble yourself over. I know you've been helping Jake, but he had it coming."

"Had what coming?" She whirled to face the crowd of angry men and yelled, "Will *somebody* please tell me what *happened* here!"

The furious shout, coming from Grace, shocked them all into silence. As one, they stared at her, stunned.

"Grace! I didn't know you were here." Hank Beaman hurried over to her and Harley ambled after him, jotting notes on a pad as he came.

"What happened, Uncle Hank?" Before he could reply she turned to the sheriff and waved a hand at the deputies holding Jake. "Is this kind of force really necessary, Harley?"

"Well, now, Grace. Take a look around. That's one tough customer. Until I get to the bottom of this, it seems advisable."

"It's all that Jake Paxton's fault," Ansel charged. "When the fight broke out, that scum picked up a chunk of wood and started swinging. He did some damage to a lot of men. Before you could get here, Sheriff, he laid Will out cold and broke Pete's arm. You want my opinion, I say they oughtta press charges."

The crowd immediately shouted agreement.

"Damned right!"

"Yeah. We'll fix the bastard!"

"Teach that woman-killer to come back here!"

"This time, by damn, we'll send that low-life to prison where he belongs!"

Frank Sheffield gave Jake's hair a vicious yank. "Ya hear that, scumbag? You're going back into a cage."

"Get your hands off me, asshole," Jake snarled and tried to twist free, but all the action earned him was increased pressure on his arm.

The men cheered when he let out an agonized groan. Encouraged by their support, Frank grinned and pulled Jake's head back at an impossible angle and brutally jammed the barrel of his gun deeper into the flesh under his chin. "Keep it up, scumbag. C'mon, fight, why don't you. Try to escape. I'll be happy to save the taxpayers the cost of a trial. All you gotta do is give me an excuse to pull this trigger."

"Fuck you," Jake managed, but his neck was bent back so far the crudity came out in a raspy growl.

Grace whirled on Harley again. "That was totally uncalled for! I demand that you put a stop to this and let him up. Right now. Have you even bothered to find out who started this fight?"

"That don't matter. This don't concern you, Grace." Ansel turned to her uncle. "Tell her to get out of here, Hank, and let us men handle this. Women don't understand these things."

"What things?" Grace narrowed her eyes at him. "Who did start this, Ansel? Who threw the first punch? It wasn't Jake, was it?"

"I done it." One of the men stepped forward with a belligerent swagger and thumbed his chest. He had a cut lip and one eye was swelling shut. "Me'n Pete. The whole shift drew straws to see who'd whip Paxton's sorry ass, and we won."

"They jumped him from behind as he was punching out for the day. My secretary saw the whole thing from the office window," Hank said wearily, gesturing toward the glassed-in second-level offices that overlooked the sawmill floor. He obvious did not want to inform on his men, but Hank Beaman was scrupulously honest. Upstairs, Mary Jo Shafer stood at the glass wall, watching the proceedings, wide-eyed.

"He had it coming!"

"Oh, just shut up, Ansel!" Grace snapped.

Ansel's jaw dropped. Color crept up his neck, and he snapped his mouth shut and swelled up like an apoplectic toad.

Grace was too furious to notice or care. "You see, it wasn't Jake's fault at all," she admonished Harley. "You have no right to treat him this way. I demand that you let him go at once."

"To hell with that!" one of the men shouted.

Grace whirled on the crowd of men with fire in her eyes and arms akimbo. "You men ought to be ashamed of yourselves! That is the most cowardly, disgusting thing I've ever heard of, ganging up on a lone man and attacking him from behind! And it must of taken you big bad men three days to work up the nerve to execute your gutless little plan.

"You listen to me, all of you. I don't care what you *think* Jake has done, that doesn't give you the right to act like a bunch of wild-eyed vigilantes. You all make me sick! Every one of you."

Some of the men had the decency to shuffle their feet and look at the ground, but most of them glared right back, their expressions surly and threatening.

"All right men, the show's over. Break it up and get out of here," Harley ordered.

"You gonna arrest him, Sheriff?"

"What for? Defending himself?" Harley shook his head. "Look, I understand how you men feel, but you're not going to do anything but bring trouble down on yourselves pulling stunts like this. Now go home, before I have to arrest some of you."

"That's not fair," Grace charged when the men trailed out. "You were ready to arrest Jake quick enough when you thought he'd started the fight. Why didn't you arrest the ones that attacked him?"

"Jeez, Grace, and I always thought you were such a peaceful little thing. Will you just let it go?"

Her mouth compressed and she tilted her chin. Harley was her friend, but at the moment she could gladly have kicked him. "At least let Jake up."

Harley sighed, but he looked at his men and nodded. "Let him up."

"But, Sheriff—"

"You heard me."

Grumbling under his breath, Frank holstered his gun, and when the other two men released Jake he grabbed the arm that was bent behind his back and jerked him to his feet none too gently. "This isn't over, Paxton," he growled in Jake's ear, and he could not resist giving his arm another hard twist."

"Ahhh! You son-of-a—"

"Stop that!" Grace ordered, and smacked Frank upside the head with her purse.

"Ow!" Frank dropped Jake's arm and grabbed his ear. "Damn. That hurt!"

"Good. Maybe you'll think twice before inflicting pain on someone else."

"You gonna let her get away with that, Sheriff? She struck an officer of the law and . . . and interfered with the performance of my duty."

"Is it your duty to abuse people in your custody?" Grace challenged with a pugnacious lift of her chin.

Harley heaved a long-suffering sigh. "All right, knock it off, both of you. Everybody just settle down?" He looked around at his deputies and jerked his head toward the door. "You men go on out to the cars. That includes you, Frank. I'll be there in a minute."

Frank's face tightened. He shot Jake a hate-filled look. "You're not always gonna be able to hide behind a woman's skirts. One of these days I'm gonna nail you, scum."

"You want a piece of me, asshole? C'mon." Jake held his hands out palms up and beckoned him in. "C'mon, dickhead. Take your best shot."

"Just stop it!" Grace stepped between the two men and poked Jake's chest with her forefinger. She was on his side but she was angry—yell-and-scream angry, stomp-your-feet angry, see-red angry—with Jake, with Harley, with her uncle, with the mill hands, with everyone. "Fighting isn't going to solve anything. Haven't you learned that yet?"

Jake looked down at her. His jaw clenched and unclenched and his eyes glittered. His face remained hard and wary, but he finally relaxed his stance.

"If you want to get even, do it the right way. Since Harley won't arrest those men, I think you should press charges."

"Ah, Grace," Harley groaned.

"Forget it. I just want to get out of here."

"But you can't come to work every day and run the risk of this happening again. You've got to take action and make them see that you won't tolerate this kind of treatment."

"Uh, about that," Hank said reluctantly. "Jake, I'm sorry, but . . . well . . . I'm going to have to let you go."

"Uncle Hank! I don't believe this! Jake didn't do anything but defend himself. Why are you firing him? It's not fair."

"I know that, Grace honey, but what else can I do? I can't let everyone else go."

"There's got to be another way of handling this."

"Drop it, Grace," Jake ordered. "It doesn't matter."

"Oh, yes, it does matter. This isn't right. You shouldn't be punished for what those men did."

"The truth is, even if the fight hadn't happened it wouldn't change anything." Hank gave Jake a regretful look. "I got a call this morning from Mrs. Ames. She ordered me to let you go."

"Verna did *that?"* Grace was speechless. Her uncle had managed the mill for the Ames family for almost forty years. He had always had complete authority over the hiring and firing and everyday operations. Until now. "Well, we'll just see about that,"

she huffed. "I'm going to have a little talk with Verna."

"Before you go off half-cocked and light into your mother-in-law, I've got to tell you, even without the order from Verna, I was going to let Jake go on Friday. Now, Grace, hear me out," he said, halting her protest with an upraised hand. "Who's at fault doesn't matter. This is a purely business decision." He turned to Jake with a regretful look. "I'm sorry, man, but your presence among the men is too disruptive."

"Yeah, well, you tried. Thanks anyway."

"But--"

"Let it go, Grace. C'mon, let's go." He turned and stalked out, leaving her no choice but to follow.

"OW! THAT HURTS."

"Oh hush," Grace snapped, and dabbed the cut above Jake's eye with the cotton ball again. He sat in a chair beside the kitchen table, while she stood between his outstretched legs. "Men! You pound one another to bloody pulps then turn around and whine like babies over a little alcohol."

"Hey, what's eating you? I was the innocent victim. Remember?"

"Huh. You haven't been innocent, Jake Paxton, since you were two years old."

He grinned and looked up at her with a dangerous glint in his eyes. "You got that right."

"I'm sure," she said in a dampening voice. "Now, hold still." She cleaned the scrape along his chin and his skinned knuckles with more vigor than necessary, then daubed both with iodine, ignoring his flinches.

Grace knew she shouldn't be taking her frustrations out on Jake, but she couldn't help it.

Although she understood that her uncle had been in an untenable position, the injustice of the situation infuriated her. She was also annoyed with herself for becoming embroiled in this sorry mess when she'd had every intention of remaining aloof.

And she'd lost her temper. In public. She almost *never* lost her temper.

"That takes care of your face and hands. Are there any other injuries that need attention?" she asked with asperity.

"A few bruises maybe."

"Well, don't just sit there. Let me see them."

"Sure. I'll have to stand, though."

Happy to relinquish the intimate position between his legs, Grace stepped out of his way and turned to get fresh swabs from the first-aid kit. She turned back just as he grabbed the bottom of his T-shirt with both hands and stripped it off over his head. She found herself at eye level with a male chest the likes of which she had never seen, at least, not in the flesh.

No, Jake was definitely not the lanky boy who had roared out of town twelve years ago. As a teenager she had gone swimming with friends, but none of those boys had looked anything like this. The only other adult male she'd seen naked had been her husband, but Charles's chest had looked puny in comparison to Jake's.

Grace's knees felt wobbly, and she gripped the edge of the table behind her and stared.

She'd had no idea that hard pectorals, a flat abdomen ridged with muscle, and a narrow waist could add up to such beauty. That beauty was not one whit diminished by the welts and purple bruises blossoming here and there. His shoulders were broad and corded with muscle. His upper arms bulged. A triangle of silky black hair covered the center of his chest and arrowed downward, swirling around his navel, which was visible just above the low-slung jeans.

Grace's mouth went dry. Her breathing became erratic and shallow. The only thought her stunned brain could process was, "Oh my."

If she had spoken the words aloud Jake could not have looked more smug. His eyes glinted at her wickedly. Clearly he knew exactly the effect he had on her and was enjoying her discomfort.

He tossed the T-shirt onto the table and stepped closer, so close his chest was inches from her face. So close his smell wafted to her, a dizzying mix of clean sweat and male. He held his arms out to the sides, and instantly her eyes were drawn to the tufts of black hair beneath those muscled arms and her stomach quivered. "See anything interesting?"

"Wh-What?" Blinking, she looked up slowly, past that silky thatch of chest hair, past broad shoulders, past the square stubborn chin that sported a raw scrape and a slight stubble, and finally met taunting eyes.

"Bruises," he said, straight-faced. "What did you think I meant?"

"I . . . uhm . . ."

"Why, Mary Grace, you're blushing. Does the sight of my body make you hot and bothered?" He stepped closer still, and Grace swallowed hard. "If you like what you see, I'm perfectly willing to be seduced."

For a moment—a dizzying, giddy moment—she was actually tempted. That scared her. Then she realized that was exactly what he'd meant to happen. Jake had always taken perverse pleasure in rattling her, in getting under her skin and making her squirm.

And she had never had the slightest idea of how to deal with him. She still didn't.

She was spared the ordeal of trying when the back door opened and Josie rushed inside.

"I stopped by the sawmill and Dad told me what happened. God, Jake, I'm sorry. Are you hurt bad?"

"Just scrapes and bruises. Nothing serious. Grace was just treating them for me."

"Are you sure? Maybe you ought to go see Dr. Watley and get x-rayed. That bruise on your side looks awful. You could have a broken rib."

He examined the injury in question and pressed on it and winced. "Maybe. You got an elastic bandage, Grace?"

"Jake, maybe you should see the doctor. If your rib is broken—"

"It won't be the first one. All the doc would do is wrap it up, and I can handle that. So do you have a bandage or not?"

"I have one," she replied tightly, and turned to rummage through the first-aid supplies in the kit. "First, though, you'd better let me put something on those wounds." She soaked a wad of cotton with alcohol and moved around to his back. Somehow, it wasn't as intimidating as his chest. Not quite.

"Jake, I'm really sorry about the job," Josie said. "Dad feels really bad about it. By the way, he said to tell you he'll drop by with your check on Friday."

He snorted. "In other words, he doesn't want me coming there to pick it up. The sight of me might incite the men again, is that it?"

"I'd like to say you're wrong, but I can't," Josie admitted with a rueful look. "Those guy aren't ever going to accept you working there. Dad did the best he could, but it just won't work. Even if he were willing to give it another shot, he can't, now that Verna's stuck her nose in." She looked at Grace. "Are you going to talk to her about that?"

"I already have. I called her the minute we got home. She claims she had no choice. That she was being harassed about him working at the mill. She even got an anonymous threat."

Verna, of course had burst into tears at the first hint of criticism. "You just don't understand, Grace," she wailed. "What was I to do? All the wives of the men at the mill were calling me constantly complaining. Then I got that awful telephone call." Grace could almost her feeling her shuddering as she cried delicately into a handkerchief. "It was terrible. He said if I didn't get rid of Jake Paxton at once he would blow up the sawmill.

"I swear I would never have insisted that Hank fire him otherwise. You do believe me, don't you, Grace?" she'd sniffed pitifully.

Of course, Grace had reassured her. What choice had she had?

"What're you going to do?" Josie asked.

"Damned if I know. One thing is certain, I've got to have a job. I'm down to my last fifty. But who the hell around here is going to hire me?"

"Hmm." Josie pursed her lips and paced the kitchen, tapping her forefinger against her chin. Finally she stopped. "There's only one solution. Grace will just have to hire you as her handyman at the shop."

Twelve

"WHAT?" Grace, who was bent over, smearing antibiotic cream on an abrasion on Jake's lower back, shot up like a released spring. Eyes wide, she sent her cousin a desperate look. "Have you lost your mind? No. No, I won't do it. I told you from the beginning that I would rent him the apartment, but that's as far as I go. I'm sorry, Jake. No offense, but that was our deal."

"Grace, you have to hire him. If you don't, no one else will."

"Great. Just imagine what it will do for my business to have him around."

"Oh, fiddlesticks. Most of your business comes from tourists passing through and the wealthy people over on the other side of the lake. They don't even know who Jake is."

"Nevertheless, the answer is still no. I don't want to get involved in this."

"Grace, you're already are involved," Josie prodded relentlessly. "Like it or not, you're involved right up to your chin. You might as well go whole hog."

"Let it go, Josie." Bare chested and magnificently male, Jake stood with his hands hooked on his hipbones, watching them, his face impassive. "If Grace doesn't want to help me, that's her choice. I've managed on my own for a good many years. I'm sure as hell not going to beg anyone for help."

The comment went straight to Grace's heart. Sharp images filled her mind—of the solitary child Jake had been, dirty and ragged, always left to fend for himself, of the brooding teenage loner, freezing everyone out with those cold stares and that go-to-hell attitude. He had been neglected and shunned so much he expected it, so he hung onto his pride by pretending he didn't need anyone, and rejecting everyone else before they could reject him.

She would be no better than all the others if she did the same. She chewed her lip, torn between her need to play it safe and her conscience.

Finally, she sighed. "Oh, all right. After the spectacle I made of myself today at the sawmill I might as well. In for a penny, in for a pound."

"Terrific," Josie crowed. "I knew I could count on you."

Jake was less exuberant. "You sure you want to do this? You don't have to, you know," he said with an edge in his voice that warned her that his feelings on charity had not changed.

"I know. Actually, I do need a man at the shop to do the heavy work. It's not much of a job, mind you, and I can't pay much, but it's yours if you want it."

He studied her for a moment, then nodded. "I'll give it a shot. And thanks."

The last, she could tell, had been difficult for him.

"Good. I'm glad that's settled," Josie announced happily, grinning from ear to ear. She was feeling pleased with herself and made no effort to hide it.

Grace glanced at the kitchen clock and jumped. "Oh, dear, look at the time." She stuffed the tube of antibiotic cream in Josie's hand. "Here, finish applying this for me. And when you're done, wrap that elastic bandage around his ribs. I've got to shower and change. Daniel is picking me up in a little over an hour."

Josie's grin collapsed. "Sure. No problem. You go ahead and get ready for your date."

"It's not a date, exactly. We're just going to Wednesday night services at church."

"Whatever." Josie squeezed some cream onto her finger and stepped behind Jake, her wholesome face set.

A half hour later when Grace returned to the kitchen Jake sat at the table, reared back in a chair balanced on its back legs. A mug of coffee sat on the table beside him. Mercifully, he once again wore his T-shirt. There was no sign of her cousin.

"Where's Josie?" she asked, looking around.

"She left as soon as she finished tending my wounds."

"Without even saying good-bye? That's odd. And not like Josie at all."

"Maybe she didn't see any point in sticking around, since you're going out."

"Mmm. Maybe. But it's not like Josie to be rude. I think I'll call her tomorrow and see if something is wrong." Grace glanced at the clock and fidgeted. She had rushed so, now she had time to kill.

Jake sipped his coffee and watched her over the top of the mug. "You look pretty."

The compliment caught her by surprise, and she blinked. "Thank you."

"I like that dress on you."

Surprised again, Grace glanced down at the emerald green garment. It was a figure-hugging knit with a modest scooped neckline, three-quarter-length fitted sleeves and a flared skirt that stopped just above her knees and flounced when she walked.

It was perhaps a bit too dressy for Wednesday night church but she knew that it flattered her and it made her feel good. She was also hoping it would arouse Daniel's interest. As shaky as she was feeling, a bit of male appreciation would be a balm. Besides, if she and Daniel were ever going to have a future together, they needed to heat things up a bit.

"A dress like that is wasted on a preacher," Jake continued, as though he had read her mind. He still watched her in that intent way of his. "He probably won't even notice how it shows off that cute little ass of yours."

"Oh!" She gaped at him, bright color rising to her face.

"You . . . you can't talk to me that way."

"Why not? It's true." Putting his coffee mug on the table he rose and walked over to where she stood. "I noticed your ass over fifteen years ago."

He was too close. Grace eased back a step, and bumped into the counter. She grasped the edge with both hands as her knees went suddenly wobbly.

Jake's mouth twitched with a hint of a smile. Leaning closer still, he braced one hand on the counter and reached out with the other to trail a fingertip along the edge of the scooped neckline of her dress. His touch barely skimmed her skin but it left a trail of fire. Grace trembled.

"You have exactly the kind of body that turns me on—small and delicate, all the right curves without being overblown. Your breasts are just the right size to fit in my hand."

Grace's color deepened. He was doing this to discomfit her, she was certain. "Stop it, Jake," she ordered, but her voice shook with the tremors rippling through her.

"Don't go out with the preacher," he murmured, ignoring her command. "Call him and break the date, and go out with me instead. We can drive over to Clearwater and go dancing. Maybe go for a walk under the stars. Just the two of us." His finger trailed along the neckline again. "How about it?"

Grace was shocked at how much the idea appealed. Excitement quivered through her. Her heart pounded. She licked her dry lips, and he smiled as his eyes followed the action.

"You want to, Grace," he whispered. "You know you want to."

"No . . . I . . . No, you're wrong."

"Then why are you shivering?"

"Because . . . because I'm frightened of you."

He frowned. He studied her face and after a moment shook his head. "You're not frightened of me, Grace. You're frightened of what I make you feel."

"That's not true," she vowed, but the blush that rose to her face gave away the lie. She sidestepped around him and hurried away. On the other side of the kitchen table she turned and gave him a cool look. "I think you'd better go. Daniel will be here soon."

Jake's face hardened as he looked at her across the width of the room. The seductive gleam was gone from his eyes. It was replaced by that steely look he normally wore. "You're a coward, Grace. And a damned selfish one, at that."

"What? I am no such thing!" Indignation swelled inside her. If there was one thing on which Grace prided herself it was giving of herself. Wasn't she on every committee for every possible type of community service? She volunteered at the nursing home, the church, and for every charity function. How dare he call her selfish.

"Oh, yeah? You don't love Daniel Street. You're merely using the man to hide from your feelings. And you're doing it with no regard whatsoever for Josie, who happens to be in love with the guy."

"What? Don't be ridiculous. Josie isn't in love with Daniel. Where did you ever get that idea?"

"My God, woman, open your eyes. Haven't you ever noticed the way she looks at him when she thinks no one is watching? There's not a shy bone in Josie's body, but whenever the preacher is around she gets tongue-tied. Then there's the way she closes up whenever you mention him. Seeing the two of you together eats her alive. Hell, she ran out of here like the place was on fire to avoid that."

Grace shook her head. "No, you're wrong." He had to be wrong. Her militant, activist cousin and mild-mannered Reverend Daniel Street? Impossible. A more incongruous pair she couldn't imagine. Besides, if anything, Grace had always assumed that Josie was sweet on Jake, given the way she had always championed him.

"It's a fact. You just don't want to face it. As long as you're involved in that tepid romance you don't have to deal with how you really feel."

"You don't know what you're talking about. I'm very fond of Da—" She stopped when Jake's mouth twitched and amended, "I care for Daniel. Very much."

"Now there's a passionate declaration," he jeered.

Grace was saved from coming up with a suitably cutting retort when Lyle's face appeared in the window of the door. When he spotted Jake he jerked open the door and stepped inside without knocking.

"What the hell are you doing in here, Paxton? Renting that apartment doesn't give you the right to come into the house whenever you please. Get out. And stay out."

"Lyle, for heaven's sake. You can't barge into my home and start issuing orders," Grace admonished, but neither man paid the slightest attention to her.

Hooking his thumbs in the pockets of his jeans, Jake leaned back against the counter, crossed one ankle over the other, and gave Lyle an insolent half smile. "I don't think so. And while we're on the subject, I didn't hear Grace invite you in."

Angry color mottled Lyle's face. "I happen to be family. It's my duty and right to look after Grace."

"Family, huh? Then what the hell are you doing sniffing around her all the time?"

"Why, you insolent cur. Get out!"

"Stop it! Both of you. I'm sick of this bickering. Anyway, this whole discussion is pointless since Jake was just leaving," Grace said, giving him a pointed look.

Jake didn't like it. His eyes glittered at her from that hard face. For a moment he didn't move a muscle, and she was afraid he was going to refuse to leave. Then he straightened away from the counter and went to the pantry, where he arrogantly rummaged through the supplies and helped himself. As he sauntered to the door he held up the can of chili and box of crackers he'd confiscated and winked. "You don't mind, do you? I haven't had time to stock my larder yet."

"No, of course not," Grace replied, but she was stunned by his audacity.

"Insufferable bastard," Lyle snarled as the door closed behind him. "Why on earth do you put up with him? The man's entirely too familiar. And dangerous. I heard he started a fight at the mill today and the sheriff had to break it up and throw him off the property."

"He didn't start the fight. The other men jumped him," she said wearily. She picked up Jake's coffee mug and took it to the sink and rinsed it out.

"It amounts to the same thing. The man is trouble. You should never have taken him in, which I'm sure you must realize by now. Why don't you just admit you made a mistake and have the sheriff evict him?"

"Lyle, will you stop it! I'm not going to throw Jake out, and that's final. Now, could we please change the subject?" She glanced at the clock again. "I don't have much time. Just tell me why you came by, then go."

"Are you going out?"

"Yes."

"With whom? That damned preacher?"

"Lyle!" she warned.

"All right, all right. I just don't know what you see in the guy, is all," he muttered, his expression sulky. "Not when you could have me."

Grace sighed. Did he have any idea how arrogant that was? "Lyle, please, don't do this."

"Why not? You know I'm crazy about you. We belong together, Grace. In my position, I can't afford to marry just anyone. You're the ideal choice. You could move back to the Willows, Verna would be happy, I'd be happy. And someday you would be mistress of the place."

And I'd be miserable, Grace thought, weary beyond words. She'd been fending off Lyle's advances for months, but the man had the hide of a rhinoceros. "Lyle, you're wasting your time. As you know, I'm seeing Daniel. Even if I weren't, I still wouldn't be interested. You, after all, are a married man."

"Is that all? My divorce from Louise will be final soon. You know that."

"Don't you think, before you take such a drastic step that ,you should at least *try* to save your marriage? You and Louise were together for six years. And I know she still loves you."

"Well that's tough. Louise doesn't have the kind of class a man in my position needs in a wife. I've explained that to her over and over. She should understand it by now."

Louise understood all right. How could she not? Lyle had walked out on her almost immediately after becoming heir to the Ames millions. The poor woman called Grace regularly to cry on her shoulder. Though she could not understand what Louise saw in Lyle, she hated for anyone to be so broken-hearted.

"You're what I need, Grace."

"I'm sorry, Lyle, but it's just not going to happen. Now if you don't mind, my date is going to be here soon."

His face darkened. "All right. I'm going," he snapped. He stalked to the door, then stopped. With his hand on the knob, he looked back at her. "But this isn't the end of it, I promise you. The next time I come courting I'll be a single man. Then let's see what you say." He jerked the door open and strode out.

Grace listened to his footsteps hammer across the porch, then the silence. A few seconds later she heard his car engine spring to life and a spin of tires on gravel as he went careening down the drive in a fit of temper.

Courting? Was that what he thought his constant harassment was? Courting?

Shaking her head, Grace sat down in one of the kitchen chairs. Guiltily, she thought about how quickly she had used Daniel to discourage Lyle. Was Jake right? Was she merely using Daniel as a shield? Honesty forced her to admit it was possible.

And if he was right about that, how right was he about Josie's feelings? Now that she thought about it, her usually gregarious cousin was unnaturally quiet around Daniel. And whenever Grace happened to mention his name, Josie quickly changed the subject. At church she always sat on the back row, and she slipped out just before service was over. By the time Daniel took his place at the door to say good-bye to the parishioners, Josie was usually long gone.

Grace remembered the time, after seeing a movie, she and Daniel had stopped at the Dairy Queen for an ice cream. Josie had been there with a couple of girlfriends, but the minute she and Daniel had walked in she'd made an excuse and left. Grace hadn't thought anything of it at the time, but now. . .

She twisted her hands together. Oh dear.

STANDING AT THE WINDOW in the darkened apartment, Jake watched with hard satisfaction as Lyle stomped down the back steps and stormed across the yard in a huff. A few seconds later he spun his wheels and took off like a bat out of hell. Jake smiled. Good riddance.

A short while later, however, his mood darkened when the good reverend arrived and escorted Grace to his car.

JAKE STARTED HIS JOB at the shop the next morning. As Grace's uncle had told her on numerous occasions, Jake was a hard worker. He spent the morning unloading the items she had purchased in Houston and, under her direction, setting up a new display in the front showroom. To her great relief, there were no suggestive remarks or salacious looks and no attempts to unnerve her. Except for being surly to her customers, he gave her no trouble at all.

It was her friends who gave her trouble.

A steady stream of locals dropped by the shop that morning, sure evidence that word had already spread that she had hired Jake. Not surprisingly, when they were sure that Jake was out of earshot, several of the women criticized her for doing so. Which was why, though dismayed, Grace wasn't surprised when Ida Bell Wheatly sailed in the door and launched her attack almost without pausing to say hello.

"I'm telling you, Grace, you'll rue this day, you just mark my word. That is, if you live."

"I'm not worried about that, Ida Bell. Jake isn't dangerous." At least not in the way Ida Bell thought. Where her emotions and her body were concerned, that was a different matter. "I never believed he killed Carla Mae. I still don't."

"Huh. You're too trusting for your own good. Just like that father of yours. You see good in people where it doesn't exist. Even if he didn't kill that girl, which I don't believe for a minute, he's still a dangerous character. Jake Paxton was born trash and he'll always be trash. You can't change that."

Grace gritted her teeth and prayed for patience. Unlike the other busybodies who had offered unsolicited advice that morning, Ida Bell didn't bother to moderate her voice. Grace was sure that Jake could hear her in the storeroom, where he was currently rearranging the inventory to make room for the shipment that was due tomorrow.

Josie, who had entered the shop in the middle of the tirade, peeked out from behind the armoir where she was hiding, and rolled her eyes at Grace at that last piece of bigoted nonsense.

"I don't believe that anyone is born good or bad, Ida Bell. Most people simply need someone to have faith in them and give them a chance."

"Humph! I believe in doing good deeds as well as the next person, but hiring that man is carrying Christian charity to a foolish extreme. You just mark my word."

When Ida Bell finally left, Josie came out of hiding, and Grace gave her a "see-what-you've-caused" look as she approached the old wood and glass display counter where Grace stood. Inside were small items, some of great value, some pure whimsy.

Her cousin grimaced. "I know. You're taking flak right now. Has it been bad?"

"Bad enough, but I guess I'll survive."

Josie leaned an elbow on the high case and raised one eyebrow. "So, how's it going with Jake?"

"So far, so good. Your dad was right, he is a hard worker." Much better by far than Charlie Snider had been. "The only negative is he has to ride in with me, since his truck still won't run." Grace wasn't at all comfortable with that, but it would be unkind and downright foolish to refuse to give him a lift.

"Well, good. I'm glad the arrangement is working out."

"It's a bit premature to make a judgement," Grace said, giving her a wry look. It was Josie's nature to try and fix things and make them turn out right. The quicker the better. "But I'm fairly sure they will."

Grace refolded a hand-embroidered piano runner and returned it to the glass case. "Will you answer a question for me, Josie?"

"Sure."

"What do you think of Daniel Street?" Grace couched the question in an offhand way and pretended to concentrate on tidying the display case, but she watched Josie closely. Her cousin's face changed in a blink, shutting down, paling. In an instant she went from animated and vivacious to stiff and withdrawn.

She stared at the feather boa Grace was draping around the other articles in the case, not meeting her eyes. "He's okay,

I guess."

"Do you think he's handsome? I mean, would you go out with someone like him?"

"Oh, he's handsome, all right. He's gorgeous. Too handsome to give someone like me a second look."

The statement shocked Grace, though it revealed a lot. "Josie Beaman, what a thing to say. There's nothing wrong with your looks."

"Grace, c'mon. I'm twenty pounds overweight and the best that can be said of my looks is I don't scare little children."

"That's not true. You have a wholesome beauty that many men find attractive."

"Oh, yeah. Wholesome, that's me. There may be some poor schmuck out there who goes for the milkmaid type, but trust me, men who look like Daniel go for beauties like you."

"But, Josie—"

"I'm sorry, Grace. I gotta go." She checked her watch, and hitched the strap of her shoulder bag higher on her arm. "Tell Jake I stopped by. Call me if you need me?"

And with that, she sailed out the door.

Grace watched her through the window. Jake was right. Josie was mad about Daniel.

~

Shortly after Josie left, Jake made a delivery to one of the homes on the lake. He came back an hour later with a sack of take-out sandwiches. When Grace tried to pay him for her half he gave her a look that could have cut steel.

"Forget it. I can afford to buy you a damn sandwich. Now where do you want me to put this stuff?"

Grace knew better than to argue.

There were no customers in the shop so they ate sitting at one of the antique tables next to the pot-bellied stove. The weather had been vacillating between winter and spring for the last few days. The night before, a weak cool front had blown through and a small fire burned in the stove to ward off the chill. The atmosphere was cozy and warm.

For several minutes they had a surprisingly companionable

conversation. Jake told her he thought the van needed a tune-up and he offered to do it for her on the weekend. Grace wouldn't hear of it unless he let her pay him. It took some persuading but she finally managed to win that argument.

After that they ate in silence for several minutes.

"This is nice," he said out of the blue.

"Yes, it is."

"I used to imagine this."

She chuckled. "Eating a sandwich in an antique store in front of a pot-bellied stove?"

His expression did not alter by so much as a flick of an eyelash, but his voice dropped to a low pitch, soft and caressing as warm velvet. "Being alone with you. Talking to you. Just looking at you."

Surprise streaked through Grace. She stopped chewing and stared at him, unable to look away from that intense green gaze.

The air seemed suddenly thick, the quiet deafening. Scattered around the store, the antique clocks ticked in hectic counterpoint to one another. A log popped and shifted in the stove with a shower of sparks. The scents of ham and pickles and burning cedar mixed with potpourri and lemon oil seemed suddenly overpowering. Grace's heart began to thump and her breathing grew erratic. She could not have said a word had her very life depended on it.

"I thought about you all the time while I was in jail."

Grace had not thought he could surprise her more than he already had, but she was wrong. "You thought about *me?* But . . . why? We barely knew each other."

He wiped his hands on a paper napkin and fished his battered wallet out of the hip pocket of his jeans. He pulled out an old photograph and handed it to her. It was yellowed and bent in the shape of his wallet.

Grace stared at the snapshot in disbelief, her chest growing tight. It was of her when she was about sixteen, taken at Tucker's Cove. She and Josie had been on a picnic with a bunch of their friends. She had been wearing shorts and a halter top and smiling happily at the camera, her hair blowing in the breeze.

"Wh-where did you get this?" She was quite certain that she'd never given him a photograph of herself. She hadn't spoken a dozen words to Jake in high school.

"I swiped it from Josie's purse during my last year in school," he replied without a trace of remorse. "I've been carrying it around every since."

"Why would you do that?"

"I told you, I've had the hots for you for years. Didn't you believe me?"

Grace slowly shook her head. "No. No, of course not. I . . . I thought you were just trying to rattle me."

"Did I?" She gave him an admonishing look, and he chuckled. "I spent most of my teen years wondering what your skin felt like, fantasizing about stripping you naked and kissing you all over, making love to you until you screamed with pleasure."

Grace sucked in her breath. She was so shocked all she could do was gape at him. No man had ever spoken to her so bluntly in her life.

He chuckled again, a wicked sound that rumbled up from his chest. "Matter of fact, nothing's changed in the twelve years since I've been gone. I go to bed every night with a hard on, thinking about you. And ever since I was about sixteen, every time I've made love to a woman I've pretended she was you."

A scalding blush washed over every inch of her body. Her mouth worked like a banked fish but no sound came out. Jake's grin grew wider.

"What's the matter? Cat got your tongue, Mary Grace?"

"Jake Paxton, I can't believe you have the unmitigated gall to say such things to me," she blurted out when anger finally overrode her shock.

"Why not? They're true. Hell, why're you so surprised? Didn't you ever guess how I felt about you back then?"

"No. Certainly not!" She tingled all over, as though a tiny electric current were coursing through her body. "The way you were always staring a hole through me, I was sure you disliked me."

"Not hardly." He chug-a-lugged the last of his cola and lobbed the can into the trash barrel in the corner. Leaning the chair back on its rear legs, he watched her. "When I was in jail I spent hours just looking at that picture of you. I used to think about someday getting out and coming to claim you."

A car pulled up outside. Jake turned his head and glanced at it through the window in time to see Etta Perkins get out of her practical four-door sedan and start up the walkway with a militant step. Wadding up his napkin and the rest of his trash, Jake tossed it after the cola can and stood up. He paused and smiled at Grace and added in a confidential tone, "I just thought you should know." He arched his back, then relaxed his stance and sauntered for the storeroom.

Not until the bell over the door jingled did Grace realize her mouth was hanging open. She snapped it shut and went to greet Etta, all the while mentally cursing Jake Paxton for the devil that he was.

Thirteen

"STOP AT THE PIGGLY WIGGLY, WILL YOU? I need to pick up a few things."

Grace glanced at Jake, her mouth compressing. She had not yet forgiven him for his outrageous remarks at lunch, and his high-handed manner annoyed her even more. Nevertheless, she turned into the supermarket parking lot. She turned off the ignition and stared straight ahead. "Please don't be long. I have an engagement tonight, and I don't want to be late."

"What? Another date with the preacher?"

His snide tone raised her irritation level another notch, but she refused to rise to the bait. "Just don't dawdle."

He gave a little snort, his mouth twisting wryly. "That's one of the things I love about you, Grace. You're always so ladylike. Believe me, I never dawdle. I might drag ass at times, but I don't dawdle. Hell, I never even use the word."

With that, he got out of the van and strolled away with that cocky, loose-limbed walk. Grace watched him, gritting her teeth. Darn his hide. Ever since lunch he'd been needling her with crude or risque comments like that, she suspected, simply to get a rise out of her. He seemed to get a perverse kick out of ruffling her feathers.

In less than a minute Jake came out of the store empty-handed. Before he ever reached the van Grace could tell by his angry stride that something was wrong. He jerked open the door and practically threw himself into the bucket seat, and slammed the door shut again. His jaw was set and his face dark as a thundercloud. "Let's go," he growled.

"But . . . you didn't buy anything."

"Just start the damned van and let's get out of here."

"Jake, you need groceries. You insisted that I stop here, and now you're not going to buy what you need? That's crazy. You can't go on eating take-out and vending-machine junk food."

"Just drop it, Grace. Okay?"

"No it's not okay. I want to know what's wrong? This van isn't budging until you tell me."

His fist clenched and unclenched against his thigh. "The goddamn store manager won't *let* me purchase anything. Okay? So now you know. Can we go now?"

Jake looked out the window. The humiliation of having to tell her was scalding. To that damned, self-important son-of-a-bitch manager and all the others around here he was less than human. He didn't even have the right to eat.

"He *what?"* She gaped at him. Then her mouth snapped shut and she reached for the door handle. "We'll just see about that! Come on."

"Where?"

She climbed out and turned to shut the door and saw that he hadn't moved. "Back into the store. We're going to buy groceries. He's not going to get away with this."

"I can fight my own battles. I don't need you running interference."

"Oh, really? And just how are you going to win this one? By taking Darwin Stiles out in the alley and beating the stuffing out of him, I suppose." Her voice was tart, her stance militant. She reminded him of a little bantam hen with her feathers ruffled.

Some of Jake's tension eased. A smile tugged at his lips. "I was thinking more along the lines going over to Bedalia to shop as soon as I get my truck running."

"And in the meantime I suppose you think you can continue to borrow from me. Well forget it. I'm through feeding you. You'll buy your own groceries and you'll do it right here, like everyone else. I've known Darwin Stiles all of my life. He's always been a self-important jerk who liked to throw his weight around, but he's not going to get away with this."

"Grace, I don't want to cause any more trouble for you."

"Oh, just hush up and come on!" She slammed the door, marched around the van and headed for the entrance with blood in her eye.

Bemused, Jake climbed out of the van and followed, the smile tugging at his mouth once again. Look out Cedar Grove. Sweet little mild-mannered Mary Grace Somerset had her dander up. And it was something to see.

He caught up with her just outside the door and strolled along with his hands in his pockets and a hint of a smile on his lips, pacing his long stride to her angry march. He suddenly felt almost light-hearted.

Inside, the store manager was nowhere in sight. They received stares and frowns from some of the customers and store employees. The ones from friends, Grace countered with a wave and a smile. The rest she ignored.

As Jake pushed the grocery cart up and down the aisles, she stayed right by his side like a bodyguard. The very idea of her defending him was ludicrous. She was delicate as a flower and couldn't weigh more than a hundred and ten soaking wet, and the top of her head barely reached his chin. Still, it pleased him that she was willing to try.

The cart was full and they were almost finished when they turned down an aisle that was empty except for one small boy who appeared to be around ten or eleven. Jake glanced at the boy, did a double take, then stopped abruptly and began to search the shelves on their right.

"What are you looking for?" Grace asked. "Maybe I can help you find it."

"Here, take this. And stay here," he said under his breath, startling her by shoving the cart handle into her hand.

"But where are—"

"Ssh." He placed his forefinger across his lips and nodded toward the boy, who had turned slightly away from them.

Taking his time, Jake ambled down the aisle, examining the shelves as though looking for something. The boy eyed him warily over his shoulder once or twice, but Jake paid him no mind. He edged down the aisle, absorbed in his search. Then, without warning, his arm shot out with the suddenness of a striking snake and he grabbed the collar of the boy's windbreaker.

"Hey! Lemme go!"

"I will, kid, when you put the stuff back," Jake said in a calm voice, holding the flailing, kicking boy at arm's length.

"I ain't got no stuff. Lemme go, you peckerwood!"

"Hey, knock it off." He gave the boy a shake. "You don't want to attract the security guard."

"Oh yeah? I'll tell 'im you're a pervert, an' you're trying to kidnap me."

Jake almost laughed at that. The kid had a smart mouth on him. He reminded Jake of himself at that age. Right down to the bumper crop of bruises he was sporting.

"And I'll tell him to check that bulge under your coat. I don't think he'll like what he finds."

"I ain't got nothin' under my coat."

"Yeah, and pigs don't stink. Don't be a chump, boy. Don't you know you've been busted already?"

"You ain't no cop," the boy charged with a surly curl of his lip.

"That's right. But there's a surveillance camera in the ceiling looking right down your neck. You try to get out of here with that stuff and your butt'll be in a sling. They'll nail you the minute you step out the door."

The boy's fearful gaze flashed up to the camera lens sticking out of the acoustical tile overhead. "Shit."

"That's about the size of it," Jake drawled. "So why don't you take my advice and put the stuff back. I'd hate to see you wind up in Juvie Hall."

He scowled and glared at Jake, but, after a brief hesitation he muttered a surly, "Aw-right."

"Smart move, kid. Now then, I'm going to stand between you and that one-eyed peeping Tom and I want you to put everything back, nice and slow, like you were just looking it over. And I do mean everything."

The boy shot Jake another killing glare and mumbled something under his breath about nosey buttheads, but he did as Jake instructed.

&

Watching the little tableau unfold, Grace was shocked and saddened. Then she was flabbergasted. She couldn't believe her eyes! Jake was shielding the little criminal while he returned the items to the shelf.

She marched down the aisle with the cart. "Jake," she said in a loud whisper, then looked around in case they were being observed. "Should you be helping that boy escape punishment? He probably needs to be taught a lesson."

The look Jake gave her was so hard and filled with so much anger, Grace stepped back a pace. "Lady, you're the one who needs a lesson. A kid doesn't lift a can of beans and franks unless he needs it."

Shock slammed through Grace. She stared at Jake, her mouth dropping. "You . . . you mean he's *hungry?* "

"Naw. He probably just wants to use the can to club somebody in the head. You know how these juvenile delinquents are."

His sarcasm made her feel about two inches high.

Grace was appalled. This was Cedar Grove, not New York or Houston or Appalachia. She knew there were poor people here, but not that poor. That there were children going hungry, right under her nose, and she hadn't even known, made her feel sick.

Taking advantage of Jake's distraction, the boy started to bolt, but Jake snagged his cheap windbreaker before he took three steps. "Whoa. Not so fast."

"Lemme go, you peckerwood. I put the stuff back like you said."

"Kid, you're not out of the woods yet. Big Brother was watching, remember. You've still got to get out those doors," Jake warned. "Just stick by Grace and me and we'll see that no one hassles you."

Loretta Babcock, a teenage girl who worked as a cashier at the store on evenings and weekends, stared when they approached the cash register, her thickly masacaraed eyes open wide. She picked up the house telephone and murmured something into the mouthpiece, never taking her frightened gaze from Jake.

"Hello, Loretta. How are you today," Grace said, smiling as she helped him stack his purchases on the conveyer.

Loretta stared at Jake, unconsciously chewing her gum so fast it popped incessantly. "Uh . . . fine, Miz Ames." She made no move to ring up the items.

Grace wasn't surprised to see the store manager come storming through the door of the little cubbyhole marked, "Office."

Darwin Stiles had been a linebacker on the Cedar Grove High School football team during Grace's senior year. He was still big, but he was developing a paunch and he was more beef than muscle.

He didn't see Grace at first. "Damn you, Paxton, I told you—"

"Told him what, Darwin?"

He stopped short. "Grace. I didn't see you there."

"Is there a problem?" she asked in a pleasant voice.

"Problem? Uh . . ." He glanced at Jake, his eyes flashing. When he spotted the boy with them he looked ready to fly apart. Darwin's mouth thinned, but he managed to rein in his temper. Finally he shook his head, his narrow-eyed gaze slicing back and forth between Jake and the boy. "No. No problem."

"Good. I wouldn't want to think this store was guilty of discriminatory practices. I'm sure the chain doesn't want that kind of black mark against them. Lawsuits are always so messy and expensive."

"Lawsuit?" Darwin's voice rose to almost a squeak. "Now, Grace. There's no call for that kind of talk."

Hate swirled in his eyes when he looked at Jake and the boy, and his jaw bulged. He simmered with fury but he didn't dare let it show. He took it out on poor Loretta instead.

"Well. Don't just stand there like a dolt," he snapped, making the hapless girl jump. "Get busy. Check out these groceries. And make it snappy. And the rest of you get back to work!" he shouted at the other cashiers, who, with their customers, were silently taking in the exchange. "I'm not paying you to stand around!"

He stormed away, but instead of returning to his office he went to talk to the security guard posted by the door.

"Damn, Grace," Jake murmured in her ear as they stacked the rest of the groceries onto the conveyer. "When you get riled you play hardball, don't you."

She sniffed and tilted her chin. "If I have to."

When Jake's purchases were bagged and paid for and returned to the cart for transport outside, they headed for the door. "You ready, kid?" Jake said to the boy who was longingly eyeing the candy display beside the register.

"Yeah, I'm comin' " he replied in a surly voice. Giving the display a last wistful look, he plodded after them, dragging the heels of his ragged tennis shoes with each step.

Behind them a buzz of conversation erupted. Among the comments that reached their ears was one from Martha Goodson, one of Ida Bell Wheatly's cronies and one of the worst gossips in town.

"Humph! You ask me, there's more to her helping him than simple Christian charity. Grace is just a mite too interested in that no-good trash for that relationship to be innocent."

"Why, Martha, surely you don't mean that. Grace Ames is a model of propriety. She would never get involved with someone like that."

"Humph. Wouldn't be the first decent woman to be led astray by a no-good man. Forbidden fruit, don't you know."

On the way to the door Jake grinned down at Grace. The mockery in his eyes inflamed her even more than the comment.

"Well, Mary Grace, is it true?" he goaded under his breath. "Do you secretly have the hots for me? Is that why you're helping me?"

"Certainly not!" she huffed, and he laughed.

The minute they walked through the door he sobered and, turning cynical again, drawled hatefully, "Well, you better get used to those kind of remarks. If you're going to cast yourself in the role of my champion, not even your sterling reputation will protect you from spiteful old biddies."

She had no chance to think of a suitable reply. The instant they stepped outside, Darwin and the security guard grabbed the boy from behind.

"We gotcha now, you little thief!" Darwin crowed, and the child let out a shriek.

Jake released the grocery cart and whirled. "Get your hands off him, Stiles."

"Forget it. This kid's a shoplifter. We caught him red-handed on video tape. He's coming with me."

"Lemme go, you piece of crap!" The boy kicked and squirmed and when that didn't get results he bit the hand closest to his mouth.

"Ow! Ow! The little shit bit me!" the guard howled. He relinquished his hold on the boy and slung his hand repeatedly. "Ow! Ow! Jesus, that hurts!"

"I'm warning you Stiles, let the boy go."

"Or you're gonna do what?" the store manager sneered. "Cut me up with a knife like you did that girl?"

"No. I'm gonna whip your sorry ass," Jake said in a deadly soft voice.

Darwin laughed. "You think you can take me, slimebucket? You don't have a prayer." He turned to the guard. "Here, hold the kid."

The guard looked horrified and tried to back away, but Darwin shoved the child into his hands. Then he turned to Jake with a nasty smile. "C'mon, tough guy. I'm gonna enjoy this."

"Jake, no!"

"Get back, Grace."

"No, stop this at once." She rushed in between the two men and held her arms out to the sides in a puny effort to keep them apart. "Fighting is not the way to settle anything. For heaven's sake, you two aren't children anymore."

"Stay out of this, Grace. It's time someone taught this creep a lesson." Jake's green eyes glittered, and she could see that he was spoiling for a fight.

Darwin, for all his pretensions of being an important businessman, was no better.

"Get out of the way, Grace." Jake reached out to move her aside just as a car roared up and screeched to a stop at the curb directly in front of them.

Harley stepped out and stood in the wedge of space between the car's body and the door. The headlights illuminated the brawlers. "All right. What the hell is going on here?"

"Harley! Thank heavens," Grace said with a sigh of relief.

The sheriff shut the car door and stepped up onto the sidewalk. He looked at Jake and shook his head. "You just can't stay out of trouble, can you, Paxton?"

"You know, Sheriff, you could find out who started this before you go pointing a finger. I was just helping out the kid."

"That boy was stealing, Sheriff," Darwin charged. "When I tried to take him into custody, Paxton here interfered. I was just about to teach him a lesson."

"You and who else, asshole?"

"Hey! Back off!" Harley put a hand on Jake's chest to hold him back and shook his head. "Jeez, you're a real hard case aren't you?"

"The kid didn't take a thing out of the store." Jake insisted. His intense gaze drilled into the Darwin Stiles. "Have you searched the boy?"

"Not yet, but we caught him on video, stuffing his coat."

"Hold still, son," Harley said kindly, squatting down on his haunches before the boy. He patted the youngster down, ignoring his sulky glare and lack of cooperation, then raised an eyebrow at the store manager. "He's clean, Darwin."

"What? He can't be. I saw the little hoodlum stuffing his coat with can goods." He shot Jake a sharp look. "He probably passed the stolen merchandise to Paxton. Why don't you frisk him?"

Jake stiffened, but the sheriff was quick to intervene. "Now, you know I can't do that unless you got good cause to suspect Jake of shoplifting."

"No, Sheriff, it's okay." Jake smiled at the store manager, unpleasantly, his eyes narrow and glittering. "You think I got the goods on me? Go ahead. Have a look." He held his arms out to the sides. The action spread his denim jacket wide, revealing the form-fitting white T-shirt underneath. It was obvious that he did not have anything under the jacket and he could not have hidden so much as a can of tuna fish in the pockets of his tight jeans.

Anger and frustration tightened Darwin's face. He glanced at the grocery cart. "He could have hidden the stuff in there." Grace had had enough. She stepped forward with her chin high. "Darwin Stiles, every item in those sacks was rung up and paid for in my presence. There is absolutely no reason for you to search them. Unless, of course, you think I would be a party to shoplifting."

"Good heavens no, Grace!" Darwin looked horrified. "Why, I'd never think a thing like that!"

"I didn't think so," she replied with daunting dignity.

"Well, that's good enough for me," Harley announced. "Looks like you made a mistake, Darwin."

The set of his jaw said he didn't think so, but he had little option but to agree. Scowling, he pointed his finger at the boy. "You're getting off this time, but I'll be watching you, kid."

"Butthead," the kid mumbled as Darwin and the guard stomped back into the store.

"What's your name, son? Where do you live?" Harley asked, and the boy shot him a go-to-hell look.

"Whadda you wanna know that for?"

"No reason," the sheriff agreed. "I was just wondering what a kid your age was doing out alone at this time of night."

"I ain't done nothin' and I don't have to tell you nothin', you peck—"

"The kid's not alone, Newcomb," Jake said, clamping a warning hand on the boy's shoulder to shut him up. "He's with Grace and me." The boy shot Jake a suspicious look, but remained sullenly quiet.

Harley's shrewd gaze slid from one to the other. "Is that right, Grace?"

She shifted uncomfortably and cleared her throat. "Why, yes.

He is." She knew the lie was written all over her face, but other than to give her a steady look, Harley let it pass.

"I see. Well, then, I guess we're all settled here. I'll be getting along." He tipped his hat to Grace and patted the boy's shoulder, though he flinched away. "You take it easy, son." Gentle and avuncular, it was a warning, nonetheless.

When Harley had driven away, the boy shuffled his feet and looked at the ground. "Thanks," he mumbled against his chest, then he cut his eyes at Jake and added with defensive bluster, "But I didn't ask for any help, you know."

Grace's heart twisted at the awkwardness of the little speech. It was painfully evident that the child had not had much practice being grateful for anything.

"Yeah, I know. But what the heck, it was no big deal. Say, look. Grace and I were about to go out for a burger. Why don't you come along?"

That was news to Grace. She opened her mouth to tell him so, but when she met Jake's eyes and read the silent message there she understood and quickly played along.

"Yes, why don't you," she said cheerfully.

The boy's gaze slid back and forth between them, suspicious as a cur dog that expected a kick. "Why would you wanna buy me dinner?"

"Hey, no big deal. I just thought you might want to come, is all."

"Yeah, well, I don't need no turkey giving me charity," the child flared back with hurt pride. "Just 'cause I let you help me, don't mean I want no handout from some do-good peckerwood."

"Hey, man. I feel like having a hamburger and fries. You want one, come along with us. You don't, then hit the bricks. It's no skin off my nose either way. C'mon, Grace." With supreme indifference, he grabbed the cart and headed for the van.

Disbelieving, Grace watched him stroll away. She glanced at the boy, then back at Jake, and hurried after him. "Jake, wait," she hissed under her breath. "We can't just leave him. That boy needs to eat."

Jake kept right on going. "Stay out of this, Grace. Let the boy have his pride."

Grace sucked in an indignant breath. She opened her mouth to tell him that you couldn't eat pride, when the boy trotted up beside them.

Sticking his hands in his back pockets, he slowed to a cocky, heel-dragging saunter and announced in a bored voice, "Aw-right. I'll go. Shit, if a dude wants to throw his money away, I'll let 'im."

Fourteen

When Grace returned from using the telephone and slipped into the booth next to Jake, his eyes held a self-satisfied gleam and a hint of a smile played around that hard mouth. "So, your date wasn't with the preacher after all."

"How do you know that?"

"I've got excellent hearing," he said, nodding toward the bank of telephones about twelve feet away. "Did your mother-in-law give you much static about missing her dinner?"

"She wasn't exactly happy about it." Which was the understatement of the year. The way Verna had carried on you would have thought that Grace was missing a state dinner at the White House. "She'll get over it though. Anyway, this is more important. Where is our little felon-in-training, by the way?"

"I sent him to the men's room to wash his hands. Did you get a load of those fingernails? There was enough dirt under there to start a garden."

"Mmm. The rest of him isn't any better. You have to wonder about his home life. What kind of mother would let her child go dirty like that? And hungry?"

Jake looked at her for a long time. "Believe me, you don't want to know."

The boy slipped onto the bench seat on the other side of the booth just as the waitress brought their order. He dived into the food with such pathetic eagerness Grace got teary watching him. The child was starved.

Before Grace had taken three bites of her dinner he had scarfed his way through a whole order of fries and most of his burger and slurped down a milkshake, all with the most atrocious manners she had ever witnessed.

While the boy was deeply absorbed in eating, Jake signaled the waitress and quietly instructed her to keep the food coming.

"So, what's your name, kid?"

He looked up sharply, suspicion in his eyes again. "Whaddaya wanna know for?" he asked with his mouth full of food.

Jake shrugged. "No reason in particular. I'm just getting tired of calling you kid and boy."

He looked at Jake a moment longer, then swallowed the bite. "My name's T. J. Tolson."

"Tolson? Is your mom Connie Tolson, by any chance."

"Yeah. Why?" T.J. asked cautiously, eyeing Jake.

"I know your mom. At least I used to. We went to high school together. I haven't seen her in over twelve years."

Grace remembered Connie Tolson. She also remembered that Connie and Jake had been an item at one time. For some reason that thought did not set well with her.

The waitress put another hamburger and fries in front of T.J., and he sent Jake a questioning look.

"Go ahead. Eat up." Jake slid the plate closer to him. "Eat all you want."

He hesitated only a second before attacking the second burger.

"So, how's your mom doing these days?"

"Okay, I guess," T.J. replied in between bites.

"How about your dad? What's his name? Maybe I know him, too."

"My ma said his name was John, but I don't remember him. He took off when I was a baby." He took a deep slurp of milkshake and went on. "Anyways, she's got herself a new boyfriend now. His name is Digger Yates. He lives with me'n ma in our trailer."

"You like him?"

"Hell no. He's—" Frowning, T.J. looked down at his plate, and stirred a puddle of catsup with a French fry. "He's okay, I guess."

"How about your mom? What's she up to these days?"

"She don't do nuthin' 'cept watch TV an' lay around with Digger and smoke pot. She used to tend bar out at The Rip Saw, but Digger, he don't like her to leave the house without him, so she had to quit her job."

"I see." When the waitress came with another shake, Jake took it from her and put it in front of T.J. "And what does Digger do?"

"Not much. Odd jobs mostly. He used to dig graves over at the cemetery when somebody croaked. That's how he got his nickname. I don't know his real name. Anyway, he got fired. Mr. Turner said he was takin' jewelry off the dead people. Digger said it was a damned lie, but he prob'ly did it."

He said the last so matter-of-factly Grace was stunned. What kind of people were these?

T.J. had shed the windbreaker to eat. Underneath, he wore a stained and faded T-shirt. Jake reached across the table and touched a livid purple spot about four inches long that wrapped around T.J.'s forearm, just below his elbow. "That's some bruise you got there. What happened?"

T.J. pulled the arm back and put it in his lap, beneath the table. He shrugged. "I fell."

To Grace's astonishment, while Jake adroitly pried more information out of him, the boy gobbled down two hamburgers, two orders of fries, two milkshakes and part of a third, and what was left he took home with him to have later.

When he was finally stuffed, they drove him home. At first, though Grace got the impression that he really did want a ride, T.J. refused, saying he could walk.

"I do it all the time. It's no big deal."

"Nevertheless, I insist. Little boys shouldn't be walking late at night by themselves."

"I ain't no little boy," T.J. replied indignantly, thumbing his scrawny chest. "I'm almost eleven."

"Oh, I'm sorry. I should have realized." Grace had to hide a grin. "But please, won't you let us drive you anyway? For my sake."

"Say yes, kid. She'll fret and worry and drive me nuts if you don't. You know how women are," Jake said in that long-suffering, male-bonding tone that men use when discussing the incomprehensible ways of women.

It worked admirably, of course. T.J. rolled his eyes and said magnanimously, "Oh-kaay. I'll letcha drive me."

He lived in a trailer park on Tobin Road, down in the Bottoms, not far from the house where Jake had grown up. Grace had driven down the road thousands of times, past the dilapidated old houses and tarpaper shacks and rusty trailers, but she'd never actually driven into one of the seedy trailer parks that lined the east side of Jasper Creek.

It looked even worse up close than it had from the road. The trailers were jammed together every which way, so close there could not possibly be any privacy. What little yard that surrounded each trailer was mostly weeds or bare dirt. There was trash and junk and beat-up vehicles everywhere.

The boy directed them down narrow dirt lanes through the maze of trailers with increasing nervousness. Finally he blurted out, "That's it up there. The last one on this row. I don't see Digger's pickup, but you'd better stop here and let me walk the rest of the way so I can sneak in around the back, just in case he's there. He gets mad if I come in late.

"Course, I don't care if the peckerwood blows his top," he added with bravado. "But my ma, she gets upset."

Jake and Grace exchanged a look. For all his big talk, the boy clearly was frightened of his mother's boyfriend. "Don't worry, kid. If you get in trouble I'll square things," Jake said, bringing the van to a stop before the trailer. "In fact, when you go in, send your mom out. I'd like to talk to her."

"Okay," he said in a distracted voice. His shoe-button eyes wide and wary, he craned his neck and searched the road behind them through the rear window before opening the cargo door."

"Oh, by the way, T.J., take this," Jake said, handing him a small card.

"What is it?"

"It's Mrs. Ames's business card. I wrote her home number on the back. If you need anything, or just want to hang out, you can reach me at the store on Main Street or you can call her house and she'll call me to the phone."

For an instant, the boy's cocky mask slipped back in place. He puffed out his chest and gave Jake a scornful look. "Why would I do that? I don't need nuthin' from you, man."

Grace noticed, however, that he slipped the card into his pocket.

"Suit yourself. But the offer is good anytime. Remember that."

T.J. shrugged, then cast another fearful glance around. Clutching his milkshake, he climbed out of the van and tore inside the trailer.

A few minutes later a thirtyish woman stepped out on the porch and came warily down the steps, squinting her eyes at them. Backlit by the harsh light coming from inside the trailer, she looked terribly thin.

As she drew near, Grace saw that T.J.'s mother was drawn and unkempt. She had a dissipated look, her bottle blond hair was frizzy and stiff with setting gel. She wore skin-tight leggings and a cheap T-shirt splashed with glitter and cinched at the waist with an elasticized belt. Her makeup had been applied with a heavy hand, but it did nothing to disguise sallow skin that had already begun to sag.

"Jake? Why, Jake Paxton, it is you. I didn't believe it when T.J. told me. How in the world are you?"

"I'm managing." He nodded at Grace. "This is Grace Ames. Grace, Connie Tolson."

"Yeah, I know. I remember you from school. You were the preacher's kid," Connie said, then added quickly, "We never ran with the same crowd or nothin', of course. An' nowadays, why everybody in Cedar Grove knows you, you being Charles Ames' widow, an' all."

"So how's it going, Connie?"

"Okay, I guess." She shifted her feet and folded her arms tight over her midriff. Her gaze kept darting down the road every few seconds in the same skittish way that T.J.'s had. In between, she batted her eyes and smiled at Jake. "I got me a man, but if I'd known you was coming back I'd a waited."

"Well, hell, I guess I missed my chance," he said, returning her flirty smile.

Connie giggled. "You never can tell. Things change, you know."

"Yeah. Hope springs eternal."

"Huh?"

"Never mind. You know, Connie," he added in a conversational tone. "Grace and I fed your boy tonight. He sure was one hungry kid."

"Shoot, Jake, you know little boys," she said with a nervous laugh. "They're always hungry. I swear sometimes I think that kid has a hollow leg. I just cain't fill 'im up. Cost a fortune to feed the little sh— uh, kid," she amended, glancing uneasily at Grace.

"Yeah, I guess it's hard to make ends meet sometimes. Maybe you ought to think about getting a job. The City Cafe is looking for another waitress, I hear."

"We do okay," she said defensively. "Digger, he takes care of us just fine."

"Good. I'm glad to hear it. By the way, we couldn't help but notice that your boy's got some mean-looking bruises on him." The icy look he suddenly turned on her took Grace by surprise. She had never seen anyone's demeanor change that rapidly. In a blink he had gone from genial to hard as nails.

Connie shuffled her feet and hugged her arms tighter, not quite able to meet that piercing stare. "T.J.'s just, uh . . . accident prone is all. Always was clumsy, even as a baby," she said with a sudden sullen edge to her voice.

"Is that right? Maybe you'd better keep an eye on him. I like the boy. I'd sure hate to hear that he'd had any more . . . accidents."

Connie darted him a resentful look. "Yeah, well, you better go now. Digger don't like for folks to come around when he ain't here."

He let several seconds tick by without answering, then nodded. "Sure. See you, Connie." He put the van in gear, then paused with his foot on the brake and gave her a long look. "Just remember what I said about those accidents."

"What was that all about?" Grace asked as they drove away.

"A word of caution to an old friend. I just hope it'll be enough."

Enough to what? Grace had no idea what he was talking about, but his tone was so icily furious she didn't dare probe deeper. They rode in silence most of the way home, but Grace couldn't stop thinking about T.J. By the time they drove through town and headed north toward the farm she could no longer keep quiet.

"That poor boy," she said with a sigh. "I can't believe his mother would spend money on pot and let her child go hungry, or not bother to see that he had a bath now and then. And that place. I've never seen such appalling living conditions."

"That's not the worst of his problems," Jake ground out with such bitterness that Grace looked at him sharply.

"What do you mean?"

He gave her a quick, searching glance. "You really don't know, do you?"

"Know what?"

"I'm talking about those bruises. I think the boyfriend is knocking the kid around."

"What? "Grace stared at him, appalled. "Are you serious?"

"You saw the bruises. The one on his arm is fresh, but he's got a fading shiner and some damned suspicious marks on his neck. There's probably more that we can't see."

"That's horrible! Jake, we have to do something."

His laugh was ugly. "God, you're naïve. What do you suggest we do? Send your preacher boyfriend over to talk to the naughty man?" he sneered.

"I don't know, but we have to do *something.* And don't dismiss Daniel so easily. He may be a minister, but he's no wimp."

"Look, I talked to her, okay. That's all we can do for now. Anyway, we have no proof. And even if we did, around here nobody gives a damn about what happens to the trash living in the Bottoms. All you decent upstanding citizens with your nice houses and warm clothes and full bellies just look down your noses and tsk about what a disgrace it is that people haven't got any more pride than to live that way.

"Hell, you haven't got a clue what it's like to go hungry or have somebody knock you around just because maybe you don't obey fast enough, or you made too much noise, or maybe just because you were there."

He turned into the driveway with his jaw set and drove into the carriage house in stony silence.

His words shamed Grace and his bitterness wrung her heart. She knew he was talking about himself as much as T.J., and the glimpse into his world was painful.

Jake turned off the ignition and reached for the door handle, but she stopped him with a hand on his arm. "Jake, listen to me," she said gently. "We may not have proof, but we do have Josie. A social worker only needs reasonable suspicion to investigate."

"Yeah, right. And if she can't find enough cause to remove T.J. it'll go worse for him," Jake stated angrily. He slammed out of the van and stomped around to the passenger side and slid open the cargo door. He was already stalking away with his sacks of groceries by the time Grace climbed out.

"Jake, wait," she called, hurrying after him. She caught up with him at the foot of the apartment stairs and grabbed his arm to stop him. "Jake, we *have* to do something. We can't just sit back and close our eyes to this. Even if he's not abused physically, that child is neglected and going hungry."

He stared into her pleading eyes, his face taut, but after a tense moment he sighed.

He sat his grocery sacks down on the steps, and when he straightened he cupped her face with both hands. This time his look was gentle and tinged with wonder. "Mary Grace." He said her name softly, simply, as though it were a benediction. He smiled, a crooked little tilt of his mouth that did funny things to her heart. "Like I said, you're too softhearted.

"Honey, there are dozens, maybe hundreds of T.J.'s in the Bottoms. What're you going to do? Rescue them all?"

"If I have to. Right now all I know is, that boy needs help."

"I know. But even if you send Josie out there, the kid's still got enough pride and grit in him to deny that anything is wrong. I've made the offer, in a way that I hope he can accept. The next move is up to him."

Grace stared up into those green eyes, frustration and a sick helplessness gnawing at her insides. She wanted to argue, but she could not.

Her shoulders slumped and she sighed. "I guess you're right. It's just so hard."

"I know."

The only illumination was the faint glow from the top of the stairs where the light was left on all the time. It cast his face in dark blue shadows and the palest yellow highlights. His eyes glittered at her through the semi-darkness, and his hands flexed ever so slightly against her face. Out in the woods behind the barn an owl hooted, and the gentle night breeze, carrying with it the fecund scents of spring, stirred her hair.

He smiled and stroked an errant lock back from her face. He watched the action, and his pupils expanded as his fingertips sank into the silky golden brown strands at her temples.

In the stillness of the night Grace could hear his breathing. She became acutely aware of the warm hands against her face and the cool breeze whispering over her arms and playing with her hair, the faint scent of turpentine that clung to Jake's hands from the refinishing work he had done that day. Most of all, she became aware of how close they were, and the intimate look in his eyes . . . and her traitorous body's reactions.

A trembling had begun deep inside her, and it was suddenly difficult to breathe. She wanted to run away from him as fast as she could, and she wanted to throw herself in his arms. The conflicting emotions tugged at her, confused her, frightened her.

She drew an unsteady breath and struggled for calm. "I . . . I'd better go inside," she said, but when she tried to ease away, one of his hands slid around to cup the back of her neck and the other encircled her waist.

"Stay," he commanded softly.

"Jake, I . . ." She shivered, unable to look away from his hard, handsome face.

"Stay." He watched her intently, those hot pale eyes tracking each tiny nuance of expression that flickered across her face, as all the while he slowly drew her to him.

She told herself to move, to stop this now, while she still could. Instinct told her that Jake would not use force if she insisted on leaving. Yet she could not seem to make her limbs obey the message her brain was sending.

Her hands came to rest against his chest, and she could feel the heavy beat of his heart against her palm. It exactly matched her own. The hand at her back pressed tighter, and from her breasts to her knees her body came into stunning contact with his.

It was like being pressed to warm rock. His strength thrilled her and unnerved her. Never in her life had she experienced this weak-in-the-knees sensation. Never in her life had she been so drawn to a man. Never in her life had she been so starkly aware of the wonderful and exciting differences between male and female.

She pressed half-heartedly against his chest. "Jake, st-stop this."

"Not yet." Beneath half-closed lids his slumberous eyes gazed at her mouth, and his head began a slow descent. Grace's heart began to do a crazy tap dance against her ribs. "Not yet," he whispered again against her parted lips an instant before his own closed over them.

The kiss was devastating. It shook Grace all the way to her toes. It was hot and wet and utterly carnal. His tongue mated with hers with uninhibited directness. Lips rocked and rubbed, teeth nipped. His big hands roamed her body with shocking familiarity.

Little currents of electricity zinged through her and fire followed close behind. She felt hot and cold all at once, and every nerve ending in her body tingled as sensation after sensation rippled through her.

Grace tried, briefly, to muster the strength and the will to resist, but it was useless. She could not think, she could only feel, and the sensations flooding her were too delicious to deny.

She was weak with hunger, on fire with need. All she could do was cling to him and return the ravenous kiss.

When Jake finally raised his head he looked down at her, his eyes filled with heat and satisfaction as he studied her dazed expression. Grace's knees nearly buckled under her and her breathing rasped from her chest like a marathon runner's at the end of a race.

He put his hand beneath her chin and rubbed his thumb over her kiss-swollen lips. "You see. You were wrong. It's not fear that makes you skittish around me. It's desire."

She sucked in a sharp breath and color flooded her cheeks. As her head began to clear, sanity returned, and she stepped back. She wanted to shout that that wasn't true, but she could not, in all honesty, do so. She settled instead for indignation. "You have a lot of nerve," she gasped. "I'm warning you, Jake. If you ever do that again you'll leave me no choice but to fire you and . . . and evict you from the apartment."

He laughed and bent to pick up his groceries. With both arms full he turned and grinned. "Now why do you make threats like that when we both know you won't carry them out?" He turned and started up the stairs. He was halfway to the landing when his soft, "Good night, Grace" floated back to her.

Fifteen

FROM THE SHADOWS someone watched with hate-filled eyes. Jake Paxton was an evil scourge that befouled everything he touched. And now he was touching Grace.

This was one more abomination for which he must pay. And pay, he would.

Sixteen

"MMM, YUM. Now that's what I call a delicious hunk of man."

The statement startled Grace. She looked around and saw that the customer who had been wandering through the store was standing at a window which looked out onto the rear of the building.

Grace's mouth compressed. She knew before she joined the woman what she would see; Jake was unloading the items that had arrived that morning by motor freight. What she had not expected to see was his impressive naked torso.

After the freezing weather they'd had only the week before, it had turned unseasonably warm, and he had stripped off his shirt. Heat flooded Grace's cheeks, but the woman next to her was too busy ogling Jake to notice. She watched him with avid eyes, her mouth slightly parted. Grace half expected her to start drooling at any moment.

Not that she could blame her. He was magnificent. He was broad shouldered and narrow hipped, and with each movement muscles bulged and rippled beneath his skin.

"Please don't tell me he's your husband," the woman pleaded, never taking her eyes from Jake.

The statement sent an odd little thrill through Grace. She gritted her teeth and shook her head. "No. He's my handyman."

"Oh, my, I'll just bet he is," the woman said with a throaty, insinuating laugh, and shot Grace a sly look. "Lucky you."

Her name was Daphne Cole. She was a wealthy divorcée who owned a summer cottage on the lake. Grace did not really know her but the woman had purchased several pieces from the shop in the past.

"Are you two . . . involved?" she asked.

"Jake and I have an understanding." That of employer and employee, Grace thought with only a trace of guilt. She had no idea what had prompted her to make the deliberately misleading statement, other than that the woman's man-hungry attitude irritated her.

"I see." Her disappointment was so obvious Grace had to hide a smile. "Well, in that case, I might as well go. You don't have anything today that I'd be interested in, at least, not in the store." Just as she was about to step through the door she turned back and said, "Be sure and tell that gorgeous man that if things don't work out here he can be handy over at my place all he wants."

It was all Grace could do to reply with a tight smile.

She fumed after the woman left. Her attitude annoyed Grace. Jake was an intelligent and hard-working man. Despite his well-earned reputation, he was several cuts above the riffraff who hung out at The Rip Saw, one of his old stomping grounds.

Jake was capable of so much more than just working as a handyman, and he certainly deserved better than to be ogled by brassy women like a hunk of beef.

The thought bothered her all morning.

After that kiss the night before, she had resolved to distance herself from Jake, and on the ride into work that morning she had been cool to him, barely speaking except to respond to a direct question. After a while he had gotten irritated and fallen silent, too.

Given the way he made her feel, she knew it would be best, and wisest, to continue in that manner. She told herself that if Jake wanted to waste his life, that was his business, not hers. Yet, she could not stop worrying about him. She was still thinking about the problem when he stuck his head in the door and asked her a question.

"What?"

"I said, where do you want me to put the new pieces?"

"Oh. Uh, I don't know yet. Let's just leave them in the storeroom until I figure something out."

"Fine with me." He turned to leave, but she stopped him. "Jake, wait a minute. Why don't we take a break and have a cup of coffee. I just made a fresh pot."

He gave her a searching look, then shrugged. "Sure. That's fine with me." He came back into the shop, stripping off his leather work gloves as he walked.

After they were settled in chairs and she had taken a few sips of coffee, she said gently, "Jake, have you ever thought about the future?"

"Some, but not often. Not lately, anyway. I'm still dealing with my past."

"That's rather futile, don't you think? Wouldn't you be better off spending that energy trying to better yourself. You don't want to be a handyman all your life, or work in a sawmill. You could go to college and get a degree, really make something of yourself, if you wanted to. You have the potential."

He took a sip of his coffee, giving her a sardonic look over the rim of the mug. "Thanks for the vote of confidence, but you're a little late."

"Jake, it's never too late to start over," she said urgently.

"What I meant is, I've already gone to college." He grinned at her astonished expression. "I have a degree in secondary education, specializing in high-school English. I've been teaching school, or trying to, for the past seven years."

Grace stared at him, her eyes wide. She was so stunned it took her a moment to recover her voice. "Why, Jake, that's wonderful! What subjects do you teach?"

"Literature, mostly. Some math."

Of course, Grace thought, recalling all the times she'd seen him in the library. Imagine. Jake Paxton, a schoolteacher. She frowned. "But I don't understand. If you have a teaching degree, why were you going back to work at the sawmill? What are you doing working for me, for that matter?"

He shot her a wry look. "What choice do I have. You're not suggesting that I apply to the Cedar Grove school board for a job?"

"Oh. I see your point. No, I guess not."

She thought for a moment, then looked at him eagerly. "But that's here. You don't have to stay in Cedar Grove. You could start over somewhere else and put the past behind you."

"God, there's that naïveté again. Hell, Grace, what do you think I've been doing for the past twelve years? I'd like nothing better than to start fresh, but every time I find a job, I no sooner get settled in, than someone sends an anonymous letter to my school board, complete with copies of newspaper clippings covering the murder and my arrest and the trials."

"Are you serious?"

"Oh, I'm serious, all right. I wish I weren't."

"What sort of things do the letters contain?"

"About what you'd expect. The writer points out that it's very doubtful that the parents of their students would approve of having a murderer teaching in their school, or that the board wants innocent children put in that kind of danger either. Then he goes on with something along the lines of, if the school board doesn't get rid of me at once, no doubt the local newspaper would be interested in the story. And, of course, he slyly reminds the board members that if that happened the parents of their students would be outraged, and rightly so."

Grace shook her head. "Jake," she began tentatively. "Are you sure about this?"

"Am I sure? Hell, yes, I'm sure. In the seven years since I got my master's degree I've worked in thirteen different schools in as many towns." Suddenly he stiffened and his eyes narrowed. "You don't believe me, do you?"

"It's not that, exactly," she denied quickly. "I just think that maybe you're being . . . well . . . a bit paranoid about the past, is all. Perhaps there were other reasons you were let go. I mean, when you were fired, did they actually tell you they'd received a letter about your past?"

"Oh, yeah, they told me. I went through some damned unpleasant termination interviews. There was never any doubt about why I was being canned."

"Did you actually see these letters?"

"Just one. Thanks to a friend who worked in the office of

the Slaton school board. She and I had gone out a few times and when the shit hit the fan, she stuck by me." He reached into his hip pocket, withdrew his wallet and fished out a creased and worn envelope. With an angry flip of his hand, he tossed it across the table to her. "She made that copy for me."

Grace looked at the letter uncertainly, and he snarled, "Go ahead. Read it. See if you still think I'm being paranoid."

He was furious, and Grace was sorry now that she had questioned him. Hesitantly, aware of his cold gaze stabbing her, she withdrew the single sheet of paper from the envelope and began to read. By the time she finished she was appalled.

"This is horrible. I can't believe someone would do such a thing. For that matter, *why* would they do it? And how did they always find out where you were?"

"It's obvious that someone is tracking me—or paying a detective to track me—someone who wants to destroy any chance I have to make something of my life. And that someone lives right here in Cedar Grove."

"Oh, Jake, no. Surely not. I hate to think that there is someone living here who would do something so awful."

He flicked his finger toward the envelope lying on the table between them. "Check out the postmark."

Grace did, and her heart sank. It had been mailed right there, in town.

"So you can forget about me leaving. I'm through starting over and having the rug jerked out from under me. I haven't a prayer for any kind of decent future until I find out who is writing these letters."

"How are you going to do that? They're not signed and they're typed, or possibly printed on a computer printer. You can't have a test run on every machine in town. And the paper and envelope are common stock."

"This person obviously hates my guts. He's probably furious that I wasn't convicted of murdering Carla Mae, so he's made it his mission to make sure I suffer. I figure my presence in Cedar Grove is going to enrage the bastard so much he'll eventually show his hand."

He took another sip of coffee and regarded her solemnly. "I also figure there's a good possibility that the writer and the killer are one and the same."

"Oh, my Lord!" Grace put her hand over her mouth and stared at him, shock and fear swirling through her. "I hadn't thought of that." Her eyes widened. *"That's* how you're planning to prove you're innocent. By drawing the killer out."

"That's right."

The bell over the front door tinkled and they looked around as Lyle entered the shop.

Jake's lip curled. He downed the last of his coffee in a single gulp and stood up. "Looks like it's time to get back to work."

"Grace, you really upset Verna last night," Lyle began the minute he walked in, but Grace barely heard him.

Frustrated, she watched Jake disappear out the back door to finish unloading the new purchases. A chill crept over her. If the killer was the letter writer, then Jake was in grave danger.

FOR THE REST OF THE DAY the horrible thought nagged at her relentlessly. Never mind her resolve to distance herself from Jake. Her concern about the attraction between them seemed unimportant, even petty, by comparison.

She tried to talk to him several times, but he seemed disinclined to discuss the matter further and cut her off before she could voice her fears. She suspected he was still angry with her for doubting him. His mood was foul for the rest of the day.

Frustrated and angry and frightened for him, she grew snappish, which was completely foreign to her nature, and he responded in kind. By the end of the work day they were snarling at one another like two pit bulls.

Just before closing, Grace had had enough, and she cornered Jake in the storeroom and told him of her fear. His reaction did nothing to reassure her.

"So?"

"What do you mean, so? Didn't you hear what I said? If the killer and the letter writer are one and the same, your life could be in danger."

"Don't you think I know that? It's a risk I'm willing to take."

"That's insane. Jake, be reasonable. You've got to leave here. Give up this idea of clearing your name. It's not worth it. Nothing is worth your life."

"That's where you're wrong. The way things are, my life's worth nothing unless I do."

"Jake, please—"

"Forget it. I'm not giving up. One way or another, I'm flushing this guy out."

Ignoring her, he stomped through the door and into the front of the store. Grace followed on his heels.

A customer had come in while they were in the back and was looking through the display of antique jewelry. Emily Perkins had spent two hours in the shop only the day before. She came in two or three times a week and never bought a thing. Grace suspected that she simply liked to be among the old things that reminded her of her childhood.

Nevertheless, business courtesy demanded that Grace break off her pursuit and greet her, but she did so with reluctance and a strained smile. "Hello, Mrs. Perkins. May I help you?"

"No, dear. I'm just browsing. You go ahead with what you were doing. I'll call you if I need you."

Grace nodded and hurried across the shop, where Jake was moving a chifforobe that was blocking an aisle. He saw her coming out of the corner of his eye and before she could speak he muttered, "Go away, Grace. I'm not changing my mind."

"But—"

"Oh, Grace, dear," Mrs. Perkins called. "I do believe I'd like to take a closer look at this brooch. Would you mind opening the case."

Before she could reply, Jake shot the old lady a hard look and snapped, "We close in ten minutes."

Emily Perkins jumped and her eyes went comically wide. "Oh! Oh, I . . . I'm sorry. I didn't realize it was that late. My, my, where does the time go," she said, darting nervous glances at Jake. "I'll just run along and come back some other time."

That was the final straw. Ever since he'd started working there he had treated her customers, locals and summer residents alike, to black looks and curt remarks.

When the old lady had scurried out Grace rounded on Jake. "Was that necessary?"

"I thought so. If you don't light a fire under that old biddy she stands around for hours."

"It wouldn't hurt you to be a little nicer to people, you know."

"Why the hell should I? They've all treated me like dirt all of my life."

Exasperated, Grace snapped, "Maybe if you didn't have such a huge chip on your shoulder people wouldn't be so quick to condemn you."

He looked ready to blow. He glared at her and clenched his jaws so tight his cheeks bulged. "Aw, to hell with it," he finally muttered and stomped out through the storeroom. A few seconds later, she heard the back door slam.

Grace glanced at one of the clocks. It was still ten minutes until closing. She was tempted to march to the back door and point that out to him, but when she looked out the window the stiff set of his back as he walked away changed her mind. Perhaps it would be best to let him walk off his anger.

She took her time closing up and totaling the day's receipts, keeping an eye on the woods behind the shop, where Jake had disappeared. By the time she was ready to leave he still had not returned. She waited another half hour, but finally she gave up and reluctantly went home without him.

By ten that evening, Jake still had not returned. Sick with worry, Grace hadn't been able to eat the dinner she had cooked for herself, and though she'd taken a long, hot bath and prepared for bed, sleep was impossible. Wearing her fuzzy chenille robe over her nightgown, she paced the parlor and checked outside the window every few minutes, but there was no sign of Jake.

"How about another beer?"

Jake looked up from his morose contemplation of the warming beer in his hand, into a pair of heavily lined and mascaraed brown eyes that were offering one helluva lot more than another drink.

The top three buttons of Charlene's blouse were undone. Leaning over him with one arm around his shoulders and her other palm flat on the table, she provided him an unobstructed view of plump breasts encased in a lacy, push-up bra.

Jake looked his fill, and wondered why the sight of that creamy flesh didn't do a thing for him. He hadn't had a woman in three months and lately he'd been horny as hell. He knew from experience that Charlene was a tigress in bed, hot and wild and insatiable.

Jake had come to The Rip Saw with the intention of getting drunk and getting laid, but his temper had cooled and, though he hated to admit it, Charlene's obvious charms seemed tawdry.

But they had once been friends, and so he played the game. Giving her a crooked smile, he stuffed a five-dollar bill into her cleavage and gave her bottom a pat. "Sorry, darlin', I'll pass. I think I'm gonna hit the road."

"You're leaving?" Her voice was pouty with disappointment. "Shoot, sugar, whadda you wanna do that for? I was kinda hoping you'd stick around until closing and go home with me." A sultry smile curved her mouth and she twined her forefinger through a lock of hair at his nape and added softly, "My old man's on a cross-country haul in his truck. He won't be back for days."

A wave of revulsion rose like bile in his throat, but he held on to his flirty smile. Christ. Had he ever found this woman attractive? Never in a million years could he imagine Grace making such an offer.

"Sorry, darlin'. Some other time, maybe."

Ignoring Charlene's pout, he slid out of the booth and headed for the door.

Outside, the night air held only the slight chill of spring. The gentle breeze carried the clean scents of cedar and pine, and after the stale beer smell of the pool hall he welcomed the freshness and breathed deeply.

Hell, he guessed that was what came of turning respectable—places like The Rip Saw no longer appealed to him. Either that, or he was getting old.

It was a good five miles to the Somerset farm. The walk here had been fueled by anger, but that had cooled, and he wasn't thrilled with the prospect of walking all that way again. Serves you right for being such a hothead.

He stuck his hands in his pockets and headed down the road. A few cars passed, but he didn't bother to stick out his thumb. What would be the point?

A quarter of a mile from The Rip Saw, Jake turned off on a little used back road. It was narrow and dark and lacked the advantage of traffic to light the way like out on the main highway, but it would cut almost a mile off of his walk home.

Home. Bemused, he realized that in only a week he had come to think of the Somerset farm as home—not the apartment, but the whole place—and all because Grace was there.

As he strode along through the darkness he mulled over their quarrel. He could concede now that perhaps he had overreacted. She, after all, had been concerned for his safety, which was surely a good sign, but it had made him furious when she had insisted that he leave. All he could think of was, she wanted to be rid of him.

He thought about what she'd said about being nicer to people and his mouth turned down at the corners. His eyes had adjusted to the darkness and he kicked a clod, sending it sailing down the road. All right, maybe—just maybe—she had a point. Maybe part of the problem was his attitude. Maybe if he were a little nicer to people they'd get off his back. He chuckled. It would sure as hell shock the socks off of most of them.

Aw, what the hell. To please Grace he'd at least give it a try. The truth was, there was very little he wouldn't do for Grace.

It seemed that fate was putting him to the test when, less than ten minutes later, he rounded a bend and came across a stranded motorist in a stalled car at the side of the road. Jake knew before he reached it who he would find behind the wheel. There was no mistaking Miss Harriet's long Cadillac.

He approached the car with caution, walking down the middle of the road so she would be sure and see him if she was looking in the mirror. With that indomitable little woman, he wouldn't put it past her to be packing a can of mace, or maybe even a gun. However, when he approached the driver's door she, as always, was sitting ramrod straight behind the wheel, her gaze fixed straight ahead. What she was waiting for, he had no idea.

The doors were locked but the window was rolled down about three inches, presumably for air. Jake tapped on the glass with his forefinger, and she jumped like he'd shot off a firecracker. "Miss Harriet?"

She glared at him and snapped, "What do you want?"

What did *he* want? Hell, she was the one stranded. "Do you need some help?"

"Certainly not. Just get along with you."

That annoyed the living hell out of him. Any idiot could figure out that Miss Harriet Tucker would not be sitting alone in her car on a lonely road at night unless she had mechanical trouble. He started to tell the old harridan to go to hell and leave her, but he reminded himself of his recent decision and held on to his temper. Barely.

"Pardon me, Miss Harriet, but I think you do. You're obviously stuck out here with a car that won't run."

She fixed him with the same fierce look he remembered from grade school and gripped the steering wheel. "I know who you are," she snapped defiantly. "You're that Jake Paxton. You were in my class one year."

"Yes, ma'am." God knew, he'd had his knuckles cracked by her ruler more times than he cared to remember. On several occasions he'd tried to intimidate her, but not even his insolent stares had fazed the tiny woman.

Had any other teacher treated him to that kind of abuse he would have walked out of class. He wasn't quite sure why he had tolerated Harriet Tucker's caustic tongue. Except that he admired her backbone, and beneath that prickly exterior she was fair. *And* she happened to be Grace Somerset's spinster aunt.

Grasping the steering wheel tighter, Harriet snapped in her starchiest schoolmarm voice, "Well, if you're going to kill me, get on with it."

Her daring almost made Jake smile. Lord, she was a pistol.

"Miss Harriet, I'm not going to hurt you. Now, would you please just pop the hood and let me see if I can get your car started."

Her sharp old eyes studied him for several seconds. Finally, with a nod, she pulled a lever and the Cadillac's long hood popped up a few inches.

"Have you got a flashlight?"

"Of course. What kind of idiot would drive around without one, I'd like to know," she snapped as she opened up her "neat-as-a-pin" glove box.

Instead of handing the flashlight to him, she announced she would hold it for him. Jake suspected she intended to use it as a club if he made a wrong move.

He walked around to the front of the car and raised the hood all the way as she climbed stiffly out. Leaning on her cane, she came to join him and held the flashlight high as he fiddled with the engine.

He quickly located the source of her problem; the wire connecting the coil and the distributor had vibrated out of the coil. He reconnected it and told her to try the engine. It started up at once and idled as smooth as a purring kitten.

"That ought to do it." Jake slammed the hood shut and stepped back, wiping his hands on his handkerchief.

He expected her to drive away, but she just sat there.

Finally she looked at him impatiently and snapped, "Well, don't just stand there. Get in."

He hesitated, feeling oddly off balance. "Are you sure you want to give me a ride?"

"Would I have offered if I hadn't been?" she said in a tart voice. "Now don't stand there dawdling. Get in."

Dawdling? There was that word again. Now Jake knew where Grace had picked it up.

He quickly stuffed the greasy handkerchief into the back pocket of his jeans and got in.

Sitting with her usual military posture Miss Harriet gripped the wheel with her white-gloved hands and drove at her standard twenty-five miles an hour, not a mile faster, nor a mile slower. Grinning, Jake started to slump down in the seat, but she snapped

"Sit up straight. Don't slouch."

He obeyed automatically, though he wasn't sure why.

They rode in silence for a while. Then, abruptly, she said, "I've seen all the repairs you've done around the farm. You've done a good job."

Jake shrugged and mumbled, "Yeah, well, they needed doing."

Another silence followed. "There are rumors going around town about you and my niece," she blurted out finally.

"I'm not surprised. If a man and woman are alone more than ten minutes in this town the nosy old biddies think they're screwing each other's brains out."

Out of habit, Jake had responded with his usual earthy cynicism, but the last word had barely left his mouth when he received a sharp rap across his knuckles. "Ow!"

"You watch your mouth, young man. I will not tolerate that kind of talk."

Jake rubbed his smarting knuckles and looked at the old woman with amazement. Holy shit, she even carried a damn ruler in her car.

"Well? Don't just sit there like a lump. Is there anything to the rumors? *Is* there something going on between you and my niece?"

"Not yet."

She sent him a sharp look, but she absorbed the implication of his terse reply in stiff silence. Several seconds tick by.

"Did you kill that girl?"

Jake's mouth twitched. Only Miss Harriet would ask that question so bluntly.

"No."

To his surprise, she nodded and replied with an equally terse, "Fine then."

"You believe me?"

"You were a disrespectful, surly little hoodlum, Jake Paxton, but you were never a liar," she said flatly.

And that, apparently, was that.

They did not speak again until she pulled into the driveway

at the farm. Jake thanked her for the ride, and as he climbed from the car, she delivered one parting shot. "I'm giving you fair warning, young man. If you hurt my niece, you'll answer to me."

He paused with his hand on the open window and looked her in the eye. "You don't have to worry about that, Miss Harriet. I'd sooner cut out my heart than harm a hair on Mary Grace's head."

She studied him. Her piercing gaze probed deep. Apparently satisfied with what she saw, she gave another of her sharp nods and drove away at her usual sedate speed.

WATCHING FROM THE FRONT WINDOW, Grace gaped when she saw Jake climb from her aunt's car. She blinked rapidly, unable to believe her eyes. What on earth was Jake doing riding around with Aunt Harriet?

It took several seconds, but once she recovered from her initial shock, she raced out the front door. However, by the time she reached the drive, her aunt's car was already cruising down the road toward the highway at her standard twenty-five miles an hour.

Burning with curiosity, Grace rounded on Jake with her hands on her hips. "Where have you been? And just what were you doing with my aunt?"

He grinned. "Didn't you know. Harriet and I are having a hot affair."

"Very funny."

Jake stepped closer, his eyes gleaming with devilment. "You waited up for me, didn't you? It's nice to know you worry about me. Why don't you admit it, you do care. Don't you, Grace? Hmm?"

He reached for her, his gaze fixed intently on her mouth, but she stepped back and batted his hands away. "Stop that." She sniffed, then sucked in a sharp breath. "You stink of beer. Jake Paxton, you've been drinking!"

"Some," he admitted.

She was so furious she wanted to hit him. Here she'd been worrying herself sick, and he'd been out carousing.

And the worst of it was, he was right; she was crazy about him. If this long, miserable evening had taught her nothing else it had taught her that much. She had no idea what she was going to do about it, but one thing was certain, she would not admit it to him.

"I did not wait up for you."

"No? Then what are you doing out here in your bathrobe?" He grinned and fingered the collar of the bulky chenille garment. It covered her from her chin to her ankles. "Very fetching, by the way. What's under it?"

"None of your business. And for your information, the only reason I'm still up is I was watching a late movie on television. When I saw you get out of my aunt's car. Naturally I was curious."

"Oh, naturally."

"However, since I'm here, I might as well give you this." She pulled a slip of paper from the pocket of her robe and slapped it in his hand. "It's your paycheck. You stormed off so fast this afternoon I didn't have a chance to give it to you. I thought you might need it. Now, if you'll excuse me, I'll say good-night."

Giving him a haughty look, she turned and marched back into the house. The skirt of the bulky robe billowed out behind her.

Seventeen

THE NEXT MORNING Jake walked into town to buy the parts he needed to repair his truck. He had planned to borrow the van, but Grace had left early, for where he had no idea, so he had no choice but to hoof it. It was no big deal. Hell, he'd walked farther lots of times.

On Saturdays Edith Hollister, the woman who worked part time for Grace at Things Remembered was in charge of the store. Since she had flatly refused to work in the shop if he was around, he had the weekends off, and he intended to devote this one to getting that heap of his running again. He was tired of being without wheels.

When he walked down Main Street he received some hard looks and people went out of their way to avoid coming into contact with him. The same thing happened when he entered Humphries Auto Supply. No one offered to help him, but neither did anyone dare to ask him to leave or refuse him service; word of Grace's genteel warning to the supermarket manager had spread. No matter how they felt, few people in Cedar Grove were willing to openly defy Grace.

While Jake was searching through the fan belts for one to fit his truck he happened to glance out the window and noticed that T.J. was hanging around outside. He was trying his best to act casual, but every few minutes he peered into the store. Jake had a hunch the boy was waiting for him to come out.

That hunch proved correct a half hour later. With no one to assist him, it took Jake that long to find everything he needed, but when he left the store T.J. was still there, leaning against the building.

"Hey, T.J. How's it going?" he said casually, as though he'd just noticed the boy.

"Okay," T.J. replied. Abandoning his slouched position against the wall, he fell into step alongside Jake. "Where you going?"

"Back to Grace's farm. I got an apartment there."

T.J. nodded sagely and gave a little skip to catch up with Jake's long stride. After a while, he looked up. "Are you really a killer?"

"Nope."

"My ma says most folks around here think you are."

"Yeah. I expect they do."

"You mean you really didn't murder that girl, like they say?" He sounded disappointed, and Jake was amused at his youthful bloodthirstiness.

"No, I didn't," he said, and they walked along in silence.

"Whatcha got in the sack?"

"Oh, a fanbelt, spark plugs and points, condenser, an air filter. Stuff like that. My truck's not running. It needs some repairs and a tune-up. I'm going work on it."

"You know how to do that kinda stuff?"

"Yeah. You want to give me a hand?"

T.J. shrugged and scuffed his heels against the sidewalk. "I guess."

Jake smiled and kept walking. Despite T.J.'s feigned disinterest, Jake could see the eagerness in his eyes.

GRACE'S VAN was in the carriage house when they got to the farm, but there was no sign of her.

With T.J. sitting importantly in the cab, steering, Jake pushed the truck out of the carriage house into the driveway, and the two of them set to work.

T.J. was inquisitive and bright and full of questions—about every tiny thing that Jake did to the truck, about Jake's lurid past, about Grace, about the farm. He eagerly hung on Jake's every word and puffed up visibly at the least word of praise. It was painfully obvious that the child hadn't had any male attention—not the right kind, at any rate.

Jake was patient and talked to him like an equal, which seemed to bolster T.J.'s confidence and put him at ease. They had been working in the driveway for about an hour when Lyle drove in and parked behind the truck.

The minute he stepped from his BMW he scowled. "If you make a mess in Grace's driveway you be sure and clean it up, Paxton," he snapped.

Jake went right on working. He didn't even bother to look up, and Lyle's mouth thinned. He didn't like being ignored.

His gaze switched to T.J. and his scowl deepened. "Who the hell are you? I know I've seen you around town. What're you doing out here, boy?"

"He's a friend of mine," Jake said in a warning voice.

"Now there's a sterling character reference," Lyle sneered. When that didn't get a rise out of Jake he turned on his heel and headed for the house. "Just see that he keeps his pilfering hands off what doesn't belong to him," Lyle warned over his shoulder.

"Asshole," T.J. muttered as he disappeared into the house.

Jake's smile was droll. "You got that right, kid."

Eighteen

REVEREND STREET looked at Grace with sad acceptance. "You're sure this is what you want?"

"I'm sure. You're a wonderful man, Daniel, and I think the world of you . . . as a friend."

"Ah, those dreaded words," Daniel said with a wry smile. He cocked one eyebrow hopefully. "And I suppose you're quite sure there will never be more?"

"I'm sure." She looked at his kind face and knew a deep regret. How foolish the heart was. By all rights, he was the ideal man for her. He was good and decent and kind, and handsome as well. They shared the same background, they enjoyed each other's company.

But he didn't make her heart race or her palms sweat or fill her with that tingly excitement with just a look. Her eyes drifted out the kitchen window, where T.J. and Jake where busily painting the picket fence. Not like someone else did.

Daniel's gaze followed hers, and he said softly, "Ahh, so that's how it is."

She guiltily jerked her gaze from Jake's muscular back and looked back at him. "Oh, Daniel, why are our hearts so foolish?" She focused longingly on Daniel's kind face. "I wish . . . I wish . . ."

He laid his hand over hers. "I know. Me, too. But our hearts have a mind of their own, it seems." He sighed heavily. "And . . . to tell the truth, I know that you're right. A match between us seemed so ideal, I guess I convinced myself that it was meant to be. But—though I'm disappointed—I'm fairly sure my heart's not broken. Nope. It seems to be thumping along just fine." He put his hand on his chest as though checking to be sure, and Grace laughed.

Relief washed through her, and gratitude for this wonderful man who was going out of his way to make this easier for her. She turned her hand over and squeezed his. "Thank you, Daniel."

"Hey, what're friends for? We are still friends, right?"

"Absolutely. The best."

"Good. Then there's no reason why we can't still attend the pot luck supper together, is there? Strictly as friends."

"None at all. I baked two pies just for the occasion," she said happily, but beneath the table she had her fingers crossed.

She had just glanced at the clock when she heard Josie's car rattle up the driveway. "Oh, excuse me a moment, will you. That's Josie. I want to talk to her about T.J. before we go. I'll be right back," she said over her shoulder as she hurried toward the front door to intercept her cousin.

Grace had feared that Daniel's car parked in the drive might spook Josie, and she had been right. When Grace stepped out onto the porch her cousin was standing in the open door of her car, eyeing Daniel's unmistakable navy blue sedan with a panicky look on her face. In another few seconds she would have climbed back in her own vehicle and taken off if Grace hadn't stopped her.

Calling to her cousin, Grace hurried down the walk. Josie aimed an accusing look her way. "You didn't tell me that Daniel would be here."

"Didn't I? Oh, well, what difference does it make? Come on inside."

"I don't know, Grace. Maybe we'd better do this another time."

"Nonsense. You're here now, so why wait? Anyway, I'm worried about T.J.," she said, taking Josie's arm and hustling her inside before she could break and run, as Grace knew full well she wanted to do.

"He's out back with Jake right now," she continued as she ushered Josie into the parlor where Daniel was waiting. Grace felt her cousin tense and try to hold back the instant she saw him, but she tugged her along anyway.

"Daniel, I told you the situation at T.J.'s. Why don't you fill Josie in for me while I go get the boy?"

Josie darted her a startled look. "Oh, no. Grace, wait—" she started to protest, but Grace hurried out with a light, "I'll be right back."

Convincing T.J. to leave his hero was not easy. In the past few weeks the boy had become a fixture, both around the farm and at the shop. He adored Jake. He tried to be exactly like him, mimicking his walk, his talk, his mannerisms—the way he sometimes stood with his legs apart and his fingertips stuck in the back pockets of his jeans, the way he often thumbed his Stetson to the back of his head when he was talking. The way the boy acted, you would have thought that Jake had hung the moon and stars in the sky.

T.J. was nowhere near ready to leave, but, with help from Jake, she finally managed to get him to come inside with her. Both Josie and Daniel had met the boy before, since he'd been Jake's shadow since the day he let him help with the truck.

As soon and she and T.J. entered the parlor, Grace stopped abruptly and rubbed her temples with her fingertips. "Oh, dear, that hurts."

"Is something wrong, Grace?" Josie asked.

"I seem to have a horrible headache. I think maybe I'd better skip the pot luck supper tonight after all. I feel a fierce migraine coming on."

"That's too bad," Daniel commiserated. "Is there anything we can do for you?"

"No, I don't think so," she said weakly. Then she brightened. "Oh, wait. There is one thing. Why don't you two go on together?"

"Oh, no. I couldn't—" Josie started to protest, but Grace wouldn't hear of it.

"No, it's perfect. You can take my pies. It would be a shame for them to go to waste. And on the way, you can drop T.J. off at his house and check on . . . you know," she said with a meaningful glance at the boy. "That thing we talked about."

"I can do that by myself, Grace. There's no need to stick Reverend Street with my company for the evening just to attend to that matter."

"Oh, but there is. That's a rough area. I know, I've been there. I really don't want you going there alone, Josie."

"Nonsense. I do it all the time."

"Grace is right, Josie. It isn't a good idea. Besides, it would be good for you to get out and socialize a bit. We never see you at any of our church socials."

"Well . . . I . . ."

"C'mon. It'll be fun. You'll see," Daniel urged, and Grace could have kissed him.

Josie continued to protest, but between the two of them, they loaded her down with pies and ushered her and T.J. out the door and into Daniel's car. As they drove down the driveway Grace watched them with a smug smile on her face.

She nearly jumped out of her skin when, behind her, someone began to clap.

She whirled around, and met Jake's sardonic smile. "Congratulations, Mary Grace. That was as devious and masterful a bit of manipulation as I've ever seen."

"I don't know what you mean," she declared with a haughty lift of her chin, then blushed scarlet under Jake's scornful look.

"Why Mary Grace, I'm shocked. Lying like that." He shook his head and tsked.

"You don't have to make it sound so terrible. I've tried for weeks to get Josie and Daniel together with no luck. Tricking her was the only way I could get her over here tonight with Daniel. She bolts like a deer whenever he's around."

"Hey, it's not terrible at all. I think what you did is great. For Josie and for us."

"There is no us, Jake. I keep telling you that," she said nervously. It was unthinkable. Impossible. Her and Jake Paxton. This town would spin like a top.

"I know what you keep telling me." He pushed away from the doorway and strolled toward her, and a shiver of excitement rippled up the back of her neck. "But your eyes and your body say something else."

He stopped just inches away and stroked the side of her neck with his forefinger, and Grace trembled. Her heart beat so fast it almost suffocated her. She felt panic well inside her. Without the protection of Daniel to fall back on she was vulnerable. She had to put a stop to this now, while she still could.

"I don't know what you mean." She stepped back and around him. "I'm sorry, Jake, but I . . . uh, I have to run into town before the pharmacy closes. I'm, uh . . . I'm out of aspirin," she improvised, latching onto the first thing that came to mind. "I really do have a headache."

He didn't believe her. She could tell by the look in his eyes. He crossed his arms over his chest. "Fine. I think I'll ride along. You don't mind, do you?"

Of course she minded. The whole object of the trip into town was to escape him, to break the nerve tingling, heart palpitating, butterflies-in-the-stomach spell his nearness evoked. "No. Not at all."

She didn't need to see Jake's mouth twitch to know the lie was written all over her face. She could feel the heat climb her neck and flood her cheeks.

In town, Jake went into the pharmacy with her. While Grace was caught in conversation with another customer, he wandered aimlessly through the store, checking out the goods on the shelves, picking up an item now and then for a closer look. At the end of the second aisle, he rounded a corner and came face to face with his mother.

Jake froze. A host of emotions welled inside him as he stared at the woman who had given him life—none of them joy.

He hadn't seen Lizzie since that morning, over twelve years ago, when that old bastard, Oscar Greely and his deputies had burst into the ramshackled shack Lizzie called home, dragged him out of bed and slapped him in irons. As they had been hauling him, kicking and fighting, out the door, Lizzie had followed along behind, cursing and screeching, "Good riddance! I hope they fry your ass, you worthless little bastard!"

That was the last he had seen or heard from his mother.

Dissipation had aged Lizzie more than twelve years should have. She was still as brassy and cheap-looking as ever. Perm frizzed hair, dyed a bright, orangy red was teased into a huge bouffant. The wrinkles in her face were caked with heavy makeup and the circles of blush on her cheeks gave her a clownish look. Mascara clumped her eyelashes together and black eyeliner circled her eyes. Both looked as though they hadn't been removed for days.

Sneering, Lizzie eyed him up and down, and erupted in a wheezy, cigarette cough. "Well, well, well. If it ain't my long-lost son. I heard you was back in town. Surprised the crap outta me, too, I can tell you. You got one helluva nerve, coming back here, you little shit. Nobody wants you here, least of all me."

In the next aisle, Grace gasped and stared.

Jake stood stone still. He didn't so much as flinch. Why did her words hurt so much. It wasn't as though he'd expected anything else. Hell, when had he ever gotten anything but abuse from Lizzie?

"Hello, Ma," he said in a flat voice. "Still the same, I see,"

"Damned right. And so are you." Her voice grew louder and nastier. Every head turned in their direction. Behind the high counter at the back of the store, even Elmer Purdee stopped filling a prescription to stare.

Lizzie's lip curled as she ran her gaze over Jake again. "You're still the same no-good, worthless bastard you always was."

Jake's jaw clenched. She enjoyed goading him. It gave her some sort of sick pleasure. If she had been a man he would have shut her up with his fist, but Lizzie knew she was safe from any sort of physical retaliation. She was his mother, and as sorry as she was, he would never strike her.

Though God knew, growing up, there had been plenty of times when he'd been tempted.

The makeup-caked wrinkles creased into a knowing smirk as she studied his remote expression. Lizzie took a deep drag on her cigarette and blew the smoke into his face. She stepped closer and stuck her face right in his. "Why'd you come back, anyway? Nobody in this town wants you here, you murdering pervert."

With precise movements, Jake turned around and returned the box of Band-Aids he had been about to purchase to the shelf. He didn't look at Lizzie or even acknowledge her existence. He simply stepped around her and headed for the door with long, deliberate strides, his eyes focused straight ahead.

Lizzie followed him. "I was glad when they arrested you. You hear that? I was glad! That meant I didn't have to look at your face no more," she sneered.

Face set, Jake walked past the gawking customers. The bell over the door set up a frantic jingle as he jerked the door open and stepped outside.

He had barely taken two steps when the bell jingled again, and Lizzie screeched, "When they hauled your ass off to prison I celebrated. You hear that, Jake? Fact is, I was hoping you'd get the chair!"

The words bounced off his back. Jake didn't slow his pace or acknowledge that he'd heard her. He drew even with Grace's van, but he walked right on past without slowing.

Lizzie reentered the pharmacy laughing. "I guess I showed the little crud."

The words jerked Grace out of her shocked stupor, and she brushed past the horrible woman and rushed after Jake. She had hoped to find him waiting in the van but when she reached it he wasn't there. She looked up and down the street and experienced a burst of relief when she spotted him over a block away.

Tossing her purse into the van, she climbed inside and started the engine. She reversed out of the parking slot with a screech of tires that caused several heads to turn, and started after Jake.

His long stride had covered another block by the time she caught up with him. She pulled up at the curb beside him, but he ignored her and kept right on walking, his face stony, eyes straight ahead. "Jake, please. Won't you get in?"

She might as well have been talking to a wall, for all the response she got. "Jake, please. Let me take you home," she entreated, cruising along beside him at idling speed. No response.

"Jake, will you *listen* to me!"

She crept along beside him for almost two blocks, but he

acted as though he didn't hear her, or see her.

Finally, Grace sped ahead a few yards, jerked the steering wheel to the left, drove over the curb onto the sidewalk and slammed on the brakes, blocking his path. Jake had no choice but to stop.

She jumped out just as his angry stride faltered to a stop and faced him squarely. "Get in the van, Jake."

His black glare switched from the askew vehicle to her. "You're attracting stares."

"Did you think we weren't when I had to trail you down the street? Now get in and let's go home."

"Go away," he snarled, and made a move to skirt around the van, but she grabbed his arm.

"I am not leaving you, Jake. I swear to you, if I have to, I'll follow you all the way home, or wherever it is you're going. So won't you please just get in now and save us both a lot of trouble?"

Angry eyes studied her determined expression. His face was so tight, Grace was sure it would feel like stone if she touched it. For an instant she thought he was going to refuse again, but finally he made an aggravated sound and got in the van.

Before he could change his mind, Grace hopped in, backed the van off the sidewalk and sped toward the farm. Every few seconds she glanced worriedly at Jake, but she remained silent. Nothing about him encouraged conversation.

He slouched in the other bucket seat and stared out the side window in silence all the way home. The instant she brought the van to a stop in the carriage house, without so much as a word to her, he bailed out and stomped up the stairs to his apartment, slamming the door behind him.

Grace did not hesitate or think about propriety or the wisdom of going after him. She simply went. He was hurting, and her compassionate heart dictated that she offer comfort.

She raced up the stairs without any idea of what she would say to him, or what she would do if he threw her out.

She half expected the door to be locked but when she tried the knob it opened and she stepped inside. He hadn't bothered to turn on any lights. She remained by the door and peered through the darkness, but she didn't see him. "Jake?"

Her voice seemed to echo in the silence. Gradually her eyes became accustomed to the gloom, and the darker shadows became pieces of familiar furniture. She turned her head slowly and spotted him in the kitchen. He stood motionless, staring out the window over the sink at nothing. Grace moved through the darkness toward him, drawn by that rigid back and the aura of pain that surrounded him.

When she drew near she saw the bottle on the counter and that he had a glass of straight whiskey in his hand. "Jake?"

"Go away, Grace," he growled, and tossed back the slug of whiskey. He sloshed another into the glass and returned his gaze to the night sky outside the window.

Grace came to stand beside him. She put her hand on his forearm, and the taut muscles bunched beneath her light touch.

"I'm so sorry," she whispered.

She expected that he would rebuff her, but he didn't say a word. She was not even certain that he heard her. He knocked back the second drink and poured another, and for a long time he just stared blankly out the window.

"When I was a kid I used to pray that she would love me," he said in a monotone, his gaze still fixed on something beyond the window, or perhaps on something long ago. "That a miracle would happen, and she would wake up one morning different. When that didn't happen, I tried everything I could think of to make her love me. I tried to be good. I tried to help around the house. I ran errands. All it ever got me was the back of her hand if I didn't move fast enough." His mouth twisted ruefully. "Once, I even brought her a bunch of wildflowers. She threw them on the floor and stomped them."

Grace stared at his profile and tried to blink back the tears that filled her eyes. Her throat felt as though she had swallowed an apple whole. She couldn't swallow past the aching lump.

The thought of a poor little boy, struggling to win his mother's love, when it should have been given freely, unconditionally, wholeheartedly, tore at her heart like sharp talons.

"When I got a little older I told myself that the drinking was the problem. All those horrible things she said to me, the way she was always knocking me around, was just the liquor talking. Later, I finally accepted that drunk or sober, Lizzie was simply a vicious person. It didn't matter what I did or said, she would always hate me."

"Oh, Jake," Grace whispered, hurting for him. If he heard her, she had no idea. He just stared out the window and talked on in the heart-rending, dull voice.

"When I was a little kid she used to jerk my pants down and beat me with the buckle end of a belt if I so much as looked at her crooked. I've still got the scars on my butt and the backs of my legs. A day didn't go by when I didn't at least get popped in the mouth or slapped up side the head. That's why I started spending as much time as I could away from the house. I'd roam the woods for hours, or hang around in town. Anything to avoid Lizzie's mean tongue and that damned belt."

Stepping closer, Grace put her arm around his waist and leaned her cheek against his shoulder, stroking his bicep with her other hand. She wasn't sure he was even aware of her touch. She wasn't sure he even knew she was there.

"By the time I was twelve I was bigger than she was, and one day when she came at me with that damned belt I took it away from her and threw it as far as I could. I told her if she ever laid a hand on me again I'd report her to the law."

He gave a little bark of laughter. "I wouldn't have, of course. By then I'd already had a couple of run-ins with the law, and I sure as hell wasn't going whining to that old bastard Greely. He'd've laughed in my face. Besides, I was ashamed to let anyone know my mother hated my guts and beat the crap out of me.

"But what the hell, everyone had to know. How could they not know, when I had more black and blue on me than normal skin tone. But no one questioned my home life or sent a case worker out to investigate, because no one gave a damn. I was just that goddamned no-good Paxton kid from the Bottoms—Lizzie's bastard—and nobody gave a shit.

"After that, Lizzie didn't hit me anymore, she just used her mouth to inflict pain. She was always screeching at me and calling me worthless and no good and telling me she wished I'd never been born. She let her boyfriends do the knocking around. And her taste always did run to mean sonsa-bitches, the kind that liked to use their fists. I fought back, but until I got my full size, I got the worst of it."

Grace, horrified at what she heard, stood silently. She had never known anyone who had been abused. She knew it happened, but only in an abstract way. From the perspective of her safe little world where parents nurtured and loved and protected their offspring, child abuse was a foreign concept that never really touched her life. Other people, people she did not know, got abused. Certainly not anyone in Cedar Grove. Jake's painful outpouring made it too real, too awful.

He took another swallow of whiskey, and gave a little snort of mirthless laughter. "It's amazing, pathetic really, how kids hang on so tenaciously to hope. Even after I gave up on Lizzie I used to lie awake at night in bed and dream of having a better life. Living in a nice house, with a mother and a father, and plenty to eat and clean clothes all the time and nobody screaming at me or hitting me."

He stopped and turned his head, and even in the darkness she saw the pain and hell in his eyes. "I used to dream of having a life like yours."

The statement wrung Grace's heart. Yes, she could imagine how perfect her world must have looked to the mistreated child he had been. That she had always taken that world for granted shamed her. At that moment she would have given anything to be able to undo all the wrong that had been done him and give him his heart's desire, for once in his life.

"Of course, that never happened. There was no way I could have what you had. By the time we were in high school I had scaled those dreams down to just one thing. One thing that represented everything good and decent and soft and loving that I had always wanted and could never have."

He looked down at her, and his eyes blazed in the gloom. The look on his face was so fiercely hungry, so determined, it sent a little thrill of alarm through her. As she met that gaze her heart began to pound and her breathing grew suddenly erratic.

"That one thing was you."

Grace blinked. She was sure she had heard him wrong. "Wh-What?"

"I meant it when I told you I've wanted you ever since I was sixteen. I used to dream about having you, about how it would be to lose myself in that sweet body of yours, to wrap myself in all that gentleness and loving until nothing else existed."

Grace's eyes widened. She stared at him, too stunned to speak. Desire that sprang from lust could be dismissed, controlled, denied, but this—this was a cry from the soul, a hunger so great it shook her to the depths of her being.

She gazed into those eyes for what seemed like an eternity, her heart going crazy in her chest, her throat so tight she could barely breathe.

"I still want that," he said in a voice raspy with need.

Spanning her waist with his large hands, he abruptly lifted her up and sat her on the kitchen counter and stepped between her legs. Their eyes were level and his blazed into hers like green fire. What she saw there sent a thrill of fear and excitement pounding through her.

"And by God," he said fiercely, "for once in my life, I'm going to have it."

Nineteen

HE GAVE HER NO CHANCE TO RESIST. Suddenly his mouth was on hers, ravenous and hot. At the same time his hands hooked beneath her knees and pulled her forward to the edge of the counter until she was straddling him. The move spread her legs wide, all the way to her crotch.

He eased back just a bit and with both hands grabbed the hem of her skirt, a soft swirly thing of gauzy pleats with tiny yellow daisies splashed all over it, and bunched up it, pushing it all the way up to her hips.

For an instant, Grace felt the cool night air against the tender skin of her inner thighs, then warmth and the scratch of denim as he stepped forward again and pressed her tight against him.

Through her silk panties, she could feel the roughness of his jeans and the swollen ridge of his arousal against that most sensitive and intimate part of her body. He was hard and hot, and the feel of him brought fire zinging to her feminine core. The sensations wrung a moan from Grace's throat.

Jake's mouth absorbed the sound, and he answered it with a growl of his own as his tongue twined with hers. She tasted the sharp bite of whiskey on his tongue. At any other time the taste would have revolted her, but at that moment she found it oddly erotic.

His hands, clasping her hips, were tense and hard. They slid under the bunched skirt and around to the back, gliding over silk panties. Callused fingers traced the top edge of the elastic, delved underneath and cupped her bottom. His fingers dug deep into the soft flesh, kneading, squeezing, pressing her closer still.

The feel of those hard, rough hands on her smooth bottom

excited Grace unbearably.

Breaking off the kiss, Jake came up for air, sliding his open mouth across her cheek. His breath left a hot and moist trail on her skin. Then the feathery warmth filled her ear as his tongue traced the delicate swirls there.

Grace shivered. Her eyes had drifted shut and her head lolled back like a flower on a wilting stem. With a little laugh, he raked his teeth gently over the arch of her neck.

"You can tell me to stop," he whispered. He nipped her lobe, then lathed the tiny hurt with his tongue. "I will, if that's what you really want."

She didn't answer, and he raised his head. "Look at me, Grace."

She responded to the soft command like one waking from a trance. As though weighted with lead, her eyelids lifted slowly. She felt feverish and shivery and slightly disoriented. Then her gaze met his, and as their eyes locked her heart began to pound.

"Do you want me to stop, Grace? Just say the word."

Her hands rested on his chest, and through his T-shirt she could feel his hard strength, the furry softness of the mat of hair that covered his chest, the pounding of his heart.

And she was aware—so deliciously aware—of that hard ridge pressing so intimately against her yearning flesh. Beneath the ecru panties, the soft feminine petals pulsed.

She looked at him helplessly. A word. A simple no. That was all it would take. She could see that in his eyes.

She could not make herself say it. Right or wrong, wise or foolish—it no longer mattered. At that moment, no power on earth could have made her deny him. No power on earth could have made her deny herself.

Her heart yearned to give him what he had wanted for so long. Her body burned to take what he was offering, what she had only just begun to realize that she craved, perhaps had always craved.

"Jake," she whispered, helplessly, too shy to do more.

It was all the answer he needed. Something flared in his eyes, something hot and urgent, and the hands cupping her rump tightened. He smiled, slowly, and it did wonderful things to his face. For the first time that she could remember, she saw happiness there.

"Grace. My Grace," he murmured, his voice rough with wonder and satisfaction. "At last."

Grace gazed into his face, usually so remote, but now so full of raw emotions, so vulnerable, and felt her heart turn over. Slowly, tenderly, she raised one hand and cupped his jaw.

He drew a sharp breath and closed his eyes. "Oh, sweetheart," he murmured in a voice that shook with the force of his feelings. "Sweetheart."

The hands around her bottom tightened. Slowly, savoring the moment, he leaned closer. Jake's head tipped to one side and descended. Grace's lifted. Her eyes fluttered shut, and as their lips drew closer a sigh shuddered through hers. She felt the soft eddy of his breath against her cheek and she moaned and clasped his shoulders and dragged him to her until their lips met in a fiery kiss that touched off an explosion.

Jake wrapped his arms around her and held her tight. He drank from her mouth as though he would devour her. Grace made an eager, incoherent sound, and her arms slid up over his shoulders and tightened around his neck.

Her legs wrapped around his hips in a move as natural as breathing. One of her sandals hit the floor with a soft thud, and a second later the other followed. The soles of her bare feet pressed against the backs of his legs, rubbing sensuously.

Shafts of moonlight beamed in through the windows, illuminating the kitchen in an ethereal blue light. Outside the wind stirred the budding pecan tree, and a barn owl hooted. A few feet away, the refrigerator hummed and clunked as the icemaker dumped fresh cubes. Two ripe bananas lay on the counter, and their too sweet smell mingled with the sharp scent of whiskey.

Neither noticed. Mouths fused, they clung together in a paroxysm of need and want, straining to get closer, as though each sought to absorb the other. Small, frantic sounds and frustrated moans issued from the pair.

Jake placed his palms against the sides of her breasts, alter-

his shoulders and clasped her legs around him tightly. "Jake, what are you doing?"

"I never intended our first time to be against a damned kitchen counter," he growled as he strode with her down the hall and entered the master bedroom. "In most of my dreams we were in a bed, and that's where we're going."

As his knee sank down in the mattress he looked into her eyes, and Grace was astonished at the hunger still burning there. "I want to feel you stretched out beneath me. I want to sleep with you in my arms. I want to make love to you, over and over, until neither of us can move."

Grace felt the cool touch of her grandmother's patchwork quilt against her back as, slowly, taking care not to break the intimate connection between them, he lowered them to the mattress.

For the first time, his weight came down on top of her, crushing her into the soft mattress. She felt the warmth of his skin, the tickle of his chest hair against her breasts, the abrasion of his jeans, still bunched low around his hips. Of their own volition, her arms encircled his neck and she looked into those intense eyes, still burning with sensuous fire and need.

She shifted beneath him, then stilled, her eyes widening. "Jake," she whispered with astonishment as she felt him stirring and swelling within her.

"Are you surprised? I've been waiting for this for at least half my life." He lowered his head and kissed her deeply with a voracious hunger, his tongue filling her mouth, claiming it, devouring it. When at last he raised his head her heart was hammering and she was caught up again in the spiraling need.

The look in his eyes made her tremble, the feel of him, hot and huge inside her, filling her, made her burn. He rocked his hips against her, watching her, and his eyes flared when she moaned. "I'll never get enough of you," he ground out as he began the plunging rocking rhythm that sent them spinning out of control once more.

Twenty

THE NEXT DAY, Sunday, turned out to be one of the worst days of Grace's life.

It started in the wee hours of the morning when she awoke and found herself lying in Jake's bed, her head on his shoulder, her fingers buried in the mat of hair on his chest and her right leg hooked over his.

At first she was so startled she almost yelped and bolted out of bed, but an instant later memory of the previous evening came flooding back and she caught herself in time to keep from waking Jake.

She closed her eyes, barely stifling a groan as the whole sequence of events that had led her to this predicament played out in her mind in great detail—from the awful scene in Purdee's Pharmacy, to her attempts at consoling, to that incredibly erotic seduction in the kitchen.

Grace did groan then, a soft rumble of humiliation and disbelief. The kitchen counter. Dear heaven, she'd had sex while perched on the kitchen counter! With Jake Paxton!

She felt like a wanton. She must be a wanton to do something like that. She'd never even fantasized about doing such a thing. How long, she wondered, had that latent tendency been lurking beneath her ladylike surface, just waiting to emerge one day when she least expected it and destroy all that she had worked her entire life to be?

One thing she knew for certain; she'd never be able to go in that kitchen again without blushing. Forget cooking.

She felt like a fallen woman. It was an old-fashioned term, but then, she was an old-fashioned woman, an anachronism she supposed, in today's modern world of premarital sex and anything goes if it feels good. She couldn't help it; that was the was the way she'd been raised. It was not only her father's teachings but simply the way things still were in small Texas towns, where, if you were female, you were either a lady or you were a loose woman.

Grace thought of how quickly she had succumbed to Jake's seduction, how enthusiastically she had participated, and felt a blush start at her toes and work its way up her body. She had not been merely loose, she had been positively . . . wanton. There was simply no other word for it.

Carefully, she lifted her leg off Jake with the intention of easing out of bed. The movement made her aware that she was still wearing her skirt. That, in fact, it was the only thing she had on, and it was bunched up and twisted around her waist.

A renewed wave of shame and dismay washed over Grace. The entire scene was one of debauchery. She was almost naked, in bed with a man, had no idea where her clothes were. The bed was a rumpled mess, she was even worse, the air around them smelled of sex and Jake reeked of whiskey. She was sticky with dried sweat, both his and her own, she was sore between her legs, she was bone tired, and she needed a bath.

She had to get out of there. She had to go home, where she could think clearly and sort things out. She certainly couldn't do that pressed up against Jake's naked body.

Sometime during the past few hours he had shed his jeans and briefs, she noticed with a twinge of resentment. She had no idea why, but winding up totally naked after sex seemed much less shameful than being partially clothed, especially when even that scant covering was in twisted disarray.

Cautiously, Grace lifted Jake's hand from where it rested on her hip and removed his arm from around her. The last thing she wanted was to wake him.

When she thought of the past few hours, what they had done together, she blushed. She wasn't ready to face him, not yet, maybe not ever, though she knew of course that she must. He lived not a hundred yards from her back door and he worked for her; she couldn't avoid him forever.

But she could avoid the morning-after awkwardness that was sure to come if she stayed. At least until she got her thoughts straight.

An inch at a time, Grace scooted over to the edge of the bed and eased off of it. She stood up, untwisting her skirt and shaking it out.

Pausing, she looked down at Jake. He lay in a pool of moonlight, stretched out on his back, his legs spread, utterly relaxed and snoring softly. As though drawn by a magnet, her gaze traveled up those long hairy legs to his sex. Even flaccid it was impressive. Grace remembered touching him, how he had felt in her hand, inside her, and her cheeks heated.

She quickly turned away and tiptoed out of the room. To retrieve the rest of her clothes and her sandals she had to entered the kitchen again. She did so quickly, keeping her eye averted from the counter and snatching up panties, bra, top and sandals and scurrying out into the living room to put them on.

In less than a minute she was dressed, if disheveled, and she quietly let herself out of the apartment and tiptoed down the stairs. Once at the bottom, she ran across the back lawn and into the house. She headed straight for the bathroom, where she stripped out of the wrinkled clothes, dumped them in the hamper and stepped into the shower.

Afterward, clean and smelling of lilac-scented talc, bundled up in her fuzzy chenille robe, she paced her room, ruthlessly and mercilessly raking herself over the coals.

Never mind the new morality, according to the standards by which she lived, what she had done was wrong. She couldn't even claim she had merely been offering comfort and succor, though she had at first tried to tell herself that. The truth was, there was much more to her feelings for Jake than compassion and pity, or even lust, though honesty forced her to admit she felt those, too. She had made love with Jake for one reason, and one reason only—because she was crazy about him.

Which was insane. Nothing could come of it. No matter how she felt about him, no matter how much she might yearn for their relationship to develop into something lasting, Grace knew that was impossible.

There were just too many things against them. For one, Cedar Grove, with all its inherent shortcomings and less-than-perfect people, was her home. Her roots were here. She loved it here. This was where she belonged. She would never willingly leave this place, but neither could she picture Jake ever being accepted here.

In addition, she had spent her entire life striving to maintain a spotless reputation and a certain position in the community. Those things were important to her. They were the foundation of her life. She couldn't just toss all that aside and involve herself in an affair, for heaven's sakes. Certainly not with Jake Paxton, of all people.

Not for a moment did she believe he wanted anything more from her than an affair. Which was just as well. Merely the thought of the complications marriage to Jake would bring to her life was mind boggling.

Finally Grace realized that she could not change the way things were or what was done. Accepting that, and that she was guilty of bad judgement and a moral slip, she vowed never to make the same mistake again, and went to bed, only to toss and turn for most of what was left of the night.

Sometime before dawn, she finally fell asleep. It seemed mere minutes later when, shortly after daybreak, she was awakened by a hard pounding on the back door. When she staggered downstairs, buttoning her chenille robe, she was not surprised to see Jake standing on the porch with a face like a thundercloud.

"What the hell did you sneak out for?" he demanded, brushing past her and into the kitchen the instant she opened the door.

He looked as though he'd just gotten out of bed. Sleep wrinkles creased his cheek, his hair was mussed and his jaw sported heavy stubble. His shirt was unbuttoned and he had stuffed his feet into his sneakers sockless.

"I didn't sneak out." The tide of color that rushed to her face gave away the lie. "Well . . . if I did it was only so I wouldn't wake you."

"You didn't want to wake me because you knew I wouldn't want you to leave. So why did you?"

"I . . . I needed to think."

"About?"

"About . . . us. About what happened."

"What's there to think about? We made love—several times—and it was great. You can't deny that."

"No. No, of course, not." She blushed under his intense stare and shoved her hands into the pockets of her robe.

"Just like you can't deny that you have feelings for me. Strong feelings. Otherwise what happened up there last night would never have happened," he said in an accusing voice, jabbing a finger in the direction of the apartment.

She looked at him unhappily, her face crimson. "No, I can't deny that. I do care for you." Care? Lord what a bland word. It came nowhere near describing what she felt for him. She wasn't sure herself just how deep her feelings went—she wasn't sure she wanted to know—but there was more there, much more, than simple caring. Or simple lust. "But, you see . .

"Oh, I knew there was a 'but.' I knew when I woke up and found you gone that you were running scared again. All right, let's have it." He looked braced for pain, staring at her in that intense way, his face set.

She gazed at him, miserable. "Jake . . . what happened last night was a mistake. It can never happen again."

"A mistake? What's the matter, Mrs. Ames? Is sleeping with the handyman just too far beneath you? Or is it just the idea of sleeping with me?"

She didn't need to see the savage glitter in his eyes to know that he was furious. Simply calling her Mrs. Ames in that sneering tone revealed that. Jake never referred to her by that name if he could avoid doing so. Wretched, she bit her lip and tried to find the words to make him understand. He didn't give her the chance.

"Hell, who can blame you? After all, I'm nothing but bastard trash from the Bottoms, right?"

She sucked in a sharp breath, appalled that he would put that interpretation on her decision. "How could you even think such a thing? Your background has nothing to do with my decision! And the fact that you work for me is unimportant."

"Is that right? Then it must be the murder charge?" His smile was nasty. "And here I thought you believed in me."

"I did! I *do!* It's just that . . ." She looked at him helplessly, unable to put it into words. "It's just so hard to explain."

"Try."

"Jake, if I were anyone else. Or if you were anyone else. Or we were anywhere other than in this town, maybe we would have a chance. But the reality is, no matter what I believe, to everyone else you . . . you're . . ."

"The local no-good and a vicious murderer," he finished for her. "And you're afraid you'll be ostracized if you get involved with me."

"Jake, please try to understand—"

"Oh, I understand all right. No matter how you try to whitewash it, the basic problem is still the fact that you're the minister's daughter and a pillar of society and I'm Lizzie Paxton's bastard. You're afraid of what people will think of you if you get involved with me."

He gave a bark of laughter, a harsh, unpleasant sound. "When it comes to defending me against injustice you wade right in and give 'um hell, but when your precious reputation is on the line you turn coward. The idea that someone might think you're less than perfect terrifies you, doesn't it, Grace? Well fine. You hang on to your halo." He marched to the door and jerked it open, then stopped and looked back at her, his face tight. "See if it keeps you warm at night."

Turning, he stormed out and slammed the door behind him so hard the window rattled.

For the first time since his return, Jake did not go to church with her that morning. Many of the parishioners were relieved and a few were downright happy, but Grace was miserable. It no longer seemed right to be sitting in the family pew without Jake by her side.

Her misery only got worse after services, during her weekly

Sunday visit with her mother-in-law.

"Did you know that the reverend attended the pot luck supper last night with Josie, of all people?" Verna fluttered happily the moment they sat down at the table.

"Yes, I did."

"You don't sound upset."

"I'm not."

"What happened," Lyle asked. "You and the preacher have a fight?"

Grace sighed. "No, we didn't. We simply realized that we weren't right for each other. We parted very amicably."

"Well, dearest, I told you all along he wasn't the man for you," Verna declared, passing the platter of fried chicken. "But even so, I must say, you're being very nice about this Josie business. Doesn't it bother you that he's going out with your cousin now?"

"No, not at all. Actually, I arranged their date."

"Why, how sweet of you. Isn't that sweet of Grace, Lyle? Although . . . I'm not at all sure that Josie is the proper choice for the reverend."

"Josie is a fine person," Grace insisted, instantly defensive.

"Oh, of course she is, dear. Of course she is. It's just that she's so . . . so unconventional. Not at all what you want in a minister's wife."

"They've only had one date. It's a bit early to starting worrying about that."

"You're right," Verna agreed. "Silly me. The important thing is you didn't make the mistake of marrying the wrong man."

Grace tensed, knowing what was coming next, and Verna didn't disappoint her.

"And now that you're no longer seeing Daniel, you're free to go out with Lyle."

"Good idea, Aunt Verna," Lyle concurred. "How about we make it tomorrow night," Grace? We could drive down to Houston and have dinner."

"I don't think so."

"Whyever not, dear?"

Grace put her fork down and looked her mother-in-law

straight in the eye. "Because I don't have any intention of going out with Lyle. Not now. Not ever. I have told you both that over and over, and I'm tired of arguing about it. If you don't stop pressuring me you leave me no choice but to stop coming here."

"Grace! You don't mean that!"

"Yes, Verna. I do." Perhaps she could have been more diplomatic, Grace admitted to herself, but she was exhausted from lack of sleep and miserably unhappy over her fight with Jake, and at that moment she simply hadn't the patience or the desire to tread lightly.

Predictably, Lyle sulked the rest of the afternoon and Verna carried on like a heroine in a Victorian melodrama. By the time enough hours had passed that Grace could politely leave without giving further insult, she had a roaring headache.

On the drive home all Grace could think of was taking a couple of aspirin and having an early night.

It was not to be.

Arriving home just before sunset, she found a morose T.J. sitting on her back porch.

"Well hello," she said, sitting down beside him on the step.

"Hi," he replied glumly, and stared down at the blade of grass he was shredding.

"Goodness, what a long face. Is something wrong?"

He shrugged. "I came over this mornin' to see Jake an' he was gone. He ain't come back yet."

"Do you mean you've been waiting here all day?"

That produced another shrug. "Didn't have nuthin' else to do anyway."

"Why, you must be starving." She put her arm around the boy's scrawny shoulders and gave him a squeeze. That he accepted the hug, when only a few weeks ago he would have rebuffed her, showed how far he had come. "We can't have that. C'mon inside and I'll get you something to eat."

She fed T.J. a cold supper of leftover ham, potato salad and coleslaw, but after only one plateful, he merely picked at the food, a sure sign that he was upset by Jake's absence.

Grace shared the feeling. She told herself it was none of her business, but nevertheless, with a sick feeling in the pit of her stomach, she, too, wondered where Jake was . . . and who he was with.

After T.J. had eaten he waited around for another hour before he gave in and let Grace drive him home.

By the time she returned to the farm it was dark and there were still no lights on in the apartment. Grace parked the van and trudged to the house feeling more despondent than she could remember ever feeling.

However, the awful day wasn't over yet. She opened the back door and stepped inside her familiar kitchen, only to jerk to a halt and gape.

Leaning back with her hips against the kitchen counter, a glass in her hand and a wry look on her face, was none other than Grace's prodigal older sister, Caroline.

Twenty-One

"WHAT'RE *YOU* DOING HERE?"

Caroline's mouth quirked. "It's nice to see you, too, Grace."

Grace was immediately contrite. "I'm sorry. I didn't mean to be rude. It's just that I've had a totally rotten day."

"And me showing up just capped it off, is that it?"

"No! Of course not." Though it was true. Caroline's visits never heralded anything good.

Ashamed of the thought, Grace hurried across the room and enveloped her sister in a hug. The smell of whiskey on Caroline's breath made her heart sink, but she forced a smile. "It's really good to see you, Caro. Welcome home."

"Thanks," she said wryly.

"It's been a long time. What brings you here now?"

"Do I have to have a reason?" Caroline snapped. "I own half this place, remember?"

"Yes, of course I remember," Grace snapped right back. "Although I sometimes wonder if you do. Especially at tax time."

She was immediately appalled with herself. She would never have made such a remark if she hadn't been so exhausted and the last twenty-four hours hadn't been so wretched.

"What the hell does that mean? You've never mentioned the taxes before. Are you accusing me of shirking my responsibility?"

"I'm sorry. Forget I said anything. It's not important. I don't mean to jump on you the minute you get home. Like I said, I'm just out of sorts." Her smile was conciliatory. "I am happy to see you, Caro. It's been a long time, and I've missed you. Please, let's not fight."

A somewhat mollified expression softened Caroline's face. "Ah, what the hell, I'm sorry too," she said, and returned Grace's hug.

"Can I get you anything? How about a cup of coffee?" Grace offered, anxious to make peace.

"No thanks." Caroline picked up the glass she had set on the counter and gave it a little swirl, making the ice cubes clink. "I already made myself a drink. I figured there wouldn't be any in the house so, as you can see, I brought my own supply."

"Oh." Grace glanced uneasily at the bottle of liquor on the counter, and Caroline laughed.

"Oh, Grace, if you could see your face. Still the little teetotaler, are you."

"It's not that. I'm just not comfortable with bringing liquor into this house. You know how Dad felt about drinking."

"Yeah, well, Dad doesn't own this house anymore. We do. And I like a drink now and then."

If Grace could believe that her sister drank just now and then she wouldn't have object too much, but Caroline tended to do everything to excess, especially if she thought you disapproved. "That's your choice, of course." Grace said, but she could not quite disguise the disapproval in her voice.

"Oh, for Pete's sake. Relax, will you? It's just one drink. It's not as though I'm committing a mortal sin."

"I know. I didn't mean to make an issue of it. Forget I said anything. Okay?"

"Sure. Why not."

"Are you hungry? It's late, but I could scramble some eggs or something."

"I could eat."

"Fine. This won't take long." Anxious to dispel any discord, Grace bustled around the kitchen, washing her hands and pulling out pans and bowls and various ingredients. "I'll cook omelettes. You like omelettes, don't you? If you don't, I'll make something else."

"Omelettes are fine." Caroline sat down at the table to get out of her way. She watched her with a sardonic expression. "You know, Grace, that's the problem with you. You worry too damned much about stepping on someone else's toes. What's the matter? Afraid someone will think you're less than perfect if you cross them?"

The criticism stung—especially after hearing virtually the same thing from Jake.

Grace whirled around to face her sister. "That's not fair, Caroline. I've never claimed to be perfect."

"No, but you sure try like hell to be."

"You make it sound as though there's something wrong in that," she said, unable to hid her hurt.

"That depends on why you're doing it."

"What's that suppose to mean?"

"Do you toe the line because of sincere religious convictions? Or because you're scared spitless you might turn out like me if you don't?"

"What?" Grace's voice was breathless with amazement. "Caro, don't be silly."

"C'mon, Grace, think about it. As a kid you were always sweet and easygoing, but at least back then you had your share of spirit and daring. And a pretty good temper when riled, too, as I recall. Then Mother died. And you and everybody else in this town blamed me."

"That's not true!"

"Sure it is. Some, like Aunt Lollie and Ida Bell Wheatly, have told me so to my face."

"Oh, Caro." Grace sat down opposite Caroline at the table and looked at her pleadingly. "Please don't pay any attention to Aunt Lollie. You know what she's like. And Ida Bell is worse."

"I know, and I don't. But the point is, after Mother died you changed. Overnight you became a regular little paragon of virtue. Back when you were in school the aunts and all the old biddies in this town held you up as the example of the ideal child. You were the perfect daughter, the perfect student, the perfect teenager. Hell, later you were even a perfect wife to Charles."

Caroline grimaced. "Personally, I don't know how you abided the arrogant little prick. I would've cut his dick off and served it to him for lunch."

"Caro!"

Ignoring Grace's shocked exclamation, Caroline took another sip of whiskey then raised her glass in mock toast. "Ah, but not our little Mary Grace. You ignored all his faults and his cheating, like a martyred angel. You've become the most admired and respected woman in town—sweet, saintly, proper Mary Grace, who never took a wrong step in her life. Or, at least, not since our mother died.

"God, Grace. The connection is plain as the nose on your face. I go a little wild and our mother keels over and dies, so you make sure your behavior is beyond reproach. Everybody thinks you're Miss Perfect, but the truth is, you're just too damned chicken to follow your instincts and cut loose now and then, the way you did as a child, for fear of bringing some divine retribution down on your head, the way I did on mine."

Beyond reproach? Caroline really thought she lived a blameless life? Grace's gaze flickered to the darkened apartment above the carriage house. Hardly.

Tears stung Grace's eyes. She blinked hard to control them. Her sister's biting assessment of her hurt. "I'm sorry," she said in a stilted little voice. "I didn't realize you regarded me with such obvious disapproval."

"Can you honestly sit there and tell me that you never blamed me for our mother's death?"

Grace opened her mouth to deny the charge, but she couldn't. "All right, I'll admit that at first I did blame you, but for heaven's sake, Caro, I was only eight years old and Aunt Lollie had filled my head with all that nonsense. But I know now that you weren't responsible. No matter what you or any of us could have done or not done, we could not have prevented that aneurysm from rupturing." Tears filled Grace's eyes and she blinked furiously to hold them back.

"Shit, don't cry, Grace. I don't dislike you. You're my baby sister and I love you. But I do worry about you. You're too uptight and controlled. For God's sake, loosen up. The world won't come to an end if you defy convention once in awhile. You don't have to be Saint Grace all the time."

Caroline looked away, her mouth set. She glanced back as a lone tear rolled down Grace's cheek, and, reluctantly, her demeanor softened.

"Aw hell, forget I said anything." She reached across the table and took Grace's hand. "Don't mind me, Sis. Sometimes I've got a real shitty attitude. Anyway, I didn't come here to fight with you either."

Grace sniffed and wiped her eyes. "At the risk of having my head bitten off again, why did you come?"

"As I said, do I have to have a reason? Can't I just drop by to see my baby sister once in a while?"

Grace smiled wanly and patted her hand. "Of course you can." But she knew that wasn't the reason for the visit. She and Caroline had never been close. The nine-year difference in their ages had been one reason. Another was the drastic differences in their personalities and lifestyles.

"Look, Grace . . . about the taxes. Hell, you have every right to be angry. I should pay my share. To tell the truth, I knew at the time they were due that I should contact you, but . . . well, I've been a little short of cash—"

"It's all right, Caro. Really," Grace assured her. "I've managed."

"How? By renting the apartment to a murderer?"

Surprise darted through Grace and widened her eyes. "You heard about that already? I thought you just got here. Don't tell me you've already talked to Aunt Lollie."

"God forbid." Caroline shuddered and made a face. "Anyway, you know that old witch doesn't speak to me unless she has to."

"Then how did you know about Jake? Oh, and by the way, he's not a murderer."

"I have my sources. Actually, that's why I came home. From what I hear, you've got the whole town in a tizzy. That's not like you, Grace."

Grace sighed. "I know. And I hate it. Since Jake moved into the apartment I've had to battle practically every one I meet. The people in this town are irrational where he's concerned."

"Hmm. Grace, you know, normally I'm all for thumbing your nose at the pious pea-brains around here, but this time maybe—just maybe—they're right."

"Oh, Caro, not you, too."

"Hey, all I'm saying is you're taking a big risk here. If this guy did kill that girl you could be in a lot of danger."

"He didn't and I'm not."

"How can you be so sure?"

"I just am. From the start I never believed he did it, and neither did two juries."

"I see." She contemplated the whiskey in her glass for a minute, her lips pursed. "I didn't really know this Jake Paxton character. I vaguely remember Lizzie's snot-nosed bastard brat running around town, but he's more your age than mine. From what I've heard lately, though, he grew up to be a real hardcase."

Grace stiffened. She didn't like to hear Jake referred to in those terms. "He was no angel in high school, I'll admit, but he never did anything truly awful. The people around here haven't judged Jake guilty because of the evidence. That was weak and circumstantial at best. In their minds he was nothing but trash from over in the Bottoms, so of course he had to be the murderer. I would think that you of all people would be more sympathetic."

Caroline laughed. "You mean because they call me trash, too?" She got up and poured herself another drink. Ignoring Grace's worried look she knocked back a big swallow. "The difference is, this Jake person got his reputation through the circumstances of his birth. Me, I'm a self-made woman."

"Caroline, don't say that."

"Why not? It's true. Honey, I've been on a slippery, downhill slide ever since I was sixteen, and I haven't hit bottom yet. It's been one helluva ride, though." She lifted her glass again. "Here's to trashy people. May we continue to annoy the crap out of the good, holier-than-thou bigots of the world. And Cedar Grove in particular."

She knocked back the rest of the drink and reached for the bottle again. Grace could no longer restrain herself.

"Caro, please. Don't you think you've had enough? Why

don't you put the bottle away and I'll cook those omelettes right quick?"

Caroline's mouth thinned. "Look, Miss Perfect, just butt out of my business. Okay? I'll decide when I've had enough. Not you or anybody else." She poured her glass full, and looking at Grace over the top, deliberately drank it down in one gulp.

"Oh, Caro, please don't do this to yourself."

"I'll do whatever I damned well please, so just get off my back!" Caroline slammed the empty glass down on the counter and stormed out of the kitchen.

"Caroline, wait!" Grace caught up with her as she was going out the front door. Her little red Corvette was sitting in the circular drive in front of the porch. Grace wondered why she hadn't noticed it when she came home. "Caroline! Where are you going?"

"Out."

"But . . . but what about dinner?"

"Screw dinner."

She jumped in the car and slammed the door, and the Corvette sprang to life with a roar. Standing on the front porch, feeling helpless, Grace watched the little fireball of a car tear down the drive and make a careening turn onto the road. Grace sighed, her shoulders slumping.

"Oh, Caroline."

Depressed and feeling a headache coming on, when she went inside she took some aspirin, poured herself a mug of coffee and curled up in her father's wingback chair by the parlor fireplace. Leaning her head against the high back, she gazed into the distance at nothing. She didn't understand her sister at all.

Growing up, Caroline had been the typical bratty minister's daughter and their parents' cross to bear. High-spirited and rebellious, as a child and as a teenager she had strained against the strict code of conduct expected of her. If something was forbidden, Caroline had been hell-bent to try it. The more people disapproved, the more determined she'd been.

She was thirty-eight now, and as far as Grace could tell, she hadn't changed a bit.

Her youthful hi-jinks had been sometimes embarrassing, sometimes unnerving and always aggravating, but she hadn't done anything truly awful until that fateful summer when she turned seventeen and ran away with the church choir director, a married man in his thirties and father of two.

It had caused a tremendous scandal, of course. Grace suspected that was at least partly why Caro had done it. She had not, however, given much thought as to what effect her actions would have on their parents, which was also typical of Caroline.

THEY HAD BEEN DEVASTATED.

The fling had lasted barely a month before Caroline's lover had dumped her. She had returned home, only to discover that the day after she had left, their mother had died suddenly and unexpectedly from an aneurysm in the brain.

The doctors had said the rupture was inevitable. The weak spot in the blood vessel had been there since birth, waiting like a time bomb to burst. It had merely been a coincidence that it happened when it did.

The locals, however, particularly Aunt Lollie, put the blame squarely on Caroline.

When you ran wild and flouted the rules of proper behavior you courted disaster, Lollie maintained. Caroline's scandalous behavior had shamed her parents and broken her mother's heart, and the strain, in Lollie's opinion, had caused the aneurysm.

A sad little smile flirted around Grace's mouth. It had always amazed her how different siblings could be. Lollie was as sanctimonious and judgmental as her brother had been kind and compassionate.

The lesson that Grace had learned from those events had been to always obey the rules. She supposed that Caroline's assessment had even been correct, to a point. Grace had always been terrified of disappointing their father and bringing disaster down on herself and her loved ones, as Caroline had done with her escapades. So, she had striven to be the model daughter and always to do the right thing.

If Caroline had learned anything from that horrible mistake, it certainly wasn't apparent. Twenty-one years ago, far from being chastened or accepting the blame the town had heaped on her for her mother's death, Caroline had reacted to the censure with defiance and continued to thumb her nose at convention. She had dressed and talked provocatively, hung out in seedy places such as The Rip Saw, and had generally run wild. Eventually she had taken off again with another lover. Currently, she was divorced from her second husband.

Periodically over the years, Caroline had drifted in and out of Cedar Grove, armored with a veneer of brittle cynicism and claiming to be happy with her life just as it was. Grace no longer believed her. In rare, unguarded moments, she had seen the pain in Caro's eyes, the abject self-hatred. She believed with all her heart that not only did her sister blame herself for their mother's death, whether consciously or subconsciously, but also, Caroline had chosen her murky lifestyle as a form of self-punishment.

Of course, Grace thought ruefully, if she were ever to confront her sister with her theory, Caro would vehemently deny it, but Grace was convinced it was true.

Grace sipped her coffee and brooded. She hated to see Caroline throw her life away, but whenever she tried to broach the subject with her, Caroline became unreasonably angry and stormed out. Like she had tonight.

Grace had to admit that a small part of her envied Caroline's daring and spirit. Now and then, she herself experienced a vague restlessness and felt an almost overpowering urge to break out of her safe, staid little world. Perhaps someday she would.

She sighed. Oh, who was she kidding? For her, the pattern was set. No matter how strong the yearnings that tugged at her, she didn't quite have the nerve to defy convention. Not after all these years.

The way she had handled this thing with Jake was proof of that.

A quick rap on the front door interrupted her depressing thoughts. Before Grace could react, Josie stuck her head inside and called, "Anybody home?"

"In here."

Her cousin came rushing in at her usual harassed speed. She was crackling with energy and positively glowing, but, except for a lightning quick glance, she would not meet Grace's eyes.

Grace fought back a grin. She hadn't known it was possible to look sheepish and happy at the same time, but Josie managed it.

"Well hi. You left so quickly this morning after church that I didn't get a chance to talk to you. How was the pot luck dinner?"

Grace had a hunch her attempt at matchmaking had been a rousing success. Ever since Reverend Street had been assigned to their congregation, Josie had sat on the last pew and dashed out the second services were over. This morning, however, her cousin had sat directly in front of the pulpit. Grace had noticed with amusement that the good reverend's eyes had met her cousin's more than once during the sermon.

Josie plopped down on the footstool in front of Grace's chair and eyed her uncertainly. "Fine. Actually . . . that's . . . that's what I want to talk to you about."

She bit her lip and glanced away. Then, as though unable to contain herself a second longer, she grabbed both of Grace's hands and blurted, "Oh, Grace, it was more than just fine. It was wonderful. It was . . . it was magic. I had the *best* time.

"I thought once we got there Daniel would go his own way, but he didn't. He insisted on eating with me, and then afterward he danced with me almost every dance, and then we went for a long walk and we talked and talked and talked. Oh, Grace, it was so wonderful. And then . . ." Her eyes turned dreamy and she exhaled a fluttery sigh of ecstasy. "Then he kissed me."

Bemused Grace looked at her practical, no-nonsense cousin and had to fight back a grin. Josie was positively radiant. A becoming blush tinted her face, and her eyes glittered with happiness. Everything about her seemed more vibrant, more alive.

Even her mousy brown hair, usually worn pulled back in a single serviceable braid, now hung loose about her shoulders in a cascade of shining curls, something Josie never would have allowed before her date with Daniel. Love, it seemed, had transformed Josie's wholesome looks into real beauty.

Grace squeezed her cousin's hands. "That's wonderful. I'm so happy for you."

Instantly guilt replaced the joy in Josie's eyes. "But you and Daniel—"

"Are just good friends. That's all we'll ever be. We both came to realize that lately."

"That's what Daniel told me last night. But you and he . . . you seemed so perfect together."

Emotion twisted Grace's heart and she smiled fondly at her cousin. "Not as perfect as the two of you," she said gently, and Josie blushed. Still, she wasn't convinced.

"But everyone in the congregation expects you and Daniel to marry. You're so suited to be a minister's wife. You were a minister's daughter. You understand what's expected of a minister's wife. You're gentle and kind and compassionate—"

"And so are you."

"No, I'm not. Not like you. I'm always stirring things up and creating controversy and wading in to do battle regardless of what people think. I'm not at all the kind of woman the people of this town want their minister to marry. Not that marriage has come up, of course," she tacked on hurriedly, turning brick red. "One kiss doesn't mean . . . that is . . ."

"Josie. Josie, listen to me." Grace squeezed her cousin's hands and gave them a little shake. "You're a wonderful, caring person. You may go about things differently than I would, but so what? You have a big heart, and that's all that matters. And it's no one else's business who Daniel marries." She made a wry face. "Besides, this town could use a little shaking up. I say, if Daniel makes you happy, then grab him."

"Grace, do you mean that?"

"Every word."

"Oh, thank you," Josie cried, flinging her arms around Grace's neck. "Thank you, so much."

Laughing, she returned the hug. "You're welcome."

When they separated, Grace turned serious. "Now that we've settled that, what about T.J.? Did you get a chance to check out his situation?"

"Yes, and I think your instincts are right. That Digger person is bad news. He got hostile when Daniel and I explained who we were and what I wanted. He yelled at the boy for bringing snoopy do-gooders home with him. I got the impression he would have knocked T.J. around if we hadn't been there. Right now, I don't have any concrete grounds for intervention. The place was a pig sty, but there was food in the house, and T.J. denied he'd been mistreated. All I can do is keep an eye on that household."

Grace grimaced. "I had hoped for something more concrete, but thanks for trying, Josie."

"Hey, that's my job."

Josie left a short while later, bubbling over with joy over the prospect of going out to dinner with Daniel after Sunday evening services. Grace smiled wryly as she waved good-bye to her from the front porch. Her cousin's new-found happiness had been the only bright spot in what had been a hellacious day.

By one in the morning, Caroline had not come home, and there were still no lights in the apartment. Was Jake up there brooding in the dark or had he gone out? Grace wondered. If so, where was he? And with whom? Where was Caroline?

By one-thirty Grace was sick with worry. She could not bear the waiting any longer. She was going to look for Caroline. Knowing her sister's penchant for raunchy dives, she had a strong hunch where she would find her.

Twenty-Two

THE GRAVEL PARKING LOT in front of The Rip Saw was jammed when Grace arrived. She drove slowly up and down the lines of cars, and sure enough, on the third row, there was Caroline's Corvette. The car was twelve years old and even at that far too expensive, but it was flashy and sporty, and that was all that mattered to Caroline.

Grace parked her van as close to her sister's car as she could and headed for the entrance. With trepidation, she pushed open the double doors and entered the bar.

The first thing that hit her was the noise—raucous shouts and laughter, blaring music, clinking glassware and the sharp crack of billiard balls slamming together all blended together to form an unholy din. The stale air reeked of beer, cigarettes, sweat and cheap perfume. A cloud of blue smoke hovered at the ceiling, barely stirred by the desultory rotation of the ceiling fans.

Grace blinked several times, but as her vision adjusted to the dim lighting, her nervousness only increased. Here and there, tawdry-looking women lounged on barstools or at tables, and waitresses in short skirts hustled among the crowd, but most of the clientele were men—rough-looking creatures, many with scraggly beards and hair and numerous tattoos who looked mean enough and tough enough to cut your heart out and feed it to you with very little provocation.

Swallowing hard, Grace gathered her courage and edged through the rowdy crowd, her nerves jumping. She craned her neck and squinted through the haze of blue smoke, searching for a particular head of blond hair.

She was about to give up and hightail it for the door when

she spotted Caroline on the other side of the room. Her sister sat on a stool, leaning with her back against the bar, her elbows propped on the brass rail on either side of her. A half-empty beer mug dangled from one hand and an amused smile played about her mouth as she watched the two men standing in front of her a few feet away.

As inexperienced and out of her element as Grace was, she could see at a glance that trouble was brewing between the pair. From the look on her sister's face, she was probably the cause of it.

Grace was halfway across the room when the first punch was thrown. In a blink a full-scale melee erupted.

A chair came sailing straight at Grace, and she screamed and ducked, throwing her arms over her head. All around her fights broke out. Terrified, her heart thundering, Grace tried to make her way through the confusion, dodging around brawling men and doing her best to keep her eye on her sister at the same time.

Suddenly, a strong arm hooked around her waist from behind. Grace screamed as she was dragged back against a muscular chest.

"What in the name of hell are you doing in here," Jake growled in her ear, even as he hauled her toward the door.

"Let me go! Jake, stop! I have to get Caroline out of here!"

"Who?"

"My sister!" she yelled above the din. "She's over by the bar!"

"Tough! She'll have to fend for herself. You're getting out of here! The cops will be here any second!"

It was all the convincing Grace needed. She quit struggling and let Jake hustle her toward the exit.

They had no sooner cleared the building than the patrol cars came screeching to a halt in the parking lot amid spraying gravel and screaming sirens.

"All right, hold it right there, you two!" an officer barked.

"Shit." Jake's arm tightened around Grace as they skidded to a halt.

She was so frightened it took a second for that voice to register. She jutted her head forward and strained to see through the shadows of the parking lot. "Harley? Is that you?"

The uniformed figure stepped forward into the pool of light. At any other time Sheriff Harley Newcomb's slack-jawed expression would have been funny.

"Grace! What the devil are you doing in a place like this!" His sharp gaze switched to Jake and swept over the arm that encircled her waist. "Is this guy bothering you."

"No. No, don't worry about Jake. I came looking for my sister. She's inside. Harley, please, get her out for me, before something terrible happens."

"Your sister? You mean Caroline? She's in there?" At Grace's nod, Harley looked pained. "Technically, this raid is being directed by the police, since it's inside the city limits. Me'n my men are just giving Chief Adams a hand." Which was usual procedure, since the entire Cedar Grove police force consisted of three men. "We're suppose to haul everyone—those inside and anyone who's making, a break for it—to the pokey."

"Jail? Oh, dear Lord." Grace made a distressed sound and put her hand over her mouth.

"Hell, Grace, I'm not going to arrest you. As for Caroline . . . Harley lifted his Stetson and raked his hand through his hair. "I'll do what I can."

He looked at Jake. "Take her home, before some of these deputies get overzealous."

"You'll get no argument from me."

"But—"

"C'mon, Grace, you heard the man." Jake hustled her toward the van and tried to stuff her into the passenger side, but she held back and shot him a disapproving look.

"You've been drinking," she said in an accusing voice. "I think I should drive."

"That's right," he shot back. "I came here to get drunk, but I'm not there yet, so give me the damned keys and get your cute little butt in the van before Frank Sheffield or some other hotshot decides to play Clint Eastwood."

Grace tightened her mouth. She was about to argue when she spotted an officer heading their way at a trot. She let out a little yelp, stuffed the keys into his hand and piled into the van. Jake bolted around to the other side, jumped in and fired up the engine. They peeled out of the parking lot with a squeal of tires and a spray of gravel just as the officer reached them.

After the pandemonium of the pool hall, the silence that descended on them once they were tooling down the highway seemed deafening. Grace glanced sideways at Jake. She hadn't seen him since he had stormed out of her kitchen at daybreak, and her heart gave a funny little lurch. She opened her mouth to explain about her sister, but his expression did not encourage conversation, and she closed it again.

He stared straight ahead, his face hard as granite. She could tell by the set of his jaw and the tiny tic at the corner of his mouth that he was furious. Whether his anger stemmed from their quarrel or her presence at The Rip Saw, or both, she couldn't tell, but she decided the wisest thing would be to keep quiet. Jake, however, wanted answers.

"Would you mind telling me just what the hell you were doing at The Rip Saw?"

"I told you, I came to get my sister."

"What the devil for? Correct me if I'm wrong, but she's a grown woman, right? Older than you, in fact."

Grace sighed. "Caroline arrived today and . . . well . . . we quarreled and she stormed out angry. The later it got, the more worried I got, so I went looking for her."

"It figures," he muttered.

After that, they rode in angry silence all the way to the farm.

When they climbed from the van the tension between them was thick enough to cut with a knife. Anxious to escape Jake, Grace offered a cool, "Thank you for getting me out of that place. It could have been embarrassing. Now if you'll excuse me, I'm going inside and wait for my sister." She started up the back-porch steps, but he took her elbow and came with her.

"I'll wait with you."

"Oh, no. That's all right. You don't have to do that."

"Yeah, I know. But I don't trust you not to go back to the bar to look for her if she doesn't show up soon. So I'll just wait."

"I won't. I promise," she declared with a touch of panic as he ushered her inside the kitchen.

"Forget it. I'm staying." He left her standing in the middle of the kitchen and headed for the coffeemaker. "I could use some coffee. How about you?"

She watched him with a vague sense of amazement as he made himself at home, moving around her kitchen as though he belonged there. It took a moment for his question to register.

"Uh . . . no. No thank you."

She glanced at the clock, then peered out the window. Wringing her hands, she began to pace.

"Take it easy, Grace. She'll be here soon."

"You don't understand. Caroline is . . . well . . . unpredictable."

"Maybe. But I wouldn't worry if I were you. From what I've seen of Harley Newcomb, he can handle her."

AT THAT MOMENT Police Chief Harley Newcomb was trying to reconcile in his mind that the miniskirted, brazen woman sitting in the back of the paddy wagon was Grace's sister. It didn't seem possible that the two could be even distantly related.

But this was Caroline, all right. She'd been about four years behind him back in their school days. He hadn't known her, but he'd sure as hell known who she was. Even then she'd been wild as a March hare. Through her antics, Caroline had made sure that everyone in Cedar Grove had known who she was.

Harley pointed his forefinger at her. "You. Come with me?"

Cocking one eyebrow, Caroline gave him a droll look. She made no move to get out of the wagon. "Well, well, well. If it isn't Wyatt Earp."

"C'mon. Hop down."

Caroline leaned back and made herself more comfortable. "Sorry, Deputy, but I'm staying right here."

Harley didn't rise to the bait. He returned her insolent look with a smile. "Well, then, we got ourselves a problem, darlin,' cause I need you to come with me. And just so you'll know, I'm not a deputy. I'm the sheriff."

"Ooooouu, the big bad sheriff. I'm impressed." She subjected him to a slow, thorough inspection that lingered unnecessarily long at the fly of his jeans. Her smile was sultry and insulting. "Sorry. Tempting as the offer is, you're not my type, Sheriff."

He smiled back. "I'm not offering. I'm telling. Now get that tight little ass of yours off the bench and get down here," he ordered, pointing to the ground in front of him. "Otherwise, I'll be forced to climb in there and haul you out, and you don't want that, I promise you."

He issued the statement in his usual friendly drawl but not even the most hardened criminal would have questioned that he meant business. Neither did Caroline. That didn't stop her from taking her time, however, or from making a lewd and insulting aside to the others in the wagon, who responded with a round of hoots and ribald comments and laughter.

Harley ignored them, and when Caroline stepped down from the back of the paddy wagon he gripped her arm just above her elbow and led her to his squad car. Her skin was satin soft beneath his callused hand and her perfume was pure seduction. It bore no resemblance to the dimestore stuff that most of the bar's female customers slathered on.

"Tell me, Marshal? Do you always take your pick of the women when you raid a joint? Well, sugar, don't think I'm not flattered, but I'm really not in the mood."

"Just get in the car, Miss."

A feline smile curved Caroline's mouth. "I think I'll pass. Like I said, you're not my type. Though you are kinda cute, in a big ole cuddly bear kind of way."

Harley opened the door of the squad car and nudged her toward the interior, but she dug in her heels. "Uh-uh, I don't think so."

"Either get in the car on your own or I'll have to use cuffs."

"Ooouu, kinky."

"All right, that's it." Putting one hand on top of Caroline's head and the other on her shoulder, Harley stuffed her into the car before she could do more than yelp. In a blink of her masacaraed lashes, Caroline dropped her air of insouciance. As Harley sauntered around to the driver's side she glared at him through the windshield and yanked at the door handle, cursing a blue streak.

"You're wasting your time," he advised when he climbed in behind the wheel and started the car. "I got the control for that door in my pocket."

"You son-of-a-bitch! You let me out of here right now!"

"Settle down. You're gonna be okay."

"I demand to know where you're taking me. Listen, pig, if you think I'm going to spread my legs for you to keep from going to jail, think again. Just you try touching me, and you'll be walking funny for a month."

"Well now, Miss Somerset, I hate to disappoint you, but I don't conduct sheriff's business that way. Even if I did, in this case I think I'd have to pass." Grinning, he gave her a quick once-over out of the corner of his eye, and drawled, "You got a nice body, an' all, I'll give you that. But to tell the truth, I'm just not interested."

Caroline's eyes narrowed. "How do you know my name? Do I know you?"

"Probably not. By the time you were breaking hearts in high school I was doing my second tour of duty with the marines. But I know who you are. You're Reverend Somerset's daughter and Grace's sister. She asked me to bail you out of trouble back there. I'm taking you home."

"Ahhh, I see." Caroline relaxed back against the seat with an insolent smile. "And do you always do what Grace wants?"

He shrugged. "She's a good woman and a good friend. If I can give her a hand, I will." He glanced at Caroline. "She came looking for you and almost got caught up in that brouhaha back there herself."

"You're kidding. Mary Grace in The Rip Saw?" Caroline gave a hoot of laughter and pulled a cigarette from her purse. "Now there's a picture."

"She was worried about you. You know you might try giving that a thought now and then. In fact, why don't you do yourself a favor and knock off this bad girl routine of yours."

"Why don't you mind your own business, Hop-A-Long?"

He ignored the jab. "You're too old to still be rebelling against your parents. Besides, they're both gone. And if you're trying to punish yourself for something, that's kinda stupid."

"Look, I don't need any advice, okay. And if I did, I sure as shit wouldn't take any from a hick sheriff like you. So just back off." Angrily, she snapped open the clasp on her purse and pulled out a lighter.

"You sure need it from someone. And don't light that thing in here. I don't like breathing smoke."

"That's too bad," she said, and gave the lighter a flick. Harley snatched the weed out of her mouth and tossed it out the window.

"Hey!"

"I said I don't like it. Light another one and I'll throw the whole pack out. And maybe you behind it."

She fumed the rest of the way home. When he stopped the squad car in the drive she grabbed the door handle, but it still wouldn't work.

"Will you release this thing!" she demanded.

"In a minute. First I got something to say."

She met his gaze with a glare. "What?"

Sitting nonchalantly with one arm draped over the steering wheel, Harley grinned. "I was just thinking—scrub off some of that war paint and trade those trashy clothes for something with a little class, and you wouldn't be a half-bad lookin' woman."

Caroline clenched her jaws. She wanted to slap him. "Fuck you, asshole," she snarled.

Harley's grin widened. "It's a mite too soon in our relationship for that, but I'm sure we'll get to it."

"When hell freezes over. Now, will-you-open-the-damned door?" she ground out through clenched teeth.

Harley shrugged. "Sure. But you think about what I said, now"

The instant the lock clicked she bailed out of the car, slammed the door as hard as she could, and stormed up the front porch steps. Harley opened his door and stepped out on one foot. "'Course, you'd have to clean up that mouth of yours too," he called over the top of the car.

He could almost see smoke coming out of Caroline's ears. She turned slowly, looked him in the eye and deliberately spewed a string of the foulest language he'd ever heard—and he'd heard plenty.

Shaking his head, Harley tsked and climbed back in the car.

Caroline stormed into the house and slammed the door so hard the oval etched glass in the center rattled.

RELIEF FLOODED THROUGH GRACE when the lights of the squad car sliced through the parlor's lace curtains. She hurried into the entryway but her sister burst inside and was halfway up the first flight of stairs before she could speak.

"Caroline. Thank heaven you're home. Are you all right?"

She stopped and glared down at Grace. "I'm fine," she snapped. "But the next time you decide to stick your nose in my business do me a favor and keep that countrified boob of a sheriff away from me."

"Harley? But he's a dear. What happened?"

"I'll tell you what ha—" She stopped, her eyes widening as Jake came out of the living and stood beside Grace.

Caroline looked him over with unabashed interest, her angry expression gone. "Well, well. Who are you?"

"Oh, I'm sorry. Caroline, this is Jake Paxton. Jake, my sister Caroline Dunn."

"Just make it Caroline Somerset. I took back my maiden name after my last divorce." Her smile broadened, and Grace's stomach lurched at the look on her sister's face. "So this is Jake. I'm so pleased to meet you."

Her voice had a come-hither pitch. So did the look in her eyes. She leaned over the banister to offer him her hand and the low cut neckline of her blouse drooped, giving him an ample view of her bosom.

If Jake noticed, he wasn't impressed. His dark expression didn't alter one whit. He gave her a curt nod and clasped her hand briefly, then released it and stepped back, turning his somber gaze on Grace. "Now that your sister's back safe and sound I'll say good-night."

"Well. That was certainly abrupt." Caroline said when he had gone.

"Jake isn't one for small talk."

"Mmm. The silent type, huh. He's really a delicious man, isn't he?" she mused, staring in the direction Jake had taken. "So dark and brooding and dangerous-looking." She gave an exaggerated shiver and rubbed her arms. "I do like that in a man."

Twenty-Three

CAROLINE WAS STILL ASLEEP when Grace left for the store, a scant five hours later. Jake's pickup was missing from the carriage house, a sure sign that he was still angry, since they had gotten into the habit of riding to and from work together.

At least, she assumed that was where he had gone. She hadn't realized how anxious she was until she arrived at the store and experienced a rush of relief at the sight of his truck parked in the back.

He was in the storeroom, crating a set of Depression glass to ship to a customer in Oregon. She tried to talk to him, but he snapped, "Leave it, Grace" and walked out, leaving her with no choice but to do as he asked.

Around noon Caroline's Corvette roared to a stop out front. Grace's spirits plummeted, but she wasn't surprised. She shook her head when her sister climbed from the car.

Caroline wore four-inch backless heels, skin-tight leggings and a knit top with a plunging neckline. She was braless, and her unfettered breasts jiggled with every step. The clinging material molded her nipples with such shocking clarity she might as well have been naked from the waist up.

"Hi, Sis. I was in town so I thought I'd drop by and see this shop of yours," she said, as she breezed in.

The plethora of exquisite furniture, china, glassware and unique accessories received the most cursory of glances. "Nice. Very nice," she murmured in a distracted voice, but her gaze darted around searchingly. Grace knew it wasn't the merchandise that had aroused her curiosity.

"Thank you," Grace replied dryly.

"So. How's business?" Caro made the perfunctory inquiry while poking her head into the storeroom.

"I'm managing. Is there something in particular you're looking for Caro?"

"What? Oh. No, I'm just looking around." She trailed her hand over the top of an eighteenth-century trestle table and edged her way over to a side window. She glanced outside and frowned. "Where is Jake? I was told he worked for you here."

"He does, but he's out on a delivery right now. I don't expect him back for a couple of hours or more."

"Oh."

The one word held such a wealth of disappointment Grace would have smiled if she hadn't felt so miserable.

"Can I get you something, Caro? A cup of tea? Or a soft drink?"

"No thanks. I really should be running. I'm going to stop by Mable Jean's and get my hair trimmed. It's a mess. I'll see you back at the house later. Bye."

She dashed out as quickly as she had dashed in.

Through the front window Grace watched her sashay out to her car with the hip-swaying, sexy saunter she had perfected in front of the mirror as a teenager. Grace saw several heads turn. Down the street, old Mr. Peabody was so busy ogling he drove his '55 Ford truck over the curb and nearly sheared the Akerman brothers right off their bench in front of the barber shop.

Grace sighed. Look out Cedar Grove. Caroline Somerset was back.

Twenty-Four

FOR THE REMAINDER OF THE WEEK Grace barely saw Jake. He drove his pickup to work, and while there he was remote and abrupt. Often Grace felt his intense stare on her but he spoke only when necessary. Every evening at precisely five o'clock he left the shop and, much to Caroline's disappointment, did not return home until late each night.

Where he spent those hours Grace had no idea. She endured several miserable evenings torturing herself with the possibilities.

On Saturday morning Grace had just poured herself a cup of coffee when Jake came out of the carriage house, and her heart did a crazy little flip-flop at the sight of him.

He carried a chain saw in one hand and had a coil of rope over his other shoulder. When he deposited his burden beneath the dead oak in the back yard she realized he was going to take the tree down.

As she sipped her coffee she watched him make several trips back and forth between the carriage house and the tree, bringing out a wheelbarrow, more ropes and pulleys, a ladder, an axe and a variety of other tools.

She watched him wistfully for several minutes, then scolded herself for wasting time on impossible dreaming when she had so much to do that weekend. There was a cake to bake for the Garden Club bake sale, and she had to go through her closet for clothes she'd promised to donate to the church resale shop. There was the house to clean and several loads of laundry to do, and the shop books to bring up to date.

Mike Kelso, her grandfather's former farmhand, had passed away yesterday so she had to cook a casserole to take to the grieving family. Also, she'd promised Verna she would be a fourth at bridge tomorrow evening if she couldn't find anyone else.

Grace had a sneaking suspicion that her mother-in-law wouldn't even make an effort to find another player; Verna was clinging to her more and more these days.

Sometime later Grace was beating cake batter when Caroline wandered into the kitchen, yawning. She was barefoot and her sleep-rumpled hair stuck out in all directions. The short robe she wore barely came to the top of her thighs. The clinging satin clearly revealed that she wore nothing beneath it.

Caroline mumbled a sleepy good morning, poured herself a mug of coffee and wandered over to the windows. Grace could barely see her out of the corner of her eye but she sensed the instant her sister spotted Jake. She perked up like a bird dog discovering a covey of quail.

"Well, well, look who's home," Caroline murmured in a throaty voice. "Mmm, nice. I always did love to see a man doing physical labor."

Grace gritted her teeth and whipped the batter harder.

"Who's the kid?" Caroline asked a moment later.

"What?" Grace looked up then. "Oh, that's T.J. Tolson. I didn't know he was here. He comes around often. He doesn't have a father at home and he's taken a liking to Jake."

"So who hasn't," Caroline drawled. "Oh, gawd, would you look at that. Be still my heart."

Grace looked up to see what her sister was carrying on about. Her gaze immediately homed in on Jake, and she received a jolt.

Spring had arrived in typical Texas fashion, bringing not just balmy but downright muggy weather. Jake had shed his shirt, and his broad shoulders and impressive chest glistened with sweat. Sawdust clung to the dark hair on his forearms and chest. Faded jeans rode low on lean hips, exposing a slightly concave, muscle-ridged belly. The faded denim cupped his butt and sex like a lover's hand.

Grace glanced at her sister, and the lascivious look on Caroline's face made her heart sink like a stone.

"I think I'll just go out and say good morning," her sister

announced, putting her mug on the counter.

"Oh, no you don't," Grace darted across the room and blocked the door. "Not like that you're not."

"What's wrong with this? I'm covered."

"Caro, there is an impressionable boy out there, and I won't have you parading around practically naked in front of him."

Caroline rolled her eyes. "Oh, all right. Maybe you're right. Actually, I probably ought to put on some makeup and fix up a bit before I go out there anyway."

She hurried out of the kitchen, and Grace heard her tearing up the stairs.

Irresistibly Grace's gaze returned to Jake. She stared at his bare torso and shivered as memories flooded her—how she had run her hands over that hard body, kissed it, tasted it. How warm and solid his flesh had felt against her palms, against her breasts." She moaned and turned away from the window, her chest so tight she felt as though it were being squeezed in a vise.

Half an hour later Caroline was back in full war paint and dressed in tight jeans and a cotton shirt, her streaked blond hair arranged in an artful windblown style. She wore no bra and the tails of her shirt were tied under her breasts. As far as Grace could tell, none of the buttons were fastened. Caro was dressed for the hunt.

&

THE BANG OF THE SCREEN DOOR drew Jake's attention. From his perch, high up in the oak tree, he saw Caroline sauntering with an exaggerated sway of her hips across the back yard toward him and T.J. Disappointment wafted through him and he returned his attention to tying the pulley rope around the limb. The only woman he wanted to see was nowhere in sight.

As he knotted the rope he heard Caroline's voice below him.

"Hi, I'm Caroline. I'm Grace's sister. You must be T.J. She's told me all about you."

The boy mumbled something, but Jake couldn't make it out. Glancing down, he saw that T.J. was shuffling his feet and staring at the ground. From far above, Jake could see that he was blushing. Even the tops of his ears were red.

Jake's mouth twisted. Women like Caroline had that kind of effect on adolescent boys, even ones as young as eleven.

Hell, he hadn't been but a few years older than T.J. when he'd gotten laid for the first time by a thirty-something divorcée who'd hired him to do lawn work. A helluva lot more than her hedges had gotten trimmed that day.

Shading her eyes with one hand, Caroline looked up and waved. "Morning, Jake. Why don't you climb down and take a break? I brought you some iced tea. You've been working so hard, I thought you might need a cool drink."

"In a minute," he called down. He tied another knot and tested the tightness of the rope, then looked down. "Yo, T.J. I got this limb secured. You hold on tight to that end of the rope. When I saw through it this thing's going to drop like a ton of bricks and jerk the rope taut, so brace yourself. When I say, you guide it down nice and slow. You ready?"

"Sure, Jake. I got it."

Leaning back against his safety belt, Jake lowered his goggles and pulled the starter cord, and the chain saw roared to life. In seconds the saw ripped through a limb as big around as Jake's waist, sending sawdust flying. Over the noise he heard Caroline squeal and scurry out of range as the wood chips rained down.

The rope snapped taut, taking the full weight of the severed limb. Jake shut off the saw and let it hang from a strap attached to his belt. He carefully released the two half-hitches holding his end of the rope.

"Okay, T.J., get set. Here it comes," he yelled. The pulleys squeaked and rumbled as he began to lower the limb. "Nice and easy now. We don't want to slip with this one."

"Hey, man, no problem. I got it," the boy called cockily, and Jake's mouth twisted.

T.J. was showing off for Caroline, trying to impress her with his strength and manly prowess, but he had to put all his scrawny weight on his end of the rope just to keep from being lifted off his feet.

When they finally lowered the thing to the ground, Jake climbed down out of the tree, or what was left of it. The trunk was denuded over halfway up. All that remained of the limbs were little stubs, which he used as steps to descend.

Five or six feet from the bottom he unstrapped the saw and lowered it into T.J.'s outstretched hands, then he jumped down, landing a few feet away from Caroline. Stripping off his work gloves, he turned and found her gazing at his body.

Taking her time, she inspected every inch of him before raising her bold gaze and giving him a sultry smile. "Very nice. I'm impressed."

Jack merely looked at her and began to unfasten the rope from the tree limb.

His lack of interest didn't faze Caroline. "Thirsty?" she asked brightly. Jake nodded, and she handed him a paper cup and filled it with iced tea from the thermos. "Sorry it's not stronger. I was going to bring you a beer, but Grace about had a fit."

"That's okay. It's too early in the day for me, anyway."

"Really?" She looked surprised, and a little disappointed. "It's never too early for me."

Jake said nothing. He drank down the tea in two huge swallows and held the cup out for another. T.J. quickly did the same.

The back screen door banged, and Jake's head swiveled in that direction in time to see Grace come out of the house carrying an armload of clothes. She headed for the carriage house and disappeared inside without once looking his way.

"You know, it's really too nice a day to be working so hard. Why don't you knock off and I'll take you for a ride in my 'Vet'?" Caroline suggested, giving him a flirty look. "She'll do over a hundred."

"Sorry. I want to finish this job today."

"Oh. Well then, how about if you and I go out tonight? We could have dinner, maybe go dancing at The Rip Saw. It'll be fun. Whaddaya say?"

"No thanks."

Grace emerged from the carriage house empty-handed and headed for the back porch. Jake watched her, his intense gaze following her like a hungry wolf tracking a lamb. *Look at me. Dammit, look at me,* he willed, but Grace did not so much as glance in his direction. *Damn you, Grace. Don't do this to us. I know you're hurting as much I am. I've seen it in your eyes. For God's sake, for once can't you just go with your heart and to hell with what the people of this town think?*

"Well, well, well. So that's the way the wind blows."

The drawled comment reeked of incredulity and drew Jake's attention back to his surroundings. He turned his head and saw that Caroline was looking back and forth between him and Grace, a bemused expression on her face.

"I don't believe it. You've got the hots for my tight-assed baby sister?" She let out a hoot of laughter. "Oh, that's rich. Talk about your impossible dreams. Give it up, handsome. Grace would never in a million years allow herself to get involved with someone like you. She's too worried about following the rules and keeping her halo polished. You'd be better off sticking to someone like me. I'm more your type anyway."

All of his life he'd been beaten over the head with that message. He was trash and not fit to even look at a woman like Grace. He'd believed it. A part of him probably always would, and it was that gnawing fear in his gut that made him lash out.

"What the hell do you know about Grace? You haven't been home enough in the last twenty years to have even an inkling of what kind of person she is or what she wants or needs."

Caroline's eyebrows rose. "Are you saying she is interested in you?"

"Forget it," Jake snapped and clenched his jaws tight. "C'mon, T.J., let's get back to work." He tossed the empty paper cup on the ground and swung away, but Caroline rushed after him and grabbed his arm.

"No, wait. This is getting interesting."

"Drop it, Caroline. I don't want to discuss Grace with you. Even if I were willing, this is not the time," he growled, casting a meaningful look at T.J., who was listening avidly.

Caroline got the message and sent the boy a coquettish smile. "T.J., honey, would you go ask Grace to brew some more tea for us, please?"

He made a face, but he took the thermos from her outstretched hand. "Sure. But if you wanted to get rid of me all you had to do was say so, you know," he said in a sulky voice, and headed for the house, scuffing the heels of his ratty tennis shoes across the grass to show his displeasure.

Caroline gave a surprised chuckle. "Well. I must be losing my touch."

"He's a smart kid." Jake folded his arms across his chest and fixed her with an unblinking stare. He didn't have to wait long.

"So tell me what exactly is going on between you and Grace?"

"Why should I?"

"Because she's my sister, and whether you believe it or not, I do love her. I don't want to see her get hurt."

"Then we want the same thing. I'd sooner cut my own throat than harm Grace."

"Really. My, my. That does sounds serious. Don't tell me you've fallen in love with her."

Jake did not hesitate so much as a heartbeat. "I've loved Mary Grace since I was seven years old."

The statement nearly bowled Caroline over. She had meant the question facetiously. She stared at him, her face slack with astonishment. "Good, Lord. You really mean it, don't you."

Her own attraction to Jake was in no way serious. He was a good-looking devil, and a brief fling would have been fun, if for no other reason than to rile the locals, but she had viewed him merely as a diversion, a sexy boy toy, someone with whom to pass the time and relieve the tedium of this visit. Yet, for an instant, Caroline felt a stab of envy that he preferred quiet, unexciting Grace to her. As a rule, her wild reputation and sexy image had men panting after her, especially the "bad boy" types like Jake.

However, the notion of a romance between her sister and this rogue with the black reputation was simply too intriguing, and her pangs of sisterly envy quickly faded as she considered the idea. The question now was, how did her sister feel about Jake? And if she was smitten, what did she intend to do about it.

Frowning, Jake shifted and glanced at the house. "Yeah, I mean it. For all the good that does me. She has feelings for me, but not enough to risk the disapproval of the people of this town."

"Oh, I don't know," Caroline mused. "She rented you the apartment. Then on top of that she gave you a job, and from what I've heard, she's defended you publicly a few times. I'd say she stuck her neck out pretty far for you. Actually, I was surprised when I heard about it." It was why she had come home, to check on the situation and toss Jake out on his ear if need be.

"Grace is a mass of contradictions," Jake said in a reflective tone. "Outside of your father, she's the most gentle soul I've ever known. It's her nature to shy away from controversy and conflict, but at the same time, she has a strong sense of right and wrong, and when push comes to shove she stands up for what she believes in."

A hint of wry humor played around his mouth. "Actually, she's really something when riled. She told Ansel Burke to shut up right in front of a gang of men, and she whacked that asshole Frank Sheffield with her purse."

"You're kidding! *My* sister hit a policeman?"

"Yeah. Right up side the head. He probably saw stars for an hour afterward."

"Oh, I love it." Chuckling, Caroline shook her head. "Maybe there's hope for her yet."

She stared at the house for several seconds, then eyed Jake askance. "I'll be honest with you. I can't for the life of me imagine a more mismatched pair than you and my sister. But, having said that, I have to admit that I think it would do her a world of good to defy convention and throw her hat over the moon for once."

"You mean have a fling? Is that the only relationship you think we could possibly share. What're you saying, Caroline? I'm good enough to fuck your sister but not good enough to be a real part of her life?" He made the crude remark without the least inflection in his voice, but the glint in his eyes told her he was furious. "Well, too bad. If all I wanted was a hot lay for a few weeks I could find that anywhere. I want a helluva lot more from Grace than that."

Caroline's eyebrows rose. In truth, she hadn't really believed that he was talking about anything more, despite his claims of love. She wasn't sure if she approved of anything more. A torrid affair might shake Grace loose from all those self-imposed restrictions she'd put on herself, and it set this town on its ear in the process, but anything more than that was . . . well . . . just too weird and unlikely to imagine.

Jake Paxton was a hunk, there was no denying that. She could see why her sister might have fallen for him. The wretched street urchin Caroline remembered bore no resemblance to the adult Jake. With his intense green eyes and jet black hair and lean, sinfully handsome face he was easily the best-looking man this town had ever seen. Or probably ever would see.

The screen door banged again, and this time T.J. accompanied Grace on another trip to the carriage house, each of them toting an armload of clothing.

Caroline glanced at Jake, but he seemed to have forgotten that she was there. He watched Grace with an expression on his face that made her heart flip-flop. She couldn't remember any man ever looking at her that way. She wasn't sure she wanted one to. That kind of intensity was almost scary.

God knew, with her past, Caroline had never been one to judge others, but when she thought of the squalor and wretchedness and abuse that Jake had known as a child, his wild reputation as a youth, the vicious murder everyone believed he had committed, she shivered.

He was a gorgeous male specimen, all right. She would give him that, but there was an aura of danger about him that was palpable, and it gave her pause. Suddenly, what had seemed like a good idea only a moment ago, now brought a wave of uneasiness.

Her relationship with her sister had always been a tense and confusing mix of love and resentment . . . and yes, dammit, even envy on her part. Grace was the good one, the perfect one, the one everyone looked up to. Caroline was the trashy daughter. The mother killer.

She closed her eyes briefly, absorbing the anguish and hurt that thought always brought.

The past and the differences in their personalities and their lifestyles had caused a strain between her and Grace that Caroline wasn't sure they could ever completely dispel.

That didn't, however, stop her from loving her.

Did she really want this man involved with her sister? Sweet, gentle Grace who had striven to make up for Caroline's sins by always doing the right thing, never rebelling or giving their father so much as a moment's worry, never taking a wrong step, never, by word or deed, committing an unkind or malicious act. Grace, who lived up to her name and bore whatever life dealt her—good and bad—with an inborn dignity and elegance that few could match. To even imagine her with a man with Jake Paxton's dark past was unsettling.

"My sister's marriage to Charles Ames was not a happy one," Caroline tossed out, testing the waters. "To him she was a trophy, and once he got her he ignored her and ran around with anything in skirts."

"Charles Ames was a stupid, self-centered dickhead."

Caroline laughed. She couldn't help it. The terse statement, issued in that flat, unequivocable voice, was right on the money. Immediately some of her misgivings eased. Any man who could read Charles Ames with such pithy accuracy couldn't be all bad.

Pursing her lips, she joined Jake in watching Grace as she and T.J. strolled back to the house. Her sister was dressed in jeans and a man's shirt that was several sizes too big for her, the sleeves of which were rolled up to her elbows. Caroline realized it must have been one of their father's.

The wind flapped the tails of the shirt around her knees and blew her honey brown hair away from her face. The casual look was a far cry from the neat little dresses and pearls that she had worn the few times Caroline had visited her during her marriage. Charles had demanded that his wife look the part of a lady of means at all times, and his mother had backed him up. They were, after all, Verna was fond of saying, the leading family of Cedar Grove.

For the first time since her return, Caroline noticed how much happier Grace looked, how much more relaxed and pretty, now that she was free of that miserable bastard. Almost any other man, Jake included, would be an improvement over Charles

Ames.

T.J. was talking to Grace a mile a minute and she listened to him as though every word were a pearl of wisdom. That, Caroline realized, was one of her sister's many graces, that innate gift of being able to make a person feel that they mattered, that what they had to say was important. It came as naturally to her as breathing.

Suddenly Grace threw her head back and laughed and ruffled the boy's hair affectionately. The simple act was typical of Grace, and Caroline felt a sharp stab of remorse for every hateful thing she'd ever said to her.

There were givers and there were takers in the world, and her sister was a giver—not just of things, but of herself, her time, her attention, her compassion and caring. Watching her, Caroline felt her heart swell with pride and love, and a fierce protectiveness as well.

"I only mentioned Grace's marriage because I would hate to see her in that kind of relationship again. I want her to be happy. If anyone deserves happiness, it's Grace."

"I agree."

Caroline let a few seconds tick by in silence, eyeing Jake surreptitiously out of the corner of her eye. "I was told she's been dating the new minister. From what I've heard, he sounds perfect for her—he's apparently a nice guy, well respected, they share the same background. Everyone expects them to marry."

On the surface the statement was merely a casual observation, but its subtle challenge was not wasted on Jake.

"Then everyone is wrong." He turned his head and impaled her with a look. "And your information is out of date. Grace broke off her relationship with the good reverend—if that's what you want to call that lukewarm attachment—and played matchmaker to him and Josie."

"You're kidding! Rabble-rousing cousin Josie and a preacher? Hmm. Interesting."

"You got that right. Josie's bound to shake up his life a bit. It ought to be fun to watch."

"Hmm. And if Grace takes up with you it'll not only shake up her life, it'll set this whole town to spinning."

"Yeah," he said with relish.

Then he smiled—a slow, full-blown devilish smile that did marvelous things to that stern face. To her amazement, Caroline realized that in addition to his dark good looks and intriguing bad-boy image, Jake Paxton possessed a disarming amount of charm.

Good Lord. If her sister really had fallen for him, even with his less than sterling reputation, it was no wonder. Caroline doubted that there was a woman alive who could resist him when he turned on the charm.

Maybe—just maybe—a good dose of Jake was just what her sister needed after all.

Tipping her head back, Caroline studied him through narrowed eyes. "I want to know one thing. And I want the truth. Did you kill Carla Mae?"

"No."

She searched his face, and after a moment she nodded. "Fine. I'll take your word for it. But I'm warning you, if I find out later that you lied and my sister comes to any harm, I'll get a gun and come after you myself. And I hope you know, that's not an idle threat."

"I can see that," Jake said slowly, studying her out-thrust jaw and militant expression. "I'll tell you the same thing I told Miss Harriet; you don't have to worry. I would never harm Grace." He cocked his head to one side. "Does this mean that you won't object to me pursuing Grace?"

"I'll do better than that. I'm going to help you win her."

Suspicion narrowed Jake's eyes. "Why would you do that?"

Caroline sighed. "Look, I know that Grace worries about me, but I worry about her just as much, though she'd probably be stunned to hear it. She needs to loosen up and live a little. And, crazy as this sounds, I think you may be just the man to help her do that."

"I see."

"Good. Now do you want my help or not?"

Jake stared at her for a long time. Finally he nodded. "All

right. So what do you suggest?"

"Well, first of all, if you're going to get anywhere with Grace the first thing we have to do is force her to accept her feelings for you."

"Yeah, right. Just how do you propose we accomplish that? I've tried everything I can think of."

"Including old-fashioned jealousy?"

"You mean deliberately make Grace jealous? Let me guess. Of you, right?"

She laughed at his suddenly wary expression. "Why, Jake, darling. What a suspicious mind you have. You think I'm just trying to trick you into going out with me, don't you? I'll admit, that part of the plan does have its appeal, but I really am just trying to help. Honest."

He still didn't look convinced, and she lost patience and threw up her hands. "Oh, for heaven's sakes! Do you have a better idea?"

He eyed her for several more seconds. "All right. I'm desperate enough to try anything. What, exactly, do I have do?"

"Don't worry, nothing too flagrant. We just want to stir the green-eyed monster, not upset Grace so much she'll never speak to you again. I'll pretend to chase you and you'll pretend not to resist too much. That's all."

Twenty-Five

By midafternoon, heartily sick of watching her sister moon over Jake, Grace headed for town. She dropped off the cake at Patsy Gorman's, who was organizing the bake sale. Then she swung by the Kelsos' to drop off the casserole and offer her condolences. She delivered the clothes to the church resale shop, took a couple of dresses to the dry cleaner's, and ran a few other errands.

The tradesmen and clerks and many of their customers were people she had known all of her life, which necessitated spending a few moments in conversation almost everywhere she went. Such was the price for living in a small town. When she'd finished her errands she put in her two hours behind the tables at the bake sale.

By the time she returned to the farm it was almost sunset. Caroline's Corvette and Jake's truck were still in the carriage house when she pulled in, but there was no sign of them anywhere. Except for a low stump, the oak tree was gone and the limbs and debris cleared away. The wood, Grace noted with pleasure, was sawed and neatly stacked in the woodpile by the back porch.

Smiling, she climbed the steps, conscious of a warm glow in her chest. As angry as he was with her, Jake had tackled that Herculean job, even though he didn't have to. No matter what people thought of him, no one could call Jake lazy.

Her smile dissolved when she entered the kitchen, just in time to meet Caroline on her way out, wearing a tight sweater and flouncy miniskirt and reeking of perfume.

"Oh, hi, Grace. You got a few calls while you were out," she said, as she hurried toward the door. "One was Aunt Harriet, and one was Sue Keatting. Something about making quilts for the poor."

She stopped with her hand on the doorknob and looked back. "Oh, and Verna called three times. I told her I'd give you the message but the old cow obviously didn't trust me to do it. And Lyle called. He wants you to call him as soon as you get in." She made a face. "Please, please, *please* tell me you're not dating that creep."

"No, of course not."

"Good. That's a relief. Well, I gotta go. T.J. wants a ride in my car, so Jake and I are going to drive him home. See you later."

She was out the door before Grace had a chance to say a word, though what she would have said, she had no idea.

From the window, she watched Caroline hurry across the yard and disappear into the carriage house. A few moments later the red Corvette came roaring out through the open double doors only to come to a screeching halt in the drive as Caroline gave the horn three quick blasts.

Jake and T.J. came loping down the apartment stairs. Both were freshly showered and dressed in clean jeans and cotton shirts.

The boy's pants looked brand new, and Grace wondered where he'd gotten them. Then she realized that Jake had probably bought them for him, and a smile fluttered about her mouth. She was touched that a man who earned as little as Jake would spend money on someone else's child.

Her smile faded as he and the boy piled into the Corvette and the little red fireball of a car roared out of sight, with her sister's laughter trailing behind.

Grace listened to the sound of the engine fading away down the road but she didn't move from the window. Soon, all she could hear was the tick of the grandfather clock in the hall and the occasional whir of the night insects tuning up.

The quiet pressed in on her. So did the loneliness. The glow in her chest was now a tight ache. Caroline and Jake were just giving an underprivileged boy a treat, a ride home in a fancy car. It wasn't as though they were going out on a date.

Even if they were, it was no business of hers, she told herself fiercely. She had made her decision. The right decision. Jake did not belong to her. He had every right to see any woman he wanted—even her sister. The thought made the tightness in her chest worse.

These feelings she had for him would fade in time—they had to.

For a few hours she had let herself be carried away. Was that so terrible? Everyone made a mistake now and then and she was human, after all.

So what if in the rosy aftermath she had dared to flirt with the idea of building a life with Jake. In the clear light of day she had faced the painful truth. The chances of her and Jake having a future together were almost nil. Even if he did manage the impossible and somehow proved his innocence, she doubted if that would make him acceptable in the eyes of some people. To them, he would always be no-good trash from the Bottoms.

Those few hours with Jake had been wonderful, and though, according to everything she'd been taught her whole life, what they had shared had been wrong, she did not—could not—find it in her heart to regret a single minute. But it was over, and to hold on to any hope that there could be more was wishful thinking. There were just too many obstacles in their path.

Grace returned the calls that Caroline had mentioned. Sue wasn't home, but she left a message with her husband that she would attend the next quilting bee. Aunt Harriet wanted to know if Grace would pick her up for church the next morning.

"My car was in the shop for a tune-up and that worthless scalawag, Billy Bob Wheatly, over at Ledbetter's station still hasn't finished with it. I won't be able to pick it up until Monday. He always was a lazy scamp, even when he was in my class."

Grace smiled at her aunt's querulous tone. "It's no problem, Aunt Harriet. I'll be by for you around ten."

"You'll have to take me to Verna's for her bridge party, too. I don't know why she had to have it on Sunday, of all days."

"It was the only time she could get everyone together."

A loud "Humph" was her aunt's only comment on that, and

this time Grace chuckled out loud. "Now don't you worry. I'll see you in the morning."

When Grace hung up she called Verna. Her mother-in-law was aflutter over her bridge party and, as Grace suspected, she had called merely to be sure that Grace would be there.

After talking to Verna, Grace thought about returning Lyle's call, but decided it could wait. She wasn't in the mood to deal with him at the moment.

Though the account books at the shop still hadn't been brought up to date, she puttered around the house, unable to settle down to anything in particular. Every few minutes her eyes strayed to the clock and her ears strained constantly for the roar of a high-powered engine.

Just at dark a car did turn into the drive, but when Grace hurried to the window and peeked out through the parlor curtains her heart sank. The white BMW belonged to Lyle. It was a new acquisition, a gift from Verna, as befitted his elevated status in the Ames family.

Grace could have kicked herself for not returning his call at once and heading him off. She should have known that otherwise he would show up in person before long. Lyle seemed incapable of taking a hint.

He got out of the car and climbed the porch steps with cocky self-assurance, adjusting his tie and smoothing back his hair on the way. Watching him, Grace shook her head. Growing up, Lyle had always been a sycophant to Charles, the self-evasive poor relation who had willingly acted as toady and yes-man to his rich cousin for the privilege of hanging out with him. Since her husband's death, however, Lyle had become puffed up with his own importance and now he fancied himself an irresistible ladies' man. He was constantly peering at himself in mirrors and preening, examining his expensive new clothes.

She responded to the first ring of the chimes, but she opened the door only a few inches. "Hello, Lyle. What brings you here?" Her tone was less than friendly.

His smarmy smile made her want to throw up. So did the overpowering cologne he wore. "Hi, Grace. Aren't you going to invite me in?"

"No. I'm busy, Lyle. What do you want?"

"Now that's not very friendly, Grace. And not at all like you. And here I thought you would help me celebrate."

"Celebrate what?"

"My divorce," he said with a self-satisfied grin. "It was final today. I thought we'd drive over to that new place on the lake and have dinner."

"No, Lyle."

"What do you mean, no? C'mon, Grace. Now that I'm a free man, there's no reason for you to keep turning me down. It's not as though you're still seeing that preacher."

Grace sighed. "Lyle, I don't *want* to go out with you. I will *never* want to go out with you. I have tried and tried to discourage you tactfully, but you leave me no choice but to be blunt. I am not in the least attracted to you. Is that clear enough?"

His smile turned to a scowl. "That's just plain crazy, Grace. I'm the most eligible man in town. Besides, everyone knows how I feel about you. I've already told several people that I mean to marry you."

"You did *what?"* Grace stared at him, appalled. "How *dare* you! How could you do such a thing?"

"Now, now. Don't go getting upset. If you'll just think about it I'm sure you'll see it's the right thing to do. As head of the family, it's my duty to take care of you. I'm sure it's what Charles would have wanted, and I know it's what Verna wants. When we marry you'll return to the Willows and take your rightful place in the family again. Then everyone will be happy."

"Everyone but me!" Grace raged. "Get out of here, Lyle. Now. And don't come back. If you do, so help me, I'll call the sheriff and have him throw you off my property."

"Now, Grac—"

"Get, I said! Or I swear I'll get my father's shotgun and fill you full of buckshot," she threatened, forgetting in her fury that the gun was at the shop. She was so angry she was shaking, a fact that finally seemed to penetrate Lyle's thick skull.

His face tightened, and he began to back away. "All right, I'm going. But this isn't the end of it, Grace. I don't give up what's mine that easy."

"I am *not* yours!" she spat, and slammed the door so hard the glass oval in the center rattled.

She spun around and stomped down the central hallway. She tried to calm herself and get a grip on her raging emotions, but it was no use. By the time she reached the kitchen she felt as though the top of her head were about to blow off, and she flung herself into a chair, put her head down on the table and promptly burst into tears.

That was where Caroline found her a few minutes later. Grace was so lost in the bout of weeping she hadn't heard the car drive up. The first she knew she wasn't alone was when her sister came bounding in.

Grace jerked upright in the chair and quickly wiped her teary eyes, but she wasn't fast enough.

"Hi. I'm back. We—" Caroline jerked to a halt in the middle of the floor. "Grace? Oh, my God. Grace," she cried, rushing to her side. "What's wrong? What's happened. Are you all right?"

"I'm fine. Really. It's nothing."

"Bullshit. Don't give me that. You were crying, for Chrissake. Did someone break in? Did they hurt you? Do you want me to go get Jake?"

"No! No, don't do that. Really, I'm all right now. I . . . I just got upset about something. With someone, actually."

"Who?" Caroline looked suddenly uncomfortable. "Look, if it upset you that much for me and Jake to—"

"No, it's not that. Not at all," she said adamantly, and felt heat rush to her face at what was, at the very least, a partial lie. Had she not been so upset over her sister and Jake going off together she would never have lashed out at Lyle the way she had and lost all control.

"Then who upset you?"

Grace sighed, knowing she had no choice but to tell her. "Lyle," she admitted, making a face and giving her swollen eyes another wipe with a paper napkin from the holder on the table.

Caroline pulled out a chair from the table and sat down, taking Grace's hands. "All right. Tell me what happened. What's that disgusting turd up to now?"

"Caro, what language," Grace scolded, but the reprimand came out on a shaky laugh.

Caroline grinned. "Can I help it if he's a turd?"

"I suppose not. After what he's done, I almost agree with you." She told Caroline about Lyle's relentless attempts to court her these past few months and her suspicions as to what was behind his interest in her, and Caro was properly disgusted.

"Now, it seems he's been going around town telling people that he's going to marry me."

"Oh, yuck! That slimy creep. I hope you bashed him over the head with a blunt instrument."

"Not quite. Although, I did threaten to shoot him," she admitted with a giggle, feeling surprisingly better just having her sister's support. They had never confided in one another about anything before and Grace was amazed at how good it felt to do so.

"Good for you! He deserved it. The very idea of you marrying another Ames gives me the willies."

"Don't worry. It will never happen." Grace shuddered and made a face. "But I hate the thought of anyone, even his cronies, thinking that it will. I could just strangle Lyle for spreading that lie."

"Don't worry, it'll blow over. Everyone knows what a weaselly little braggart he is." She gave Grace's hand a pat. "You okay now?"

"Yes. I feel much better. I guess I just needed to let off steam."

"It does help. In my opinion, you should do it more often, and in more ways than just having a good bawl." She stood up and pushed in her chair. "Well, if you're sure you're going to be okay, I'm going to run. Jake is probably wondering what's taking so long."

"You're going out?"

"Not really, Jake and I are just going to pick up a pizza and eat it at his place. I just came in to tell you I wouldn't be here for dinner."

"Oh. I see."

"Well, I'm off. See ya." At the door, Caroline looked back and winked. "Don't wait up."

Twenty-Six

THE NEXT DAY, as the parishioners stood around outside the church after services, the hot topic of conversation was the flourishing romance between their minister and Josie Beaman.

Moving from one cluster of people to another, Grace and Harriet heard little else discussed. Grace was at first shocked, then angered to discover that many disapproved of the match. By the time they joined the group that included her Aunt Lollie, Grace was fuming so, she temporarily forgot about Jake and Caroline, and the fact that her sister hadn't returned to the house until well after midnight the previous night. Grace knew because she had been awake, tossing and turning in her lonely bed.

"Well, I, for one, think it shows poor judgement on his part," Ida Bell Wheatly huffed. "The woman is simply not a suitable companion for a man of the cloth, and that's all there is to it. I say, we get the elders and deacons to talk to him. Afterward, if he still insists upon continuing this unsuitable relationship, we should ask him to leave."

"I agree," Martha Goodson chimed in. "Don't get me wrong, I like Josie. She's a pleasant enough person and she attends church regularly, but she's just a bit too unorthodox for my taste, if you know what I mean. And no offense, Lollie—I know she's your niece and all—but I just don't understand what he sees in her. He's such a handsome man, and Josie is . . . well . . . rather plain."

"You're absolutely right, Doris, and no offense taken, I assure you." Lollie's thin lips puckered as though they were on a drawstring. "Lord knows, I love that girl, but she's no beauty, and that's the God's truth. My sister was a lovely woman but unfortunately

Josie got her looks from her father, and the Beamans always were a homely lot."

"Humph! It's not her looks that concern me," Ida Bell said with a sniff. "It's her character."

That was too much for Grace. "What, may I ask, is wrong with Josie's character?" she demanded in a frosty tone, staring straight at Ida Bell. "My cousin happens to be one of the kindest, most giving, hardest-working people you'll ever meet."

"That may be, but she's an agitator. Always stirring up trouble, beating the drum for some cockamamie cause or another." Ida Bell looked to the other women for support. "Remember all those protests and demonstrations she ramrodded in high school and college. Why, I heard she was even arrested at a sit-in once."

"That's right. Oh, dear. What if this thing between the reverend and Josie gets serious? She'd hardly make a suitable minister's wife."

"That's right," Ida Bell concurred. "And she hasn't changed one iota since her school days. Why, just look at that job of hers—running all over the county, poking her nose into other folks' business, hauling people into court for no good reason."

One of those whom Josie had hauled into court, as Grace recalled, had been Ida Bell's shiftless older son.

Normally she would have skirted the topic in the interest of peace, but not this time. "If you're referring to Kenneth, may I remind you, that he hadn't paid a dime of child support for his three children in over a year. While he's out drinking almost every night, his ex-wife and those babies, whom he abandoned, are having to draw food stamps just to eat."

Ida Bell puffed up like a toad and her face turned a mottled red. "My Kenneth is a good man. He works hard. He deserves to relax and enjoy himself. Besides, that Mary Beth tricked him into marrying her by getting pregnant. He never wanted all those children."

"Then Kenneth should have kept his pants zipped," Grace snapped.

The other women, with the exception of Harriet, gasped and stuttered and fluttered their hands. From the way they carried on you would have thought that the Virgin Mary had just spewed a string of foul obscenities.

"Mary Grace!" Aunt Lollie gasped when she'd recovered enough to speak coherently. "What in the world has gotten into you? I've never in my life heard you make such a crude remark."

"Now, now, Lollie, we all know how Grace bends over backward to be kind. She's just being loyal to her cousin."

"Oh, hush up, Martha! You too, Lollie" Harriet thumped the ground with her cane and shot the group a quelling glare. "Whether or not Josie is family is beside the point. Grace is right. You ought to all be ashamed of yourselves. Josie Beaman is the salt of the earth. Maybe she's a bit more zealous than most, but her heart's in the right place. Personally I think she'll make an excellent minister's wife, one who'll work hard to help people.

"And as for you, Lollie Madison, a fine aunt you are! The girl's not even my kin, but I think a sight more of her than you do."

"Now, see here, Harriet—" Lollie began, but that's as far as she got.

At that moment the roar of a high-powered engine intruded.

"Oh-my-word! Would you look at that!"

At the woman's horrified drawl, Grace and the others turned around, and her heart plummeted.

"Well!" Lollie huffed. "What did you expect. You know what they say about birds of a feather."

The bright red Corvette zoomed past the church with the popping roar of glass pack mufflers. Occupying the passenger seat, her long hair streaming behind her, was Caroline.

Jake sat behind the wheel.

Twenty-Seven

On the edge of the disapproving crowd, one pair of eyes glittered with approval as they followed the low-slung red car and its two occupants until they were out of sight.

What a delightful, if unexpected, turn of events. Elation blossomed inside, but the watcher knew there was danger in letting it show. Only the merest smile was allowed to curve those thin lips. But the watcher was pleased.

For weeks now nothing had been going right. Anger and frustration had built until the watcher had been considering drastic measures, but now it looked as though that wouldn't be necessary. Things were finally beginning to swing in the right direction. Oh yes, the watcher was pleased. Very pleased.

Twenty-Eight

"ARE YOU ALL RIGHT?"

"Me? Of course." Grace took her eyes off the road just long enough to glance at her aunt. "Why wouldn't I be?"

"I thought maybe you were still upset over what happened back at church."

"Oh, that. I probably shouldn't have lost my temper, but I couldn't just stand there and let them criticize Josie that way. It was just so unfair. I hope I didn't embarrass you."

"Oh pish tosh. Embarrass my foot." Harriet scowled and thumped her cane on the floorboard of the van. "You were right. And if you ask me, it's high time you let fly. There's nothing wrong with a little righteous anger, you know."

Grace ground her teeth. *Oh Auntie, not you, too. Why did people keep saying that to her? You would think she was a pressure cooker just waiting to blow.*

Harriet folded her gnarled hands over the top of the cane and stared straight ahead, sober as a judge, but when Grace glanced her way again she saw her aunt's stern mouth twitch. A second later the old lady added wickedly, "Besides, the look on Lollie's face was priceless. I wouldn't have missed seeing that for the world. You shocked the garters right off her and those other 'holier than thou' old crows."

"Why, Aunt Harriet, what a thing to say," Grace said, chuckling.

"Humph. It's the truth. Anyway, we're getting off the subject. I wasn't talking about that little set-to with Lollie and her cronies. I thought maybe you were upset about your sister and that Jake person."

Grace's smile faded, and the painful tightness in her chest grew worse. Ever since the previous night her heart had felt as though it were clamped in the jaws of a vise. The reminder of Jake and Caroline together squeezed it tighter. "No, not at all," she said, trying to sound unconcerned. "I told you, I never believed that Jake killed that girl. Caroline is in no danger."

"That's not what I meant. I'm worried about you. I know it must hurt you to see them together."

"What?" The comment sent a dart of alarm zinging through Grace. She shot her aunt a startled glance, and Harriet snapped, "Watch where you're going!" when she almost ran off the road.

Grace righted the van and tried to calm herself and at the same time appear as though the comment had aroused no more than amused surprise. "I don't know what you're talking about," she said with a shaky little laugh. "Why on earth would I care if Jake and Caroline are seeing one another?"

Her aunt made an aggravated sound and thumped her cane again. "I swear, Mary Grace, you never could lie worth a fig. I may be old, but I'm not blind. I've seen the way he looks at you when he thinks no one is watching, and I've seen the way you look at him. Two worse love-sick fools I've yet to come across."

"Aunt Harriet!"

"And don't bother denying it. Back there at the church when that car went by you looked as though someone had driven a stake through your heart." The alarm that Grace felt must have shown on her face because her aunt quickly added, "Oh, don't worry. No one else noticed. They were all too busy passing judgement on your sister and Jake."

"I see." Grace turned into her aunt's driveway and brought the van to a stop beneath the sprawling sweet-gum tree. Gripping the steering wheel tight, she stared straight ahead. "You don't have to worry about me, Auntie. I'm not going to go off the deep end and do something foolish."

Harriet put her hand on Grace's arm, and when she spoke her voice had lost its crispness. "Child, you know that I love you as though you were my own. I'll admit, I've revised my opinion of Jake Paxton somewhat. Once you get past that moody exterior he's not nearly so bad as he tries to make out. He's intelligent and a hard worker, and I don't sense any viciousness in him—not the kind that would make him capable of murder at any rate. However, that's just my opinion, and that and fifty cents will buy you a cup of coffee at the diner. What I'm trying to say, child, is there are just a few too many shadows in that man's past. If I thought you had a prayer of finding happiness with him I'd support you, you know that. But..."

"I know," Grace said softly, patting her aunt's bony hand. Gratitude and love for the tiny woman rushed up inside her to mix with the pain, bringing tears to her eyes. "I know."

"Why don't you skip Verna's card party? I can get a ride with someone else. I could tell her you took sick at the last minute."

Grace blinked the moisture from her eyes and attempted a wobbly smile. "Thank you, dear, but I wouldn't dare. Verna would have the vapors. Plus, she'd never forgive me."

"All right, but you'd better brace yourself. Remember, Ida Bell and her cronies are in Verna's bridge club. You're going to get an earful. Those women are going to jump on this like a dog on a meaty bone."

~

Her aunt had not exaggerated. The trouble was, on arriving, Grace had no idea just how much her patience would be tested, or that, once her tolerance level was breached, she was even capable of such stunning fierceness.

It started when Doris Rinequist arrived at the Willows, breathless with the news that she had seen Jake and Caroline having dinner together at the City Diner. They had barely taken their places at the card tables when she began to dish the details.

"That fancy red car of Caroline's was parked out front, so naturally I glanced in the window as I drove by, and sure enough, there they were, bold as brass, sitting at the front table." She paused in dealing the cards and lowered her voice in that confidential manner people use when relating something shocking. "They were acting real friendly too, laughing and talking like they were real close, if you get my drift."

"My Fred said he saw them shooting pool at The Rip Saw earlier. Can you imagine? Shooting pool on the Sabbath."

Grinding her teeth, Grace shuffled the other deck of cards with a sharp riffle. How was that different from playing cards? And what, she wondered, did Martha think Fred had been doing at the bar, passing out Bibles?

"Huh. I'll bet that's not all they were doing."

"Well, I for one, don't know why everyone is so surprised," Martha sniffed. "All of her life, Caroline has done the most outrageous things."

"Now, now, ladies," Verna admonished in her twittery, Southern-belle voice. "Be nice. Remember, Caroline is Grace's sister and Harriet's niece."

"Well, I'm sorry, but truth is truth, and everyone knows that Caroline is as wild as a March hare," Ida Bell stated emphatically. Still smarting from their clash in the church yard that morning, she cast a gimlet stare at Grace as though daring her to deny it. "Grace knows that as well as anyone. Don't you, Grace?"

With an effort, she managed a stiff smile. "My sister is high-spirited, and perhaps she doesn't always make wise choices, but she's not as bad as you ladies are painting her."

"High-spirited! Is that what you call it? Humph! She ran off with a married man when she was just a teenager and caused her own mother's death. She's had affairs with God alone knows how many men and has already divorced two husbands. Now she's taken up with a killer. If that's not no-good trash, I don't know what is."

Grace saw red—actual little dots of fiery color dancing before her eyes. She slammed the deck of cards down and shot to her feet so quickly her chair tumbled over with a clatter that startled shrieks out of several women. It went skittering across Verna's beloved mirror-polished oak floors and crashed against an antique curio cabinet where it came to a stop. Every eye in the room fastened on Grace in fascinated horror as she bent forward and slapped her palms flat on the card table, bringing her face down until it was just inches from Ida Bell's.

"You sanctimonious, hypocritical, mean-spirited old busybody," Grace hissed through her teeth.

Ida Bell was so shocked her eyes nearly bugged right out of her head. She shrank back, holding her cards pressed against her ample bosom, her mouth agape.

"Once and for all, Caroline did *not* kill our mother. The aneurysm in her brain would have ruptured at that moment in time, no matter what.

"Furthermore, I don't know how you have the unmitigated gall to call my sister trash. You, of all people. I happen to know that twenty years ago you tried to seduce my father."

That brought gasps all around and a sputtered denial from Ida Bell.

"I . . . I did no such thing!" she cried, but a fiery color crept up the folds of her neck and she could not meet any of the eyes that fixed on her. "Y-You're lying."

"No, you're the liar. You see, I was there, Ida Bell, playing dolls under my father's desk. You came in to see him on some flimsy pretext and propositioned him. I was only nine at the time, but I understood enough to know what you were up to. You even tried to kiss him. My father, being the kind of man that he was, tried to discourage you gently but you wouldn't take the hint. You left him with no choice but to use firm measures. He had to practically throw you out of his office."

"That's . . . that's not true! I never—"

"Oh, it's true, all right. After he put you out, my father dandled me on his knee and told me that you were upset and didn't know what you were doing, and that I wasn't to mention it, and until now I haven't. But I will no longer stand by and listen to you vilify others when you are hardly an angel yourself."

All around, scandalized murmurs erupted from the other women. Grace straightened and flashed a look that silenced them cold. "As for the rest of you. I wouldn't get too smug if I were you. There's hardly one among you that doesn't have some dark little secret. It might surprise you what I know. As a child, I played under my father's desk a lot."

With that oblique threat delivered, she headed for the door.

Verna jumped up and hurried after her. "Grace! Dearest, where are you going?"

"Home."

"But . . . you can't! What about the party?" Verna grabbed Grace's arm, stopping her. "Dearest, please don't go away angry. This isn't like you at all. We can straighten this out. I'm sure you didn't mean all those things you said."

"Oh, I meant them, all right." Grace looked back at the room full of women. "One more thing. Jake Paxton is *not* a killer."

She shook off Verna's arm, snatched up her purse from the hall table and stalked for the front door.

"Well, I never!"

The huffy comment floated out of the parlor an instant before she slammed the heavy mahogany door behind her.

Grace couldn't get to her van quick enough, and she burned rubber for a hundred feet down the half-mile long asphalt drive. She was so furious she was halfway home before she realized she had left her aunt behind.

~

IT DIDN'T HELP HER OUTLOOK to arrive home to the sound of music and laughter—Caroline's laughter—coming from the apartment. Grace was sorely tempted to march upstairs and throw both of them out. But, of course, she couldn't throw her sister out, since she was half owner of the farm. And since they'd become so chummy, Grace doubted that Caroline would allow her to toss Jake out on his ear, even if she could make herself do so.

Fortunately, she managed to retain a modicum of control, enough, at any rate, to know that she'd already made a big enough spectacle of herself for one day.

A miserable night of tossing and turning did little to calm Grace. All through the next morning at the store she felt as though her chest contained a swarm of angry bees. Aside from a terse hello when she arrived, she didn't speak to Jake, and he kept his distance.

She was short tempered and edgy and so restless she was unable to settle down to anything constructive. She paced back and forth among the artfully displayed antiques, needlessly adjusting a lamp shade here, a whatnot there.

In the clear light of day, however, she was not so much still angry with the gossiping busybodies—such was the life of a small town, and always would it be so. Mostly, she was upset with herself. Grace stopped pacing the showroom and cast a jaundiced eye toward the back workroom, where Jake was stripping an antique halltree. And she was angry with Jake.

In a few short weeks, she, who hated strife and violence in any form, who never got embroiled in controversy, who had never so much as exchanged a cross word with anyone outside her immediate family, had defied public opinion, faced down a gang of angry men and an irate store manager, hit a police officer, told off her lecherous cousin by marriage, got into an argument in the church yard with one of the town's most notorious gossips, and then to top it off, had lashed out at the woman and revealed her scandalous secret in front of a roomful of women.

And the reason for every one of those lapses in conduct could be attributed directly to Jake Paxton. The man had turned her well-ordered life upside down and she had no idea how to right it.

By now, word of her tirade was sure to have spread all over town. Making a face, she folded her arms and stared out through the bay window at the front of the store. She could hear them now:

"Would you believe it? Sweet little Mary Grace Somerset had a wall-eyed, hissy fit, right there in front of everybody. A regular table-pounding, foot-stomping temper tantrum. And she said the most scandalous things about Ida Bell. Just wait until you hear..."

Grace sighed. She would probably never live it down.

Her disposition was not improved by the steady stream of visitors who dropped by the shop, all with the hope of confirming the juicy tale they'd heard.

"I heard you let fly at the bridge party last night."

"Regular cat fight, that's what I heard."

"Is it true about Ida Bell?"

"So, you let Ida Bell have it, did you? About time somebody did. The woman's poison. I'm just surprised it was you."

"Who knew you had such a temper?"

"Do you think she really did have an affair with your father?"

The last, whispered with prurient avidity, very nearly snapped the tenuous hold Grace had managed to regain over her emotions. As it was, she barely managed a terse denial, couched in tones so icy they would have caused frostbite in a person with more sensitivity.

Shortly after that encounter, while Grace was still seething and in no mood to put up with more aggravation, Caroline arrived.

"What do you want?" she all but snarled the instant her sister entered the store.

"Now there's a pleasant greeting." Caroline made her way through the cluttered shop with her usual hip-swaying saunter and an amused smile on her face. "Something wrong?"

"No. If you're looking for Jake, he's in the back."

"Actually, I came to talk to you." She leaned her hip against the counter and eyed Grace with a cat-that-ate-the-cream look. "I heard that you stood up for me last night at Verna's hen party."

"Where did you hear that?" Grace couldn't imagine that any of the women who had been raking her sister over the coals with such relish would have called Caroline and repeated what had been said, and it was too soon for the gossip to have filtered back to her. Caroline was on the tail end of the local gossip grapevine.

"Aunt Harriet."

Oh, Lord. She had forgotten about her aunt. Again.

Grace had telephoned her first thing that morning to beg her forgiveness for running out on her, but her aunt had cut her off midway through the apology.

"Pish tosh. It's not as though I was stranded. This is Cedar Grove, not Houston. Any one of those women would have given me a ride home."

"But I should have remembered and taken you with me."

"You don't seriously believe I would have gone, do you? And miss the commotion that erupted after you left? Not on your life. You never heard such a ruckus, everybody clucking and carrying on, accusations flying and feathers ruffled. Ida Bell was huff-ing and puffing and trying to defend herself. Her face turned the most interesting shade of purple. Got her come-uppance, but good. It was a sight to behold. You should have been a fly on the wall. Child, you shocked everyone so, some were speculating that you were having a nervous breakdown, brought on, it was suggested, by the strain of living in such close proximity to Jake."

They hadn't been far wrong, Grace thought with a little inward sigh.

"Did you really blow up and call Ida Bell Wheatly a sanctimonious, hypocritical, mean-spirited old busybody?"

"Caroline, please. Last night I lost control and said a lot of things that I shouldn't have. It was wrong of me, and I regret it. And I certainly don't want to talk about it."

"Oh my gawd, you did!" Caroline crowed. "It's written all over your face. Oh, that's rich! Damn, I wish I could have been there to see it."

"Could we just drop this, please?"

An avid twinkle danced in her sister's eyes. "Did Ida Bell really try to seduce Dad, or did you just make that up?"

"Caroline, stop it! I said—"

"What's all the fuss about?" Jake came out of the back room, wiping his hands on a rag. "I could hear you two all the way in the back."

"Oh, hi, Jake. Wait'll you hear this."

"Caro," Grace warned, but her sister forged ahead as though she hadn't spoken.

"Grace lost her temper last night and told off the town's biggest gossip."

Jake's gaze shot to Grace. "Is that right?"

"And you haven't heard the best of it yet. She was defending both of us."

"Caroline could we drop this please? I told you, I don 't want to discuss it. It was a mistake and I'd like to forget it ever happened."

Agitated and anxious to put an end to the discussion, Grace came out from behind the counter and walked to the window. Folding her arms tightly across her middle, she presenting them with her back.

Jake came over and leaned his shoulder against the window frame next to her. "So. What brought this on?"

"I said, I don't—" A figure on the other side of the street caught her attention. Grace frowned and narrowed her eyes. "Isn't that T.J.?"

"Where?" Straightening, he turned and peered out the window at the boy scurrying by on the opposite side of the street. "Yeah, that's him. Where the hell is he going?"

Since the night Jake had stopped T.J. from shoplifting at the Piggly Wiggly, the boy had been a regular visitor. Every afternoon, the minute school let out, he made a beeline for the shop.

Sometimes he helped Caroline. She paid him for dusting the furniture and bric-a-brac and vacuuming, but mostly he just hung out in back with Jake until closing time. Almost nightly they took the boy to the farm with them and either he or Grace fed him dinner before driving him back to the trailer park. Neither of them could stand the thought of the boy going hungry.

"Why won't he look this way?" Jake tensed and his head jutted forward. "Wait a minute. Isn't he limping?"

"Why, I think you're right."

"What the hell?" Jake snatched open the door and stalked outside. Standing on the sidewalk in front of the shop, he cupped his hands around his mouth and shouted, "Yo! T.J.! Where you going, pardner?"

Grace stepped just outside the door onto the small stoop and watched. Across the street, T.J. hurried faster.

"Something is wrong, Jake. He's acting peculiar. Why won't he look at us?"

"T.J.? Dammit, boy, what's the matter with you?"

"I ain't got time to stop, Jake," the boy called back, but he kept his face averted.

"To hell with that," Jake growled almost to himself. Cupping his mouth again, he shouted, "Dammit, boy, you get your ass over here. Now! Or I'll come and get you."

The order drew several startled looks from passersby. Some of them turned to scowls as they recognized Jake, but when Grace moved to stand beside him no one offered to interfere.

Across the street, T.J. drew to a halt but he merely stood there, staring at the ground, his shoulders slumped.

"Get over here, T.J."

"Ah, Jake, do I gotta?"

"Move it!"

His chin rested on his chest and he dragged his feet but he came, cutting diagonally across the street in the middle of the block. He no longer even tried to disguise his limp.

"He's hurt," Grace whispered. Beside her, Jake grew ominously still. When the boy came to a stop before them he reached out with one finger and gently lifted his chin.

Grace couldn't help herself. She cried out and her hand flew to her mouth. "Oh, my Lord!"

T.J.'s face was a battered mess.

Twenty-Nine

JAKE'S FACE DARKENED and his jaws clenched. "Who did this to you?"

One side of T.J.'s face was bruised a livid purple and black and so swollen his eye was almost shut. His lower lip was cut and puffed up to twice its normal size.

T.J. tried to turn his head away, but Jake wouldn't let him. "Tell me."

"Nobody did nothin'. I fell."

"Bullshit."

"Okay, I didn't fall. I . . . I got into a fight at school."

"Try again."

"It's the truth!"

"Kid, I've been in enough fights to know that no eleven-year-old inflicted this kind of damage. Now, I want to know who did this to you, and I want to know now."

"Jake, perhaps we should continue this inside where it's not so public." Grace made the suggestion with a meaningful glanced around. Several people had stopped on the street and were taking in the little tableau with unabashed interest.

Jake shot them a hard stare and took T.J.'s arm. "You're right. Anyway, I want to get a look at the rest of him and see what other injuries he has."

Grace experienced another rush of alarm. That thought hadn't occurred to her.

"What's going on? Why did you run out like th—"

Caroline's jaw dropped. "Oh, shit, kid, what happened to you?"

"That's what we're about to find out," Jake snarled and herded the boy into the back room. Grace tried to follow, but at the door he blocked her way. "You'd better wait out here. I think he'll be more comfortable stripping down if it's just me with him."

Grace's motherly instincts were outraged. "But if he's hurt badly he may need me. He's just a little boy."

"He's eleven, Grace," Jake said with a look that spoke volumes.

"But— Oh."

"Yes, oh. Look, I know you're worried, but just give us a few minutes, okay."

It was the longest few minutes of Grace's life. Pacing back and forth in front of the storeroom door, she wrung her hands and glanced at the grandfather clock in the corner each time she walked by it.

"Take it easy, Grace. That kid's a tough little nut. He'll be okay."

"I can't believe this has happened, Caro. How could anyone do such a thing?"

"You're so naïve. Hell, Grace, the world is full of vicious low-lifes." Something in her tone caught Grace's attention, and at her questioning look, her sister shrugged. "My last husband used to knock me around. He enjoyed hurting me. I think it made him feel powerful."

"Oh, Caroline," Grace whispered, appalled. "Why didn't you tell me?"

Her chin came up and she looked away. "What could you have done? Anyway, my shrink says I deliberately choose destructive relationships. But hell, what does she know?"

"You're seeing a psychiatrist?"

"Now and then. And she's a psychologist, actually. It's no big deal." She gave a dismissive shrug. "Anyway, I've about decided to quit."

Grace was going to question her further, but just then they heard T.J. shriek, "No, you can't! Don't do it, Jake!"

She was already taking a step toward the door when it opened and Jake came stalking out with T.J. right on his heels. The boy's shirt was unbuttoned and he was white as parchment, making the bruises on his body stand out in vivid contrast. He hung onto the back of Jake's belt in a pathetic attempt to hold him back. "No, Jake. Please!"

"What is it? What's wrong?"

"Somebody beat the crap out of him. The poor kid's black and blue all over. And I think he may have a pelvic fracture. It's hard to say for certain. No one's bothered to take him to a doctor." Jake's face was a rigid mask of fury. At that moment he looked capable of committing murder.

"Oh, my word." Feeling sick, Grace pressed her hand against her stomach. "Who? And *why,* for heaven sakes?

Jake shot T.J. a narrow look and the boy's expression turned sullen. "He's sticking to his story, but I think he's lying through his teeth. My guess is, Digger threatened him with worse if he told anybody."

"Nuh-uh. I ain't a'scared of Digger Yates," T.J. blustered, puffing out his scrawny chest. "I was in a fight, just like I told you. An' you cain't prove I wasn't."

"Oh, T.J." The thought of this small boy being struck by Digger Yates was so appalling it brought tears to Grace's eyes. Digger was a huge man and strong as an ox. Her face softened and she touched his uninjured cheek gently. "Sweetheart, it's all right. No one blames you for being afraid. But we want to help. If Digger did this, you have to tell us so that we can fix it where he can never harm you again. Do you understand?"

"There ain't nothin' to fix. I was in a fight," he muttered stubbornly, staring at his shoes.

"Yeah, well. Maybe so," Jake said. "But I think I'll take a little ride out to the trailer park anyway."

T.J.'s head snapped up, his eyes wide with panic. "No, Jake. You cain't!" He latched on to Jake's arm but he easily shook off the boy's hold and stalked for the door. Everything about him radiated anger, from the set of his shoulders to the icy glint in his eyes.

"Jake! No!" Frantic, T.J. turned to Grace and wailed, "You gotta stop him, Miz Ames! He's gonna go beat up Digger."

"What! Jake, you can't! You'll be arrested." If he didn't get himself killed. Digger had at least fifty pounds on him and was built like a gorilla.

She might as well have saved her breath. He didn't even slow down.

"No, Jake!" Grace rushed to the door and tried to block his path. "Listen to me. We'll call Josie and let her handle this. It's her job. She'll know what to do. If you go over there you'll just get in trouble."

"Call Josie if you want, but that bastard's going to answer to me. Now, get out of my way, Grace."

"No, I won't le—"

He ended the argument by simply grasping her upper arms and lifting her to one side. Then he stalked out.

"Oh, this is bad. This is real bad." Tears streaked T.J.'s cheeks and his eyes held terror. "You gotta stop him, Miz Ames. That Digger, he's a mean son-of-a-bitch. He don't fight fair, neither. He'll kill Jake for sure if he can."

She hesitated only an instant, then rushed to the telephone. Her hands shook as she punched out the number.

"Sheriff's Office."

"Sheriff Newcomb, please Sara. This is Grace."

"Oh, hi, Grace. Say, I heard about your run-in with Ida Bell. Good for you! What did the old witch have to say for herself?"

"Sara, I'm sorry, but I can't talk right now. I need to speak to Harley. It's an emergency."

"Sorry, Grace, he isn't here. I think he's down at the diner getting a piece of Thelma's peach pie. You want me to beep him?"

"Yes, please. And tell him to come to my store at once."

"Sure thing."

Grace immediately dialed Josie's number at work. While the phone on the other end of the line rang she fidgeted. "You've got to be there. Please, please, please be there."

"Social Services, Beaman speaking," Josie snapped.

"Oh, thank, God. Josie, it's Grace." As quickly as she could, Grace filled her cousin in on what had transpired. She had barely finished when Harley's patrol car screeched to a stop in front of the shop.

He bailed out almost before the engine stopped, dashed up the walk, took the steps in one leap and burst through the door, his hand on the butt of his gun. His stance and expression said he was ready for trouble.

His gaze picked out Caroline first, then darted to Grace. "I got here as quick as I could. What's the trouble, Grace?"

For an answer, she grabbed T.J., who had been skulking behind an armoire trying to look invisible. She nudged him forward until he stood in front of Harley. The boy kept his head down and drew circles in the carpet nap with the toe of his dirty sneaker. T.J. didn't trust lawmen.

"This," Grace replied, raising T.J.'s face for Harley's inspection.

The sheriff pushed his Stetson back with one finger and tipped his head to the side. Frowning, he whistled softly between his teeth. "Son-of-a-gun."

"T.J. claims he was in a fight, but Jake thinks his mother's boyfriend did this to him," Grace explained in a voice that shook with anger and fear. "Now Jake's on the way out there to confront Digger. There's going to be trouble, Harley. Bad trouble. Please, you've got to do something."

"Calm down, Grace, I will. You live out in the Jasper Creek Trailer Park, don't you, son?"

T.J. nodded, but returned his gaze to the carpet the instant Grace released his chin.

"It's trailer space eight-nine," she supplied.

"You're going to have to shake a leg, Sheriff," Caroline drawled, speaking up for the first time. "Jake's already on his way, and he's madder than a grizzly with an impacted tooth. Matter of fact, I think I'd better ride along with you."

"Whoa. Back up there. This is official business. Besides, it may get messy."

"Hell, do you think I've never seen a fistfight before? Anyway, without a guide, it'll take you half an hour to find the right place in that maze of trailer houses." Caroline slung her purse strap over her shoulder and headed toward the door, crooking her finger at him as she went by. "Come along, cowboy. We don't have time to argue about it. The mood Jake was in, if we don't get there fast, all that will be left of this Digger guy is a greasy spot."

Harley stared hard at her retreating back and pulled on his lower lip, but after only a few seconds he started out after her. "Grace, you'd better call Josie over at Social Services and tell her what you suspect."

"I already have," she called after him. "She's meeting me at the Clinic.

~

"Uh, Marshal Dillon. Maybe you didn't get the message. We're kind of in a hurry here."

"Yeah, I know."

"Well? Aren't you going to turn on the siren?"

Harley glanced at Caroline. "There's not enough traffic to slow us down. Besides, do you want to draw attention to the fact that you're riding in a squad car? Everyone will assume you went and got yourself arrested."

She snorted. "You think I care what the local yokels think?"

He glanced her way again, considering. "Yeah. I think you do. Matter of fact, I think you care a whole helluva lot more than you want to admit."

"Oh, pul-leeze. Look, Sheriff, I've got a news flash for you. I'm the local bad girl. I do whatever the hell I please, and if somebody doesn't like it, hey, that's tough. If I gave a rat's behind about what people around here liked or didn't like, why would I always be rubbing their noses in it?"

The squad car went over the Jasper Creek bridge, and Harley made a sharp right onto Tobin Road. The road followed the creek. Except for a few gentle curves, it was fairly straight, and he stepped on the gas. Soon they were doing over sixty.

"I don't know. Maybe you do it just to prove them right. I read somewhere that people live up or down to what they perceive to be others' opinion of them. Maybe you believe that no matter what you do, folks around here are always going to blame you for your mother's death anyway, so you might as well shock the socks off of them. Or else maybe you think you really are to blame, and playing the part of loose woman is your way of punishing yourself."

"Oh, Lord. Just what I need, a hick marshal who fancies himself a shrink." Caroline rolled her eyes, then shot him a disgusted look. "Spare me your amateur analysis, will you."

Harley shrugged. "Just trying to help. And like I told you before, I'm not a marshal, I'm the sheriff."

"Whatever. And like I told you before, I don't need help. Not from you or anybody." Folding her arms tight, Caroline looked out the window. "Anyway, you're wrong."

"I see. Then you haven't been hanging out with Jake just to stir up folks around here?"

"Of course not." He shot her a skeptical look, and she grimaced. "Well, not entirely, anyway. For your information, Jake Paxton happens to be a good-looking man with a ton of sex appeal."

"I wouldn't know about that." Up ahead, Harley saw the faded sign that read Jasper Creek Trailer Park, and he lowered his speed. "You may be right, though. He's been turning female heads around here since he was about fourteen. Still, I'm surprised you're giving him a whirl, seeing as how your sister is sweet on him."

Caroline's head whipped around. She stared at him with her mouth slightly agape. "Well, well. How perceptive of you, cowboy."

"So you do know."

"Yes."

"And you don't feel bad about what you're doing to Grace?"

She didn't say anything for several seconds. Then she sighed. "If you must know, that's exactly why I am seeing Jake—to goad Grace into admitting her feelings for him."

"Ahh, I see. So you're not interested in him yourself?"

"No."

Harley looked at her and grinned. "Good. That makes things a lot less complicated."

"What things? What's that supposed to mean?"

"We'll talk about it later." Ignoring her mystified expression, he braked and turned into the trailer park. The rear end of the patrol car fish-tailed when it hit the sandy trail that passed as a street but he quickly righted it. "Okay, which way?"

Caroline was still studying him with a perplexed frown. "What? Oh. Hang a right just beyond that utility pole. Okay, now, where the road forks up ahead, take the left branch." She guided him through the rabbit warren of rusted and battered trailer houses. As they cruised through the maze the black and white patrol car drew suspicious stares from children and adults alike. To the people of the Bottoms, a police car meant just one thing: trouble.

Finally the monstrosity that was T.J.'s home, came into view. None of the homesites were anything to brag about but the Tolson trailer, with its peeling robin's-egg blue paint, sagging porch and junk-filled minuscule yard, made some of the others look almost livable.

"That's it," Caroline said, but Harley was already braking to a stop behind Jake's truck, which was parked in front.

"YOU GET OUT OF HERE, JAKE PAXTON. You hear me! You can't just force your way into a person's home," Connie whined. "Digger knows about us. If he comes home and finds you here, he'll kill you. What're you doing? You can't go in there?" she cried when he opened the closet door in the tiny bedroom.

Jake made a face. Not even a Chihuahua dog could have hidden in that crammed closet. Shutting the door, he looked at the woman and felt a spasm of distaste. Christ, he couldn't believe he'd ever touched her. She was as slovenly as this dump she called home. He didn't know how anyone could stand to live in such a cramped space.

The entire trailer consisted of two bedrooms—neither much bigger than a closet—a bath, a nothing kitchen and a living room that barely held a couch, a TV and a tiny table. He knew, because he'd just searched every inch of the place.

"Where is he?"

"I told you, I don't know. Digger comes home when he feels like it. What do you want with him, anyway?"

"I tell you what I want with him. That son-of-a-bitch beat the hell out of T.J. Did you see him do it?"

She turned pale and her gaze flickered away from his . . . I don't know what you're talking about. T.J. ain't been beat."

She was lying. Jake could see it in her face. His hands curled into fists at his sides. God, what kind of mother let someone knock her kid around?

The answer came to him at once; one like his own. He vividly recalled the blows he'd suffered at the hands of several of Lizzie's men friends over the years. He could imagine all too well what T.J. had suffered. And what he was feeling. "The hell you don't. Your son looks like he went ten rounds with a gorilla. Don't tell me you didn't notice. What the hell kind of mother are you anyway? How can you stand by and let a sorry piece of trash like Digger Yates abuse your son?"

"You don't understand," Connie whined, wringing her hands. "It's hard makin' ends meet an' raisin' a kid. Real hard. Digger takes care of me'n T.J."

"Yeah, I've seen how he takes care of the boy."

A vehicle pulled up outside, and his gaze darted out the open door in time to see Sheriff Newcomb and Caroline climb out of a squad car. Grinding his teeth, Jake pushed open the torn screened door and stepped out. Connie sidled out right behind him.

"I suppose Grace sent you?"

Harley didn't even blink at his belligerent tone. "Yeah, she was a bit worried."

"If you were hoping to arrest me you came all this way for nothing, Sheriff. Digger isn't here."

At the dilapidated little porch, Harley stopped, propped one foot on the bottom step and braced his hand on his knee. Caroline stopped just behind him and stood to one side, watching. The sheriff pushed back his Stetson with his forefinger and squinted up at Jake. "Actually, I thought you might need a little help."

Startled, then immediately suspicious, Jake scowled, but Harley turned his attention to the woman. "You Ms. Tolson?"

"Yes. And I'm so glad you're here. Jake forced his way into my house and searched it. I . . . I want you to arrest him."

"Well, now, ma'am, I sure would hate to do that. I'm sure Mr.

Paxton here was just trying to make a citizen's arrest. Isn't that right, Jake?"

He studied Harley's amiable smile through narrowed eyes, but he nodded. "Yeah, right."

"A-Arrest? You mean Digger? Wh-what for?"

"Well now, ma'am, your boy's in pretty bad shape. You know anything about that?"

"Why n-no. No, I don't. An' Digger don't neither. Did, uh . . . did T.J. tell you Digger hit him?"

"Well, no, ma'am. Truth is, he didn't," Harley drawled, and the relief in Connie's eyes was clear. She looked almost faint with it. "The boy claims he was in a fight at school."

"He was. Honest, Sheriff Newcomb." She fluttered her hands and fidgeted. Her gaze darted all around but never met either Jake's or the sheriff's eyes. "That boy. I swear, he's such a trial. Gets into one scrape after another. I'm real sorry if he's caused you any trouble."

"Hmm. No, he didn't cause any trouble. But you can expect Ms. Beaman from Social Services to be out to talk with you about this . . . uh . . . fight real soon."

"What for? I said we didn't—"

"It's routine in cases like this, Ms. Tolson. You just answer her questions and if you didn't have anything to do with causing your son's injuries, you'll be okay." He shot Jake an uncompromising look and jerked his head toward the vehicles. "C'mon, Paxton. Let's go."

Jake stared at that implacable expression, his own just as unyielding. "I think I'll wait awhile longer."

"That'd be trespassing. The lady doesn't want you here, Jake. Now do us both a favor and just come along."

"Bad as I hate to side with the fuzz, I gotta admit he's right, Jake," Caroline put in, sending Harley a wry look. "You aren't going to do T.J. any good by getting yourself thrown in jail."

For an instant he hesitated, his jaws clenched tight. "Crap." He started to stalk away, but he barely took two steps when he turned and pointed his finger at Connie.

"You tell Digger that T.J. had better not get into another 'fight' because if I ever see another mark on the boy I'm going to beat your boyfriend's sorry butt into the ground."

Thirty

"DAMMIT, JAKE, are you *trying* to get me to lock you up?" Harley muttered when they were out of earshot. "You can't go around threatening people that way. Jesus Christ, at least have the good sense not to do it in front of an officer of the law. By rights, I oughta cuff you and haul you in. If that woman wasn't so ignorant she'd know she could slap you with a whole truckload of charges."

"Who gives a rat's ass?"

"You'd better. The people of this town got a real low tolerance level where you're concerned. Right now, you haven't broken any law so they can't do a damned thing about you being here except complain. But you so much as spit on the sidewalk, and they'll be all over you like a duck on a June bug."

"It'd be worth it. She was lying, dammit. She knows what happened to T.J."

"I know."

"Then what the hell was going on back there? Why didn't you arrest her and go looking for Digger?"

Harley stopped by the patrol car. "Look, I'd like nothing better than to send Digger Yates to prison and let the inmates have him. Even hardened criminals have no use for child abusers. But as long as the boy denies that Digger hit him, we don't have a case."

"We? No, *you* don't have a case. Those bruises on T.J. are all the evidence I need. And I say Digger Yates deserves to have the piss stomped out of him."

"That may be, but if you're smart you'll take my advice and stay away from him. I'd hate to have to lock you up."

"Is that right?" Jake sneered. "Funny, I seem to recall you were one of the deputies who arrested me twelve years ago."

"You're a real hardcase, aren't you, Paxton. That wasn't personal. I was just doing my job. Hell, man, I'm trying to help you. No more supporters than you've got in this town, I'd think you'd welcome a friendly gesture now and then."

"That all depends. Why would you want to help me?"

"Suspicious bastard, too, aren't you." Harley opened the door and got in the car. As he started the engine, he rolled down the window and looked up at Jake. "For what it's worth, I never was convinced you murdered that girl."

"YOU MEAN THERE'S NOTHING YOU CAN DO?"

"I'm sorry, Grace. I wish I could. In my opinion Jake is right, those injuries didn't come from another kid. But as long as T.J. claims they did and denies that his mother or her boyfriend beat him, my hands are tied."

Grace glanced at the door of the treatment room. T.J. was on the other side with Dr. Watson, getting every cut and scrape cleaned and treated. A few would require stitches. Luckily, his pelvis wasn't cracked, as Jake suspected, just badly bruised. "So, we have to let him go back to that environment? Is that what you're saying?"

"For now, I'm afraid so." Grace made a pained sound, and Josie put her arm around her. "I know. I'm sorry, Grace. Look, I'm going to take the kid home and I'll talk to the mother and try to put a scare into her. I'll tell her if T.J. sustains any more injuries she might lose her son and go to jail. I don't know how much good it will do, but at least she'll know that we're watching her."

THE NEXT AFTERNOON, Grace watched Jake out the window of the shop as he maneuvered a tea table into the back of a customer's minivan. A box of china and an Eastlake chair sat on the sidewalk beside the vehicle, waiting to be added to the load.

It had been a good sale. The shop turned a healthy profit and the customer was delighted with her purchases. Grace suspected that the woman owned one of the vacation homes on the other side of Lake Kashada. She wasn't from around there, that much was obvious by the way she chattered away to Jake as she stood beside the van's open cargo door.

Straightening, he said something to the woman and smiled, and Grace's heart gave a little bump. The customer, though somewhere in her sixties, was no more immune to that roguish charm than Grace. She laughed and fluttered her hands and twinkled at him prettily. From that distance Grace couldn't be sure, but she thought the woman blushed.

Grace smiled. She had to give Jake credit. Lately he had been making an effort to be pleasant to the customers, strangers and locals alike, though he hadn't had much success with the latter.

Most either looked right through him as though he were made of glass or else met his overtures with a glacial stare and a few clipped words meant to keep him at a distance. Actually, she had to admire his restraint. At times the snubs had been so insulting she had been certain he would snarl back at them, but he had persevered, most of the time with a locked jaw, she strongly suspected.

After yesterday's episode, however, she hadn't known what to expect from him this morning. He had been in a black rage when he'd stormed out of the shop the day before, and when he'd returned, his mood had been so dark and withdrawn not even Caroline had dared to go near him last night.

Her sister had told her what had taken place at the trailer park. Though Grace understood Jake's frustration and anger, she was relieved that he hadn't found Digger. If he hadn't gotten himself beaten to a pulp by that Neanderthal, he would probably have ended up in jail on an assault charge.

She could only hope that, now that he'd had a chance to calm down, he would leave the matter to the authorities.

Jake lifted the Eastlake chair and carefully squeezed it into the van beside the tea table. Grace's gaze lingered on the rippling muscles in his arms and back, then drifted down to admire the way the faded jeans molded that compact behind. She stared for several moments, until she realized that her heart had speeded up and breathing had became shallow and labored.

Chiding herself, she started to turn away when an old rattletrap car screeched to a stop on the other side of the street and a man jumped out. Her eyes grew wide as he cut diagonally across the street, heading for Jake with a quick determined stalk.

"Oh, my Lord. Digger!"

He was almost on Jake, who was still bent over, his upper body inside the van, when she noticed that Digger was carrying something in his hand.

As he strode nearer he raised the object and slapped it across the palm of his other hand several times, and she saw that it was a piece of scrap lumber, a two-by-four board roughly the length of a baseball bat.

Fear shot through Grace, and as Digger rounded the end of the van she dashed for the door and snatched it open. "Jake! Watch out!"

GRACE'S SCREAM snapped Jake's head around. Over his shoulder he caught a glimpse of Digger's ugly face twisted with rage and the blur of the club as he drew it back to swing. Jake ducked and tried to lunge to the side, but the warning had come a shade too late, and the board caught him in the shoulder.

He cried out in pain as the force of the blow spun him around and slammed him against the door opening, catching the sharp edge across his back.

The elderly lady beside the van screamed.

"You son-of-a-bitch!" Digger bellowed. "I'll teach you to come bothering my woman while I'm gone!"

He swung the board again, but this time Jake saw the blow coming and made a dive for Digger's knees. The board whizzed over his head and slammed into the side of the van. The woman held her head between her hands and screamed every breath.

Digger went sprawling backward and hit the ground hard with a loud, "Ooomph!" and Jake came down on top of his legs. With a roar of rage, Digger kicked out, and Jake had to roll away quickly to avoid a blow to the groin. In a continuous roll, he sprang to his feet.

"You son-of-a-bitch! I'm gonna kill you!" Digger lumbered up and came at Jake swinging.

Jake ducked the first blow, blocked the second with his forearm, then swung a punch of his own, but his injured shoulder and Digger's size worked against him. When the punch landed, it hurt Jake almost as much as it hurt Digger. As the hulk staggered back under the blow, Jake turned away and grabbed his shoulder and bent over, groaning.

The next thing he knew, Digger blindsided him. Rushing in from the side, he landed a powerful right on Jake's jaw and sent him sprawling. He fell over the box, and there was a sickening sound of china shattering as he went down hard on his injured shoulder.

"Aaaggh!"

Passersby gawked, but did nothing to intervene. As people stopped to watch, a small crowd gathered.

Digger picked up the board again and charged Jake while he was still rolling on the ground in agony, holding his shoulder. "I got you now, you son-of-a-bitch! I'm going to kill you!" His face contorted in murderous rage, he drew the board back.

A shotgun blast rent the air.

Digger stopped in his tracks, the downward swing of the board arrested. Both he and Jake looked up and saw Grace, standing on the steps of her shop, holding the gun.

The old lady by the minivan screamed and screamed, and the onlookers, who had all fallen back in fright, were gesturing and talking in excited voices.

Grace ignored everyone except the ape-like figure standing over Jake. Looking him in the eye, she pumped the action, putting another round in the chamber, and pointed the gun at Digger's midsection.

"Get away from him," she ordered. "Now! Or so help me, the next shot is going right in your gut." Grace was shaking with fury and determination. She had never been so angry in her life.

"Oh, yeah? That's big talk, girlie. You ain't got the balls to shoot me." He took a step closer to Jake and raised the board again.

Without so much as a blink, Grace brought the butt end of the shotgun to her shoulder and squinted down the barrel, pointing the end directly at Digger's belly. "Just try it."

He hesitated, staring at the icy fury in her eyes, the board still suspended. His jaw bulged and his mouth thinned. Finally, cursing, he lowered the board. "You bitch," he snarled. "I'll get you for this. See if I don't."

"Touch her, and I'll—" Before Jake, who was still writhing in pain, could gasp out the rest of the threat Digger delivered a vicious kick to his ribs.

"Ahhh!"

"You'll what, Paxton?"

"Stop that!" Grace came down the steps, her eyes blazing. "You sorry excuse for a human being. I ought to shoot you for that. Now, drop that board. Do it now!"

Frantic and panting from exertion, Caroline pushed her way through the front of crowd just as Digger tossed the board aside. "Grace! What's going on?"

She stopped short and goggled at the shotgun. "Oh my God! Was it *you* who . . . who fired that thing?" she asked, gasping for breath. "I her-heard the shot three blocks away. I was afraid you'd . . . been hurt. I ran all . . . the way."

"I'm fine. Caro, would you see to Mrs. Leeks, please?" Grace nodded toward the elderly woman who was still screaming hysterically, but her gaze never left Digger.

"Sure."

"Now, you," she ordered, jabbing the gun at Digger. "Get away from him. And get those hands up and keep them up."

"All right. All right. Just don't shoot!"

Harley came roaring up in his patrol car and had to tap the siren several times to clear a path through the crowd. He bailed out and rushed up onto the walk, his eyes widening as he they switched from Grace to Digger to Jake, who was still on the ground.

"What in the name of hell is going on here?"

"It's that Jake Paxton, Sheriff," a man in the crowd shouted. "I told you he'd be trouble."

"Yeah," someone else agreed. "You should of locked him up soon as he showed his face."

"Arrest him, Sheriff.

"Jake did not start this," Grace snapped.

"All right now, just hold on, people! Everybody settle down and let me sort this out." As the crowd's grumbling settled down, Harley turned to Grace. "You can put the gun down now, Grace."

"Not until you've got that animal in handcuffs."

Harley's eyebrows rose at her adamant tone. "Now, Gra—"

"No. I mean it, Harley. He tried to kill Jake. He would have if I hadn't stopped him. And he's the one who started this. He attacked Jake from behind for no reason." She sent a furious look at the crowd. "You all know that's true. You saw what happened. And you heard Digger say he was going to kill Jake."

"Well?" Harley's gaze swept the people in the front of the crowd. "How about it? Is that what happened?"

Clyde Ledbetter, who had run over from his service station as soon as the fight started, shuffled his feet. "Well . . . yeah, Digger did come after him with a two-by-four when he wasn't looking."

Under Harley's penetrating stare several others reluctantly corroborated the statement.

"And did any of you hear Digger threaten Jake?

"We did, Sheriff," Dwayne Ackerman said.

"That's right," his brother Dewey concurred at once. "Saw the whole thing, too, from over yonder on our bench and came a run-nin'. That feller there would a kilt Jake for sure, if Grace hadn't scared the pants off him with that shotgun blast."

"That's good enough for me. Thanks guys." Harley patted each elderly twin on the shoulder. "I'll need to take your statements later, if you could come down to the station."

The two old men puffed up with pride at being called upon to give an official statement.

"Be glad to, Sheriff."

"You bet."

Harley cuffed Digger, read him his rights and stuffed him into the back of the patrol car. Grace lowered the shotgun and hurriedly stuck it inside the shop, then rushed to Jake's side.

"Are you all right? Is your shoulder broken?"

"No, I don't think so," he replied with a grimace. "Just give me hand up, will you?"

The muscles in her arm quivered from holding the heavy weapon for so long and as she tried to help him to his feet they felt like rubber. Caroline had her hands full with Mrs. Leeks, who was still sobbing hysterically, and Grace had to call Harley over to help her. Between them, they got Jake into the delivery van.

"Tell Caroline that I'm taking him to see Dr. Watley and ask her to close up the shop for me, will you?"

"Sure thing." Harley gave the top of the van a slap to send her on her way and turned to the crowd. "Okay, folks, let's move along. Show's over. There's nothing more to see."

Thirty-One

With the main characters in the drama gone, the spectators slowly dispersed, talking and speculating among themselves as they scattered and went on their way. Among them, on the edge of the crowd, one who had witnessed the little drama from start to finish was quiet. Keen eyes were thoughtfully watching as Grace drove away with Jake. Another interesting development. This one had even more potential than the last.

The watcher smiled. Patience had paid off. Jake Paxton was so stupid. In twelve years he hadn't learned that no matter what he did or where he went he would always be doomed to failure.

His kind was fit only to wallow in degradation and shame and wretchedness. Soon he would have to give up and accept his fate. That was the only kind of life he would ever be allowed to have. Anything else was intolerable.

It would have been so simple if he had gone to prison as he should have. The thought of him locked up in a tiny cell like an animal for the rest of his life, enduring unspeakable depravities and humiliations at the hands of the other inmates, brought an almost orgasmic pleasure.

The smile faded, replaced by seething anger. It wasn't fair that Jake had managed, just barely, to escape that fate, not once but twice. He had put the watcher to a lot of trouble over the years. Now, without knowing it, the fool had just provided the means to his own downfall.

Thirty-Two

"I STILL THINK we should drive over to Bedalia and let a doctor look at your shoulder. This cut could probably use a stitch or two, as well."

Grace rinsed the bloodied washcloth in the pan of warm water on Jake's dining table. When she'd wrung it out she bent once again to carefully clean the cut on his cheek. Digger had been wearing a ring when he'd caught Jake with the blind side punch and it had ripped an inch-long gash that would probably leave a scar.

"Quit fussing, Grace. I keep telling you, my shoulder isn't broken."

Jake sat in a chair, stripped to the waist, an ice pack on the shoulder in question. A hideous bruise in the shape of the two-by-four had already formed under his skin.

"You could have at least waited at the Clinic until Dr. Watley got back from that house call. Just to be sure."

"I'm sure. I can move it just fine. It's sore is all. So just drop it."

Grace folded her mouth into a tight line. It was either that or burst into tears. She had held together through that awful scene, and afterward while she'd driven Jake to the Clinic, then home, but now she was beginning to suffer a delayed reaction. She felt wobbly and fragile, as though she would shatter into a million pieces at any moment, and her knees seemed to have turned to rubber.

Worst of all, her emotions were in tatters. When she had seen that animal swing that two-by-four at Jake's head her heart had stopped.

She had realized in that split second that she loved Jake Paxton deeply, more than life itself, and that if she lost him she would not want to live.

Now, fear and anger and love swirled together inside her like a boiling cauldron.

She finished washing the cut and dumped the washcloth in the pan of water. "It seems as though all I do lately is clean up your cuts and bruises," she grumbled as she soaked a cotton ball with alcohol.

"Hey, I didn't start the fight, remember."

They heard Caroline's sports car come up the driveway and enter the carriage house below. Grace expected her to come running up the stairs to see after Jake, and was surprised when her sister went into the house instead.

"If you hadn't gone to the trailer park none of this would have happened," she snapped, and swabbed the cut, less than gently, with the alcohol-soaked cotton ball.

"That bastard knocked T.J. ar— Ow! Dammit, you're hurting me worse than Digger did."

"Oh, really?" Planting her hands on her hips, she clenched her jaws and fought to control her rioting emotions. "Why don't I just go get Caroline to come up and take my place. I'm sure you would rather have her attention anyway," she snapped.

Fighting tears, she whirled around and would have stomped out, but Jake snagged her wrist. "Whoa. Come back here. What's the matter with you? Why are you angry with me?"

Grace raised her chin and refused to look at him. "I'm not angry," she lied. "I'm simply tired of tending you and getting nothing but complaints."

"Bullshit."

"What?" Her head whipped around.

"You heard me. Why don't you tell me what's really bugging you."

"Nothing."

"C'mon, tell me, Grace."

She ground her teeth. Her nerves were frayed almost to breaking point and his relentless prodding snapped the last thread.

"All right, I will! I am sick and tired of being upset. Ever since you came back here I haven't had a minute's peace. You've completely turned my life upside down, Jake Paxton. At every turn I've been forced to defend you, when I swore from the start that I would not get involved. I've insulted and alienated people I've known all my life, I've lost my temper and argued in public and made a spectacle of myself. I even hit poor Frank Sheffield. I've been worried sick over T.J., and over your safety. And now, on top of everything else, that horrible fight. *That's* what's bothering me."

"But that's not all, is it, Grace?"

She shot him an aggravated look, her mouth pinching. "Is it?"

"No! It's not! You seduce me and claim to care about me and then turn around and start dating my sister. I am sick to death of watching the two of you together!"

He looked up at her for so long that Grace began to squirm. "Are you jealous, Grace?"

"Certainly not."

"No? It sure sounds that way."

"Well, you're wrong." She tugged her arm, but he tightened his hold. "Will you let me go?"

"No. Never."

"What?" She looked at him sharply, blinking.

"I don't want Caroline," he said softly. "The only woman I want is you. The only woman I've ever wanted is you. I love you, Grace."

The soft declaration took her breath away. Her heart seemed to turn over in her chest. She looked down into that dark, sternly handsome face, those intense green eyes, and was so filled with emotion she felt as though she would burst. Tears filled her eyes and her chin wobbled.

"Do you mean that?" she whispered, barely getting the words past her aching throat.

"I've never meant anything more in my life."

"But you and Caroline—"

"Are friends. Nothing more."

Relief gushed through Grace like a hot tide, and her tears spilled over. "Oh, Jake," she said achingly. "I've been so miserable."

He pulled her to stand between his legs and looked up at her tenderly. "I know. At least, I hoped you would be."

She leaned back in the circle of his arms, her eyes growing wide. "You mean . . . you and Caro were deliberately *trying* to make me jealous?"

"Yeah," he admitted a bit ruefully. "I'm sorry, Grace. I never wanted to hurt you, but it was the only thing we could think of to make you admit your feelings. I was desperate. Please don't be angry." He circled her waist and pulled her close, pressing his face against her midriff.

Wrapping her arms around him, she sighed and laid her cheek against the top of his head. "I'm not angry. I probably should be, but I'm not. I guess, because you were right."

He stilled. Slowly, he pulled back and looked into her eyes, his own smoldering. "Does that mean that you do love me?"

A soft smile curved her mouth, and she looked at him tenderly and stroked her fingers through the hair at his temples. "Yes, I love you, Jake. I love you so much it hurts."

His arms tightened around her and he closed his eyes. "Thank God."

Circling her waist with his hands, he eased her back a step and stood up, sending the ice pack tumbling to the floor with a thunk.

Then she was in his arms, where she wanted to be, crushed against that bare chest, her fingers curling in the mat of silky hair as their lips met and clung in a kiss so rife with emotion her heart swelled painfully and tears seeped from beneath her lowered lashes. It was not a kiss of carnal desire, but a pledge of love, a bonding of souls, a promise of forever.

When it was over their lips clung, then parted slowly. Grace opened her heavy eyelids and looked up into the greenest eyes she had ever seen.

"Say it again. I want to be sure I'm not dreaming."

Grace smiled, knowing what he wanted to hear. "I love you,

Jake Paxton, with all my heart and soul."

His pupils flared and the look in his eyes was so fiercely loving she felt as though she were drowning in those green depths. "I love you too, Grace. God, how I love you."

She surged forward and snuggled her face against his bare chest, and his arms wrapped around her. For a long time they just stood there, holding each other tight, savoring the love that they had so nearly lost, and that was now theirs to share.

"Come on," he said softly at last, and turning, one arm still looped around her waist to hold her close against his side, he led her down the hall to his bedroom.

Grace went as in a dream, her steps slow and measured her head resting on his shoulder, but when he pulled her down on the bed and began to work open the buttons than ran down the front of her skirt, from waist to hem, she awoke.

"Jake, darling, we can't. You're hurt."

"Ah, sweetheart, the way I feel right now, nothing could cause me pain."

"But, Jake—"

"Shh."

"But—"

When he couldn't hush her any other way, he simply covered her mouth with his.

The protest dissolved on Grace's tongue. The kiss was a tender ravishment. Her mouth flowered open, and Jake's tongue dipped in repeatedly, drinking from her sweetness like a man dying of thirst. "You taste like heaven," he murmured as he rubbed his mouth back and forth over hers. "I'll never get enough of you. Never."

The passionate avowal sent Grace's heart soaring. Her husband had never been a passionate lover. Charles hadn't made love; he'd had sex, and that had always been more a matter of dominance than pleasure. Whatever scant attraction he had felt for her had faded within months of their marriage.

Jake strung a line of kisses up the side of her neck, and Grace sighed and tipped her head to one side to give him better access, her whole body responding to the caress with an aching quiver.

She felt like a woman awakening from a long, comatose sleep. She had never before experienced the exquisite sensations that Jake aroused in her so easily, with a mere touch, a look.

Jake eased back and smiled and ran his forefinger over her kiss-swollen lips. "You see. No pain. Now, where was I?" he murmured, and went to work on the buttons once more.

The gold-rimmed white buttons were big square things that were difficult to handle, but he managed to undo every one without the least trouble. He grasped the edges of the green linen skirt and spread them wide. He stilled for a moment, gazing almost reverently at her slender body.

"I used to dream about doing this back when we were in high school. About stripping away your proper clothes, one by one, and looking my fill."

"Jake!" Color crept over Grace's face and chest.

"I used to wonder what kind of panties you wore, those full brief type or bikini." He looked at the tiny scrap of white satin and lace visible through her pantyhose and smiled. "I'm glad to see I was right."

Grace blushed crimson again, and his smile widened.

He bent his head and placed his open mouth against her belly. His hot breath seeped through her pantyhose and skated over her skin, filled her navel, sending a delicious shiver through her.

Grace sank her hands into his hair and winnowed her fingers through the thick strands, ran them over his scalp, luxuriating in the freedom to touch and caress him.

Distantly, with that small part of her brain that still functioned, she thought of her vow never to let this happen again, but she could not drum up even the slightest bit of guilt or remorse. How could this be wrong, when it felt so right? So absolutely perfect? So meant to be?

Her hands drifted down the back of his neck, then over his broad shoulders and back. His skin was warm against her palms, the muscles hard.

"I have to admit, though, my adolescent fantasies ran more to a garter belt and stockings. I used to imagine making love to you while you were still wearing them."

"Jake Paxton! You didn't!"

"Yep." He grinned. "We'll have to try it sometime. For now, let's get rid of these." Getting to his knees, he peeled down her pantyhose and sent them sailing, then lifted her slightly, stripped away her knit top and did the same with it.

He paused and stared at her body, clad in only two tiny wisps of satin and lace. Tracing the edge of her bra, he ran his fingers down to the front closure and casually, effortlessly, flicked it open.

Her breasts spilled from the fragile cups and into his waiting hands. With a sigh of satisfaction, Jake bent his head and flicked one nipple with his tongue. The sensitive nerve endings tingled and the bud swelled and hardened. He treated the other to the same sweet torture, and a little moan rippled from Grace's throat.

Jake stripped away the tiny panties and tossed them aside, then sprawled out on his belly between her legs, half covering her. As his flesh met hers she moaned again, and he gave a low chuckle. "I like that sound." His lips closed around her nipple, drawing it into the hot wetness of his mouth to suckle deeply.

"Oh, Jake. Oh." Eyes shut, Grace rolled her head from side to side on the pillow. Her back arched with the rhythmic tugging, her fingers digging deep into the firm flesh of his shoulders.

He raised his head and looked at her. "Do you like that, sweetheart?"

"Yes. *Yes!* Oh, Jake!"

In restless passion, her hands ran over his shoulders, his neck, down his chest. Her fingers threaded through the silky hairs, tugged, kneaded.

As Jake lavished the same attention on her other breast his broad palm slid downward. Grace whimpered when his hand stroked her belly. The whimper turned to a moan when his seeking fingers found the moist core of her desire.

He lifted his head from her breasts and looked down at her, his face taut and flushed with passion. "Oh, sweetheart, I wanted to make this last, but I can't wait any longer."

With jerky movements, he stood up and stripped off his jeans, briefs and socks in one quick movement and kicked them aside.

When he returned to Grace, she smiled. Her arms enfolded him, and as their lips met, Jake slid his hands beneath her hips, lifted her and thrust deep.

Grace gasped, her body taut and trembling as she absorbed the shock, his heat, his hardness.

He stilled. "Did I hurt you?"

"No. No!" Her hands clutched his bare shoulders. "I . . . oh, Jake."

Bracing up on his forearms, he looked at her, and his frown faded. Seeing in her flushed face and dazed eyes the helpless passion she could not hide, he smiled, a slow, loving smile that softened his stern face. "I know, sweetheart. "I know."

He rotated his hips against her, and the smile deepened at her little groan. He repeated the action.

"Oh . . . please." It was both a cry for mercy and a plea for more.

Lowering his head, he nibbled the sensitive skin beneath her jaw. With a slow undulation, he moved within her. The warm, moist heat of his breath filled her ear as he whispered, "Ah, Grace. My love."

His tongue dipped into the fragile shell, wetting it, stroking it, the tiny thrusts matching the rhythm of his rocking hips.

Making a desperate little sound, Grace arched her back, her fingernails digging into the hard muscles of his back.

Jake grunted. Abruptly, he abandoned his teasing torment. His breathing grew harsher, his movements stronger, more deliberate. Grace wrapped her legs around him and matched his urgent movements, her hips rising to meet each powerful thrust. "Oh, God, Grace! Yes! *Yes!*"

"Ja-aake!"

A SHORT WHILE LATER, lying naked in Jake's arms, cuddled against his side, Grace realized that she had never been so happy before.

She smiled to herself and absently twined her fingers through his chest hair.

Jake's encircling arm rubbed up and down hers with hypnotic slowness. "Grace?"

"Mmm?"

"Do you remember the first time we met?"

She thought for a second. "No. Not really."

"I do. You were five years old. I was seven. You were in Humphries Hardware store with your parents. You were watching the electric train that old man Humphries had on display."

She raised up and looked at him, her eyes wide. "You're kidding. And you remember that?"

He looked at her with that intense stare that used to frighten her, and her heart skipped a beat. He stroked her cheek with his free hand. "I remember everything about you."

"Oh, darling." She turned her head and kissed his palm, then snuggled her head back into the crook of his shoulder and sighed.

"I had sneaked into the store to watch the train myself," he continued in a reminiscent voice. "And to enjoy the cool air-conditioned air for a few minutes before old man Humphries discovered me and chased me out. When I saw you, I forgot all about the train.

"The contrast between us was painfully obvious to me, even at that tender age." His chest lifted with a little snort of laughter. "As usual, I was dirty and barefoot, wearing hand-me-downs that were little better than rags that some church group had given Lizzie.

"But you . . . God, you were so pretty and so perfect with your golden curls and big blue eyes and your pretty clothes. You were spotless and fairylike. I remember you were wearing a frilly pink organdy dress with matching socks and patent leather Mary Janes. Those pink socks were trimmed with lace. I'd never seen lace on socks before. I thought you were a princess.

"I just stood there, awestruck, and stared at you," he mused.

Grace tipped her head up on his shoulder, and she saw that his face had a faraway look. She sensed that, for some reason, this was more than just a random memory from childhood.

"At first you didn't notice me. When I sidled into the store you were standing there, absolutely enthralled, looking with an expression of wonder at that little train chugging around the store. Then you happened to see me staring at you and you got this frightened look.

"You panicked and turned away to run back to your parents, but in your rush you fell and skinned your knee. Of course, right away you started bawling, and your mother came running. I was afraid at first that she was going to hit you for crying. Jesus, I was shocked when she gathered you in her arms and hugged and kissed you and wiped your tears and talked to you in that soft voice.

"I'd never seen anything like it. Whenever I cried I got a slap or a kick from Lizzie."

"Oh, Jake, no." Grace looked up at him in anguish, hurting for that little boy.

He shrugged, as though it didn't matter, but Grace could see that it did. "Most of the time Lizzie was so soused she hardly knew I was around, which suited me just fine. When she sobered up enough to notice me, all I got was the rough edge of her tongue and knocked around, so mostly I just stayed out of her way.

"But standing there in that hardware store, watching your mother comfort you, seeing the love and tenderness in her face as she crooned to you and wiped your tears . . ." Jake shook his head. "I was mesmerized. All of my life that scene has stuck with me. To have a mother like yours, the security and warmth and love that you had, for years was my most secret and cherished childhood fantasy."

Every word of the poignant story wrung Grace's heart. She rose up again and looked at him with tears in her eyes. "Oh, my darling. You must have hated me."

He smiled tenderly and stroked a lock of hair away from her face. "No, I could never hate you. You were my own secret fairy princess. Oh, I'll admit, at first I was envious. You had everything that I didn't, that I would never have. Later though—about the time you entered junior high school—I saw in you the same gentleness and sweetness of character that I'd seen in your mother, and I fell head-over-heels in love. I've loved you ever since."

"Jake!" Grace stared at him, flabbergasted. "All this time? I don't believe it. You had all those other girls, and you never even spoke to me."

"I didn't dare. To me, you were all that was soft and gentle and loving in a world that was mostly harsh and ugly. Even before I was accused of murdering Carla Mae, I knew I had about as much chance of ever having the love of someone like you as I did of flying to the moon. So I merely looked and yearned. And dreamed."

"Oh, Jake, I wish I'd known," she said in a quivering voice. She gazed at him, her heart nearly breaking with pity and love.

Jake's mouth quirked. "What would you have done? Defied public opinion, maybe even your parents, and gone out with me? I don't think so. You were so timid back in those days, and so afraid of me, you would have probably run screaming."

Grace bit her lip. She wanted to deny the charge, but it was true. Jake had unnerved her. She felt so ashamed. "I'm sorry," she whispered.

"Don't be. I would never have approached you. I didn't think I had the right. But all that's changed now. It took me years, but I finally realized that if you want something you should go after it with all you've got. Because you never know what kind of blow fate will deal you next."

He picked up her hand and kissed her palm, watching her all the while. The warm caress sent shivers racing through her.

"After the trials I left Cedar Grove, swearing I was through with this town and everyone in it, including you. I was going to start over and make something of my life and put those first hellacious twenty-one years behind me.

"But you continued to haunt my dreams. The memory of you made all the other women I met pale by comparison. "So I came back—for two things; to prove that I didn't kill that girl, and for you. I knew from the start that I might never win your love, but at least I would know it wasn't because I hadn't tried."

Thirty-Three

THE NEXT MORNING Grace awoke with a start. Disoriented at first to find herself in a strange room, cuddled against a warm male body, she sucked in a sharp breath. Then memories of the previous night returned, and she smiled and snuggled her face back on Jake's shoulder and relaxed . . . until her drowsy gaze happened to encounter the clock on the nightstand.

"Oh, my heavens!" Jerking to a sitting position, she threw back the covers and scooted for the edge of the bed. Before she could stand, a hard arm hooked around her waist from behind.

"Whoa. Where're you going, gorgeous?" Jake's sexy voice rumbled in her ear.

"Let me go, Jake. I'm late. Oh, I can't believe it! I overslept. I've never done that in my life."

"What's the rush?"

"I've got to open the shop. And you should be getting ready for work, too."

"Mmm, there's no rush." He propped his sandpapery chin on her shoulder and murmured sleepily, "I've got pull with the boss."

"Jake Paxton. Get out of that bed this instant. We should both be leaving in ten minutes."

"Slave driver."

"Up."

"I got an idea. Why don't we take a few days off and stay here? Just the two of us."

"I can't do that. Since Edith quit, I don't have anyone to cover for me at the shop. Now let me go." She plucked at his encircling arm but she couldn't budge him.

"Shoot, is that all? I can fix that." He snatched the telephone off the bedside table and punched out a number. "Who are you calling?"

He smiled mysteriously. "Hi, Caro. Listen, Grace needs a few days off. Can you—" He stopped and a lazy grin curved his mouth. "Yeah. Everything's great." Another pause, and then a masculine chuckle. "Mmm. Yeah, I'll say. Uh-hmm. Yes she did. Uh-huh. That's right. All night."

"Jake, what are you telling her?" Grace made a grab for the telephone but he fended her off easily. "Say, listen, Caro, can you mind the shop for a few days?"

"*Caro?* Are you crazy?"

"Great. Come on up when you get ready and Grace will give you the keys and whatever instructions you'll need." He started to hang up, then paused. "Oh, and Caro. Thanks."

He replaced the receiver and gave Grace a smug look. "She'll be up in a few minutes."

"Jake, Caroline can't run the shop. She doesn't know anything about antiques. And she has no experience working in retail sales."

"How do you know? Have you asked her?"

That stopped her cold. "Well . . . no. But, I just assumed—"

"You shouldn't make assumptions about people, sweetheart. And you might be surprised at what your sister knows and what experience she's had. Anyway, she'll do fine for a few days. Everything in the store has a price tag on it and you're not expecting any new shipments for the rest of the week. She can reconcile a cash register. So what's the problem?"

"Well . . . I . . ."

He turned her head around with a finger on her chin and kissed her. The kiss was affectionate and hot, and a stunning experience so early in the morning. By the time he lifted his head her eyes were glazed and she'd forgotten what they were discussing. He took shameless advantage immediately.

"Just think," he murmured against the side of her neck as he nibbled the tender skin there. "This is Wednesday. We could have . . ." His tongue batted her earlobe, then he nipped it gently. ". . . five whole days off. And if we . . ." He mouthed her ear, his hot breath filling it. ". . . don't tell anyone . . ." His tongued delved into her ear and swirled, and Grace trembled. ". . . where we are . . ." He let the thought trail off tantalizingly and took her mouth in another long, heated kiss.

When he lifted his head he grinned wickedly. "So how about it? You wanna play hooky?"

"Mmm," she said dreamily. "That sounds like heaven."

WHEN CAROLINE CAME IN a short while later, Grace was in the kitchen making breakfast, something she had been sure she would never be able to do. Not in that kitchen. She still got a tingle whenever her gaze strayed to a particular spot on the counter.

She didn't hear her sister enter and didn't know she was there until Caroline said in a sultry voice, "Well, well, well. I would never have believed it if I hadn't seen it with my own eyes."

Grace whirled and saw Caroline leaning negligently against the door frame, her arms crossed. She smiled. "Good morning, Caro."

Starting at Grace's bare feet, Caroline's gaze inspected every inch of her, slowly climbing her legs and taking in Jake's shirt, which reached almost to her knees, her whisker burned mouth and neck, her glowing eyes, and finally her tousled mane.

"It certainly must be. From the look of you it must have been one helluva night, too."

Grace blushed but she met her sister's amused look head on. "It was."

The straightforward statement sent one of Caroline's brows arching skyward. "So, you've finally kicked over the traces, have you? Thank goodness. It's about time."

"All I know right now is I'm very happy," Grace said with a light laugh as she turned back to beating pancake batter. "By the way, my keys are by my purse on the table right behind you."

Caroline retrieved the keys and returned to the doorway, twirling them around her finger.

"So, where is Jake?"

"He's shaving."

"Mmm. Tell him to try that *before* you go to bed," she drawled, eyeing Grace's abraded skin.

"Caro!"

Caroline's expression turned serious. "I just want to know one thing. Do you love him?"

A soft look entered Grace's eyes as she looked over her shoulder at her sister. "Oh, yes. I love him."

"It's not going to be easy, you know."

"I know."

"Which reminds me, what do I tell people if they ask where you are?"

Grace stopped beating the batter, surprised and a bit unnerved by the question. Some of her happiness faded as the full consequences of her action sank in. She loved Jake, and she wanted to believe that they could somehow overcome the past and build a life together. Still . . . a lifetime of circumspect living was difficult to break, she discovered. The thought of revealing her and Jake's relationship to the world frightened her.

Her first gut instinct was to avoid becoming embroiled in a controversy. At that point she had no idea which way her relationship with Jake was headed or if they *could* work out a future together. If he even wanted that. She wasn't Caroline.

She couldn't—wouldn't—stir up a furor without a good reason.

"I doubt that anyone will ask about Jake, but if they ask about me, tell them I've gone to an antique auction out of state."

Caroline's eyebrows rose. "I don't believe it. You *are* going to lie."

"She doesn't want anyone to know about us," Jake said from the doorway.

Grace whirled around guiltily. The anger and hurt in Jake's eyes made her feel terrible. "Jake, I . . ."

"Why don't you just say it, Grace. You're ashamed of me."

"No!"

"No? It sure looks that way to me."

"Uh, look, I think I'll go and let you two hash this out in private," Caroline said, backing out the door.

Her footsteps clattered down the stairs, but neither Grace nor Jake moved. They stared into one another's eyes. hurt and guilt simmering in the air between them.

"Jake . . . darling. You're wrong. Please don't be angry with me. I . . . this just isn't the right time. We've just gotten together."

"Ah, I see. To you this is just a fling. No point in making it public knowledge and ruining your spotless reputation, when it will end soon, right?"

"No! That's not it at all! I just think we need a little time. Both of us."

"Time for what?"

"To . . . to get to know one another better. To be sure of. . . well . . ."

"Our feelings for each other?" Jake gave a mirthless little bark of laughter. "Maybe you're not sure, but I thought I made my feelings pretty damned clear. Hell, woman, I bared my soul to you."

Stricken, she recalled the words he'd said to her the night before, how he had silently loved her and longed for her most of his life. Miserable, she ran to him and wrapped her arms around his waist, burying her face against his chest. "Oh, Jake, darling, I'm sorry. I'm so sorry."

He held her close and lifted her face. "Just answer one question. Do you love me, Grace?"

The look in his eyes, so hot and full of love, filled her with choking emotion. Like a geyser, hot and insistent and irrepressible, it rushed up inside her, swelling her heart to overflowing. She gazed up at him with all she was feeling swimming in her eyes. "Yes," she said in a quavering whisper. "Oh, yes, Jake. I love you so much."

Something flared in his eyes. He cupped her face with both hands. "Do you mean it?"

The hint of doubt in his voice, in that strong face, wrung her heart. Smiling tenderly, she turned her head and pressed a kiss into his palm. Placing her hand over his, she held it close against her cheek and met his gaze. "Yes, I mean it. I love you, Jake Paxton, with all my heart and soul."

He closed his eyes briefly, and a shudder rippled through him. The next instant, he snatched her close against his bare chest and wrapped his arms around her as though he meant never to let her go. He laid his cheek against the top of her head and whispered fiercely. "Then that's enough. For now, that's enough."

Thirty-Four

"I DEMAND THAT YOU TELL ME where Grace is. She didn't attend church Wednesday night, and she missed the quilting bee at Verna's today, without calling to say she wouldn't be there, I might add. And I tried calling the farm, but there's no answer. I even drove out there and knocked on the door. Is she sick?"

Caroline looked at Lyle with distaste. She had followed Grace's instruction and told everyone else that she was on a buying trip, but she couldn't resist goading Lyle.

"She's fine. I expect she's up at Jake's apartment. She's been tending to him ever since the fight with Digger."

Which was partially true. Jake didn't need any tending, but Grace had been up there for four days now. If those two didn't come up for air soon she was going to have to march up there and roust them out. She was running out of excuses for Grace's absence.

"What!" Caroline almost laughed out loud at Lyle's livid expression. "This situation is absolutely intolerable. Something must be done to get rid of Paxton."

The bell over the door tinkled, but Lyle was so wound up he barely acknowledged Harley when he walked in. The sheriff winked at Caroline and stood to one side, leaning against the wall, his arms crossed over his chest, taking in the tirade with a faint twist to his mouth.

"Verna told me about that disgusting brawl," Lyle spat. "She was in town getting her hair done and she saw most of it. I couldn't believe my ears. Grace fired a shotgun and held it on a man! This is all Paxton's influence. I knew all along that he was trouble. I warned Grace not to take him in, not to give him a job, but would she listen? No. She's too compassionate for her own good. What she needs is a strong man to lean on, someone who will take her in hand and guide her."

Caroline hooted. "Who? You? What a joke."

Lyle swelled up like a toad. "Are you insinuating that I am a wimp?"

"No. I'm not insinuating anything. I'm saying it straight out."

She watched with glee as his face turned purple. He looked like he wanted to hit her. Finally he drew himself up and looked down his nose at her. "I'm hardly concerned with what you think about anything. Considering who and what you are, your opinion isn't worth worrying about."

Harley stiffened. He abandoned his casual post against the wall and walked up to the counter. "That sounded awfully close to an insult, Lyle. I sure hope you didn't mean it to be, 'cause I don't stand for anyone insulting a lady in my presence."

"A lady?" Lyle scoffed, but Harley's hard look instantly erased his sneering expression. "Caroline and I were just having a friendly disagreement," he said resentfully.

He scowled at Caroline again. "I've a good mind to drive out to the farm and put a stop to this foolishness Grace has gotten herself into, once and for all."

"I wouldn't, if I were you," Caroline advised. "She wouldn't take kindly to that, I promise you. Anyway, didn't you and Grace quarrel the last time you were at the farm? As I recall, she told me she'd thrown you out and told you to stay out of her life."

She could see that he was incensed and embarrassed that Grace had told her about the disagreement. That tickled her pink.

"Nonsense," Lyle blustered. "Grace has had plenty of time to get over that little tiff. Besides, I have a right to look after Grace. She's still part of my family."

"Jeez, you're a pompous ass," Caroline said, rolling her eyes. "When are you going to get it through your thick head that you don't have any rights where my sister is concerned? And remember, the last time you were at the farm, Grace threatened to have Harley throw you off her property if you ever bothered her again."

"Grace didn't mean that."

"Oh, she meant it all right."

"Nonsense. She was just in one of those moods you women get into."

Harley leaned his elbow on the counter and looked Lyle in the eye. "I gotta warn you, Lyle, if you ignore Grace's warning she'll have a perfect right to charge you with harassment and stalking, and if she does, you better believe that I'll damn well arrest you."

Lyle was getting more angry by the second. He looked like the top of his head was about to blow off. "May I remind you, Sheriff Newcomb, just who it is you're talking to? The Ames family runs Cedar Grove, and without our support, you could find yourself out of a job."

"True," Harley replied, unfazed. "But as long as I am sheriff, I'm going to do my job the right way."

Lyle glared for several seconds, then stormed out in a huff, setting the bell over the door to jingling.

"Well, well. I'm impressed. You handled that very well," Caroline said, eyeing the sheriff with reluctant admiration. It annoyed her that she found him attractive. He wasn't her type at all. She didn't waste her time on small-town, good-old-boy or straight-arrow types, and most especially not lawmen, and Harley was all three.

"Well, thank you, ma'am. Glad to be of service."

"Could you just drop the ma'am business? It makes me think of little old ladies in shawls sitting in rocking chairs. I'm not quite there yet."

"Whatever you say, sugar."

She narrowed her eyes at him. "You can drop the sugar crap, too."

Harley merely grinned.

"So what brings you here, Hop-A-Long? Did you just stop by to shoot the breeze, or just to help me get rid of that dickhead,

Lyle."

"Now, sugar, I told you to cut out that talking dirty. I don't like it. And it's not at all attractive in a woman."

"Tough. It's the way I talk. If you don't like it, there's the door."

"Now Caroline, you know you only talk like that to shock people. It's not you at all. I remember how you were, growing up. A little headstrong and spirited, but not really bad. How could you be, with your upbringing?"

"Aren't you forgetting something? I ran off with a married man when I was seventeen. Most people around here call that pretty bad."

"Shoot, if you want my opinion, that yahoo you ran off with was more to blame than you. After all, he was a married man in his thirties and who seduced a young and impressionable teenager."

Caroline's expression was wry.

"All right. So you made a big mistake when you were just a kid. That doesn't mean the die is cast."

"In Cedar Grove it does. God, where have you been all these years?" she argued stubbornly. "Besides, I like my life and it's none of your business."

"What if I made it my business?"

The question startled her. "Why would you want to?"

Harley rubbed the back of his neck. "Damned if I know."

"Men," she muttered, rolling her eyes.

"There's going to be an Easter picnic in the park next Sunday after church," he said out of the blue. "I thought maybe you'd like to go with me."

"Me? Go to a church social? With you?"

"Yep."

She laughed and drawled, "Well you thought wrong. I'm not interested. You're not even my type."

Harley was undaunted. He merely grinned. "How do you know? That's like saying you don't like a dish when you haven't even tasted it."

"I don't have to taste rattlesnake to know I wouldn't like it.

"You think I'm a snake?"

No. She thought he was a nice man, and that's what scared her. "Look, Sheriff, we don't have anything in common, okay? I'm not interested."

"Sure you are. You just don't want to admit it. What's the matter? Afraid you'll ruin your reputation?" He winked and headed for the door. "I'll pick you up after church about one."

Caroline was so stunned she was speechless for once. He stopped and looked back. "Oh, and when you're packing our picnic basket, remember I like my chicken fried extra crispy and potato salad made with a touch of mustard."

"You can take your potato salad and stick it up your—" He wagged his finger at her. "Ah, ah, ah. Remember what I said, no dirty talk."

Caroline's mouth dropped. "I'm not going!" she yelled, when she recovered her senses, but he had already strolled away down the sidewalk with that fluid, hip-rolling cowboy gait.

Thirty-Five

NURSING A BEER, Connie lay sprawled on the sagging sofa in her trailer, feeling sorry for herself. Damn that Digger anyway. He'd been in jail for five days, and he was furious with her because she hadn't gotten him out. The bastard. Like she was supposed to get the money for his bail out of thin air.

But that wouldn't cut no ice with Digger. When he did get out he'd probably beat the crap out of her, worse than he had T.J.

She glanced down the short hall toward the bedroom where her son was sleeping. That was another thing. Thanks to her sniveling kid, that busybody, Josie Beaman, or her preacher boyfriend, or both, were constantly on her case. Always snooping around, checking up on her.

So Digger had knocked the kid around a little. So what? All kids got whacked now and then. She had. Plenty of times. How else was you gonna keep the little brats in line, she'd like to know.

She took another swig of beer and wiped her mouth with the back of her hand and glared at the flickering image on the TV screen. To top it all off, the frigging sound had gone out on the television. What was she? A damned lip reader, for Crissake.

Shit. Her life sucked.

And it was all Jake Paxton's fault. He could have run Digger off and taken his place if he'd wanted to.

Connie's skin tingled at the thought of it. Jake was even better-looking than he'd been at sixteen when they used to get it on, down at Neeson's Cove. He was bigger too, his shoulders wider, that lean body all filled out with muscles. She'd bet under them jeans and T-shirt he was all sleek and sexy, not a hairy gorilla like

Digger.

She wondered if he was as good a lover as he'd been as a teenager. She'd sure like to find out.

She snorted. Fat chance of that happening. He knew what she wanted. She'd sent him plenty of signals. But no. He acted as though he thought he was too good for her, anymore.

Huh! He wasn't no better'n her. Just Lizzie Paxton's bastard and probably a murderer to boot. He had one helluva nerve, looking down his nose at Connie Tolson. She'd sure as hell been good enough for him to screw fifteen years ago.

She heard a thump out back by the trash can. Shit. Those damned cats again. Last time they'd had a fight out there they'd scattered the smelly garbage all over the place. Old Mr. Landers, who ran the trailer park, about had a hissy fit. He threatened to have her evicted if she didn't fix her garbage can so the varmints couldn't get into it.

"Meow!"

Holding the long-neck bottle in the loose circle made by her thumb and forefinger, Connie heaved herself off the sofa, staggered down the hall to the back door and flung it open. "Shut up and git the hell outta here!" she yelled. "There are people around here trying to sleep!"

The garbage can clattered. Cursing, Connie staggered down the steps and around the end of the trailer. "I said git—"

The blow struck the back of her head, hard enough that she collapsed onto her knees and saw stars. She went sprawling, face first into the dirt, half in and half out. She felt a sharp pain in her back. Then another, and another, and she realized finally that she was being stabbed.

"N-No. Please, n-no," she begged. She tried to roll over onto her back and raise her arm to ward off the blows, but her assailant was stronger and the knife kept plunging into her over and over.

She moaned and slipped into darkness.

Thirty-Six

"DON'T GO."

Grace laughed as she allowed Jake to pull her back into his arms. "Darling, you know I don't want to leave you, but I have to. If I didn't attend estate sales and auctions I would soon be out of business."

"Send Caroline."

"I can't do that."

"Why not? She'd love it."

"Because she'd probably pay three times what everything was worth and bankrupt me."

It was true that in the four days her sister had covered for her at the shop she had shown an amazing aptitude for retailing. Much to Grace's surprise, she'd apparently also developed an interest in antiques. The night before, when Grace had dashed down to the house to get a change of clothes Caroline had actually been studying a book on the subject. However, that in no way qualified her to buy.

"Ah, c'mon. Give her a chance. We'll stay here and handle the shop. At least that way we'll be together." He grinned wickedly. "We could even try out that old horsehair sofa in the storeroom."

"Jake! We'll do no such thing."

"Why not? We could hang the Out to Lunch sign on the door and lock it."

"You're insatiable."

"Hmm. And you love it," he murmured, nuzzling her neck.

"I love you." She turned her head and kissed him. He tried to deepen the caress but she made a tormented sound and pulled back. "None of that. If I'm going to get to Palestine in time to preview the estate I have to go. And you have to go to work. I'm sure Caroline needs your help with the heavy work."

"Slave driver," he growled, but he patted her bottom as she climbed into the van. Holding the door open, he leaned inside for another kiss. "You're coming straight home, aren't you?"

"Yes. It'll be after closing time before I could possibly get back."

"Good. I'll be here. If you're real good, I might even have dinner ready."

"You're spoiling me."

"Honey, you ain't seen nothin' yet," he drawled. His eyes grew serious as they roamed her face, and he touched her cheek with his fingertip. "Having you to spoil is something I've fantasized about for years. I mean to enjoy it to the hilt."

He shut the door and slapped the top of the van. "Now go on. And be careful."

"I will."

She waved and drove off down the gravel driveway. Jake watched her until she was out of sight. God, he loved that woman. And she loved him. Mary Grace Somerset loved him.

Grinning, he took the stairs two at a time. For the first time in his life he believed in miracles.

While he was shaving, the wide double doors of the carriage house slid open and a moment later Caroline went roaring down the drive in her racy little car. Jake grinned and swiped another strip of shaving cream off his cheek. The shop didn't open for another hour. Caroline's enthusiasm for the work was almost comical. If she wasn't careful she was going to turn out to be a responsible upstanding citizen.

Half an hour later Jake was about to climb into his truck when two patrol cars turned into the drive. He stopped and watched them through narrowed eyes. There were no sirens or red lights flashing, but the way they came roaring up the drive gave him a bad feeling in his gut.

They came to a screeching halt, one on either side of him, and in an instant the four uniformed men were out of the cars, guns drawn and braced on top of the open doors, pointed straight at him.

"Freeze, Paxton!"

Jake recognized the voice as belonging to Frank Sheffield, the driver of the second car, but his gaze went to Harley. "What the hell is this, Newcomb?"

"I said *freeze!*" Frank yelled again. "Move another inch and I'll blow your head off, scumbag."

Jake gritted his teeth, but he didn't move. That idiot Sheffield was itching for an excuse to shoot him."

"Take it easy, Frank. I'll handle this," Harley cautioned. "You're under arrest, Jake," he said, squinting down the barrel of his .357 Magnum. "Up against the wall and spread 'm. Nice and slow, like."

Jake glanced from Harley to Frank and at the taut faces of the other two deputies. Slowly, seething, he turned and complied. At once Frank rushed up and poked his revolver in Jake's back with more force than necessary and kicked his legs wider. The action smashed Jake's face into the rough barn siding and he felt a splinter break the skin of his cheek.

"Move," Frank hissed in his ear. "Please move. Just twitch. Give me an excuse to blow you the shit away."

"Fuck you, asshole."

The barrel of Frank's gun rapped him over the right ear and pain exploded in Jake's head. For an instant he saw stars.

"Dammit, Frank! I told you, no unnecessary force. Now back off!" Harley bellowed.

"He's a no good murdering son-of-a-bitch and—"

"I said get away from him!"

The gun barrel in Jake's back pressed deeper, and he held his breath. Then Frank released him and the other two deputies took his place.

While one of the men frisked him the other stood to one side in a ready position, arms extended, his gun held in a two-handed grip, pointed at Jake's head.

"He's clean."

"Good. Cuff him."

As the young deputy complied, Harley came forward, holstering his revolver.

"What is this about, Harley?" Jake demanded through clenched teeth.

"Chief Newcomb, to you, dickhead."

Both men ignored Frank's outburst. Jake's furious gaze blazed at the sheriff. Harley met it with heavy resignation. "Murder one."

Murder. The word went through Jake like an electrical shock. Oh, God, not again. Not again. Tamping down his emotions, Jake managed a sarcastic smile and a smart-assed tone. "Is that right? Who am I suppose to have murdered this time?"

"Don't play dumb. You know who!" Frank took a threatening step toward Jake, but a look from Harley stopped him.

"Jake Paxton, you're under arrest for the murder of Connie Tolson. Be advised that anything you say can and will be held against you. You are entitled to an attorney. If you cannot afford an attorney, one will be provided . . ."

As Harley continued to advise him of his rights in that droning monotone Jake squeezed his eyes shut. Grace. Oh, God, Grace.

Thirty-Seven

DUSK WAS FALLING when Grace reached the city limits of Cedar Grove. Anxious to get back to Jake, she drove through town a little faster than the law allowed. She smiled and waved to a couple of people on the street and returned Mr. Peabody's honk when he drove past her going in the opposite direction, but the gestures, expected courtesies in a small town, were automatic. Grace's mind was on getting home as quickly as she could. It had been a fruitful business trip, but the day had seemed interminable.

Soon, though, she would be home, and in Jake's arms.

She smiled to herself. She was behaving like a schoolgirl in the throes of first love, but she couldn't help it. Happiness bubbled through her like sparkling wine. Complications and problems lay ahead for them. She knew that. Maybe more than they could handle, but she would face those when the time came. For now she could feel only joy. She was in love—truly in love—for the first time in her life, and it was glorious.

Out of habit, she glanced at the shop as she drew near. Grace frowned. It was long past closing. The store should have been in darkness, but the interior was lit like a Christmas tree. Someone had switched on every lamp in the place.

On top of that, Caroline stood in the bay window, looking searchingly in her direction. Even from that distance Grace could see that she was agitated. Her sister spotted her and waved her arms, then darted for the door, and Grace applied the brakes. By the time she had pulled over to the curb Caroline reached the van. The look on her face sent alarm streaking through Grace.

Caroline, who strolled through life with a perpetual "don't

give a damn" attitude, was so breathless and upset she could barely talk.

"Oh, God, Grace, thank heaven you're finally back," she panted, latching on to the window opening before Grace could get out of the van. "You've got to go down to the sheriff's office. Right now. Jake's been arrested."

"Arrested! What for?"

"I'm not sure. That damned Harley isn't releasing any information. I even called him myself, but he wouldn't tell me anything except that they were in the middle of a felony investigation. The rumors are flying around town, though, fast and furious. Grace, you'd better get down there right away."

Thirty-Eight

THE SHERIFF'S DEPARTMENT, the three-man Cedar Grove Police Department and the County Jail occupied a squat, one-story, red brick building across the street from the courthouse, an equally unprepossessing edifice of identical red brick and white trim. The only difference was that the courthouse had three stories and sat in the middle of the town square. Everyone in Cedar Grove referred to the building as simply, the station house.

Growing up, Grace had never set foot in the place, but after her marriage she'd had occasion to enter the station house more times than she cared to recall to pick up Charles after his frequent arrests, usually for being drunk and disorderly or speeding. It was during those frequent and humiliating visits that she had become friends with Sheriff Newcomb.

Grace shoved open the double doors of the building and marched inside with fury and fear eating her alive. How could Harley have arrested Jake? There must have been some mistake.

The thoughts echoed in her mind as she crossed the beige linoleum tiles. Several people sat in the old wooden chairs that lined the hallway, but Grace paid no attention to them.

The young woman at the front desk looked up and smiled when she drew near. "Grace, hi. It's good to see you."

She did not bother with the niceties. "I want to see Chief Newcomb, please, Betty Sue. At once."

Harley must have heard her. He stepped out of an office down the hall. "Grace. This way," he said, motioning.

As she approached him she realized that he looked grim. There was a weary tightness around his eyes and his hair stuck up in tufts, as though he'd been running his hands through it. His eyes met hers with pity and a sad resignation, and her alarm increased tenfold.

"What's this about, Harley? Why have you arrested Jake?"

"C'mon into my office and we'll talk." He escorted her inside and closed the door. Grace's nerves were screaming, but she allowed him to seat her in front of the tan metal desk. He walked around to the other side and took his seat.

The room had only one window, which looked out onto Main Street. Through the uncurtained glass she could see that darkness had fallen. The overhead fluorescent fixture flooded the room with harsh light that glared unmercifully down on dingy walls and scuffed beige linoleum.

Harley leaned back in his chair, folded his hands over his stomach and assumed an indolent pose, but Grace noticed the restless tapping of his forefinger against the back of his other hand. It also registered on her, in an oddly disconnected way, that Harley was beginning to thicken a bit around the middle. He looked at her from beneath half-closed eyes and said gently, "I arrested Jake for questioning in the murder of Connie Tolson, Grace."

She sucked in a sharp breath. *"What? "*

"I'm sorry. I truly am. I've known for a while how you felt about the guy. But I had no choice. All the evidence points to him. The D.A. thinks we have enough to file charges."

"Connie Tolson is *dead?"* At Harley's nod she gave a little cry and put her hand over her mouth.

"Her body was found behind her trailer this morning. Since, technically, Jasper Creek and all of the Bottoms are outside the city limits, that puts the case in my jurisdiction."

"That's horri— Oh, my Lord, T.J.! That poor child. Is he all right? Where is he?" She rose halfway out of the chair as she asked the questions.

"Relax. He's with Josie for now. Until she finds a suitable foster home for him, anyway."

Grace slowly sank back down onto the chair. She was shaking inside. The news was so stunning she could hardly take it in. The unthinkable had happened. Again. There had been another murder in Cedar Grove. And, like the first time, Jake was being blamed.

That thought stiffened her spine, and she looked at Harley, her expression challenging. "What evidence do you have against Jake?"

"Well . . . to start with, Ms. Tolson was stabbed twenty-two times, the same kind of frenzied overkill that was used on Carla Mae. Also the killer printed the word "BITCH" in blood on her forehead."

"Oh, God." Hugging her arms tight, Grace closed her eyes and shuddered.

Trying to pull herself together, she forced away the grisly image and sat up straighter. "Let me remind you, Harley, that Jake was not convicted of Carla Mae's murder."

"True. But he wasn't acquitted either. The only reason he wasn't tried a third time was the cost, and the lack of additional evidence it would take to get a conviction. You know as well as I do that most folks around here are dead certain he did the killing. And they're going to think it's mighty suspicious that within a couple of months of Jake's return there's another murder."

"You can't arrest a man just because everyone *thinks* he's guilty."

"True. But added to the obvious similarities in the killings, there was that fight between Jake and Digger Yates."

"What does that have to do with the murder? I told you, Digger attacked Jake. He was merely defending himself."

"Maybe. But no less than twenty people heard Digger tell Jake to stay away from his woman."

"He only went out there because of T.J. He has no interest in Connie Tolson."

"Maybe not, but that's how it sounded to the people who witnessed the fight. We've already talked to about ten of them."

Wringing her hands, Grace pressed her lips together and looked away. "He didn't do it. He couldn't have done it." The words tumbled automatically from her tongue, but they struck a chord. Her gaze swung sharply back to Harley. "When did this murder take place?"

"Last night. Somewhere between one and four in the morning."

"Then Jake couldn't have done it!" A fierce elation exploded inside Grace like a starburst. Her smile stretched wide. "Jake was with me last night."

Thirty-Nine

MILD SURPRISE flickered in Harley's eyes. "Really? What time did he leave you?"

"He didn't." His eyebrows rose. So did Grace's chin. "Jake was with me all night. He's been with me for the past five days and nights, ever since I took him home after the fight with Digger Yates."

The chief sat forward abruptly, frowning, and braced his forearms on top of the cluttered desk. "You're sure about this, Grace?"

"Of course I'm sure."

"Then why didn't Jake tell me he was with you? All he would say was he was at the apartment. When I asked if anyone could verify that, he told me to go to hell."

Grace stared, speechless. There could be only one reason for Jake's silence; he was protecting her reputation. In that stunning moment, the enormity of what he was willing to sacrifice for her revealed a depth of love that took her breath away.

Remorse flooded her when she remembered her reluctance to allow their relationship to become public knowledge. She felt humbled and ashamed—and so profoundly touched that tears filled her eyes and her chest ached.

"Grace? Are you all right?"

"I'm fine. I'm absolutely wonderful," she said with a watery smile. "Oh, Harley, don't you see? Jake was protecting my reputation."

He looked skeptical. "No offense, Grace, but a man would have to love a woman a powerful lot to do that. He's risking prison. Maybe even the death penalty."

"I know."

"Grace--are you sure you're not just trying to cover for the guy?"

"No." She stared at him, her eyes widening. "You think I'm lying. No! I tell you I was with Jake for five days and nights at the apartment, just like I said. You can ask Caroline, if you don't believe me! Except for when she was at the shop, she was in the house the whole time."

"Take it easy, Grace. Look, I'm sorry. I didn't mean to insult you, but I had to be sure. We got a nasty murder on our hands and a town full of people who are going to be convinced that Jake Paxton is the killer. But if you say you were with him, I'll accept your word. However, I wouldn't expect too many others to, if I were you."

"I don't care. Jake is innocent. And I insist that you release him at once."

Harley studied her determined expression. "You're absolutely sure about this Grace? I don't mean to question your honesty. I've known you and your family all my life. For the last several years I've considered you a good friend, and to my knowledge you've always been arrow straight, but—"

"Harley—" she began, but he held up his hands to cut her off.

"No, hear me out, Grace. I been around long enough and seen enough of mankind to know that love can make people do crazy things—things they wouldn't ordinarily even consider doing. If that's what's happening here, if you're just trying to protect Jake because of some blind faith you have in him, tell me now. Because once I leave this room, there's no going back. If you're lying, you could be in serious trouble."

"I told you the truth, Harley. Jake was with me last night."

"And you're willing to swear to that in a court of law? In front of your friends and neighbors and all the other people in this town."

"Yes," she said without hesitation.

He examined her face a moment longer. Then, be nodded and hove to his feet. "All right, Grace. I'll see to Paxton's release.

Wait here."

He opened the door and stepped out. She heard him issue an order to someone to bring Jake to his office and to get his release papers ready.

Immediately, Grace heard Frank protest. "*What?* The hell with that! You'll release that murdering son-of-a-bitch over my dead body."

Grace stood up and peeked out the door in time to see Harley grab Frank by the collar and shove him against the wall. "You listen to me, Frank," he snarled in the young officer's face. "I've been cutting you some slack because Carla Mae was a member of your family, but if you ever refuse to obey my orders again I'll personally kick your butt out of here. You got that?"

"Jake killed that woman, sure as shit," Frank muttered, with a defiant thrust of his chin. "Just like he killed my cousin twelve years ago. We got him dead to rights this time."

"Not according to Mrs. Ames. She says he was with her."

Even from where she stood, Grace saw the shock that flashed over Frank's face. Before nightfall, that same look would be repeated all over town.

"She told you that? She actually *admitted* she'd spent the night with that lowlife bastard?"

"Yeah. Now do as I say and go get Paxton."

Releasing him, Harley headed back toward his office, but halfway there he stopped and looked back. "Oh, and Frank. No rough stuff this time. That's an order."

Less that five minutes later Jake walked into Harley's office. Grace, who had been fidgeting in her seat, jumped up, and the sight of her brought a flash of intense emotion to Jake's face. Her name spilled from him like a soft exultation. "Grace."

His hair was rumpled and stubble was beginning to shadow his jaw. His face had a haggard look, but she could see by the tautness of his body and the icy glitter in his eyes that he was furious. In front of his right ear, a trickle of blood had dried in a line from his temple to his jaw, and that side of his face was swollen and had turned purple.

"Oh, Jake, you're hurt." Grace rushed to his side and her eyes widened as she got a good look at the swollen gash and matted blood above his ear. She turned on Frank, who had escorted him in and was keeping a resentful watch on Jake's back. "Who did this to him? Was it you?"

"So what if it was? He had it coming. He's lucky I didn't bash his head in."

"Try it, asshole. and you'll be eating teeth," Jake snarled.

"Why, you—"

"Can it, Frank!" Harley barked.

The young officer shot his chief a sullen look but he backed off.

Grace, however, wasn't ready to let Jake's attacker off that easily. Bristling, she stepped up to Frank and poked him in the chest with her forefinger. The top of her head did not quite reach his chin.

"How dare you brutalize a man in custody. Frank Sheffield, you're nothing but a foul-tempered, swaggering bully. You always have been." She poked him again. "You use your position as a law officer to run roughshod over people. You're a disgrace to the uniform you wear. Someone should have taken you behind the barn and whipped the stuffing out of you years ago to show you how it feels. Then maybe you'd think twice before flying off the handle and abusing people."

Frank was so flabbergasted all he could do was gape. Everyone knew that Grace was a gentle soul with an even temper. No one had ever known her to so much as raise her voice in anger. Now here she stood, toe to toe, giving a blistering tongue-lashing to a man who was easily twice her size. And she wasn't finished yet.

"And don't give me that 'my poor cousin' bit either. Others may fall for that but I don't. You never cared two beans for Carla Mae and you know it. You're just using her death as an excuse to let fly with that nasty temper of yours." That delicate finger stabbed again—so hard Frank flinched. "Well you're not going to get by with it this time. I'm going to see to it that Jake files a complaint against you."

"Forget it," Jake growled. "I got better ways of getting even." A tic pulsed beside his tight mouth as he cast a murderous gaze at Frank.

"Why you son-of-a—"

Jake tensed as Frank tried to push Grace out of the way to get to him, but Harley was on his feet in a flash and stepped in between the two men.

"Dammit, Frank! Am I going to have to suspend you? Now knock it off."

"You heard him! He threatened me! You gonna take the side of a known killer over mine?"

"Jake is *not* a killer," Grace insisted in a furious voice. Out of patience, Harley bellowed, "All right! Everybody *back off!*"

Silence fell instantly, but the air in the small office vibrated with tension. Harley's hard stare switched from one taut face to the other. When satisfied his order would be obeyed, he focused on his sullen deputy and jerked his head toward the door. "Get out of here, Frank. And take care of that paperwork like I told you."

Frank didn't like it, but he went.

Harley took his seat behind the desk again. He looked at Jake, who remained standing with his fists clenched, and waved to a chair. "Have a seat, Paxton. You too, Grace."

Jake's eyes narrowed. "What is this, Newcomb? Are you going to grill me in front of her?"

"No, hardcase. As a matter of fact, I'm letting you go. Grace here is willing to swear that you were with her at the time of Ms. Tolson's murder."

Jake's head whipped around. "You told him?"

"Yes." She smiled tenderly at his stunned expression. "I told him everything."

"Do you realize what you've done? The gossips will eat you alive. Your reputation will be in shreds."

"I don't care. You're a million times more important to me than what others think."

Surprise flared in his eyes. It was followed at once by a look of intense adoration, and Grace felt a strong tug on her heartstrings. That her love meant so much to him was incredibly humbling. That, even after the past five days, he so obviously had not expected her to declare it, made her incredibly sad.

"Just to verify her story, how long were you and Grace together," the sheriff interjected.

Jake dragged his gaze from hers and met Harley's. "Since the fight with Digger until this morning when she left for Palestine."

"You see. I told you he was innocent."

"It would appear so. The question now is, if Jake didn't kill Connie Tolson, who did?"

"This is just a wild guess, mind you," Jake drawled with heavy sarcasm. "But how about the same person who murdered Carla Mae twelve years ago?"

"Hmmm." Ignoring his derision, Harley leaned back in his chair and tugged at his lower lip with his thumb and forefinger. "That would be my guess, too. If that's so, that means for the past twelve years there's been a vicious killer living right here in Cedar Grove."

Grace gasped and shuddered. Then her eyes widened and she looked at Jake. "That matches your theory that the person who wrote those letters was the killer!"

"What letters?" Harley questioned.

Jake appeared reluctant to reveal the information. His past dealings with lawmen had not inspired trust.

"Tell him, Jake," she urged. "You can trust Harley."

He hesitated, but finally he did as she asked. Still tugging at his lower lip, Harley listened intently. His eyebrows rose when Jake told about getting his college degree, but other than that he showed no reaction. "Do you have these letters?"

"Just one. At the last school where I taught, in the little town of Slaton, out in West Texas, I had a friend working as a secretary for the school board. She filched the letter and gave it to me."

"You got it with you?"

"It's in my wallet, which your men took when you brought me in."

Harley stepped to the door and bellowed down the hall. "Frank! Get in here with that stuff"

In mere seconds Frank stalked in with a paper and a bulky envelope and plunked them down on Harley's desk. "Here's the release form and his personals," he said grudgingly. After casting Jake one last glare he turned and stomped out.

"Check these, then sign the release and you're free," Harley said, tossing the brown envelope to Jake.

He dumped the contents onto the corner of Harley's desk and returned the small items—some change, comb, handkerchief, pocketknife and keys—to his pockets. After checking the contents of his wallet, he pulled out a folded envelope. "I want it back," he said, as he handed it over.

"Sure. Mind if I make a copy?"

He nodded his head, and Harley left the office. While he was gone, Jake took a pen from Harley's desk and scrawled his name to the bottom of the form.

Harley was back in less than a minute. "I noticed the local postmark on the envelope. And you said the writer sent newspaper clippings, too?"

"Yeah. A large manila envelope full of them. But my friend couldn't risk swiping those, too."

"Did she happen to tell you what newspapers the articles were clipped from?"

"Mostly from the *Bedalia Chronicle* and the *Cedar Grove Herald*."

"Hmm. Give me a list of all the places where you taught and I'll make some calls to the local school boards in those towns and have them send me what they've got."

Leaning back, Harley propped his elbows on the arms of the chair and steepled his fingers together. "Whoever wrote those letters means to make sure that, one way or another, you take the blame for Carla Mae's murder. If that person is Carla Mae's killer and he also killed Connie Tolson, he obviously wants everyone to think you're guilty of both crimes."

He looked at Jake and raised one eyebrow. "Do you know anyone who hates you enough to frame you for two murders?"

"In this town? Hell, throw a rock in any direction and you're liable to hit someone who meets that criterion."

Harley worried with his lower lip some more. "Hmm. Of course, that's not the only possibility. I don't like to think so, but there is a chance that we could be dealing with more than one murderer. This could be a copycat killing."

"Why would someone duplicate a murder from twelve years ago? One that Jake stood trial for twice?"

"Could be the perpetrator had some sort of sick admiration for the first killer's technique. Or maybe Ms. Tolson had an enemy we don't know about, and Jake being back in town provided him with a convenient scapegoat. Or maybe it was just a coincidence and the two murders are unrelated."

Jake scowled and shook his head. "I don't believe in coincidences."

"Neither do I, but at this point I can't rule out any possibility."

"Am I free to go now?"

"Sure."

Jake stood up and took Grace's arm. "C'mon. Let's get out of here. This place gives me the willies."

Jake stopped short. "You don't still consider me a suspect?"

"Nope."

"Why not? Everyone else will, regardless of what Grace says."

"Probably. But Grace is the most honest person I know. If she says you were with her, then I believe her. Also, like I said before, I wasn't convinced you were guilty the first time."

For several seconds Jake regarded the sheriff in silence. Fairness on the part of a lawman was something new in his experience, something with which he was not altogether comfortable. Harley's gaze did not waver under that intense scrutiny, however, and finally Jake nodded.

"Thanks."

"Oh, mind if I give you both one more piece of advice? If I were you, I'd keep a low profile. Let Caroline continue to run the shop for a while, Grace, and you and Jake make yourself scarce until the furor this is going to cause dies down a bit."

"No," Grace declared with a pugnacious lift of her chin. "That's exactly what we are *not* going to do. Jake hasn't done anything wrong. Neither have I by loving him. We're not going to hide or in any way act guilty."

Harley blinked at her militant stance and even Jake looked surprised. "Okay, if that's the way you want it."

On their way out of the station, Grace and Jake received several hostile stares, mostly from the officers on duty. He ignored them, but Grace glared right back. "I still think you should file a complaint," she said loud enough that the three officers around the front desk could hear her.

"Yeah, right." Jake snorted. "What planet do you live on, anyway?"

Reaching around her, he pushed open one of the swinging doors and urged her through it. Outside, without slowing, he hustled her down the steps to the van, which she had parked at the curb.

"But what Frank did was wrong," she protested as he opened the passenger door. He climbed into the van and closed it behind him.

When she climbed in behind the wheel and started the van he sat slouched in the bucket seat, staring straight ahead. His jaw was tight and anger glittered in his eyes but he looked bone weary.

She didn't speak again until they were out of town. "Jake, you can't just let them get by with brutality. You have to fight back through legal channels."

He turned his head and looked at her. She practically vibrated with righteous ire on his behalf. "I've never known anyone like you. Honey, this is the real world. I've got about as much chance of getting justice in this town as I have of getting elected mayor." He slumped farther down in the seat and rested his head on the back. "Besides, I'll be lucky if I can just manage to avoid getting lynched."

"Don't say that."

"Why not? Ole Harley was right, you know, when he said everyone's going to blame me. And they're going to crucify you when they find out about us." He rolled his head on the back of the seat and looked at her. "Are you going to be able to handle that?"

"Yes." She turned into the driveway and drove, without stopping, into the carriage house. The only light in the cavernous building was the single bulb hanging from the central rafter, which was left on all the time. Its weak glow barely illuminated the interior of the van, casting Jake's face in blue shadows and palest gold highlights. Still gripping the wheel with both hands, she turned to him.

"I won't pretend that I don't care. My life here is important to me. I love this town, and I love most of the people here, shortcomings and all. It matters to me what they think of me. But . . . if I have to, I can live without their approval. What I can't live without, I've discovered, is you."

The slow smile that curved Jake's mouth was tender, and when he spoke his voice was softer than it had been. "Ah, sweetheart, you're really something. I used to dream of hearing words like that from you, but I never really thought I would."

He opened the door and got out. As he came around the front of the van to her side she watched him. A troublesome thought was taking shape in her mind. Jake loved her, but he'd never once hinted at a future for them. She had the horrible feeling that he had grown up so in awe of her and the kind of life she'd had—that he was still so in awe—that he wouldn't allow himself to even consider a permanent relationship.

Jake opened her door, and when she stepped down he put his arms around her waist loosely. Resting her palms on his chest she searched his face. The musty smells of a time gone by—old harnesses and reins, horse liniment and axle grease—mingled with the scent of metal and rubber and gasoline. From the far corner of the carriage house came the soft scrabbling of a mouse, and beside them the van engine popped as it cooled.

"Jake, how do you see us in say . . . five years? Ten? Fifteen?"

He looked surprised at the question. "I don't know, I haven't thought that far ahead."

Haven't, or haven't let yourself, she wondered.

"I've learned it doesn't pay to make too many plans. Life has a way of shooting you down when you do."

"I see."

"Why do you ask?"

"Because . . . well . . . Jake, I love you. More than I had thought it was possible to love anyone. But that love has a high price tag for me. Many people are going to disapprove of us. Some, many of my friends included, may even turn their backs on me. Certainly, no one in this town will ever think of me in quite the same way again."

He stiffened as though bracing for a blow and his face grew remote, but she pressed on. "Even so, I'm willing to toss my hat over the rainbow for you and defy public opinion and turn my back on everything and everyone I have always valued. But . . ."

"Ahh, here it comes. I figured there was a but."

"But only if I can be sure that it will be worth the sacrifice."

He frowned. "What the hell does that mean?"

"It means that I have to know . . . well . . . that what we have is . . . something I can depend on." It was as close to coming right out and asking what his intentions were as Grace could make herself come. As it was, she felt like some sort of Victorian maiden.

Biting her lower lip, she waited and prayed that he would get her drift, but he merely watched her with that taut look of dread on his face. Beneath her palms she could feel the tense way he held himself, as though waiting for a fatal blow.

"If you're trying to tell me you've changed your mind—"

"No! No, that's not what I'm saying at all."

"Then what are you saying?"

Grace wanted to scream. Her mouth tightened and she stared at him, utterly frustrated. He was never going to say what she wanted to hear, she realized. That left her with only one choice. "I'm saying . . ."

Oh, Lord. Never, not in her wildest dreams, had she ever imagined herself doing what she was about to do. Jake's scowl deepened. She grimaced and bit her lip. Then she drew a deep breath and screwed up her courage.

"What I'm trying to say is—Jake, will you marry me?"

Forty

THE STUNNED LOOK on Jake's face would have been funny had his answer not been so important to her. His jaw actually dropped. He stared, slack jawed without a trace of his usual harsh, go-to-hell expression.

"Marry you!" He practically croaked the word, and with so much astonishment that she was insulted.

"You said you love me," she returned in a tight voice.

"*Marry* you?"

"Oh, forget it," she snapped, and tried to pull out of his arms, but Jake wasn't having any of it.

"Whoa. Wait a minute. Don't be mad." She struggled, but he tightened his hold and pulled her close. "I didn't mean anything by that, sweetheart. You caught me by surprise, is all."

Grace glared, her mouth tight, but he barely noticed.

"Marriage." He shook his head as though trying to clear it. "Whew. I still don't believe it. *You* are asking *me* to marry you?"

Grace turned her head to one side and tilted her chin at a haughty angle. "If the idea is that distasteful to you, please forget I asked."

"Honey, that's not it at all. And believe me, I won't forget this, not if I live to be a hundred. Over the years, I've had a lot of fantasies about you. I've imagined making you fall in love with me. I've dreamed about coming back to town, successful and rich, and sweeping you off your feet. I've pictured making love to you more times and in more ways than you can count. But I didn't dare let my fantasies go as far as marriage. Hell, the last thing I ever expected was for you to propose to me. I'm sorry, honey, but I'm bowled over. You're going to have to give me a minute to take it in."

She slanted him a sidelong look. "Then you don't completely hate the idea?"

"No! Hell, no. I can't think of anything I want more. It's just—"

"What?"

He looked at her tenderly and cupped her face with one hand. His gaze held love and wonder, and something else—something vulnerable, a sort of hopeless longing that tore at her heart. "Sweetheart, have you thought this through? I mean, c'mon, Mary Grace Somerset and Jake Paxton—that's not exactly what most people would call a match made in heaven.

"You're the great-great-granddaughter of the town's founder, the daughter of a minister and the most respected and admired woman in town. I'm the bastard of a mean-spirited drunken slut, a man whom everyone believes is a cold-blooded murderer."

An uprush of emotion welled inside Grace, filling her heart to overflowing and melting away every last iota of pique. She put her hand over the one that cupped her cheek and looked at him with all the love she felt shining from her eyes.

"Oh, Jake. The circumstances of your birth aren't important. You had no control over that. It's the man you are inside that counts. All your life you've been judged harshly and treated worse, but despite that you are a good and decent man. You've managed to survive some horrendous things that would have felled a lesser man. Then you pulled yourself up by your bootstraps and got an education. Under that hard exterior you're kind and caring and fine." She turned her head and pressed a lingering kiss into the center of his palm, then held it against her cheek again. "That's the man I love. That's the man I want to marry."

His eyes blazed down at her like green fire as she rubbed her cheek against his palm. The fierce hunger in his face made her heart sing. Smiling she raised both hands and stroked his temples, the short silky hairs over his ears. Her gaze held his, open and warm and honest, and her voice became a feather caress. "Will you marry me, Jake?"

Through her stroking fingertips she felt the tremor that rippled through him, saw the flare in his eyes in that instant when he set aside the past and its limits and fears. "Yes. God, yes!" he growled as he snatched her hard against his chest.

He kissed her with a depth of feeling that took her breath away. Her ribs hurt, he held her so tight, but Grace didn't care. Aching with love, she clutched him and gave herself up to that kiss of commitment.

When Jake finally lifted his head he studied her intently for several moments. He still could not quite believe what had just happened. Surely this was a dream. He was bound to wake up any moment. Miracles like this just didn't happen—not to him.

But this was no dream. Grace was solid and warm in his arms, and she was looking up at him as though he were the most wonderful man in the world, those guileless blue eyes swimming with tenderness and love. For him.

The wonder of that filled him with awe. Until now, he had never known true joy, or that it could be painful, but his heart was so swollen with happiness it felt like a giant aching knot in his chest.

Still, he felt a moral obligation to give her one more chance to change her mind.

Smoothing an errant strand of hair away from her face, he smiled crookedly. "You're not getting much of a catch. All I've got to my name is that beat-up old truck and about fifty bucks left from the last paycheck you gave me. I've got a miserable past and no future at all. Hell, I can't even get a job in my field. You could do a lot better."

"No. I couldn't." Though the words were softly spoken, her emphatic tone and the sincerity in her eyes left no room for argument. Barely able to swallow around the lump in his throat, Jake could only stare at that beloved face and marvel at the quiet determination he saw there.

"Are you finished trying to scare me off?" she asked with a knowing little twitch of her lips.

"Yeah. I gave you your chance but you blew it. Now you're stuck with me."

"Good."

"It's really going to shake things up when word about us getting married leaks out. You do know that, don't you?"

"Word isn't going to leak out. We're going to have Daniel announce our engagement at church on Sunday."

His mouth dropped again. "You can't be serious." Just when he thought she couldn't surprise him any more, she did.

"I most certainly am."

She smiled with serene determination and that little tilt of her chin that he was beginning to recognize. Slipping her arms around his waist, she laced her fingers together at the small of his back and leaned back in the circle of his embrace. "And afterward we're going to attend the church picnic. What's more, every day we're going to go about our business as usual. We'll walk around town with our heads high and smiles on our faces. If anyone wants to be friendly—then fine. If they want to snub us, that's their problem . . . and their loss."

Jake stared at her, the oddest sensation zinging through him. His gentle lamb was turning into a tiger right before his eyes.

A slow grin spread over his face. "Jesus, honey. When you do decide to take a stand you sure as hell pull out all the stops don't you?"

OUT OF COURTESY, Grace felt she owed it to her family and Verna to break the news to them before the public announcement on Sunday.

Of course, they had no choice but to tell Caroline immediately. She had seen the van drive in and was waiting on the back porch for them to come out of the carriage house. The instant they did, she pounced.

"For heaven's sakes! What were you two doing in there all this time? Here I've been waiting on pins and needles to find out what happened. Why on earth you would want to make out in that drafty old barn when you have a perfectly good apartment upstairs is beyond me."

"Caroline Marie! We were not making out," Grace admonished. "We were discussing something."

"Oh, yeah? Then why is Jake wearing your shade of lipstick?"

He grinned and took a handkerchief from his hip pocket to wipe his mouth. "It was an intimate discussion."

Cocking a hip, Caroline swept him from head to toe with a sultry look, her blasé persona dropping back into place like a theater curtain. "Uh-huh. Well, at least you're out of the slammer. What'd you do, Grace? Go his bail?"

"I didn't have to. We managed to convince Harley that he arrested the wrong man. Why don't we go inside and we'll tell you about it."

When they were seated at the kitchen table Caroline frowned at Jake. "What happened to your face?"

Gingerly, he touched the swollen ridge above his right ear. "Frank Sheffield got a little enthusiastic when they arrested me."

"Huh. He always was a prick. What'd Harley pick you up for anyway? There's all sorts of rumors flying around town."

"Murder one."

"What! "She sat forward, her nonchalant facade crumbling like dust. "Whose murder?"

"Connie Tolson," Grace supplied. "She was killed some time between two and four this morning."

"But Jake couldn't have done it. He was here with you."

"Exactly."

Caroline's eyes widened. "You mean . . . you told Harley that? I can't believe it." She let out a hoot of laughter. "Oh, man, just wait until this gets around!"

"That's not all," Jake drawled. Grinning, he scooted his chair closer to Grace and draped his arm around her shoulders. "You want to tell her? Or do you want me to do it?"

Grace reached up and took the hand that dangled over her shoulder. She glanced up at him with an impish smile. "Well I don't know . . ."

"For heaven's sake, somebody say something!"

Grace laughed and relented. "Jake and I are getting married."

"Wh-what?"

"She proposed to me," Jake put in with a smirk, and earned himself a sharp elbow jab in the ribs.

"What?"

"Ow. That hurt."

"Good. That's what you get for being so ungentlemanly. You're never going to let me forget that, are you?"

"Nope."

"Hey! You two knock off that sickening lovey stuff or I'm going to smack you both. Now explain yourselves."

"There's nothing to explain. Jake and I are in love and we're going to get married."

Caroline stared, her mouth agape. Then she turned to Jake. "Were you serious? Did she really propose to you?"

"Yep."

She looked askance at her sister. "You're really going to go for it? Despite all the brouhaha that's sure to come?"

"Yes."

"Well hallelujah!" Throwing her arms wide, Caroline surged up out of the chair and enveloped them both in an exuberant hug.

Forty-One

THE NEXT MORNING, over a cup of tea in the main parlor at the Willows, Grace told her mother-in-law of her plans. When she'd finished, she sat quietly in the fussy French Provincial chair and watched Verna's face pale.

"You . . . you *can't* be serious."

"I'm very serious, Verna," she said gently. "Please try to understand. I love Jake. Very much. And I am going to marry him, just as soon as we can make the arrangements."

"Oh, dear Lord. Oh, dear *Lord!* "Verna clamped one hand over her mouth and shook her head. "No. No, this can't be happening. It can't be. It's too horrible."

"Verna . . ."

"How *could* you? How could you even consider such a thing? How can you do this to me?" Her voice wobbled and tears filled her eyes as she gazed piteously at Grace. "Haven't I always loved you. Haven't I always treated you as though you were my very own daughter?"

"Yes, of course. But that has nothing to do with this."

"It has everything to do with this! You are an Ames. How can you lower yourself to actually *marry* Jake Paxton?" Verna grimaced and shuddered. "Oh, Lord, the shame of it will be devastating. I don't know how I'll ever be able to hold my head up in this town again. My son's widow, the woman I welcomed into my home, the woman who I had hoped would be the mother of the next generation of Ames children, marrying that sorry murdering trash. How can you dishonor my dear Charles's memory that way?"

Grace had come there with nothing but sympathy for Verna,

knowing she would take the news hard. Verna would be upset if she married anyone but an Ames, which meant Lyle, since he was the last of the line—but Jake Paxton? Oh, no, that was simply too much for her fluttery, status-conscious mother-in-law to abide.

Grace had come prepared for histrionics and pleading and dramatics, perhaps even anger, though guilt and emotional blackmail were more Verna's style. Grace had known it would not be pleasant but she had intended to listen with understanding and offer what comfort she could. She was not prepared, however, to sit passively and listen to the man she loved being maligned.

A few months ago she might have held her tongue, but not now. That mild-mannered, malleable Grace no longer existed.

She set her cup down on the tea cart with a decisive click and stood up. She looked down at Verna. The woman, with her dainty Southern-belle ways and her tears and quavery voice, had been manipulating everyone around her all her life. Grace had always known that she was doing it, but Verna's machinations had seemed harmless, even amusing . . . until now.

Unmoved, she stared straight into Verna's moist eyes and made no attempt to hide her displeasure. "Listen to me, Verna. Jake Paxton is not a killer, nor is he trash, and I won't stand for you or anyone else calling him that."

"No, you're wrong. The man has . . . has beguiled you. He's no good! Everyone knows that. If you marry him, you will be no better." Verna put her face in her hands and wept. Her silk-covered shoulders heaved piteously. "Oh, Grace. Grace. How can you dishonor my dear Charles's memory this way?"

Clenching her jaws, Grace stood taller. "Dishonor Charles? That would be difficult, considering."

Verna's head came up and she looked at Grace with tear-drenched eyes, her expression a mix of affront and wariness. "Why, whatever do you mean? My Charles was a prince. He had breeding and class. After being married to him I don't know how you could even look at someone like Jake Paxton. I would think you'd feel dirty." To emphasize the statement, Verna wrapped her arms tightly around her body and shuddered, grimacing as though she just swallowed a dose of quinine. "Lizzie Paxton's bastard."

The comment made Grace so angry she saw red. "Trust me, Verna. You don't want me to start making comparisons between Charles and Jake. Your son would lose by a mile."

Verna gasped and placed her hand over her chest as though she'd been stabbed in the heart. "What nonsense! My Charles was a man among men."

"Your precious Charles was a spoiled, irresponsible, self-centered liar and cheat. He had no ethics nor morals. He drank too much, and he was unfaithful to me practically from the start of our marriage."

"Heavens, that doesn't matter," Verna declared with an airy flutter of her hand.

"It mattered to me."

"My dear, all men have their little peccadillos. That's just the way they are. The other women were diversions, but you are the one Charles chose for his wife."

"Am I supposed to be grateful for that? Well I'm not! And you're wrong about men. Jake is none of those things. He's a decent, caring, loving man whom I can trust completely, and I am honored that he loves me and wants me for his wife."

She snatched up her purse and turned for the door but stopped and looked back at her mother-in-law. "I am going to marry Jake. I will let you know exactly when. You can attend and wish me happiness, or you can stay away. The choice is yours."

THERE WERE TWO FUNERAL HOMES in Cedar Grove. Almost everyone in Grace's circle used the Smythe and Turner Mortuary when it came time to say good-bye to their loved ones. Connie Tolson's funeral was held at Potts and Potts, who routinely handled services for the county's indigent and Cedar Grove's less prosperous citizens.

Harley advised Grace and Jake not to attend. Many people, though shocked, accepted the alibi she had given him, but there were some who did not, and sentiment among them was nasty.

Digger Yates's trial was set for late June. As yet he had not been able to post bail, but Harley was letting him out of jail long enough to attend the funeral. To avoid possible trouble, he thought it would be best if Jake were not present.

He and Grace, however, could not bear the thought of T.J. being all alone at his mother's funeral. In addition, Grace was concerned that staying away would give the appearance of guilt, and she was determined not to do that.

Together, they picked T.J. up from the home where he was staying. The lady providing foster care had seen to it that the boy looked presentable. His face had a scrubbed look and his hair was slicked back and neatly parted. He wore the new shoes, dress pants, white shirt and necktie that Grace had purchased for him.

He looked self-conscious and kept running his forefinger beneath his shirt collar, but he didn't complain. He sat quietly—too quietly for T.J.—during the drive to the funeral parlor. His face was so pale the freckles across the bridge of his nose stood out like paint splatters.

Never in his young life had T.J. attended a funeral, Grace discovered through gentle questioning. That his first one would be his own mother's brought the sting of tears to her eyes.

The loud, hate-filled whispers and gasps began the instant the three entered the mortuary and signed the guest book.

"Just look at that. Can you believe he had the gall to come here? And with that dear boy?" Ida Bell said in a loud murmur.

Martha tsked. "It's a disgrace, that's what it is. The sheriff ought to have arrested him. Decent people shouldn't have to rub elbows with the likes of him."

Grace heard the whispers and she was sure that Jake had also, but they held their heads high and ignored them, both aware that every eye in the place was on them.

Though stoic, T.J. was obviously scared as they walked down the aisle of the small chapel. Grace and Jake flanked him, each with a hand on his shoulder, and she could feel the tremors that vibrated through his scrawny frame. His young face was pinched and solemn, his bony shoulders erect, but when they reached the open casket and he saw his mother, waxy and grotesquely stiff in death, his composure deserted him.

With a sob, he turned and flung his arms around Jake, burying his face against his middle as great, racking cries tore from deep in his soul.

Without hesitation, Jake wrapped his arms around the boy, cupping the back of his head in his big hand to hold him close, and let him sob out his grief.

The awful sounds wrung Grace's heart. She bent over T.J., patting his back and murmuring words of sympathy in his ear, but she had never felt so helpless or useless in her life. Apparently, no matter how bad they were, a child still loved his parents.

When the first wave of grief had eased a bit, T.J. was embarrassed and self-conscious under the pitying stares of the people filing in, but he couldn't seem to stop crying. Tactfully, Jake edged him over to the first pew that was reserved for family members. T.J., Jake and Grace were the only ones there.

Once seated, T.J. struggled to get control of himself. He sniffed and his breath hitched over and over piteously, and he scrubbed his cheeks and eyes with the heels of his hands. Wordlessly, Jake fished a clean handkerchief out of his pocket and handed it to him. The boy wiped his eyes and blew his nose loudly, then sat with his eyes downcast, the white square of linen balled up tight in his fist.

Reverend Street and Josie arrived with Caroline and Aunt Harriet. Connie Tolson had not been a regular church goer, but Daniel had agreed to conduct the service. He stopped to offer condolences to the child and talk to Jake and Grace while Josie, Caro and Harriet slipped into the chairs on either side of them. Grace smiled at them, grateful for the family show of solidarity.

Somber, recorded music flowed from hidden speakers. The cloying sweet smell of flowers and air freshener and that nauseatingly sweet chemical smell that permeated funeral homes drifted on the air-conditioned air.

People came in, filed past the casket with appropriate reverence, then took their seats. Quite a few had turned out for the funeral, most because of the sensationalism surrounding Connie's death. Grace was certain that over half of them, especially those friends and acquaintances of hers who were there, hadn't even known Connie, but for T.J.'s sake Grace was glad to see the chapel filling up.

There was a brief stir when reporters and photographers from both the Bedalia and Cedar Grove newspapers entered and starting snapping pictures, but the Pottses, father and son, quickly swooped down on them and firmly ushered them out.

Daniel walked up to the pulpit and opened his Bible, and the music faded away. "Friends, neighbors, beloved families, we are gathered here today in this tragic hour to say good-bye to a fallen sister . . ."

Most of Daniel's eulogy was directed at comforting T.J. The sentiments were tender without being cloying, and, at least to Grace, extremely touching. Her throat closed up and tears ran down her cheeks as she listened to the hymns, the prayers, and Daniel's thoughtful words, and she wondered what was going to become of the poor, motherless boy beside her.

Daniel offered up his final prayer and everyone stood and prepared to file past the casket one more time before it was sealed and transported by hearse to the cemetery. Suddenly an electrified hush fell over the crowd, and no one moved as Harley and Digger Yates, whom the sheriff had allowed to listen to the service from the vestibule, came into the chapel. Frank Sheffield took up a post by the door while Harley, with a firm hand on the Digger's arm, led his prisoner down the aisle.

Dressed in the jeans and plaid shirt he'd been wearing when he attacked Jake, Digger looked out of place among the somberly dressed mourners, but Grace supposed his attire was preferable to jail issue coveralls. He appeared more subdued than she had ever seen him, his face set, his massive shoulders slightly slumped.

When they reached the casket, Harley released him and stepped back a pace to give him a degree of privacy. Digger stared at Connie for perhaps ten seconds, then, with a keening wail that startled everyone, he flung himself across her body and began to howl like a banshee.

T.J.'s eyes bugged out, and he pressed closer to Jake's side. "Cripes. He's freakin' out."

Harley pulled him off of the casket and turned around to guide him to a seat. Digger stumbled a few steps under Harley's guidance, but his blubbering wails cut off abruptly and he jerked to a halt when he spotted Jake.

"What the hell is *he* doing here?" he demanded, but even as he asked the question his muscles bunched for an attack, and with a yell he launched himself at Jake. "Murdering bastard! I'll kill you! I'll kill you, I swear I will!"

Jake instinctively shoved T.J. into Grace's arms and turned to shield them both from harm. He tried to stand, but Digger plowed his squat body into Jake like a pro linebacker, sending Jake and the chair, and three of the people seated in the row behind him flying backward. Screams and shouts went up all around, amid the crash of folding chairs. Digger came down on top of Jake, fists flying.

"Goddammit, Yates!" Harley roared, wading into the melee after him. Frank came charging up to help, pushing out of his way the people who crowded into the aisle, craning their necks for a look at the brawl. "Step aside. Clear the aisle. This is police business. Get back! Get back!"

He finally shoved his way through the crowd and between them, he and Harley pulled Digger off of Jake.

"Digger, you sorry son-of-a-bitch, I warned you about starting trouble."

"I'll kill him! I'll kill the sorry low-life woman-killer." Digger raged, fighting to be free.

"Oh, knock it off, Yates," Harley snapped. He shoved him at Frank. "Here. Get him outta here. Take him back to the jail."

"No! You said I could go to the gravesite! Why don't you arrest Paxton? He killed her. Everybody knows he done it!" he screeched as Frank and another deputy dragged him out of the room.

Harley offered Jake his hand and hauled him to his feet, and Grace rushed forward.

"Are you all right? Oh, Jake, the cut over your eye is open again," She moaned, dabbing with a tissue at the blood running down his temple.

"It's okay. Leave it be." Jake's voice was strained and hard, despite his level tone, and she knew he was struggling to hold onto his temper. As he raked a hand through his hair murmurs began to float to them from the crowd.

"Can't say I'm surprised."

"What'd he expect, showing his face at the woman's funeral this way?"

"The sheriff shoulda let Digger loose on him, if you ask me."

Calmly, Jake straightened his coat and tie and retucked his white shirt. His frosty gaze swung around and met the accusal in the eyes of the onlookers. Many shifted uncomfortably and looked away.

"You okay, Jake?" T.J. asked timorously, stepping close. The boy looked shaken, and frightened out of his mind. Grace wanted to punch Digger herself. The boy had enough to deal with without being subjected to a brawl at his mother's funeral.

Jake looked down at the frightened boy and his expression softened. So did his voice. "Yeah. I'm fine, sport. C'mon, let's go."

He held out his hands, one to T.J. and one to Grace. She smiled at him as their fingers linked, and together the three of them walked by the casket one last time, then back down the aisle with their heads held high.

~

"I STILL DON'T SEE WHY I have to stay here," T.J. muttered in a sullen voice, casting a resentful glare at the neat white frame house. He sat between Jake and Grace on the truck seat, slumped down on his spine in an attitude of utter dejection. His head was tucked so low his chin rested on his chest.

"Because it's the law. Until a permanent home is found for you, you have to stay in foster care," Jake said patiently for at least the fifth time since leaving the cemetery.

"Why can't I stay with you'n Grace?"

"Because we're not foster parents."

"You could be, I bet. If you wanted."

The accusatory tone in T.J.'s voice wrung a sigh from Jake, and he looked over the boy's head at Grace, a plea for help in his eyes.

She put her hand on T.J.'s arm and looked at him sadly. "Sweetheart, it's not that easy. And it takes time to apply and get approved." She didn't add that, until the murderer was caught and Jake was cleared, they didn't stand much chance of being approved, not even with Josie in their corner. "I promise that Jake and I will visit you and take you out for outings, and you can still come by the shop whenever you want. It won't be so bad. But you have to give it a chance. Won't you at least do that?"

T.J.'s sulky mouth twisted. "Oh-kaay. But I'd still rather live with you and Jake."

The words twisted Grace's heart. Her eyes met Jake's as she pulled the boy into her arms and whispered in an aching voice, "Oh, sweetheart, I'd rather you did, too."

"Did you mean it?" Jake asked after they left T.J.

"What?"

"About wishing that T.J. could live with us."

She glanced at Jake's profile, trying to gauge his feelings, but he stared straight ahead, his eyes on the road. "Yes. I meant it. Would you mind?"

"Mind? Hell, no. I think it would be great. If I could afford it, I'd take in all the T.J.s in the world."

Tears threatened as Grace gazed at Jake's profile. The statement not only revealed the bigness of his heart, it echoed with the pain of his own childhood. She loved him so much in that moment it hurt.

Forty-two

GRACE INVITED the rest of her family for dinner the next evening so that she and Jake could break the news to them all at once. Josie and Daniel were practically inseparable nowadays, and since she and Jake needed to talk to Daniel about making the announcement after church service on Sunday, Grace invited him as well.

Both Caroline and Jake teased her about that, saying her real motive was to prod the good reverend into proposing to Josie. Grace, of course, denied any such intent. But . . . if things happened to work out that way, well . . .

The reactions to the news varied.

Aunt Lollie—being Aunt Lollie—proved the most difficult from the very start. The gossip about Grace and Jake had spread like wildfire, and when Grace called to invite her to dinner she had to endure a long lecture before she could finally get a word in and issue the invitation. Lollie immediately asked if "that Jake person" would be there, and when Grace had replied truthfully, her aunt had sniffed and declined.

Coaxing and wheedling did not budge her. Finally Grace ran out of patience and let loose with anger, something Lollie had never experienced before. She, like most other people, hadn't even known that Grace had a temper.

In no uncertain terms, Grace informed Lollie that she would either come to dinner and listen to what she had to say or she would not be welcomed in Grace's home in the future. Shocked, her aunt quickly agreed.

Lollie arrived in a high snit, and throughout most of the evening she made a project out of ignoring Jake and tried to punish

Grace by affecting an offended silence. Unfortunately, it did not last. The announcement, made after dinner, ended her sulks and threw her into a fit of the vapors.

The way she carried on, you would have thought that her niece had suddenly declared her intention to join a satanic cult or become a nude dancer in a girlie bar, or something equally sleazy and abhorrent. She shrieked and wailed and fluttered about as though she were about to expire.

Grace and Josie did their best to calm her, but Caroline merely looked on with disgust, while Jake sat ramrod stiff and the other two men shifted uncomfortably and looked everywhere but at the silly woman.

Only Aunt Harriet seemed unmoved by Lollie's histrionics. She endured the scene for only a few moments, then thumped her cane on the floor and snapped, "Lollie Madison, you hush up that caterwauling this instant, or so help me I'll wallop you with my cane!"

To everyone's surprise, Lollie's keening shut off in mid-wail like turning a spigot. She shrank back on the sofa with her hand over her mouth, her wide-eyed glare fixed warily on her nemesis, but not another sound came from her mouth.

Harriet nodded. "That's better. Now then, I'm going to say my piece." Her gaze went from Grace to Jake. "I don't mind admitting, if it were up to me, I would have chosen differently for my niece."

"Well, I should hope so."

"Shut up, Lollie." Harriet shot her a silencing look. "As I was saying—I would have chosen differently." She fixed her gaze on Jake, and pointed a bony finger at him. "Not because of those charges against you. I'm willing to give you the benefit of the doubt there, since you were never convicted. But the fact is, right or wrong, guilty or not, you come with a lot of baggage, young man, and that's not what I want for my niece.

"However, it's Grace who's doing the choosing, not me. And certainly not you, Lollie Madison. Thank the Lord. My niece obviously loves you, young man. If you love her and you swear to treat her right, you have my blessing."

"*Harriet!* You *can't* mean that!"

"Don't you go telling me what I mean, Lollie. Grace is a grown woman and perfectly capable of making her own decisions. If she wants to marry Jake Paxton—or Beelzebub himself—it's none of your business or mine. But just so you know, I happen to think that Jake will do just fine by Grace if you and others like you will just leave him alone."

"Well! I never!"

"Thank you, Aunt Harriet." Standing together, each with an arm around the other's waist, Grace and Jake exchanged a glance and a smile.

But her aunt wasn't through. "However, I'm not too proud to admit that I have been wrong before. I sincerely hope I am not this time." She walked purposefully up to Jake and thumped his chest with the handle of her cane. "But I'm warning you right now, young man, if any harm comes to my niece because of you, I will personally get a gun and blow you to kingdom come. You have my word on that."

There was a collective gasp. Every eye in the room was on the incongruous pair.

Harriet had stood barely an inch over five feet in her youth. Now she was slightly hunched with age and frail as a bird. She had to crane her neck to meet Jake's eyes, but she did so fearlessly.

Staring down at the tiny woman, Jake's expression was impassive, but he had to bite the inside of his cheeks hard in order to fight back the grin that threatened. He didn't put it past the old tartar to really whack him with that thing if she realized he was amused. How the hell did someone that small have the audacity to try to intimidate someone his size? God, the women in Grace's family were really something.

"Yes ma'am. I understand. You don't have to fear that I would ever harm Grace, because I won't. I love her, and I'm going to do my best to keep her safe and make her happy. You have *my* word on that."

Harriet studied his face and Jake stared right back, two strong-willed people taking each other's measure and recognizing a worthy opponent. Finally Harriet nodded. "You'll do."

The reactions of the others were not as dramatic, for which Grace was grateful.

Hank Beaman expressed reservations, but Josie was as delighted as Caroline. "I knew it! I knew you two belonged together," she crowed when Harriet had finished speaking her mind. "For heaven sake's, the poor guy has been in love with you since we were all kids."

"How did you know that?" Grace asked, shocked.

"Oh, pul-leeze. A blind man could see that, the way he practically devoured you with his eyes. Take it from me, this was fated." Josie glanced around, then asked in a low murmur, "Have you told Verna yet?"

"Yesterday morning."

"Oh, boy. I'll bet she had a hissy, didn't she?"

"You could say that. Actually, I lost my temper and said some things that were probably better left unsaid. I regret that."

"Oh, well, look on the bright side. That means it'll probably be a long time before you're invited back to the Willows to sit through one of those long, boring Sunday dinners."

Grace smiled wanly. She doubted that she would ever be invited to the Willows again for any reason.

Daniel, seeing his duty, insisted on talking with Grace and Jake privately, first together, then separately. At first she was afraid that Jake would balk at that. The fiery emerald glitter in his eyes made it clear he wasn't pleased, but he held his tongue and went into the study with Daniel with his jaw set in a hard line.

They were gone for what seemed like hours. Grace was a wreck the entire time. She fidgeted in the parlor with the others, her gaze alternating between the mantel clock and the door into the hall, certain that any moment the two would either come to blows or Jake would come storming out in a rage.

She had no idea what passed between them, but whatever Jake said obviously satisfied Daniel. When they finally emerged they were smiling and talking as congenially as a pair of old friends. The instant they walked into the parlor Jake's gaze sought her out like a heat-seeking missile zeroing in on its target. His sexy mouth curved in a slow smile, and he winked, and, for the first time that day she relaxed.

Forty-Three

Driving home from church on Sunday, Grace sat in the passenger seat and stared straight ahead.

"Are you all right?"

"Don't worry, I'm fine."

Caroline reached over the back of Grace's seat and patted her shoulder. "Of course you are. What're a few glares and snubs? You expected those."

"Yes. Of course." Grace did not bother to point out that the reaction to the engagement had been a bit harsher than that. Gasps and murmurs of outrage and disbelief had rippled through the congregation like shock waves. Afterward, though they were obviously uncomfortable, a few good friends had come up to them and offered good wishes, but others, people she had known all of her life, had turned their backs when she and Jake had come out of the church.

Caroline chuckled. "I haven't been inside a church in . . . shoot, I can't remember. But am I glad I went today. Did you see Martha Goodson? Her eyes bugged out like they were on stems. And Ida Bell almost swallowed her tongue. I wouldn't have missed that for the world."

"I'm glad you enjoyed yourself," Grace said in a dry voice. The only reason her sister had attended the service was to witness the appalled reactions of the parishioners when they learned that she and Jake were to be married. Caroline's unexpected attendance had created almost as much of a stir as the news of Grace's engagement.

Jake turned into the driveway and drove around to the back, bringing the van to a stop in front of the carriage house. He turned off the ignition and reached across the space between the seats and took her hand. "Are you sure you're all right? You've been quiet since we left the church."

"Yes. I'll admit, I'm a little shaken. I guess I just didn't expect that much animosity and disapproval, but I'll get over it. Don't worry."

They had barely entered the house when Josie and Daniel arrived. No sooner had the couple climbed from Daniel's car than Harriet's huge old Cadillac came purring up the drive behind them.

"My goodness, what is this?" Grace said as the trio came trooping in together through the back door.

"We came to be sure you were all right." Daniel took both her hands in his and looked at her with concern.

"Of course I am. Why does everyone keep asking me that?"

"Grace, are you sure?" Josie questioned gently. "That wasn't a very pleasant scene at church."

"Oh, quit fretting, you two. Grace knew what she was getting into. She can handle it. She's my niece, after all." Harriet plunked herself down at the table and thumped her cane on the floor. "Caroline. Make yourself useful and pour me a cup of coffee."

"Yes ma'am," Caroline said, rolling her eyes.

"Aunt Harriet is right. I'm fi— Now who in the world is that?" Grace said as yet another vehicle pulled into the driveway.

Caroline twitched back the curtain over the kitchen sink. Her mouth tightened as she watched the lanky figure climb from the car and amble across the yard to the back porch. "It's the law."

She marched across the kitchen and glared at Harley through the screened door as he climbed the steps. "What're you doing here?"

"Now is that any way to talk?"

"Did you come to arrest Jake again on some trumped up charge? Or maybe it's Grace you're planning to drag away in handcuffs this time. Or is it me?"

Harley sighed. "Knock it off, Caro. I'm not here to arrest anybody, and you know it. I told you I'd be by to take you to the picnic this afternoon."

"And I told you, I'm not going."

"None of us are going," Jake announced.

"Oh yes we most certainly are."

Scowling, Jake swung around. "Grace, you can't be serious. After what happened at church? It'll be worse at the picnic. Why put yourself through that?"

"Because we have just as much right to be there as anyone else. And because I live in this town and I intend to go on living here. I am not going to let anyone tell me how to live my life, especially not a bunch of sanctimonious old busybodies like Ida Bell and her cronies. Nor are we going to slink away and hide when we haven't done anything wrong. The food is prepared and the picnic basket is packed. As soon as we change clothes we'll be ready to go."

Harriet's cane thumped. "That's my girl. And I'll go with you."

"If you don't mind, Josie and I would like to join you, too," Daniel announced, and her cousin quickly murmured agreement.

Leaning his hips back against the counter, Harley glanced at Caroline. "Count me and your sister in, too."

Astonished, Grace looked from Daniel to Harley, her eyes growing moist. "It's sweet of you to offer, but supporting Jake and me would put you both in terrible positions. Daniel, you could lose your congregation over this. And you'd be risking your job, Harley. People around here expect you to find a reason to arrest Jake, not befriend him. We appreciate what you're both trying to do, but we couldn't ask you to make that kind of sacrifice."

"Grace is right," Jake agreed. "There's no reason for you to jeopardize your positions for us."

"The people of this town pay me to enforce the law and protect them, but I pick my own friends. If the mayor wants my badge, then he can have it." Folding his arms over his chest, Harley looked at Daniel. "I don't know about you, Reverend Street, but I got me a hankerin' for some of Mary Grace's fried chicken. It's the best in the county."

"So I've heard." Daniel smiled at Grace. "I hope you made enough for all of us."

❧

They arrived at the park all together. As expected, they drew stares and angry murmurs as they made their way through the throng already gathered. Grace and Jake led the way, searching for a table big enough to accommodate them all, and each of them was laden with picnic baskets and thermoses, folding chairs and blankets.

"Just remember, this isn't a date," Caroline grumbled. "I'm only doing this for Grace's sake."

Grace and Jake heard Harley chuckle, and they exchanged an amused look. Her sister had been sniping at the sheriff ever since they left the farm.

"Hey, this is great," T.J. enthused.

On the way to the park they had picked him up, and he bounced along with the group of adults excited as a pup. That didn't, however, stop him from slipping in a complaint now and then about his foster home.

"Look! They're gonna play softball. I never get to play at fussy old Mz Bordon's," he grumbled, cutting his eyes around at Grace to see what kind of reaction that drew. "She's afraid I might break out her windows or somethin'."

Grace had been appalled to learn that T.J. had never been on a picnic before. Determined that he would enjoy this one, she had outdone herself. Her baskets contained fried chicken and ham, deviled eggs, potato salad, baked beans, coleslaw, green salad, three kinds of pies, two cakes and cookies.

Throughout the meal Grace ignored the glares they received and was determinedly gay, though she was aware of Jake's watchful concern. T.J., oblivious to the tension all around him, had a wonderful time. His appetite, as usual, was tremendous, but he was torn between sampling everything in the appetizing spread and rushing off to join the other boys on the baseball diamond.

A few people were friendly, if a bit uncomfortable. A couple of women of Harriet's generation were bold enough to pull Grace aside and demand to know if she had lost her mind. Her dear departed parents were probably turning over in their graves, one had the nerve to say, and was treated to a cool set down by Grace. She was a bit ashamed of herself for the sharp way she had spoken, but she took comfort in knowing that her father was probably cheering her on from above.

After the meal, Daniel went to talk to an elderly parishioner. As Grace, Caroline and Josie began cleaning up the mess and packing away the leftover food, Jake and Harley wandered off to check on T.J.

A short while later, the work done, the women were sitting in the shade of the trees, drinking iced tea and fanning themselves, when they heard screaming.

"What on earth?"

"Lord-a-mercy!" Harriet exclaimed. "Sounds like somebody's dying."

The screaming continued without let-up and others began shouting.

Grace, Caroline and Josie stood up and looked in the direction of the sounds.

"It's coming from down by the river," Caroline said, cupping her hand over her eyes and squinting.

"Well, don't just stand there gaping. Go see what all the fuss is about. And one of you come back and tell me as soon as you find out," Harriet called after the three younger women as they began to trot away, joining the others who were heading toward the river.

"What is it? What's happened?" Grace asked a man who raced passed them carrying a coil of rope.

"The Colemans' little girl fell in the river," he hollered over his shoulder.

"Oh, no. She'll be swept away."

The three women took off running as fast as they could. This stretch of the Hawbeck River was treacherous. The deep, fast-flowing currents contained strong undertows and eddies that had claimed many swimmers over the years. At the moment, swollen from spring runoff and recent heavy rains, the river harbored dangerous snags and debris as well.

As they neared the river Grace saw Jake sitting on the bank, snatching off his boots. Beside him, Harley was waving his arms and shouting orders at the other men. They reached the bank just in time to see Jake jump up and shuck out of his shirt and jeans and launch himself into the water.

"Jake!" Grace screamed. She covered her mouth with her hand and stared, horrified, as he swam away, bobbing in the current like a cork. A hundred yards or so ahead of him, the small head of a child was barely visible over the top of the log to which she clung.

Harley snatched the rope from the man who had passed them and tore along the bank, paralleling Jake, yelling to him all the while. Grace ran after him.

"I'm going with Grace. Josie, you go back and tell Aunt Harriet what's going on," Caroline yelled as she started after her sister.

Every now and then Jake disappeared beneath the water, and Grace moaned and frantically searched the surface until he popped up again. She raced along the bank after Harley, stumbling and tripping every few feet, trying to keep her eye on Jake and at the same time negotiate the rough path at a dead run. A painful stitch stabbed her side and she skinned both knees and the palms of her hands, but she was barely aware of discomfort, or of the other people yelling and rushing along the bank with her.

Yard by yard, Jake was gaining on the child. The little girl clung to the log like a leech. Her high-pitched screams sounded piercing and heart-wrenching over the roar of the river and the shouts of the people on the shore.

Jake was within ten feet of the little girl when her grip on the log slipped. The swift current grabbed her like a piece of flotsam and hurled her downstream, tumbling head over feet.

Harley shouted and Grace screamed. So did many others who watched helplessly as the tiny child was swept out of Jake's reach.

Another chorus of shouts went up when the girl was carried into the middle of the river toward a snag, formed by a log and other debris that had caught on a submerged obstruction, some thirty yards or so downstream.

Harley yelled something to Jake and he seemed to redouble his efforts, although he appeared to be almost as much at the mercy of the raging river as the child. The waters tossed and hurled him about like a rag doll.

As the horrified people on shore watched, the little girl slammed into the log. Abruptly, her screams ended. Her T-shirt caught on a branch, and for an instant she hung there, limp and lifeless. Everyone shouted encouragement to Jake as he fought to reach her. He was within a few feet of the snag when the T-shirt ripped and the child slipped beneath the water and disappeared.

Jake slammed into the log, and for a few seconds he simply held on, breathing hard. Then he gulped in a huge breath and dove beneath the surface.

"Jake!" Grace skidded to a stop beside Harley on the bank across from the snag. "Wh . . . Where is h- . . . he? I don't se- . . . see him!"

"I don't know," Harley snapped, his face tense as he scanned the river and at the same time worked feverishly to tie a loop in the end of the coil of rope.

Frantic, Grace searched the surface of the water. Her eyes darted among the snag, along the opposite bank, downstream, but there was no sign of Jake or the child. *"Jake!"*

Agonizing seconds ticked by. Grace wrung her hands and prayed. Please, God, please let him be all right. Don't take him from me. Not now.

Others reached the spot and stood tense and watchful. The water roared. A woman began to whimper, and someone else cursed.

Grace remembered all the people who had drowned in the treacherous waters. In her mind she pictured Jake caught beneath that pile of debris, helplessly entangled and fighting for his life. A scream began to build in her throat. Jake! Jake, where are you?

Then, with startling suddenness, he broke the surface on the other side of the snag, shooting up out of the water like a rocket. A cheer went up from the crowd, then another when they saw that he had the child in his grasp. Grace put her hand over her mouth and began to weep. "Jake. Oh, Jake."

"It's okay, sweetie," Caroline crooned, putting a comforting arm around Grace's shoulders. "He's safe now. Look, he's holding on to the log. And he's got the little girl. It's okay. Everything's going to be fine."

Harley began bellowing orders. "All right you men, line up behind me and grab on to this end of the rope. Hurry! Dammit! And when I say pull, put your weight into it!" Cupping his hands around his mouth, he yelled, "Jake! Here comes a rope. Grab hold!"

He whirled the lasso over his head a few times then sent it sailing out over the river. Jake made a grab for it, but missed, and everyone groaned. "Hold on! Hold on! We'll try again!" Harley shouted as he hauled the rope back in.

On the second try, Jake managed to snare the line. Hampered by the need to keep the child's head above water and hold onto the log at the same time, and extreme fatigue, Jake's movements were slow and awkward, but finally he had the lasso looped around his chest under his arms. Turning onto his back, he held the unconscious little girl high against his chest, gave the signal to the men on the shore and let go of the log.

"Pull! Pull!" Harley bellowed. The rope snapped taut and the current caught them, swinging them out into the flow. Its force jerked the line of men forward a step before they could dig in their heels. *"Pull! Pull, dammit!"*

Water foamed and bubbled over Jake's head and shoulders as the men on shore dragged him against the force of the current. Tense and fearful, Grace watched, unconsciously digging her nails into Caroline's palm. It seemed to take forever, but finally they dragged him out of the main current into the shallows by the shore.

Harley and two other men jumped into the water to give assistance. One man lifted the limp little girl from Jake's chest and handed her to someone on the shore, while Harley and the other man grasped Jake's arms and dragged him up onto the bank.

Coughing and sputtering, he lay back in the grass utterly exhausted, his feet still dangling in the water. "How you doing? You need a doctor?" Harley asked, kneeling beside him. All he received in the way of a reply was more coughing.

Jake was in the middle of a paroxysm when Grace pushed her way past the crowd gathering around the prostrate child and dropped down beside him.

"Oh, sweetheart, are you all right?" She ran her hands over him frantically, and made an agonized sound when she discovered several deep scratches on his chest and back. Finding a deep gash on his thigh she sucked in a hissing breath. "This needs stitching, I'm sure."

"There should be an ambulance here any minute to take him and the kid to the hospital over in Bedalia," Harley said. "Frank put in a call for one from the patrol car."

"No hos . . . pital," Jake gasped, stirring.

"Here now, you just lie quiet until the paramedics get here." Harley tried to hold him down, but, shaking his head, Jake pushed away his hand and struggled to a sitting position. "Ho-How's the . . . little gi-girl?" he sputtered between coughing spasms.

Caroline arrived in time to hear the question. "Daniel's giving her CPR. I think he's got her breathing on her own. She's bruised and scratched up, but it looks like she'll recover, thanks to you."

At that moment, as though right on cue, the little girl started to cry, and everyone around cheered and laughed. That outraged wail was the most wonderful sound any of them had ever heard.

Harley looked abashed at Jake. "I'm sorry I couldn't help you in the river. I never was much of a swimmer. I'd be lucky to save myself if I got out in that current."

"That's okay. I was glad to have someone . . . on shore I could c-count on to . . . throw me a li-lifeline."

"Oh, Jake, darling. You scared me half to death, but I'm so proud of you." Looping her arms around his shoulders, Grace covered his face with kisses and held him close, as the distant wail of a siren drew louder.

T.J. came up on Jake's other side, and his admiration bordered on awe.

The father of the little girl came over and shook Jake's hand and said somberly, "I can't thank you enough for what you did. Not many men would have jumped into that raging current. Not many would have survived it if they had. I know I wouldn't have. Me'n my wife, we just want you to know how grateful we are. We'll be forever in your debt, Mr. Paxton. If there's ever anything we can do for you, you just say the word."

"Don't worry about it," Jake said, looking uncomfortable. "I was glad to do it."

Several others, some of the very ones who had snubbed him only that morning, came over and commended him for his quick thinking and bravery. Jake appeared ill-at-ease and slightly suspicious, but he endured all the praise stoically.

From somewhere blankets were found and wrapped around the child and Jake, and several men's handkerchiefs were folded into a pad and tied around the gash in his thigh to stop the bleeding. Within minutes the paramedics arrived and loaded the little girl into the ambulance for the trip the hospital.

Grace argued with Jake that he should go too, but he wouldn't hear of it. She was so upset, as a compromise, he finally agreed to let Harley drive them to the Clinic so Dr. Watley could sew up his leg.

With Daniel on one side and Harley on the other, they helped him to his feet, but when they turned to head back to the van, Frank Sheffield stepped in their path.

Grace edged Daniel aside and took Jake's arm, moving in close to his side. She felt him tense as he fixed the deputy with a steady stare. "What do you want, Sheffield?"

Frank turned his Stetson around and around in his hands and shuffled his feet. He looked at Jake, then the ground, out at the river, then back at Jake. "I, uh . . . I just wanted to thank you. Susie Coleman—the kid you saved—she's my niece. My sister Darlene's girl."

"You don't have to thank me. I would have done the same for anyone."

"Yeah, well . . . maybe so, but I'm grateful all the same. My whole family is." Frank hesitated, then stuck out his hand. Jake's eyes narrowed. His gaze went from Frank's face to that outstretched hand, then back. Finally, slowly, he extended his own. Frank pumped Jake's hand vigorously. "Thanks, Paxton. Thanks a lot."

He started to let go, but Jake tightened his grip and stared straight into the young man's eyes. "I didn't kill your cousin."

For several tense seconds, Frank studied Jake's face. Then he nodded.

Forty-Four

FROM THE EDGE OF THE CROWD, hate-filled eyes watched as old friends and allies came up to Jake and offered thanks and praise. Oh, how that galled. That he should be a hero in the eyes of the local citizens was so deeply offensive the watcher wanted to scream.

Jake hopped on one foot toward Grace's van, his arms looped over the shoulders of the reverend and the police chief—the two most respected men in town. And there was Grace, scurrying along after them, carrying his clothes and full of concern.

All this gratitude and anxiety for a man like that. It was disgusting.

He should have drowned. Why hadn't he just drowned? Instead, people were beginning to treat him like . . . like an equal.

It was intolerable.

Forty-Five

"I CAN WALK ON MY OWN."

"Shut up, hardcase. Doc Watson said stay off that leg for the next twenty-four hours, and that's what you're going to do."

"Harley is right, Jake," Daniel said. "Besides, you're so dopey from that pain shot he gave you I doubt that you could stand."

"You could at least take me to my own place," Jake groused.

"We'll take you where it'll be easiest for Grace to look after you."

"I can look after myself. I don't need a nursemaid."

Ignoring him, Harley and Daniel maneuvered Jake through the back door. Inside the kitchen they stopped and looked at Grace. "Where do you want him?"

"This way." She held open the swinging door for them to follow her into the main hall. Another hall, one not quite as wide, bisected the main one at the halfway mark. Grace led them down the left branch and into a bedroom at the end.

"You can't put me in here," Jake protested. "This was your father's bedroom."

"That's right, it was. But it, along with the rest of the house, is mine now—at least, half mine—and I can do anything I want with it," she replied in a brisk tone. "It so happens this bedroom is downstairs, therefore convenient. Plus, it has a big bed, so you should be comfortable here."

She hurriedly turned down the covers and plumped the pillows. "Just put him right here."

"There you go, hardcase," Harley said as he and Daniel lowered Jake onto the bed. He lay back on the pile of pillows with a sigh and closed his eyes.

"Is there anything else we can do for you, Grace?"

"No, I think I can manage fine now. Thank you, Harley. You too, Daniel, for all your help."

"Hey, no problem. After what Jake did, it was the least we could do. But you just give a holler if he gives you any trouble and I'll come over and take care of it," Harley said with a grin.

One of Jake's eyes opened and his baleful gaze fixed on the sheriff. "Oh, yeah? You and whose army?"

"I told you he was a real hardcase," Harley said. Laughing, he and Daniel waved at Grace and went out the door.

"Are you comfortable? Do you need anything?"

"Don't fuss, sweetheart. I'm fine," Jake insisted as she bustled around him, plumping pillows and straightening the covers.

Paying no attention to his protests, she fetched a glass of water from the bathroom and shook out one of the tablets Dr. Watson had prescribed. Jake balked, insisting he didn't need any more pain killer, but she stood over him while he swallowed it down. When he was done she returned the glass to the bathroom and while there she used the facilities. A few minutes later, she reentered the bedroom and found him fast asleep.

She stood over him, her heart swelling as she looked down on that beloved face, his expression softer, more vulnerable in sleep. Dear God, how she loved him.

The sound of voices floated to her from the kitchen. She assumed that Caroline and Harley were still sparring. All during the picnic and on the drive home they had bickered and fussed and taken potshots at one another. Or rather, Caro had taken potshots at Harley.

It was getting dark. In the gloaming the trees were purple silhouettes against a darkening fiery red sky and the fields glowed a luminescent rose. Grace sat down in the big winged-back chair by the window and gazed out at the lovely sight.

At some point she must have dozed off, because she awoke with a start two hours later in pitch darkness to the sound of Jake calling her name.

"I'm here. I'm coming." She jumped out of the chair and hurried to the bedside, fumbling for the lamp switch.

At last she located the knob and gave it a turn, and as light flooded the room she looked at Jake anxiously. "What's wrong? Are you in pain?"

"Yeah. I need to go to the john."

"Is that all?" Grace exhaled a relieved sigh. From his urgent tone, she had thought he was in agony.

"What do you mean, is that all? My bladder's about to burst."

Chuckling, even as her cheeks turned pink, Grace threw back the covers and helped him to the bathroom.

After she had him settled in bed again, she brought him a dinner tray containing three ham and cheese sandwiches, a huge bowl of vegetable soup and a tumbler of milk, all of which he devoured with his usual hearty appetite.

When Grace had dealt with the dishes she showered and put on a nightgown and robe and returned to Jake's room, prepared to keep an all-night vigil by his bedside.

She sat down beside him on the bed. "How do you feel?" she asked, laying the back of her hand against his forehead to check for fever.

"Fine."

"Is there any pain?"

"Not much."

"Oh, Jake, I was so scared—"

"Shh." He hushed her with a forefinger against her lips.

"It's over, and everything turned out all right. Forget it. Okay?"

She gave him a watery smile and nodded, and he removed his finger.

"Is there anything else you want?"

A hint of a smile played about Jake's mouth, but there was no amusement in his hot gaze. It skimmed downward over her neck and shoulders and came to rest on creamy breasts, swelling above the low-cut neck of her deep rose nightgown. When he looked up, his eyes were a dark, stormy green. "Yes," he said in a husky voice. "You."

A surprised giggle shot up out of Grace's throat. "Jake! You know we can't."

"The hell we can't."

"But . . . but your leg—"

"You just let me worry about my leg."

He unbuttoned her robe and removed it. For a moment he simply stared at the form-fitting bodice of rose lace. He reached out and traced one long finger along the edge of her gown, leaving a trail of fire on her skin. Grace's eyes grew cloudy as a delicious shiver ripped through her. Smiling, Jake slipped the finger into her cleavage, hooked the low neck of the gown and tugged her closer.

Grace did not even try to resist. When Jake touched her in that way, looked at her with that smoldering heat in his eyes, her common sense flew out the window and her will and her flesh turned as weak as a soggy noodle.

"We'll take it nice and easy," he whispered.

With slow, deliberate movements that sent little tingles racing over her skin, he eased first one, then the other strap from her shoulders.

At his urging, Grace slipped her arms free, and the lacy garment slid down her body to puddle in soft folds around her waist. Bracing up on one elbow, Jake touched the tip of his tongue to one nipple. It peaked instantly, and Grace gasped as he toyed with the bud, mouthing it gently. Moaning, she threw her head back and clutched his shoulders, digging her nails into firm muscles as the sweet torment went on and on. At last he drew the tender bud deep into his mouth and suckled with slow, strong suction.

Grace made a little keening sound. "Darling. Oh, my love."

Cold air hit her wet flesh as he abandoned the nipple to lavish the same attention on the other breast. Grace arched her spine and clasped his head, pulling him closer, wanting, needing more.

She was almost delirious with pleasure when Jake eased back onto the pillow, pulling her with him. "Lift your hips, love," he murmured, pushing her nightgown downward. She obeyed without thought, and as the nightie slithered to the floor, Grace found herself lying half over Jake.

He felt warm and wonderfully alive. After the scare of almost losing him she could not touch him enough, and her hands ran frantically over his chest, his flat belly, down his thighs, over his burgeoning sex. Her hand cupped and stroked and gently squeezed. Jake lay with his head back, his teeth gritted.

He felt warm and wonderful and masculine and sexy, and her heart raced like a runaway train when her breasts pushed into the silky mat of hair on his chest. Then her knee bumped against his bandage, and she stiffened and jerked her hand back. "Jake, I don't think—"

"Don't think," he gasped. "Just feel. Feel how much I want you. How much I need you." He took her hand and guided it back where he wanted it, and as her fingers enclosed his velvet hardness he moaned.

"Did I hurt you?" Grace tried to snatch her hand away, but Jake tightened his hold and chuckled.

"Hardly. Just relax, sweetheart. Forget about my leg."

He lifted her until she was stretched out full length on top of him. He rocked his hips against her and chuckled again at her gasp of pleasure. "Now, I want you to do exactly as I say."

As his mouth played with her ear he murmured instructions in a deep voice that sent fire sweeping from Grace's toes to the roots of her hair.

"Ja-aake!"

He laughed wickedly and ran his fingertips down the groove of her spine, all the way to the shadowy cleft at its base. "Do it," he ordered, and that sexy growl made dust of her weak protest.

Shyly at first, then with growing boldness, she complied. "Is this what you mean?" she asked in a sly, provocative voice.

"Yes, that's the way," Jake groaned. "That's it. Yes. Oh, God yes."

"Ahhhhh, love."

Forty-Six

"No, no. Don't get up. I just want to shake your hand, young man," Dewey Ackerman said, extending his gnarled hand across the table to Jake.

"Me, too," his brother Dwayne echoed. "That was a mighty fine thing you done, yesterday, boy. A mighty fine thing. That poor little mite woulda been a goner if it wasn't for you."

"That's right," Dewey added, not to be outdone by his twin. "An' me'n Dwayne, we just wanted to tell you we're right proud of you." He looked around, then leaned forward and added confidentially, "Never did believe all those things that was said about you, nohow."

"Thanks," Jake replied dryly, but neither old man caught the skepticism in his voice.

Gregarious as always, the Ackerman brothers continued to chat with Jake and Grace until Doris came and placed their lunch order on the table. Excusing themselves, the Ackermans left the diner to return to their spot on the bench outside the barbershop next door.

Grace's lips twitched. "You should feel flattered. It isn't often Dewey and Dwayne stir from their bench for anyone."

For the past twenty years, ever since the brothers had retired and sold the barbershop to Floyd Digby, they had spent the better part of each day on the bench, playing checkers, gathering and dispensing the latest gossip and monitoring the comings and goings of the townspeople. During the day, they left their bench only for meals and nature's call.

Jake grimaced and picked up his hamburger. "I wish they hadn't bothered. I don't know why everyone is making such a fuss."

"They're making a fuss because you did a courageous thing."

"It wasn't courageous at all. It was impulse. If I'd taken time to think about it I probably wouldn't have done it."

"Ah, but the point is, you did."

He scowled and she fought back a grin as she tucked into her sandwich. Poor Jake. Praise and gratitude were things he had received precious little of in his life, and he did not know how to handle them.

The congratulations and praise had been pouring in all morning. Much to Jake's discomfort, a steady stream of people had come by the shop to thank him for saving the little girl's life. On the way to the store that morning, one man had even stepped up to the van to commend him while they had been stopped at Cedar Grove's one and only traffic light. Jake was clearly the man of the hour, and not at all comfortable in the role.

Now that word of his deed had spread, the general opinion of him had altered. People were beginning to voice the opinion that whoever had killed Carla Mae, and possibly Connie, too, it couldn't have been Jake. The consensus seemed to be that only a low-down, craven coward could have hacked up a woman in that brutal way, and Jake Paxton was no coward. Anyway, whoever heard of a cold-blooded killer risking his own life to save someone else?

"You might as well get used to it, you know," Grace advised. "You're a hero now."

"I'm no hero. I'm the same guy I've always been. The one everyone here wanted to see fry twelve years ago."

The bitterness in his voice made her wince, but she understood it. "I know. But now a lot of them are beginning to realize that there is much more to you than that surly bad-boy image you worked so hard to project." She reached across the table and put her hand on his arm. When he looked up and met her eyes they were soft with entreaty. "Give them a chance, darling. You'll find that most of them are nice, decent people."

He grunted in response, and she raised her eyebrows. "Is it so horrible, having folks be nice to you?"

Jake's mouth twisted. "It just doesn't seem natural," he grumbled. "It's weird."

Grace laughed and picked up her egg salad sandwich.

Weird or not, during the following week Jake was forced to accept that the town's overall attitude toward him had changed. When he walked down the street people waved and called a greeting. Store clerks were friendly to him. People he met in stores and on the street stopped to chat. Even Grace's Aunt Lollie stopped by the shop to offer to help with the wedding, which was scheduled for a week from Sunday. She also sang his praises all over town. To hear Lollie talk, she had known all along what a sterling young man he was.

However, the changes were due to more than merely Jake's good deed and his recent, if somewhat strained, attempts at cordiality. Namely, Grace's aunt.

Verna Ames might have been the richest woman in town and she definitely held a high opinion of her position, but Miss Harriet Tucker was the undisputed social leader of Cedar Grove.

She was, after all, the great-granddaughter of the town's founders, the president of the Cedar Grove Historical Society, past president of the Woman's Club and the Garden Club, chairwoman of the annual Founder's Day celebration and charter member of the Knitter's Guild, the Quilter's Guild and the Duplicate Bridge Club.

In addition, for forty-three years, Miss Harriet had taught seventh-grade English to the children of Cedar Grove. There was hardly an adult in town under the age of fifty-five—from the mayor right down to Ollie Adams, who drove the town's only garbage truck—whom she had not had in her class, and most of them, at one time or another, had felt the sting of her ever-ready ruler.

To Miss Harriet they were all still young whipper-snappers. She knew them inside out—their strengths, their weaknesses, their character flaws. It was difficult, if not downright impossible, to put on airs with or exert any authority over, or for that matter, in any way oppose a woman who had whacked your knuckles for throwing spitballs or marched you by your ear to the principal's office. Miss Harriet didn't take any guff off of anyone, and when she voiced an opinion, people listened.

Her full support and constant championing of Jake, plus the rescue of the little girl, had put a different light on things, and Harriet's friends had all hastily lined up behind her.

There were a few diehards, of course. Ida Bell and Martha and their friends refused to believe anything good about Jake, and Lyle made no secret of his hatred for him. When the engagement had been announced, Lyle had flown into a rage, and with the tide of support for Jake growing he had become more and more vocal with his opinions. He had made the remark more than once in public that he would rather see Grace dead than lose her to the likes of Jake Paxton.

However, despite Lyle's blustering and the vicious tongues of the gossips, day by day, support for Jake grew.

Grace was beginning to feel hopeful for their future.

Forty-Seven

THE SITUATION WAS INTOLERABLE. Unbearable. It could not be allowed to continue.

Everyone was beginning to revise their opinion of Jake Paxton. Some were openly expressing doubts that he could have murdered Carla Mae. Even the Sheffields. Just because he saved that silly, sniveling brat from drowning.

The fools! Stupid, ignorant fools! Couldn't they see that Jake was no good? He was trash! Worthless. He deserved to suffer. To be locked away with the other dregs of humanity

The watcher seethed with impotent rage. The time had come to teach Jake a lesson he would never forget.

Forty-Eight

On Saturday, the weekend after the picnic, Verna walked into the shop, and Grace's spirits fell. She should have known that things were going too well. The last thing she wanted was to get into another argument with her mother-in-law.

"Hello, Verna. What are you doing here?" she asked in a less than cordial voice. Verna had never set foot in the shop before. She had disapproved of Grace going into business and becoming independent, and refusing to visit was her way of punishing Grace for doing so.

"Hello, dear. My, my, what an attractive little store you have." She walked slowly around the main showroom, smiling and running her fingertips over the surface of tables and settees, fingering the fringe on lamps and picking up bric-a-brac. "I didn't realize you had such a knowledge of antiques or such excellent taste. Why, I might even find something suitable for the Willows here."

The old Grace might have eagerly jumped at that dangled bait, but not the new Grace. "Verna, we both know you're not here to shop. So why have you come? Frankly, after our last meeting, I'm surprised."

Dropping any pretense of interest in the merchandise, Verna rushed to Grace and took her hands and gazed at her with imploring eyes. "Oh Grace, dearest, that's why I'm here. I can't bear to leave things the way they were. You're like my very own daughter, and this animosity between us is breaking my heart." On cue, Verna's eyes filled with tears and her chin started to wobble. When Grace failed to respond, Verna squeezed her hands tighter.

"Please, Grace. I'm an old lady, all alone in the world except for you and Lyle. I need you."

It was blatant manipulation. Grace knew that. Still, she felt a twinge of pity. "I don't know, Verna. After all that was said, I don't see how—"

"Oh, but that's all in the past. I realize now that I was wrong about Jake. It appears that I misjudged him terribly. He's proven himself a man of courage and strong moral fiber. It takes a big person to overcome the origins and upbringing he had and become a decent person."

Grace winced at that, but Verna rushed right ahead. "I'm so ashamed for my earlier attitude and all the horrible things I said. Please say you'll forgive me, Grace. I shall just die if you don't. I lost my darling son. I can't lose you, too."

The tears that banked against Verna's lower eyelids spilled over and ran unchecked down her cheeks, and Grace's tender heart melted. She put her arms around the older woman and pulled her close, patting her back as she sobbed daintily against her shoulder. "Hush. Hush, now. It will be all right. You won't lose me. I promise."

"Really?" Pulling back, Verna looked hopefully at Grace and dabbed at her eyes with a lace-edged hankie. "Oh, my dear, you've made an old woman so happy. So very, very happy." She stopped and flashed Grace a tragic look. "But what about your young man. Will he forgive me?"

"I don't know, Verna. I can't speak for Jake."

"But you will talk to him, won't you? Try to make him understand?"

"Yes. I'll try."

"Oh, I know! Perhaps you could both come to dinner tomorrow after church?"

"Oh, Verna, I don't think . . ."

"Please, Grace. At least ask your young man."

Grace hesitated, biting her lip, but she couldn't deny that imploring look. "All right. I'll ask him, but I can't promise anything."

THE MOMENT HE RETURNED from making a delivery Grace broached the matter. His answer was not unexpected.

"No. Absolutely not. You can go if you want to, but I don't want to have anything to do with that woman."

"Jake—"

"No, Grace. I'll do damn near anything for you, but I draw the line at socializing with Verna Ames."

Disappointment wafted through Grace, but when he had that flinty look in his eyes she knew better than to argue. She couldn't really blame him either, considering his history with the Ames family.

"I understand," she murmured in a subdued voice. Immediately Jake's tense stance relaxed and his harsh expression softened. Stepping close, Grace rested her palms on his chest and fiddled with the third button on his shirt. "Did you mean what you said? Would you really do almost anything for me?"

Smiling, he looped his arms around her and laced his fingers together at the small of her back. An indulgent smile played about his mouth. "As long as it's legal and doesn't involve anyone named Ames."

"So . . . if I asked for a very special favor, even if it was something you would detest, you'd do it?"

"Just name it."

She stared at the button she was fingering, then looked up into his eyes. "Before we get married, I want you to try one more time to make peace with your mother."

"What!" His scowl returned, darker than before. "Grace, you don't know what you're asking."

"Please, Jake, do this for me. She's your mother. There has to be some way to heal the bad feelings between you. Won't you at least try?"

He frowned, his expression a mix of exasperation and love. "Sweetheart, you don't understand. Not everyone had the kind of family you knew growing up. You saw Lizzie that night at the pharmacy. She hates me. She always has."

"Oh, no. Surely not. She's your mother."

"Ah, Jesus." Releasing her, Jake raked a hand through his hair and walked to the other side of the room. Grace watched his tense back and waited. Finally he swung back and looked at her. "You just don't get it, do you? Grace, there are mothers and there are mothers. Lizzie doesn't have a maternal bone in her body, or an ounce of feeling for anyone but herself. Growing up, I was just a brat she got saddled with, a nuisance and an expense she resented. She detests me. She always has. I accepted that years ago."

"Please, Jake. At least try. Maybe she's changed. Maybe she regrets the things she's done. I feel terrible that we're planning a wedding and not even inviting her. Please. Won't you do this for me?"

He sighed and ran his palm down over his face, his shoulders slumping. "All right. She'll probably spit in my face, but if it's that important to you I'll talk to her."

Forty-Nine

JAKE DROVE HIS TRUCK along Tobin Road with his jaw set so tight his teeth ached. He passed the Jasper Creek Trailer Court and kept going. The seedy cluster of mobile homes where T.J. had lived marked the beginning of the Bottoms. Actually, the trailer court was the more upscale section.

God, he hated coming back here. He hated being reminded that this was his world, this was where he'd come from. He wanted to turn the truck around and get the hell out of there.

But he couldn't. He'd promised Grace.

With every mile the houses and trailers and tarpaper shacks got more run-down and seedy. This was the poor section of Cedar Grove, the part the tourist and summer folks over on the lake never saw. Here were the indigent and the lowliest workers, domestics, handymen, waitresses, cooks and yardmen. Some were decent hardworking people down on their luck. Some were lazy and worthless. Some were simply mean and shiftless riff-raff without an ounce of ambition or drive who blamed all their troubles on everyone else.

Here yards were overgrown with weeds and strewn with junk. Dirty, barefoot children in ragged clothes played in the areas of packed dirt around the front doors. They were all pot-bellied and skinny and big-eyed from lack of proper nourishment. Jake knew that, because he'd once been one of them. As he drove by they stopped what they were doing, to stare at him.

He saw fat, shapeless women in faded cotton dresses sitting in listless silence on sagging front stoops and porches. They all looked the same—straggly hair, rough, worn skin, an occasional slip strap drooping down an arm, a cigarette dangling from the corner of a mouth or from nicotine-stained fingers. Surly men in dingy, tank-top style undershirts stared at Jake with distrust. They all looked to be in their fifties or better, but he knew that many were in their thirties and forties, some even in their twenties, but life and booze and hopelessness had taken their toll. Such was the life of grinding poverty.

Shit, he'd sooner die that return to this.

A couple of miles past the trailer park he turned down a rutted dirt track that passed for a driveway and stopped before the dilapidated frame house. He switched off the engine and sat, staring at the place that had been his home for the first nineteen years of his life.

The place looked much the same as it had twelve years before, except that it was more dilapidated than ever and there was more junk in the yard. The house leaned in on itself from every side, which was probably all that kept it from falling down.

Once, many years ago, it had been a neat farmhouse. Its original owners had even embellished the eaves and front porch with fancy Victorian woodwork. Most of that had long since rotted and fallen off. The house hadn't seen a coat of paint in Jake's lifetime and the exterior was a weathered gray. A few curling paint chips in protected places were all that was left of the original blue paint and white trim. An ancient divan, with stuffing coming out in several places, sat on the front porch, along with numerous empty beer cans.

Jake's upper lip curled. *Fuck.*

The chickens that scratched and clucked among the weeds scattered, squawking and flapping their wings as he climbed from the truck.

Someone had crudely patched the rotten spot in the porch, but from the squeaks the boards made as he walked across them they needed to be replaced again. He half expected Lizzie to appear in the doorway or bellow out a demand to know who was there, but the only sound from inside was the drone of the television. Jake stepped to the torn screened door and looked in.

His mother lay sprawled on the sagging sofa. While Oprah talked to a woman about juvenile crime, rumbling snores came from Lizzie's open mouth. The hand on her stomach held a can of beer tilted at a precarious angle. Several more empties lay on the linoleum beside the couch.

Jake opened the screened door and stepped inside. He turned off the television and walked over to the couch. For a moment, he stood looking down at the woman who had borne him. It was the middle of the afternoon, and already she was in a stupor. Disgust and pity and a host of other emotions, all unwanted, rose up inside him, making his chest hurt.

His jaw clenched. Dammit, he was either the world's biggest sap or a glutton for punishment. He shouldn't feel anything for her but revulsion and hatred. That was all she deserved from him.

"Lizzie." He reached down and shook her shoulder. "Lizzie, wake up."

She mumbled something and batted at his hand as though shooing a fly.

"Lizzie."

Her eyes blinked opened. They were unfocused and bleary at first, then they cleared. She frowned. "What the hell are you doing here?"

"I need to talk to you."

"Oh, yeah." She sat up, scratching her belly. Her dyed red hair frizzed in all directions and her makeup looked as though it had been on for days. An unpleasant smell emanated from her, a combination of sweat, cheap perfume and beer. She lifted the can of beer to her lips, but when nothing came out she tossed it on the floor with the others. "Well, I ain't got nothing to say to you, so just get the hell out of my house and stay out."

"In a minute. First I've got some things to say to you."

"Maybe you didn't hear me. I said get your sorry ass outta my house."

"Dammit, Lizzie, will you just listen for a minute. I came here to try to patch things up between us."

"What the hell for?"

"For one thing, we're family, all either of us has as far as I know."

She let loose a nasty chuckle that caused her belly to jiggle. "You think I care? Shit, I didn't want you when you was born. I sure as hell ain't got no use for you now."

Jake's jaw tightened. That shouldn't have hurt. It wasn't as though he hadn't known. But dammit, it had hurt. Like hell.

Jake wanted nothing so much as to get out of there. To leave this place with its ugly memories, this woman to her hate. If it wasn't for the promise he'd made to Grace he'd walk out and never set eyes on the boozy old bag again.

"Look, I know you don't have any motherly feelings for me." She snorted at that but he gritted his teeth and forged on. "Maybe you never will. That's probably asking too much, given our past. But, hell, couldn't we at least try to be civil to one another?"

Giving him a sardonic look, Lizzie lumbered up off the couch and staggered into the kitchen. Jake heard the refrigerator open, and a moment later he heard the pop and hiss of a can tab being opened. "So you want me to be civil to you, huh?" She came weaving back to the doorway between the living room and kitchen and leaned against the jamb. She lifted the can and took a long pull. When done she wiped her mouth with the back of her hand and cackled. "Why don't you come out and say what you really mean?

"Meaning?"

"That you want your mama to love you," she jeered.

Jake stiffened as though he'd been slapped, and she cackled again.

"Shit, didn't you think I knew? You think I didn't catch those soulful looks of yours when you was a brat? The way you used to scurry around trying to please me? At least when you was a little 'un. When you got older you was just a snotty delinquent. I'd'a thrown you out when you started back-talking if it wouldn't've brought the law down on me."

"I see," Jake said dully.

"Yeah, well just so you do, lemme spell it out for you. You got about as much chance of me giving a shit about you now as you did then."

"Fine. If that's the way you want it." He strode toward the door, but when he reached it he stopped and looked back. "Just so you'll know, the main reason I came out here was to tell you that Grace and I are getting married."

"Grace? You mean the preacher's daughter? The one who was married to Charles Ames?"

"Yes."

Lizzie took another swig of beer and chuckled. "Oh, that's rich. Little Miss Pure as the Driven Snow Grace has really got a thing for Ames men, don't she? First Charles and now you."

Jake froze. He felt as though he'd just had all the air punched out of his lungs. "What did you say?" he demanded in a deadly whisper.

Lizzie staggered to the middle of the room and stood there, swaying. "I said your girlfriend's hooked on Ames men. First she spread her legs for Charles, now you. You think she knows you're brothers?"

"Jesus. Are you saying . . . ?" He stopped. The idea seemed so preposterous he couldn't believe it. "Are you telling me that Franklin Ames was . . . my father?"

For an instant Lizzie looked triumphant. A second later the realization of what she'd done penetrated her alcoholic fog and her smirk collapsed. Her expression turned sullen, but fear swam in her eyes. "I never said that."

"Oh, yes you did." Jake walked back into the room. Lizzie took a quick step back and stumbled. She landed awkwardly, sprawling hard on the sofa. Jake bent over her, one hand braced on the back, the other on the arm. At any other time the combined stench of her body and dirty upholstery would have turned his stomach, but he was totally focused on getting an answer from her and barely noticed. "You said I was an Ames. That Grace was attracted to Ames men."

"That was a mistake."

"Yeah, and you made it. I tried for years to get you to tell me who my father was and you laughed in my face. No more. You're going to tell me the truth, old woman. All of it. I'm not leaving here until you do."

She glared up at him with pure hatred, but this time it had no effect. He stared right back, unmoved.

"All right, you little prick. You want to know if Franklin was your father? Well, the answer is yes. How does that grab you? You're an Ames. Old Franklin's first born, as a matter of fact." She snickered. "Damn, how that has always galled the snooty bitch he married."

"You mean his wife knew?"

"Not at first, but she found out. That old fool Franklin got drunk one night and got to feelin' bad about abandoning his kid and he blubbered the whole thing to her." Lizzie gave another beery chuckle. "I sure woulda like to been a fly on the wall that night. That Verna, she musta had a wall-eyed fit. She made old Franklin's life miserable after that.

"You were born ten months after Franklin married Verna Phelps, and over a year before she whelped that sniveling brat of hers." Lizzie laughed cruelly, and he could see the perverse pleasure gleaming in her eyes. "That's the main reason I kept you around. Just knowing you existed made old Franklin and that snotty wife of his antsy as hell. Franklin gave me a monthly allowance to keep quiet. Since his death, Verna's continued to send the checks each month."

That surprised him, and it must have shown on his face.

Lizzie cackled again. "I told her that I have the proof of who your father was in an envelope, tucked away in a safe place, with instructions that in case I should die of anything but natural causes, it's to be opened. I don't trust that old bitch not to murder me, now that Franklin's not around."

Jake straightened. Numb, he stood still as stone and stared in the distance at nothing. He hadn't had a clue. He remembered all the times he'd passed Franklin Ames on the street. The man hadn't even looked at him.

"Knocked the props out from under you, didn't I?" Lizzie's

taunting statement drew his attention. She smiled at him evilly. "How does it feel to know that all those years you shoulda been living the good life up there at the Willows? You coulda had nice clothes and good food and a fancy car, same as that little prick Charles. It always tickled me to see you living like a little sewer rat, knowing you was entitled to a share of the Ames fortune."

"Why? For once in your sorry life, just tell me why?"

"Cause I hated Franklin," she snarled. "I hated him for picking that prissy Verna over me, when he'd been makin' it with me for years. I was good enough to screw but not to marry. For knockin' me up and leaving me saddled with his brat. That's why."

Jake stared at the venom in her eyes, and his stomach twisted. It wasn't even him. She hated his father, and he'd been an easy target for that hatred.

"Charles musta been delighted when you was arrested," she jeered. "That snooty little asshole wasn't the type to take kindly to having you as a brother."

Jake sucked in a sharp breath. "Charles knew about me, too?"

Lizzie shrugged. "Probably. The way Verna always doted on him like he was the Prince of Wales or somethin' I figure she was bound to have told him."

Prickles skittered down Jake's spine. For years he'd tried to figure out who had killed Carla Mae, but he hadn't been able to come up with anyone who had a motive for the crime . . . until now.

Ever since he could remember there had been bad blood between him and Charles, and by association, his cousin Lyle. Charles had been an arrogant dickhead, and Jake had just plain never liked him, but maybe the reason for Charles's animosity had gone deeper. Jake had always chalked up their eagerness to testify against him at the murder trials to that animosity, but maybe that too was an oversimplification."

"I don't like that look on your face," Lizzie said, frowning. "What're you thinkin'?"

Jake shot her a cold look and headed toward the door. Lurching to her feet, Lizzie staggered after him. "What're you up to? You come back here!"

Ignoring her, Jake strode from the tumble-down shack, his face hard with anger and purpose.

"Jake! Jake, wait! You gotta keep quiet about what I told you. You hear! You can't tell anybody. You can't!"

Jake marched across the packed dirt yard as though he hadn't heard a word of her frantic shouts.

"Did you hear me? You can't tell!"

He opened the driver's door on his truck, then paused and looked at her over the top of the cab. "Oh, yeah? Watch me."

"Damn you! You worthless piece of shit! If you spill the beans you'll ruin everything! Verna will stop sending the money!"

"Tough."

Fifty

JAKE DROVE STRAIGHT to the sheriff's office. Driven by an urgency that had him wound tight as a spring, he shoved through the double doors of the station house without breaking stride or slowing.

He didn't bother to check in with the desk sergeant. He headed straight for Harley's office.

"Hey, wait a minute," the pretty officer behind the front desk yelled. "You can't just barge in there! Wait!"

Jake heard footsteps pounding down the hall after him but he kept going. The venetian blinds on the door and the glass inner wall of Harley's office were open, and Jake could see him sitting reared back in his chair, his booted feet propped on his desk and crossed at the ankles as he perused a piece of paper.

Without bothering to knock, Jake thrust open the door and went inside.

Harley glanced up, a look of mild surprise on his face. "Well, hello, hardcase. C'mon in, why don't you?" he said dryly.

"I have to talk to you."

Sergeant Bailey skidded to a halt just outside the door, out of breath and agitated. "Sorry, Chief. I tried to stop him."

"That's okay, Betty Sue. Just go on back to the desk. I'll handle this."

"Well . . . if you say so."

She cast a disapproving glance at Jake as he closed the door in her face and shut the blind. He quickly did the same to the other blind, ensuring privacy.

Leaning back in his chair with his hands folded over his middle, Harley watched with interest, and when Jake finished he cocked one eyebrow. "Okay, hardcase, what do you have to talk to me about that's so important?"

"I think I know who the killer is."

Harley's expression remained placid, but the slight tensing of his body revealed his interest. "Really? Who?"

"Charles Ames."

"What?" Harley chuckled. "Look, I know the guy was a worthless asshole, but I have a hard time thinking of him as a killer. Anyway, what possible motive would he've had to kill Carla Mae?

"Jealousy, maybe—I'm not sure. But I think I know why he tried to pin her murder on me."

"Oh, yeah?"

"He found out that he and I were brothers."

Harley's feet hit the floor with a thud. "You're *what?* "

Quickly, Jake filled him in on what he had just learned. Harley listened with amazement, his mouth hanging open.

"Charles had to have hated the thought of us being related. But even more, he would have hated the thought of possibly having to share the family fortune if it ever came out."

"Hmm. I don't doubt you're right about that."

"I thought about it on the way here, and it explains a lot. Like why he seemed to hate me so much when we barely knew each other, why he went out of his way to goad me, but always when he had a crowd of friends around him. He didn't have the guts to pull that shit when we were one on one.

"Hell, the guy had everything, but he always wanted whatever I had." Jake shrugged. "A pair of athletic shoes, a jacket, a girl, you name it—it didn't matter. If he couldn't take it from me—which he never could—or get something better and show me up, he tried to destroy what I had.

"Once someone put sugar in the gas tank of my Harley. I can't prove it, but I'm sure it was Charles. And you've got to admit, he was damned anxious to testify against me in the trial."

"So you think he was jealous of you and Carla Mae?"

"I don't think, I know. He'd been after her for months, but she wouldn't give him the time of day. I figure, when I dropped her off that night, he forced her into his car—"

"You mean kidnapped her?"

"Yeah. You know what he was like. When Charles wanted something he thought he ought to have it. It pissed him off good that she preferred me. And if he knew we were makin' it together, which he probably did, he had to have been livid. I figure he raped her and she fought, which made him even more furious, and he killed her—maybe accidentally, maybe not."

"Well, now. In theory, that all makes sense, but it's not hard evidence. Plus you're forgetting something. All the evidence points to one killer. Charles Ames was long dead when Connie Tolson was murdered."

"Did you ever know Charles to do anything without his cousin tagging along? Lyle was his own personal toady and fan club all wrapped in one. He'd get down on all fours and wipe Charles's boots just for the privilege of hanging out with him."

"That's the God's truth. I never saw anyone kiss ass like old Lyle used to."

"That's why Charles kept him around—to stroke his ego. If Charles killed Carla Mae you can bet that, at the very least, Lyle was there when he did it." Jake fixed Harley with an intent look. "Remember, the semen found in her body was from two men, neither of which was me."

"Hmm." Harley leaned back in his chair and tugged at his lower lip. "So, you're saying you think Lyle took his turn at raping her and was an accessory to her murder, and he killed Connie in the same way so that you would take the rap? Why? What reason would Lyle have to frame you?"

"The same reasons Charles had—jealousy and greed. Think about it. If I was a threat to Charles I'm even more of a threat to Lyle. If I could have proved in court that I am Franklin Ames's son, Charles might have been forced to share the Ames fortune, but Lyle would lose all claim to it. In Texas, cousins don't inherit when there is a direct heir."

"You got a point there." An arrested look came over Harley's face. "And Lyle's been going around telling people he'd rather see Grace dead than married to you."

"He *what?*" Fear snaked through Jake. He stared at Harley.

"The wedding is a week from tomorrow. Jesus. I've got to call Grace."

He reached across the desk and snatched up Harley's telephone. His hand shook as he punched out the numbers. Taut as a violin string, he listened to the ringing at the other end.

Answer. Answer, he silently commanded, but after the seventh ring he hung up. "She's not at home." He shot Harley a desperate look and fought to battle down panic.

"Maybe she's at the shop."

"No. Caroline has started taking over for her on Saturdays."

"Why don't you call anyway. Maybe she decided to work today for some reason."

"Yeah, maybe," he said, but he didn't believe it. He quickly punched out the number, and when Caroline answered he snapped, "Caro. It's Jake. Is Grace there?"

"No. She's off today, remember."

"I know, but I thought she might have come in. Do you know where she is?"

"She's supposed to be at home."

"I see. Okay, thanks." He hung up and looked at Harley. "She's not there. Dammit! I'm going to find that prick, Lyle and—"

"Now take it easy. Take it easy. Grace could be anywhere. Hell, she might be outside, or in the shower."

"Yeah, maybe," Jake mumbled without conviction. "She was there about an hour and a half ago when I left the farm, and she didn't say anything about leaving." He paced in front of the desk and tried to calm himself, but it was no use. With a curse, he swung toward the door. "Dammit, I can't stand this. I'm going to find Lyle."

"Whoa, there, hardcase. Not so fast." Harley stood up and plucked his Stetson from the rack. "*We* will find Lyle. I don't want to have to throw your ass in jail again. Grace and Caro would come after me with a gun. Besides, we don't have much to go on, but I wouldn't mind asking him a few questions myself."

DARN. Holding the receiver with its droning dial tone away from her ear, Grace gave it a sour look then slammed it back on the hook. Why did people always hang up just as you answered?

The fingerprints on the receiver caught her eye, and she glanced down at her dirt-encrusted hands and made a face. She could never seem to remember to wear gardening gloves. Ruefully, she looked down at her knees. They had fared no better. Beneath her cutoffs, both were caked with mud.

With a shrug, Grace recrossed the kitchen and shouldered open the screened door. Five minutes later she was once more kneeling in the flowerbeds along the driveway, digging up a clump of *Caladium* bulbs with a trowel, when Verna's car turned into the drive.

Straightening, Grace waved a dirt-caked hand as her mother-in-law climbed out of the car and hurried toward her. She sent up a silent thank-you that Jake wasn't there. Something about Verna set his back up.

"Hi. This is a surprise. What brings you out here today?" she called, but her smile faded when she saw Verna's expression. She knew at once that something was wrong. Dropping her trowel, she stood up. "What is it?"

"Now dearest, stay calm," Verna advised, which, of course, had the opposite effect. Grace's anxiety doubled.

"I knew it. Something's happened. Tell me."

"It's Harriet. She collapsed right in the middle of the bridge tournament."

"Oh, no!" Grace gasped and put her hand over her mouth. She stared at her mother-in-law and felt the blood drain from her face.

"I know, dearest. I know," Verna sympathized, patting her arm. "But don't you worry, she's on her way to Bedalia by ambulance right now. Some of the others wanted to call you, but I said I would come break the news to you myself."

"Thank you. I . . . I appreciate it." Grace dithered, wringing her hands, too upset to think straight. "I've got to go to her."

"Of course you do. I'll drive you. You're in no condition to be behind the wheel of a car. But first you must clean up and change."

"Oh, but I—"

"Grace, dearest, you can't go like that. Just look at you. Why, you've even got dirt on your face." Taking her arm, Verna hustled her around the house and in through the back door. "Now you just go wash up and change, and I'll write a note for Caroline and Jake so they'll know where you are."

"Oh, of course. I . . . I hadn't even thought about that. Thank you, Verna. I don't know what I'd do without you."

"Nonsense. That's what families are for. Now you just run along and get ready and we'll be on our way."

IT DIDN'T TAKE THEM LONG to find Lyle. In a town the size of Cedar Grove, a flashy car like his BMW stood out like a hooker at a tent revival.

Spotting it parked in front of the City Diner, Harley pulled the patrol car in behind it. Jake was already out of the car and striding toward the door by the time Harley shut off the engine. "Oh Christ. Jake! Hold up!" he yelled as he bailed out and hurried after him.

Jake stormed into the diner and made a beeline for Lyle, who sat at the counter, flirting with the waitress. When he reached him, Jake slapped both hands down on Lyle's shoulders and spun him around on the stool.

"Wha—?"

Jake thrust his forearm against his neck and bent him back again the bar, holding him there. Lyle's face turned purple and his eyes bugged out. "Where's Grace," Jake snarled in his face. "What have you done with her, you creep?" He clenched his jaws and struggled to resist an overpowering urge to plant his fist in Lyle's weak-chinned face.

"Hey, whoa there. Back off, hardcase," Harley commanded, grabbing Jake's arms from behind and pulling him away.

"If he's harmed her in any way I'm going to—"

"Knock it off!" Harley warned. He gave him a shake for good measure. Pointing a warning forefinger in his face, he hissed for Jake's ears alone, "Dammit, don't go making threats in a public like that. Lot of folks, if they heard you, wouldn't take kindly to that kind of thing, especially coming from you."

Jake wanted to shout that he didn't give a rat's ass, but one look into Harley's face and he clamped his mouth shut and glared daggers at Lyle, who was coughing and sputtering.

"Wha-What the hell is wro- . . . wrong with . . . him? I was ju-just sit . . . sitting here and he . . . attacked me."

"Yeah, well, Jake's a little unstrung right now."

It was late afternoon, too early for the dinner crowd, so there were just a few people in the diner, but the commotion had drawn their attention. Harley swept a look around and smiled. "It's okay, folks. Just a little difference of opinion.

Nothing to worry about," he said jovially. "Just go on back to what you were doing."

Turning back to Lyle, he jerked his head toward the door and said, sotto voce, "Let's take this outside."

"Take what outside? What's this about?" Lyle glared from Harley to Jake and back. "You'd better be careful of the company you keep, Sheriff. This is an election year, you know. A lot of folks around here don't like to see their sheriff buddying with a killer."

"Why you—"

"Easy, Jake." Other than to give him a warning look, Harley ignored Lyle's jab. "It's outside or the station. What's it gonna be, Lyle?"

He cast a surly look between the two men, then, still holding his throat, he stomped toward the door. The instant they were outside on the sidewalk he spun to face the sheriff. "All right. What is this about?"

"First of all, when was the last time you saw Grace?"

"Grace? I don't know. Thursday, I think. Yeah, it was Thursday. Why?"

"You haven't seen her today?"

"No."

"Where have you been the past couple of hours?"

"Right here at the diner." Lyle frowned. "What's this all about, Sheriff?"

"I suppose Ina can verify that?"

"Sure. So can a half-dozen other people. What the hell is this? Are you accusing me of something?"

"No, no. Take it easy. We just thought you might help us locate Grace."

Lyle shot Jake a venomous look. "If Grace is missing, Paxton's the man you ought to question, not me."

"Up yours, dickhead," Jake snarled.

Lyle bristled. "Why you scum—"

"All right, knock it off. Both of you." Harley barked. Two elderly ladies walked by, and the sheriff tipped his hat and smiled. "Miz Sneed. Miz Lehmann. How're you ladies today?"

"Just fine, Sheriff."

"Lovely," they replied in unison.

When they were out of earshot, he turned back to Lyle and, as casually as though he were discussing the weather, he said, "Out of curiosity, would you mind telling me again where you and Charles were the night Carla Mae was killed?"

Lyle could not have looked more shocked had Harley punched him in the stomach. His face paled and his eyes widened. "Wh-Why do you ask? That case was settled twelve years ago. We all know who did it," he blustered, casting a hate-filled glance at Jake.

"No one's been convicted. Until that happens, the case stays open."

"I see." Lyle swallowed hard and shifted from one foot to the other. "Still, I don't see the point in this questioning. Charles and I told you everything we saw," he insisted belligerently, but his eyes darted away, not quite meeting Harley's.

"Some new evidence has surfaced. I'm just verifying facts, that's all. So where were you and Charles at the time that Carla Mae was killed?"

Lyle became more agitated by the second, and his voice became almost shrill. "Just like we told you before on numerous occasions, we were at the Willows, watching a movie on video."

"Hmm. What movie?"

"Uh . . . *Back to the Future*."

"I see. And was Verna there with you?"

"Yes. Yes, she was. Say . . . what is this? Why are you asking me these questions?" Lyle's expression grew hostile. "Surely you don't suspect *me?* This is outrageous! If you think I'm going to stand still for th—"

"Calm down, Lyle. Nobody's accusing you of anything." Beside him, Jake cursed under his breath and made a restless move, but he shut up when Harley sent him a warning glance.

"Good. Because I'm not answering any more questions unless my attorney is present."

"Really. Now why would you think you need an attorney?" Harley said, giving him a speculative look.

For an answer, Lyle returned it with a furious scowl. "I don't have to put up with this." Without another word he stomped around his car to the driver's side and got in, slamming the door behind him. Seconds later he roared away.

"He did it, dammit. You could see the guilt written all over his face."

"Maybe," Harley said, staring after him. "One thing for sure. He didn't watch *Back to the Future* that night. Unless I'm mistaken, and I don't think I am, it didn't come out on video until a year after Carla Mae was murdered."

Jake gave him a sharp look. "He lied."

"About the movie. And I suspect about their whereabouts, too. But it's not enough to hold him on. On the stand he'd swear he forgot what they watched that night. It's been twelve years. A jury would probably believe him, even though when something shocking or tragic happens, people usually remember exactly what they were doing at the time, right down to the tiniest detail."

Jake cursed again. "So what're you going to do?"

"For the time being, nothing—except keep an eye on old Lyle. He never was the brightest guy around. Now that he knows we suspect him, he just might get careless. In the meantime, I suggest you go home. Grace is probably there by now."

"Yeah, you may be right," Jake conceded, casting a last grim look in the direction that Lyle had taken.

Harley clapped Jake on the shoulder. "C'mon. I'll give you a lift back to the station so you can get your truck."

Fifty-one

"*TEE-JAY! Tee-Jay, where are you?*"

T.J. pretended not to hear Mrs. Bordon calling him as he made his way through the woods behind her house, heading for his favorite hideaway.

She probably wanted to try to get him to eat something yucky again, like that liver and onions she'd served for dinner the night before. Barf city. He'd sooner eat dirt.

The old lady was driving him nuts. She was always so cheerful. And there was the way she licked her fingers and slicked back his cowlick whenever he got within reach. Yeah right, like he really wanted old lady spit in his hair.

She'd given him so many hugs he was gonna be black and blue all over. And when she hugged him his face always got squashed right up against her big ole pillowy bosom, and she smelled like that menthol rub junk.

But the worst thing of all was when she dragged out those dumb board games and those jerky old jigsaw puzzles. They were so lame.

If he had to be stuck in foster care, why'd they have to put him with an old lady? Why couldn't he be with somebody like Jake?

Jake was cool. So was Grace.

A mile or so from Mrs. Bordon's house, T.J. pushed through the dense bracken and stepped into a large clearing around a secluded cove that was part of Kashada Lake. He stopped at the edge of the clearing and looked around, but, as usual, there was no one there. No one had come there since he'd found the place, even though there was a road of sorts that led into it from the highway. T.J. wondered why, but he didn't waste a lot of time worrying about it. It was all right with him if he had a neat spot all to himself.

He stepped out into the clearing and headed straight for the enormous tree at the edge of the woods on the opposite side.

The oak was so huge it was awesome. He'd discovered this place and the tree the first day he'd stayed at Mrs. Bordon's, and he'd come here every day since. With its low swooping branches that almost touched the ground in places, the oak was easy to climb, and it made an excellent hiding place. Even if old Mrs. Bordon came looking for him—and no way could he picture her tromping through the woods—she'd never find him up there in the tree.

Agile as a monkey, T.J. scrambled up over the huge limbs until he reached an exceptionally broad one about twenty feet above the ground. The branch was so wide he stretched out on it flat on his back and there was still room to spare.

He bent one knee, propped his other ratty tennis-shoe clad foot on it and peeled the banana he'd filched from the bowl on Mrs. Bordon's kitchen table. One hand beneath the back of his head, munching contentedly, he gazed up at the sky through the canopy of leaves and thought about his hero.

Jake knew a lot about car engines and motorbikes and building model airplanes and really neat stuff like how to sharpen a knife and where to find fishing worms and the right way to break in a catcher's mitt. And he knew how to fix just about anything. And he was brave, too.

When he'd dived into the river after that girl, T.J. had thought for sure that Jake was a goner. He'd never seen anything like it. He stuffed the last of the banana into his mouth and stacked both hands behind his head.

When he grew up, he wanted to be just like Jake.

Fifty-two

ON THE DRIVE BACK TO THE FARM Jake tried to tell himself that Harley was right. Grace was probably there waiting for him. He was letting his imagination run wild.

It didn't help. No matter how much he lectured himself, he couldn't shake that little niggle that something was wrong.

Anxiety had his stomach in a knot by the time he reached the farm. The instant he turned into the drive, Grace's sister came tearing down the front porch steps, frantically waving a piece of paper in her hand.

Caroline, whose usual gait was a slow, sexy saunter, who rarely bothered to hurry for any reason, who certainly never abandoned her sardonic air, pounded across the yard, her movements jerky and awkward, stumbling in her haste.

The hair on the back of Jake's neck stood on end.

He stomped on the gas and roared up the drive, then slammed on the brakes when he reached her.

"Jake! Oh, God, Jake. He's got Grace!"

"Who's got Grace? What do you mean?"

Caroline was white as parchment. The wild-eyed look of terror on her face sent his heart caroming.

"Here! Read this! I found it on the kitchen table when I got home just a few minutes ago."

He took the piece of paper she thrust through the open window at him. It was a note on plain paper that had been folded in half. Cold fear grabbed him by the throat the instant he unfolded it.

The letters used to form the words had been cut from magazines and newspapers and pasted on the page. The ominous message was simple and direct . . . and chilling.

IF YOU WANT TO SEE GRACE ALIVE AGAIN, COME TO NEESON'S COVE. ALONE.

Nothing else. No name, no hint of who the writer was.

"Jesus."

Jake dropped the note as though it were on fire and slammed the truck's gearshift into reverse.

"Wait!" Caroline shouted, clinging to the open window with both hands. "I'm coming with you."

"No. You stay put and call Harley. Tell him to get over to Neeson's Cove as quick as he can."

"But—"

"Just *do it!*"

"Okay, okay! But hurry, Jake!"

He didn't bother with an answer. The truck shot backward out of the drive like a rocket and screeched to a rocking stop in the road. For a few seconds dirt and gravel flew from beneath the spinning rear wheels. Then they got traction and, fishtailing slightly, the truck roared away.

Wringing her hands, Caroline watched him for only a few seconds before breaking into a run. She didn't stop until she reached her car, inside the carriage house. The keys were in the ignition, where she always left them when at home. She scrambled in behind the wheel and fired up the hot little sports car. Making a sharp U-turn inside the cavernous building she sent the car careening out through the double doors as though it were jet propelled. Before she reached the end of the drive she had punched out the number of the station house on her car phone.

"Sheriff's Department," Betty Sue answered on the second ring.

"Let me speak to Harley," Caroline demanded, tucking the phone between her hunched shoulder and her chin as she made the turn onto the road. "It's an emergency."

"I'm sorry, but Sheriff Newcomb has gone home. Can someone else help you?"

"Get some deputies out to Neeson's Cove. Quick, before there's a murder."

"A murder? Who is th—"

Caroline hit the disconnect button and tossed the phone on the passenger seat. Gripping the steering wheel harder, she set her jaw. She didn't know Harley's telephone number, but she sure as hell knew where he lived.

Fifty-Three

GRACE TWISTED HER HEAD AROUND and looked out the rear window. "You passed the turn."

"Don't worry about it, dear."

"But . . . that was the road to the Bedalia highway. We need to turn around."

Verna glanced at her and smiled. "No we don't. We're not going to Bedalia."

"Not *going!* But I've got to get to the hospital. I've got to be with Aunt Harriet!"

"Harriet isn't in Bedalia."

"What do you mean? The nearest hospital is there. Did they take her to Houston? Oh, God, is her condition that serious?"

"She didn't go a hospital."

"What? But . . . you said . . . I don't understand. If she's not in the hospital, where is she?"

"As far as I know, at home watching television."

Grace stared at her mother-in-law. An uneasy feeling began seeping into her bones. "Verna, what's going on? If Aunt Harriet is all right why did you tell me she had collapsed?"

"To get you to come with me, of course." She glanced sideways again, and the expression on her face sent a chill down Grace's spine. "It was easier this way."

"What do you mean? Where are we going?"

The question was rendered moot as Verna slowed the car and turned down the narrow dirt lane that wound through tall pines to Neeson's Cove.

Grace's scalp crawled. The cove, once the favorite gathering spot for Cedar Grove's teenagers, had been the scene of Carla

Mae Sheffield's grisly murder. Almost no one came here anymore. Grace hadn't visited the spot in twelve years, and she didn't want to now.

"Verna, turn around. I don't like this place."

"That's understandable, given its history. But I'm afraid this is our destination."

"Verna, please. Neeson's Cove gives me the willies. It's a place of death."

"Which is precisely why we're going there. Can you think of a better place to die?"

Grace's head snapped around. "What? What are you talking about?"

"In a few minutes you're going to die at Neeson's Cove, in the exact spot where Carla Mae was killed. So will Jake."

The appalling statement, rendered even more terrifying by Verna's matter-of-fact tone, sent a chill racing down Grace's spine.

"Verna, if this is a joke, it's not funny. Either turn this car around, right now, or stop and let me get out and walk. I am not going to Neeson's Cove, and that's final."

Verna just smiled and kept driving.

Grace looked at her—really looked at her—for the first time since she had arrived at the farm. Verna was dressed in tan twill slacks and a plain dark brown shirt. Her fingers were bare, and she wore flat-heeled, lace-up shoes.

Grace's uneasiness grew. Verna never wore slacks or sensible shoes. And she'd never known her mother-in-law to leave the house without a ring on every finger. Certainly she would never have entertained the idea of going to a duplicate bridge tournament dressed the way she was.

Verna was dressed—unbelievable as it seemed—for physical activity. Like tromping through the woods . . . or committing murder.

Oh, God. Was Verna really planning to kill her?

The lane leading to the cove had fallen into disrepair over the last twelve years. Weeds had grown over the road in places and deep ruts and potholes made the going slow and rough. They reached a narrow section between tall pines where passage was particularly difficult, and Verna had to slow the car to a crawl.

Had Verna gone mad? Her behavior seemed to indicate so. Grace had no intention of sticking around to find out. Surreptitiously, she wrapped her hand around the door handle.

"Try it, and I'll shoot you where you sit."

Grace's head snapped around. Her blood ran cold when she saw that Verna had a gun. Driving with her right hand, she held the lethal-looking weapon in her left, the butt resting in her lap. The obscene black hole in the end of the barrel was pointing squarely at Grace's heart.

She stared at that small, deadly circle and shivered.

The car broke through the trees into a wide clearing that arched around the inlet like a huge letter C turned on its back. Verna stopped the car but left the engine running. She motioned with the barrel of the gun. "Get out. And don't try anything."

"Verna—"

"I said, get out."

Slowly, never taking her eyes off of her captor, Grace did as she was ordered. Verna got out on the other side and came around the front of the car, the gun pointed at Grace all the while.

T.J. JERKED AWAKE, blinking, his heart pounding. At first he didn't know what had wakened him. Then he heard it—the purr of a car engine nearby.

Rolling over onto his stomach, he peered cautiously down through the leaves just as a long, wine red car pulled into the clearing.

A moment later the passenger door opened and Grace climbed out of the car, then Mrs. Ames got out on the driver's side. To his amazement she had a gun, and she was pointing it straight at Grace. T.J. hugged the limb tighter and watched, his eyes wide.

"NOW WALK OVER TO THAT BIG OAK." Verna ordered.

Grace's stomach churned and gooseflesh rippled up her arms and shoulders. She had been trying not to look at that particular tree.

It was enormous. The tree was known as the Tejas Oak. It had been huge long before the white man had ever set foot on this continent. Three grown men, standing fingertip to fingertip with their arms outstretched could not reach around the trunk, and the spreading branches spanned more than a hundred feet, some dipping so low in places they almost touched the ground.

In the past, small children and teenagers alike had climbed all over those ancient, gnarled limbs. Kids had made forts and played Swiss Family Robinson and young lovers had necked among the wide boughs, hidden from view.

That had all changed twelve years ago, after Carla Mae Sheffield had died a gruesome death beneath the sheltering arms of the Tejas Oak.

As she drew near the tree on trembling legs, Grace's eyes were helplessly drawn to the ground at its base. After all this time she knew it had to be her imagination, but she was almost certain she could still see the dark stain where Carla Mae's blood had pooled.

"Stop. Now, turn around."

Trying not to think of the grisly act that had been committed on the very ground on which she stood, Grace obeyed. The fury in her mother-in-law's eyes made her shiver.

"Verna, why are you doing this?"

"Why? I don't know how you have the nerve to ask such a question. Did you truly believe I would let you dishonor my son's memory and do nothing?"

Confusion swirled through her brain. Grace was so terrified she couldn't think. "I . . . I don't understand."

"After being Mrs. Charles Ames, how could you take up with trash like Jake Paxton? How *could* you, Grace? Him, of all people."

The shock of disbelief left Grace momentarily speechless. She stared at Verna, dazed. "That's what this is about? You lied, didn't you. You haven't changed your mind about Jake at all. You're going to murder me just because I fell in love with him."

"That's part of it."

"Oh, Verna."

"Don't look at me like that! I am fond of you. I don't want to do this, but there's no other way. I can't let you marry Jake.

"This is all his fault, you know. None of this would have happened if he hadn't come back here. I've tried every way I could to get rid of him. If Sheriff Newcomb had arrested him for that Tolson woman's murder like he was supposed to he would be in jail awaiting trial now.

"Oh, my God," Grace whispered, her blood running cold. "*You* killed Connie Tolson, didn't you?"

Verna shrugged. "She was Bottom trash."

The ease with which she dismissed a human life sent a chill through Grace. She wrapped her arms around herself to combat the shivers rippling through her body.

"Jake was supposed to have been blamed. I thought that surely this time he would be convicted and go to prison. It was absolutely intolerable that he wasn't twelve years ago."

"You're the one who has been sending those letters and clippings to Jake's employers, aren't you?"

"Yes. I had to make sure that he failed at whatever he tried. He should have gone to prison, but since that didn't happen I made sure that he would never make anything of his life. I wanted him to suffer."

"Why? What has Jake ever done to you that you would do such a horrible thing?"

Verna's expression turned ugly. "His very existence is an abomination to me!" she spat. "He's an Ames. My dear departed husband's bastard with that slut, Lizzie Paxton."

"What?" Grace gaped, so startled she was speechless, and Verna laughed.

"It's true. Franklin was sleeping with the whore even after we married. Jake was his firstborn. That made him a threat to my son. I couldn't allow that."

"You mean . . . y-you killed Carla Mae as well?"

"No. Charles did. But that was really Jake's fault, too, so he should have been the one to take the blame.

"My poor son. I never meant for him to know about Jake. I

knew it would hurt him. But he learned the truth one night when he overheard his father and me arguing about Franklin's bastard son. The discovery incensed him. For months he seethed over it, hating Jake, hating his father. For years he was obsessed with trying to find a way to get rid of Jake.

"When he found out that Jake was seeing Carla Mae on the sly it was the last straw for Charles.

"He and Lyle saw her riding behind Jake on his motorcycle that night. Naturally he was angry, so, they followed them here and watched them from the bushes while they copulated like animals. Can you blame Charles for being furious? After all, he had tried to date Carla Mae for months but she would never go out with him. Yet she eagerly spread her legs for that Bottom trash. Charles decided to teach her a lesson."

"Teach her a lesson? He killed her!"

"That was an accident. The stupid girl fought him. She kept on fighting even after he and Lyle had taken what she had given away so freely to Jake, and that, of course, made Charles lose his temper.

"Afterward, he panicked and confessed to me what he'd done. It was then that I saw a way to get rid of Jake and protect my son at the same time."

"You had Charles and Lyle point the finger at Jake."

"Yes. If things had worked out the way I planned, Jake would have spent the rest of his miserable life in prison." Verna's cold smile made her shiver. "While he was awaiting trial, and all during the proceedings, I used to daydream about him suffering in prison at the hands of the other inmates." Her smile faded, and she shot Grace a venomous look.

"But he got lucky and had a hung jury. And now, thanks to you, instead of being charged with the Tolson woman's murder, he's wriggled free again. He even has some of the townspeople on his side after his heroics at the picnic last weekend. The next thing you know he'll become respectable. I can't allow that to happen."

Grace was still grappling with the knowledge that the man to whom she had been married for five years was a cold-blooded murderer. The horror she felt overshadowed even her fear for an instant. "Charles killed Carla Mae," she whispered. "Oh, my God. Charles killed Carla Mae."

"Now you can see why I can't let Jake go on living. Up until now it was enough that he merely suffered, but now he has to die.

"He'll be here soon. I left him a note telling him where to find you. He will be blamed for your murder, of course. But this time I'm not going to take the chance of him getting off again. This time, after he kills you he's going to be so filled with remorse he's going to commit suicide."

She raised the gun, and Grace's blood ran cold. "Verna, you can't do this."

"You've left me with no choice. I can't run the risk that bastard will somehow learn who his father was. I can't. Lyle isn't much, I'll admit, but at least he's a genuine Ames, not Franklin's by-blow by that slut. I'm sorry, Grace, but it has to be this way."

T.J. WAS SO SCARED he was sick to his stomach. He had to do something. He couldn't let Mrs. Ames kill Grace. But what could he do? He eased down the tree to a lower branch, then to a still lower one, until he was merely eight or ten feet above the two women. He looked around for a weapon but there was nothing.

"VERNA, PLEASE."

"Don't whine, Grace. It's not becoming a lady. Just be glad I'm going to shoot you. It will be over quickly this way. It would be better, of course, if I stabbed you to death like I did that Tolson woman, but I'm sentimental, I guess. I simply can't bring myself to do that to you."

Was she supposed to be grateful for that? Grace wondered in a panic.

"Good-bye, Grace, dear. I am sorry. Truly. I do hope you believe that."

Verna's hands tightened around the butt of the gun, and Grace moaned.

Out of nowhere, like the spread legs of a giant tarantula, a banana peel splatted against Verna's face. She screamed, and jerked the trigger.

Grace screamed and jumped as the bullet went high and knocked a small branch off the tree, sending shredded leaves raining down.

Shrieking, Verna hopped around, slapping at the clammy thing stuck to her cheeks. Grace turned to run but something dropped out of the tree in her path, and she screamed again. So did the creature from the tree.

"It's me! It's me, Grace," the boy yelled when he recovered his senses.

"T.J.? Oh-my-God! What're you doing here?"

"C'mon! Run! *Run!*" He grabbed her hand and took off running, and together they plunged into the woods.

Panting and straining for all they were worth, they dodged trees and jumped logs and tore through underbrush. Grace had no idea where they were headed. She didn't think T.J. did either. They just ran.

"Graaace!" came Verna's enraged shriek from somewhere behind them.

The hair on Grace's nape stood on end.

"Ohhh, ohhh, ohhh," T.J. whimpered, casting a wild-eyed look over his shoulder.

They could hear Verna thrashing through the undergrowth after them. Grace's heart beat so hard it felt as though it would explode from her chest at any second. Sweat poured from both her and T.J. but despite their exertion the boy's face was white as chalk.

Brambles and tree limbs snatched at their clothing, caught in Grace's hair, scratched their faces and arms. Gasping for breath, they pounded on, oblivious to everything but the woman pursuing them.

"Stop, Grace! You can't escape me!"

"Ohhh, ohhh."

A bullet struck a tree to their right, and instinctively both Grace and T.J. ducked and screamed.

JAKE'S HEART NEARLY STOPPED when he heard the gunshot.

The first thing he saw when he drove into the clearing was Verna's car. He gritted his teeth and hit the steering wheel with his fist. Verna! Of course. Dammit, he should have realized.

He stomped on the brake, threw the gearshift into park and bailed out of his truck before it came to a complete stop.

He hit the ground braced for trouble. Turning in a circle, his gaze darted around the clearing, but there was no one there. He stopped and listened, but for a moment his heart was pounding so hard it drowned out everything else. Then he heard it—a distant thrashing in the underbrush.

Spitting out a curse, he took off at a dead run.

A STITCH DEVELOPED in Grace's side, forcing her to run with a limp and bent over.

"C'mon, Grace. That bad lady's gonna git us!" T.J. cried, tugging frantically at her hand.

She stumbled along after him as fast as she could. They splashed through a small stream and struggled up the bank on the other side, dodged around a huge fire-ant mound, squeezed between a tight stand of loblolly pines, and abruptly came up against an impenetrable barrier.

They skidded to a stop and stared, horrified. Stretched out as far as they could see to the right and the left hung a curtain of briars and vines, so dense it would have been impossible to push your hand through it. They looked around, looked at one another, and T.J. began to whimper.

"You see," Verna panted behind them. "Di-didn't I say you . . . you co-couldn't escape me."

Grace and T.J. whirled around. Instinctively she grabbed the boy's arm and tried to pull him behind her, but he jerked free and placed himself squarely between Grace and Verna, bristling, "Don't you hurt her!"

A cruel smile tilted Verna's mouth. "My, my. How touching."

"Verna, let the boy go," Grace pleaded. "He's just a child."

"Now, Grace, you know I can't do that. He's heard too much and seen too much. Besides, this will add a nice touch.

Jake will appear even more remorseful for killing an innocent child." She raised the gun, holding it at arm's length in a two-handed grip, and took aim.

"No, Verna, wait!"

"There's no time. Your lover will be here soon and I have to be ready for him. Good-bye, Grace."

Fifty-Four

As he tore through the woods Jake heard the sirens screaming along the dirt track that led to the clearing. It sounded like Harley was bringing the whole force.

Jake hadn't prayed since he'd been about five, but he prayed now—prayed like he'd never prayed before. *Don't let me be too late. Please, God, let me get there in time. I'm begging you. Please.*

He jumped the stream, dashed around the stand of pines and stopped cold. Straight ahead, her back to him, stood Verna, and she was drawing a bead on Grace. Unbelievably, T.J. was with her, but he had no time to wonder why.

Terror clawed at him. Verna was too far away. He'd never reach her in time. All he could do was distract her.

"Grace! Run! Run!"

Startled, Verna cried out and spun around. "You!" Still holding the weapon at arm's length, she pointed it straight at Jake and fired.

In midstride he halted as though he'd hit a glass wall. The impact of the bullet spun him around and slammed him to the ground.

"NOOOO!" Grace shoved T.J. aside and leapt across the space that separated her and Verna, just as her mother-in-law began to swing the weapon back toward her and the boy. With a furious cry, Grace lowered her shoulder and slammed into her with all her might, ramming her back so hard they both toppled forward.

They hit the ground in a heap. Verna's loud "Humph!" when Grace came down on top of her was immediately followed by an ear-splitting explosion.

"Verna?" Grace scrambled off her, and Verna slowly rolled partway onto her back. She stared, wide-eyed, up through the canopy of trees, a shocked expression on her face. Then her eyes closed and she went limp.

"Jake! Oh, Jake!" Sobbing, Grace scrambled across the rough ground toward him, partly on all fours, partly in a stumbling, lurching crouch. From several feet away she saw the blood that blossomed out over his shirt on the right side, just above his jeans, and panic filled her. Dropping down beside him, she cupped his face in her hands. "Jake? Can you hear me? Talk to me. Oh, Jake, don't die. You can't die."

His face was white, his eyes closed. She pressed her fingers to his neck and whimpered with relief when she felt a pulse.

Blood oozed from the hole in his side and spilled onto the ground. She looked desperately around. He would die if she didn't stop the bleeding.

When Harley and Frank Sheffield and three other deputies burst through the brush moments later Grace was bent over Jake, nude from the waist up except for her bra, desperately pressing her wadded-up blouse against the ugly wound.

Fifty-Five

"HE'S GOING TO BE ALL RIGHT, GRACE. Jake's a tough one."

"You listen to him, honey. As bad as I hate to agree with the big lug about anything, he's right this time."

Not in the least fazed by the dig, Harley gave Caroline a lazy smile and winked.

She rolled her eyes but said nothing.

Wringing her hands, Grace made another circuit of the room. "He'd lost a lot of blood by the time we got him here. And he's been in surgery over two hours, already. That can't be a good sign. And the doctor wasn't very encouraging about his chances. Oh, God, what if they can't save him?" Her voice broke, and tears filled her eyes.

"Here now. None of that," Harriet commanded with a thump of her cane. "That young man is going to be right as rain, and I don't want to hear any more negative talk."

"Oh, for heaven's sake, Harriet, leave the girl be. She has every right to worry over her young man." Lollie's hand fluttered over her heart. "That was such a brave thing he did. Why, I just want to weep when I think about it."

"Oh, hush up, Lollie."

In that mysterious way peculiar to small towns, word of the happenings at Neeson's Cove had spread faster than a message on cyberspace. Within half an hour after the ambulance had brought Jake to the Bedalia Hospital, the two aunts had come bustling in to lend their support.

Barely ten minutes later Josie and Daniel had arrived, then Josie's father, who had come straight from the sawmill. An hour later, amazingly, Frank Sheffield had shown up, hat in hand and looking shamefaced and worried.

At least a dozen people, including the Ackerman brothers, had called offering to donate blood, if Jake needed it.

After all that, Grace wouldn't have been surprised to see Ida Bell and Martha walk in the door and prostrate themselves on the floor.

Sitting slumped in one of the vinyl-covered chairs beside the two old ladies, T.J. listened to the adults, his gaze darting from one to the other. Finally he stood up and went to Grace and laid a hand on her arm. "Jake's gonna be okay, ain't he, Grace?"

The small voice stopped her cold. One look at that painfully young, too pale face, the awful fear in those eyes, and her heart seemed to crack right open. Remorse flooded her. Dear Lord, how could she have been so selfish? T.J. loved Jake, too.

She snatched the boy into her arms. T.J.'s scrawny arms locked around her waist, and the tightness of his hug spoke volumes about the terror that gripped him. Pulling him close, Grace rested her cheek against the top of his head and squeezed her eyes shut. "You bet he is, sweetheart," she vowed in a fierce whisper. "Jake's going to be just fine."

When they had loaded Jake in the ambulance for the drive to Bedalia, Harley had ordered Frank to take T.J. back to Mrs. Bordon's, but the boy had balked at that and Grace had backed him up. She had convinced the sheriff to allow him to come along. Now she was glad she had. How awful the waiting would be all alone.

"Mrs. Ames?"

Grace spun around. Her heart began to pound when she saw a middle-aged man dressed in surgical scrubs standing in the doorway. He wasn't the young doctor she had met earlier, and for some reason that frightened her even more. She reached blindly for T.J.'s hand, squeezing it tight. "I'm Grace Ames."

"I'm Dr. Weisman, Mrs. Ames," he said, stepping forward to shake her hand. "I assisted Dr. Wright during Mr. Paxton's surgery."

It seemed to Grace that the doctor looked terribly weary and downcast. Fresh tears rushed to her eyes, and her chin began to quiver. "How . . . how is Jake?"

Dr. Weisman rubbed the back of his neck. "It's really too early to say for certain, but . . . if pure cussed stubbornness is any indication, he's going to be great.

"He's in ICU at the moment. He needs to rest, but he's so worried about you he's threatening to get out of bed and go look for you. I told him you were all right, but he won't believe it until he sees for himself. It's against procedure, but under the circumstances I'm going to let you see him for a few minutes."

Grace's smile had begun to blossom even before he finished speaking. "Oh, thank God," she whispered through her tears. "Thank God."

When the doctor led her into the ICU cubicle, moments later, Jake was flouncing on the narrow bed, determined to fend off the two harried nurses who were trying to calm him. "Grace. I've . . . got to see . . . Grace."

"I'm here, Jake. I'm here."

At the sound of her voice he immediately stilled. "Grace." He struggled to focus on her as she leaned over him. Raising a trembling hand, he touched her face. "Are you . . . all . . . right?"

"I'm fine, my darling." She took his hand in both of hers and kissed each knuckle, then clasped it against her heart.

Jake sighed, and in an instant he was asleep.

Tears spilled from Grace's eyes and splattered, unnoticed, on their joined hands. "I'm absolutely wonderful," she whispered.

FIVE DAYS LATER, Grace sat beside Jake's bed writing thank-you notes to the people who had sent flowers. From the number of bouquets in the room and all the ones he had passed on to other patients, it seemed as though that included at least half the population of Cedar Grove.

"If they're going to have daytime television you'd think they'd at least put something on that was worth watching," Jake grumbled as he channel surfed.

Grace smiled to herself. For the last two days Jake had been growing increasingly grumpy, a sure sign he was getting better.

The door opened partway and Harley stuck his head inside.

"Hi. Me'n Caro have somebody out here who's real anxious to see you."

Before either Jake or Grace could ask who, T.J. ducked under Harley's arm, and tore across the room. "Jake!"

"Hey, whoa there, son." Harley grabbed the back of T.J.'s shirt, halting him just an instant before he flung himself on top of Jake. "Take it easy. You don't want to hurt your pal all over again, do you?"

T.J. looked horrified and embarrassed all at once. "Gee, I'm sorry, Jake. I guess I forgot."

Caroline laughed and ruffled his hair. "He's been about to bust a gut to see you."

"Hey, pardner, don't worry about it. The bullet hole's on the other side. So how about a high five?"

Jake held up his left hand and the boy complied with the typical macho male greeting. Then their eyes met for several seconds. "C'mere, you." Grabbing the boy's hand, Jake tugged him against his chest in a one-armed hug, and T.J. responded eagerly.

When he released him T.J. sniffed and surreptitiously wiped his eyes before looking at his hero with real interest. "You really got a hole in you?"

"Well . . . it was a hole. It's more of a scar, now."

"Can I see it?" he asked, eyeing Jake's bandaged side with ghoulish avidity.

Grace shivered and shook her head. Males.

"Sure. When I get out of the hospital and these bandages come off, I'll show it to you."

"Cool."

"What's this I hear about you being a hero? I understand the mayor's going to give you a medal this afternoon."

"Yeah. We were on our way to the town meeting," Caroline put in. "The whole town's turning out."

"I wish I could be there to see that."

"Aw, Jake, I didn't do nothing," the boy protested lamely, digging into the industrial grade hard-pile carpet with the toe of his tennis shoe, but you could tell he was pleased. "I just threw an ole banana peel, is all."

"Yeah, right into Verna's face. And if you hadn't, Grace would be dead now. You saved her life, and I want to thank you for that."

Jake stuck out his hand, and when T.J. took it he pumped the boy's hand hard. "Thanks, T.J. I owe you."

"Well, c'mon, boy. You've seen your hero. Now we'd better shake a leg if we're going to make that ceremony." Harley put his hand on T.J.'s shoulder and looked at Caroline. "C'mon, sweet thing. We gotta go."

"Don't tell me what to do, cowboy."

"Why, sugar, I wouldn't dream of it. But if you're riding with me'n T.J., that train is pulling out of the station." Grinning, he steered the boy out the door.

"Insufferable lout," Caroline grumbled, but she hastily kissed Grace and Jake and hurried out. "Harley Newcomb, don't you dare go off and leave me . . ."

Bemused, Grace shook her head. "Do you think those two will ever make a go of it."

"Could be. Stranger things have happened. Look at us, for instance."

"I suppose you're right. I hope so, anyway. It would be nice to have my sister here in town."

Grace moved to stand by the bed, and as she fluffed pillows and straightened his covers Jake captured one of her hands. "Grace, we have to talk."

She gave him an arch look. "You're not going home early, and that's that, so don't try to sweet talk me. You know what Dr. Weisman said."

"No, it's not that."

"Oh. Well, in that case, fine." He patted the mattress, and she sat down on the bed beside him. "So, what did you want to talk about?"

Jake picked up one of her hands and ran his forefinger over the delicate skin on the back, tracing the fine bones that lay beneath it. "Harley brought an attorney to see me this morning. I told him to go ahead and file those papers we talked about."

"Are you sure that's what you want to do? You don't have to for my sake, you know."

"I'm sure. The name Paxton isn't anything to brag about and I'll be damned if I take the name Ames. Franklin didn't see fit to claim me when he was alive, and I don't want his name now. Tuckers founded this town. I figure that's a name that deserves to live on. I'd be proud to carry it."

"Thank you, darling." She grinned and punched his arm. "I guarantee you're going to score points with Aunt Harriet."

"Yeah, I thought of that," he drawled slyly.

He continued to explore her hand. "The attorney also said he didn't foresee any problem getting a favorable ruling on my claim as Franklin's son to the Ames estate. Especially now that Lyle is out of the picture."

"That's wonderful, darling."

Lyle, who was in jail awaiting trial, had confessed to his part in Carla Mae's murder, though, on the advice of the slick Houston lawyer he'd hired, he had later recanted. However, both Harley and the District Attorney were certain that the confession would hold up in court. All evidence had been preserved since the case had remained unresolved. The state was confident that the confession, along with DNA tests on the semen samples taken from the victim's body would be enough to convict.

"I hope you'll still think so when I tell you what I plan to do." He looked up from his contemplation of her hand. His expression was a strange blend of hope, determination and entreaty. "First of all, I don't want to live at the Willows when we're married. I'd rather we lived at the farm."

"If that's what you want, that's fine with me."

Actually, Grace was relieved. She had never been truly comfortable living in such opulent surroundings, and now the Willows would always hold bad memories for her of Charles and Verna. She had not been looking forward to returning there, but she would have done so for Jake. He had been cheated out of living there as a child. He deserved to now, if that was his choice.

If he was planning to sell the place, she hoped he was prepared to wait several years. Buyers for an estate the size of the Willows weren't easy to come by. Certainly, no one around Cedar Grove had that kind of money.

"I can't live the life of the idle rich, either," Jake continued. "I want to do what I trained for and never got the chance to do. I want to teach school."

"I'm sure you could get a job at the high school."

"Actually, I was thinking of turning the Willows into a school. A place for underprivileged and problem kids. Sort of a combination school and home, where they can live and get an education and a decent start in life."

Surprise rippled through Grace. "You mean for boys like T.J.?"

Jake's mouth twisted wryly. "I was thinking more along the lines of the kind of kid I used to be. I made T.J. look like a choir boy."

A great uprush of emotions filled her chest, swelling her heart to overflowing. She felt pity for the boy he'd been and so much love and pride for the man he'd become she could barely breathe. She smiled tenderly, letting all she was feeling shine from her eyes. "Oh, Jake. Darling, I think that's a wonderful idea."

"Yeah? You do realize it's going to cost a bundle, don't you? I can probably get the state to chip in but it'll still take a big chunk of the profits from the Ames's holdings every month. We won't starve, but we won't be living as high as you did when you were married to Charles."

Smiling, Grace leaned forward and brushed his lips with hers. When she drew back she looked into his eyes and whispered, "I can't think of a better use for all that money."

Jake's relief was almost palpable. He put his arms around her and kissed her with a depth of passion that took her breath away. When he finally ended the kiss she was trembling, and her head lay weakly against his chest.

The wedding had been postponed until the following month. As far as Grace was concerned, it couldn't pass quickly enough. Much more of this and she would end up attacking the poor man.

Jake ran his hands slowly up and down her back. She sighed

and snuggled closer, as even that gentle caress sent little tremors of fire coursing through her. "There is one more thing. Well . . . two, actually," he murmured against her hair.

"Mmm. What's that?"

"How do you feel about letting the boys at the school farm your land? We could start an ag program, and they would learn a useful trade. How about it?"

"I think that's a wonderful idea, darling."

"Hmm. And how would you feel about us adopting T.J.?"

Grace sat straight up and stared at him. "Are you serious?"

"Yeah." He frowned when she continued to gape. "Of course, if you hate the idea—"

She stopped him with a kiss—a hard, possessive, thoroughly rapacious kiss that quickly threatened to flame out of control. When she finally pulled back her eyes glittered with love and laughter. "Foolish man," she murmured. "I love the idea."

Epilogue

FIVE WEEKS LATER, dressed in a new navy blue suit, a thin but otherwise healthy-looking Jake paced the length of a small room, checking his watch every few seconds. He jingled the change in his pockets, straightened his tie, then checked his watch again. "Dammit, shouldn't we be starting by now?"

"Hell, man, will you calm down? At this point most grooms are getting cold feet. I've never seen a man in such a hurry to get himself hitched. It's downright weird."

"Hurry, my ass. It seems like I've been waiting for this day for most of my life." Jake shot Harley a wry look. "What's weird is I've got a sheriff for a best man. What the hell was I thinking?"

Harley laughed. "Life works in mysterious ways. But don't worry, it won't kill you to have a lawman for a best friend."

"Who said I was your friend?"

Harley laughed and shook his head. "You're a tough nut to crack, aren't you, hardcase."

Unable to stand it a moment longer, Jake opened the anteroom door a crack and peered out. The pews in the sanctuary were packed. The small family wedding they had originally planned had grown into a full-fledged production. In the past weeks he had somehow gone from pariah to something of a local folk hero, and apparently folk heroes didn't have quiet weddings.

"Jesus, it looks like the whole damned town is out there." He shut the door again and resumed his pacing.

Lounging against the wall as though he hadn't a care in the world, Harley watched Jake make another circuit of the room. "Speaking of weird, how would you feel about having a sheriff for a brother-in-law?"

Jake jerked to a stop. "You're kidding. You and Caroline? She actually said yes?"

"Well . . . not yet. But I'm working on it. I figure one of these days I'll finally wear her down." Harley grinned. "I'm a patient man."

Jake shook his head. For the life of him, he couldn't think of a more mismatched pair than Grace's wild sister and this "good ole boy" sheriff . . . unless maybe it was him and Grace.

The thought brought a smile. Hell, maybe it wasn't such a bad idea after all.

From the other side of the door came a sudden crescendo of organ music. "That's our cue," Harley announced.

Abandoning his slouch, he opened the anteroom door and he and Jake marched out into the sanctuary and took their places before the altar, facing the congregation. Grace's aunts were sitting in the front row on the bride's side. Lollie smiled and fluttered her fingers at him coyly. Harriet merely nodded with stern approval.

As the organist played softly, first Josie, then Caroline came slowly down the aisle wearing similar dresses of coffee-colored silk and carrying small nosegays.

Jake barely saw them. His gaze riveted to the back of the church. His palms began to sweat. What if she didn't show up? What if this was all a cruel dream?

With a flourish, the organist began to play "The Wedding March," and suddenly there was Grace. She walked toward him exactly the way he had imagined a thousand times, breathtaking in a pale green dress and a matching picture hat, an enormous bouquet of pink roses and baby's breath cradled in her arm. She was being escorted down the aisle by none other than their soon-to-be-son, T.J., looking proud as a peacock.

Jake's heart pounded like a wild thing in his chest. Grace smiled at him serenely, and when they reached him and T.J. solemnly gave him her hand he felt such incredible joy it was almost painful.

Never taking his eyes from Grace, he drew her to the altar. There, before Grace's family and a good portion of the town, flanked by Josie and Caroline on one side and Harley on the other, with the Reverend Daniel Street officiating, Jake and Grace repeated the solemn vows that bound them together in love, forever.

Meet Award-Winning Author

Ginna Gray

www.ginnagray.com

Ginna Gray has been making up stories since before she could read and write. By the time she was ten years old she knew that she wanted to be a writer when she grew up. Marriage and family came first, however, but when she put her youngest child on the bus for the first day of kindergarten she went home and started writing. In 1983, she won the Golden Heart Award, given by Romance Writers of America for the best unpublished traditional romance. Two days later the book sold and Ginna's writing career was born.

She has received the *Romantic Times* Lifetime Achievement Award, Romantic Times Award for Best Traditional Romance and a Readers' Choice Award. She has been a finalist in the Romance Writers of American Rita Awards, three times. Her books have been on the Waldenbooks Romance Bestseller List, *USA Today* paperback bestseller list and the *New York Times* paperback bestseller list.